NEVER TRUST A STRANGER

This Large Print Book carries the
Seal of Approval of N.A.V.H.

NEVER TRUST A STRANGER

MARY MONROE

THORNDIKE PRESS

A part of Gale, Cengage Learning

GALE
CENGAGE Learning·

Farmington Hills, Mich • San Francisco • New York • Waterville, Maine
Meriden, Conn • Mason, Ohio • Chicago

GALE
CENGAGE Learning

Copyright © 2017 by Mary Monroe.
Lonely Heart, Deadly Heart.
Thorndike Press, a part of Gale, Cengage Learning.

LIBRARY OF CONGRESS CATALOGING-IN-PUBLICATION DATA

Names: Monroe, Mary, author.
Title: Never trust a stranger / Mary Monroe.
Description: Large print edition. | Waterville, Maine : Thorndike Press Large Print,
    a part of Gale, Cengage Learning, 2017. | Series: Lonely heart, deadly heart |
    Series: Thorndike Press large print African-American
Identifiers: LCCN 2017005685 | ISBN 9781410497772 (hardcover) | ISBN 1410497771
    (hardcover)
Subjects: LCSH: African American women—Fiction. | Online dating—Fiction. |
    Large type books. | BISAC: FICTION / African American / Contemporary Women.
Classification: LCC PS3563.O528 N48 2017 | DDC 813/.54—dc23
LC record available at https://lccn.loc.gov/2017005685

Published in 2017 by arrangement with Dafina Books, an imprint of
Kensington Publishing Corp.

Printed in the United States of America
1 2 3 4 5 6 7 21 20 19 18 17

*This book is dedicated to Gloria Malone of Alliance, Ohio —
one of the best teachers on the planet.*

ACKNOWLEDGMENTS

I am so blessed to be a member of the Kensington Books family. Selena James is an awesome editor and a great friend. Thank you, Selena! Thanks to Steven Zacharius, Adam Zacharius, Karen Auerbach, Mercedes Fernandez, Lulu Martinez, the wonderful crew in the sales department, and everyone else at Kensington for working so hard for me.

Thanks to Lauretta Pierce for maintaining my website and sharing so many wonderful stories with me.

Thanks to the fabulous book clubs, bookstores, my readers, and the magazine and radio interviewers for supporting me for so many years.

I never thought I'd be celebrating the release of my *twentieth* book, especially when so many people predicted I'd be a one-book wonder (the same ones ask for a free book each time I release a new one . . . ha ha).

I have one of the best literary agents on the planet, Andrew Stuart. Thank you, Andrew. Without you I would still be answering phones and running out to get coffee for my bosses at the utility company instead of writing full-time.

Try to be a rainbow in someone's cloud.
— Maya Angelou

CHAPTER 1
LOLA

February 2015

"Would a man with everything going for him marry a woman he met on a sex club website?" This question had been burning a hole in my brain for weeks, but I'd just drummed up enough nerve to ask it today.

Joan Riley was the only person I could ask. She had been my BFF since elementary school. She knew almost every one of my deep, dark secrets, and vice versa. We had done things that could have sent us to jail, or gotten us killed.

With a curious look on her face, Joan repeated my question. "Would a man with everything going for him marry a woman he met on a sex club website?"

"I asked you first," I said impatiently.

Joan gave me an incredulous look. "Now what the hell kind of off-the-wall question is that?" she asked, rolling her big, brown eyes. "And why are you asking *me*?"

I let out a loud sigh and slid my tongue across my bottom lip. "You, of all people, know that there is nobody else I can ask such a bold question. The thing is, I'll be thirty-three years old this year."

Joan shrugged. "So? So will I."

"I don't want to wait too long to have my first child."

"Then don't. As much action as you are getting between the sheets these days, you can have a baby whenever you're ready, honey."

"That's true. But the only men I sleep with 'these days' are members of our online sex club." I couldn't believe how casual I sounded. I'd just made a statement that was as bold as the question I'd asked.

"You don't have to be married to have children, and you don't have to look for a baby daddy on the Internet. If we walked down the street right now, we'd see at least half-a-dozen sperm donors who would love to make you a mommy." Joan snickered. Then she paused and cleared her throat. From the mischievous look in her eyes, I could tell she was gearing up to mess with me. "If you want to get pregnant in a more sophisticated way, there's that sperm bank on Pike Street."

We occupied a booth in Jocko's Bar and

Grill that Sunday afternoon in February, a week after the Super Bowl. Jocko's was a popular sports bar located across the street from our favorite San Jose mall, which was about half an hour's drive from where we lived in the suburb of South Bay City, California, in the heart of Silicon Valley.

No matter where Joan and I went together, we were always two of the hottest women on the premises. We received equal attention from the men we encountered. They admired my smooth cinnamon-colored skin, thick, black hair, and pearly white teeth as much as they admired her light brown complexion, jet-black hair, and heart-shaped face. We were both petite, and Joan had had a baby but her body parts were still as firm and perky as mine. We were enjoying our lives, and spending time drinking together in a bar was one of our favorite pastimes.

Today was warmer than usual for Northern California this time of year so we wore jeans, Windbreakers over halter tops, and sandals. There were other women in the crowded bar, but almost every man's eyes were on us.

I was the designated driver, so I was still slowly sipping my first and last Cadillac margarita. Joan had just finished her second, but she wasn't even slightly buzzed. My girl was from a huge family of seasoned drinkers, so she was much more alcohol friendly than I was. She licked salt off the rim of her empty glass, and then she signaled the waiter to bring her another drink.

I glanced around the bar. I didn't see any men I'd be interested in enough to sleep with so I could get pregnant. I returned my attention to Joan. "I'm serious."

"So am I!"

"Then give me a serious answer." I gave Joan an exasperated look. "And please do me a favor and don't mention sperm banks or sperm donors again. I don't want to raise a child on my own. I want a husband." I paused and took another tiny sip of my drink. "Some of the men in our club are the cream of the crop. Handsome, intelligent, and they make a lot of money. A couple of weeks ago, I received date requests from two doctors, a lawyer, and a software company executive."

"A couple of weeks ago? You haven't heard from anybody since then?"

I heaved a sigh and nodded. "A dishwasher and a mailman left messages in my club inbox yesterday. The mailman lives in Denver with his mother. He's coming to California to visit his sister next month. The dish-

14

washer lives in Vegas in a Section 8 apartment with his sister and her five kids. He's coming up here on a Greyhound bus next week to visit his brother and wants me to spend time with him in his brother's trailer!"

"Humph! The nerve of some people! I hope you didn't respond to those two."

"No, I didn't. I wish low-end men would stop asking me for dates. There's nothing wrong with them, and some are hot and really sweet, but you and I have both been down that road. I've had some fun times with broke dudes. Someday I'll probably hook up with a few more on that level again, even though they can't afford to show a woman as good a time as a doctor or a lawyer."

"Tell me about it. But getting jiggy with a dude in a trailer — who came to town on a *Greyhound bus*? OW! Girl, some of the men on the Internet have more nerve than a terrorist. Oh well. We can't stop sad sacks like them from trying to sleep with us, and it is kind of cute and flattering. Last month I received requests from a busboy, a maintenance man in a low-rent apartment building, and a discount store security guard. Even though they were gorgeous and a lot of women raved about them on the club's review board, I didn't respond. I deleted their messages right away."

"Sometimes I wonder if we're missing out on something real good by not accepting dates with club members in the low-income bracket. I checked the reviews for the dishwasher, and most of them were good."

"So what? If you can drive a Rolls-Royce, why settle for a Toyota? Last night I received requests from a judge, a real estate mogul, and a TV producer. The bottom line is, *all* of these men joined a sex club to have casual sex, not make babies." Joan snickered again. Then she finally got serious. "I'm sorry, so get that pitiful look off your face and go on," she told me, waving her hand in the air.

"What about the members who post comments on the club's blog and in their review section about how they developed a serious relationship with a fellow member? Some even got married!"

Joan gave me a steely look and a nod. "Oh yeah. Quite a few."

"Let me rephrase my first question: Do you think any of the high-end men in the club would marry women like *us*?"

"Who the fuck cares, Lola? I already have a handsome, intelligent husband who makes tons of money. And anyway, almost every single one of the men I've dated in the club is already married or in a committed relationship."

"Well, I'm not married or in a committed relationship, so I care," I said firmly. "I just want to know if you think there's a chance one of the club members I've been with, or one I haven't been with, would marry me knowing I've slept with a bunch of other members."

"Pffft!" Joan waved her hand in the air again. "Get real, girl. If you marry a club member, he's doing the same damn thing we're doing, so he'd have no room to talk." She glanced at her watch. "What's taking that damn waiter so long to bring my drink?"

"Don't you think you've had enough? The tequila that they put in the margaritas here is the strongest spirit I've ever come across," I said with a mild grimace, wanting another drink myself.

"No, I don't think I've had enough. I know there's going to be another showdown when I get back home, and I can't face it without a lot of strong 'spiritual' help."

CHAPTER 2
LOLA

A few minutes later, our waiter set another margarita on the table in front of Joan. She wasted no time taking a long drink. Her eyelids had begun to droop, and her light brown nose was now a bright red. Other than that, nobody could tell she was drunk.

After a mighty belch, Joan wiped her lips with a soggy napkin and looked at me with her eyes narrowed. She belched again and snapped her fingers. "What about what's-her-name?"

"What's her name who?"

"Miss Black Piggy — I mean Shirelle, your daddy's ex. She married that architect she met online and had three kids. And don't forget about her niece, Mariel. She met her husband through the same club. You told me yourself that Shirelle and Mariel are living like queens. They have children, big fancy houses in upscale neighborhoods, fat bank accounts, and all of the other shit every woman wants. And neither one of them is half as hot as you or me. I wonder if those two hoochies managed to hold on to their husbands, though."

"Oh! Didn't I tell you?"

"Tell me what?"

"I bumped into one of Shirelle's cousins at the beauty shop last month. She told me that Shirelle is happier than ever and Mariel is pregnant again. She's also very happy."

"Oh? Humph!" From the harsh tone of Joan's voice, I couldn't tell if she was disappointed, jealous, or both. "Well then. All that should answer your question about men marrying women like us that they met online."

"Joan, the dating site where Shirelle and Mariel found their husbands is a regular dating site. The kind that can advertise on TV. The club we belong to was created exclusively for people who want to hook up with other members only to have sex. You will never see a TV commercial about our site."

Joan hunched her shoulders, drank some more, and then swallowed with a grunt. The alcohol had finally begun to affect her. She gave me a curious look with her glazed, red eyes. "Well, like I said, I already have a handsome, intelligent, rich husband. Don't tell me you've fallen in love with one of your Internet hookups."

"Well, I —"

She cut me off and started wagging her finger in my face. "Honey, I advise you to forget about making a *love connection* with any of the men in the club. Didn't I tell you when I turned you on to Discreet Encounters that it was only about *discreet encounters*? Just straight-up, consensual, casual sex! And I've told you more than once to have a good time as often as possible, but don't go falling in love with any of the dudes. I — wait a damn minute! Is this about *'BigBen,'* that well-hung Native American casino honcho from South Dakota that you were with last month? He's one of the few single club members you've dated."

Just thinking about my encounter with BigBen made me want to laugh and cry at the same time. With his flawless bronze skin, chiseled features, and long, jet-black hair, he was too good-looking for his own good, and for everyone else's. "I have no male friends because they're all jealous of my good looks," he had told me at least half-a-dozen times during our three-hour date. "I can't keep a woman because no woman wants to be with a man who is more beautiful than she is," he'd told me, also at least half-a-dozen times. He had booked a room in an adult motel with mirrors on the ceiling so he could look at himself during sex. To bring him down a peg or two, I did something I rarely did in bed with a man: I checked my watch right in the middle of his orgasm. And I made sure he saw me. That shut him up, but just for a few moments. The stunned expression on his face was priceless. He suddenly gripped the sides of my head with his hands, gazed into my eyes, and said, "I can tell that you're intimidated by my good looks and can't wait to leave, but I'm used to women behaving like you when they get around me. You should stick to plain men until you feel more confident being with an extremely handsome man like me." I had had enough by then, so I told him, "Honey, you can count on that." I slid out of that vibrating bed, got dressed in record time, and left that motel literally running.

When Joan had asked me about my date with BigBen the next day, I'd told her he had an awesome body and that he'd been a good lover, but I didn't tell her how much he'd bragged about his handsome features throughout the date. I had stopped sharing all of the details of my dates with her, and I was sure she had stopped doing so too. Last year she'd teased me for days about the Spaniard who'd had a heart attack in bed with me. Even more so than I'd teased her about the midget she'd almost accidentally smothered to death with her legs around his neck while he was performing oral sex on her.

I shook my head to clear my thoughts and returned to the present moment. "The man I'm thinking about is better than BigBen. Remember Calvin Ramsey, that fine-ass truck driver who lives in San Jose?"

Joan's jaw dropped. She looked at me like I had suddenly turned into a big pumpkin. "You think a *truck driver* is better than a casino big shot? Girl, please. Your 'date' with that truck driver last week was in a coffee shop. All you did with him was drink coffee and talk! For all you know he could be bankrupt, psychotic, and have a teeny-weenie. And you haven't even heard from him since."

"So what? Before I met Calvin in person, he and I had communicated online several times, so I know a lot about him. I really like him. He's not like any of the other men I've dated or communicated with. Not even the ones I've been with who I didn't meet on the Internet." I paused and cleared my throat. Just thinking about the handsome truck driver — who was also a war hero — made me tingle. "I don't want to rush into anything, but I think he might be the man I've been looking for all my life. If he is, I hope nothing happens to screw it up. . . ."

"Well, the most likely thing to 'screw it up' is your stepmother, Bertha. Just like she screwed up things between you and that marine who wanted to marry you that time."

"*Pffft!* Maurice turned out to be a straight-up jackass anyway. I read in the newspaper a while back that he's doing time in prison for beating the woman he married into a coma. And before that, he'd done time for dealing drugs and human trafficking. I'm glad Bertha busted up my relationship with him." I sniffed and blinked hard before I spoke again. I didn't like the amused expression that was on Joan's face now. I gave her a threatening look just to make sure she knew I was still dead serious. "Besides, Calvin and I have something in common."

"And what's that?"

"His parents are deceased, too, and the few relatives he has, he's not too close to. Just like me."

"You really opened up to that truck driver, huh?"

"Joan, I wish you would stop downgrading his line of work. At least he's not a drug dealer or a pimp. Every man can't be a doctor or a lawyer or in some other big-time profession. Long-haul truck drivers deserve a lot of respect because they're doing a job that *somebody* has to do. I'm sure the average man wouldn't enjoy driving a big truck for hours on end and risking his life just to transport merchandise."

"You're right. Driving an eighteen-wheeler is just as respectable as any other profession. At least Calvin gets to travel from state to state, and he makes lots of money."

"And to be honest with you, I'd still like Calvin if he drove a *garbage* truck and didn't make a lot of money. It's been years since I met a man who's made me feel so relaxed in his presence." I took my time making the next statement because I had a feeling it was going to ruffle Joan's feathers even more. "I even told him about Bertha."

"You have got to be kidding!" Joan clapped her hands together like a seal, threw her head back, and laughed so loud and long, everybody in the bar turned to look at her.

"Can you laugh a little louder so the people out on the street can hear you too?" I hissed.

She stopped laughing and gave me a look

that was part incredulous, part angry.

"What's wrong with you, Lola? Why would you waste your time telling a random sex partner — who you haven't even had sex with yet and hardly know — about your crazy-ass stepmother?"

"Woman, you have no room to talk! Didn't you tell me that you told some of your partners about your 'crazy-ass' husband?"

"Oh yeah, I did tell you that." Joan giggled and looked embarrassed. "And each one I told felt so bad for me, they were extra nice. It helps for me to talk about the mess I'm in with whoever wants to listen. Other than my meddling family and you, that is. So, what all did you tell Calvin about Bertha and her useless, rotten-ass children?"

"I didn't go into a lot of detail about Libby and Marshall. Talking about them takes a lot out of me, physically and mentally. Besides, there is so much to tell about them, it would have taken me a few hours just to scratch the surface. I focused on Bertha and how she's using Daddy's death-bed request to manipulate me. Calvin laughed when I told him how when I was a teenager she used to show up at the places my dates took me to. And, believe it or not, he actually said it was very noble of me to be so devoted to her. He feels sorry for her,

25

and he told me that karma is going to reward me for my kindness someday. I swear, he's the most sensitive man I've ever come across."

"All that's easy for him to say. I'm sure he wouldn't say that if he knew Bertha," Joan decided. "You said his screen name is 'RamRod'? I think 'DudleyDoRight' would suit him better."

"I wish you wouldn't make fun of Calvin. There's nothing wrong with his being sensitive," I snapped. "I like that quality in a man. Family is real important to him too. He used to live with his elderly uncle in Chicago, who manipulated him left and right. But he said it never bothered him. And he even said that he is always eager to help out a family member or a friend in need."

"You might be right, you know. Calvin could be just what you need." Joan paused and gave me a thoughtful look. "When you first told me about him, I checked out his club profile. I admit, he's no baboon in the looks department. I think he's as hot as they come."

"And he's not a wimp. An ex-marine truck driver. How macho is that? He would never let an elderly woman like Bertha run him off the way Maurice did."

"Humph. But no matter how hot, sensitive, and macho this Calvin is, I think you're getting way ahead of yourself. You're thinking about having babies and spending the rest of your life with a man you've seen in person only one time."

I sighed. "I guess I should really be more patient. If Calvin's not the one, and if I'm lucky, my ship will eventually come in. I hope it hasn't already come in and I missed it."

"I hope your ship wasn't the *Titanic*. . . ."

I rolled my eyes and gave Joan an annoyed look. "I knew I could count on you to say something that'll keep me from sleeping tonight. Thanks."

"You're welcome."

CHAPTER 3
JOAN

With three margaritas in my belly when we left Jocko's an hour later, I was feeling real good. My head was spinning and I couldn't even feel the ground beneath my feet as we walked to the parking lot across the street. But I knew I would not be feeling the same way when I got home.

There was a three-car accident on the freeway, so it took twice as long for us to get back to South Bay City.

Lola parked her aging Jetta in front of the posh high-rise I lived in with my husband, Reed, and our fourteen-year-old son. I was horrified to see Reed staring out the front window of our eighth-floor condo with a tight look on his face. I sucked in some air and shook my head. Lola snickered.

"Uh-oh," she said, giving me a hopeless look. "Reed doesn't look too happy."

"So what else is new?" I moaned. "Lola, will you please pray for me?"

"You don't have to ask me to do that. I pray for you all the time," she said gently as she patted my shoulder.

My buzz suddenly didn't feel so strong anymore. I gave Lola a one-armed hug before I tumbled out of her car and sprinted toward the entrance of my building. Before I could even scan my security card to unlock the door to the lobby, Reed buzzed me in. When I reached our floor and got out of the elevator, he was standing in the hallway in front of our door with his hands on his hips.

"So you finally decided to come back home, huh?" he barked. He looked as slovenly as he always did when he was at home. His thick, gray-and-black hair was matted on both sides and sticking up on top like a Mohawk. It was almost four p.m. and Reed was still in his flannel bathrobe and house shoes. It was hard to believe that last year he'd been voted the "best dressed man" in the lodge he belonged to. He had not even shaved. A mask of stubble, half of it gray, covered the lowest part of his face. "Where the hell have you been this time, Joan?"

"Out! O-u-t!" I yelled as I brushed past him. As soon as I got inside, I kicked off my shoes and headed toward the living-room couch. Reed headed in the same direction.

"I can see that!" He was so close behind me I could smell his hot, sour breath on the back of my neck. "I can tell that you've been drinking too!"

"And I'm going to drink some more," I snarled, my eyes fixed on the liquor cabinet across the room. I whirled around to face Reed, looking him up and down. "You could have at least combed that crown of thorns on your head and shaved. You look like hell."

"I feel like hell too," he said in a weak voice and with a profound pout on his face. "I want to know where you've been for the past three hours."

I sighed and brushed past him again, ignoring his question. He followed me down the hall to our huge bedroom.

"Joan, talk to me!" he ordered. "Where were you and who were you with?"

"I was with Lola," I said casually as I dropped down onto the unmade bed with my purse still in my hand. "I told you when I left here that I was going to go hang out with Lola for a while."

"You've been with Lola all this time?" Reed yelled. He stood in front of me with his arms folded and a scowl on his face.

"Yes, 'all this time,' " I yelled back. I was

glad that Reed Junior was spending the weekend with my in-laws. He had never witnessed one of our tirades, and I was going to make sure he never did. "You ought to know by now that I come and go as I please!"

Reed grunted, unfolded his arms, and scratched the side of his neck, then he plopped down next to me. "I was worried that something had happened to you, that's all," he whimpered with a puppy-dog look on his face. "You're a beautiful woman, Joan. There are a lot of predators out there just waiting to grab a female like you." I could understand him being concerned about criminal activity. However, when he said that he was "worried" about me, what he really meant was he was worried about me fooling around with another man. "If anything ever happened to you, like if I *lost* you, I wouldn't want to go on. . . ."

I rolled my eyes and gave him a disgusted look. I was not in the mood to listen to *another* one of his veiled suicide threats. It was an extremely sensitive subject in our house, and I avoided it like the plague.

Reed had attempted to take his life a couple of years ago because I had threatened to divorce him. From that day on, the fear of his committing suicide hovered above my head like a black cloud every time we had a showdown.

"Why don't you let me enjoy a little more freedom now and then?" I rose, still clutching my purse. I didn't trust Reed, so I never let my purse out of my sight when he was in the house. I had caught him rooting through it more than once. He was the most suspicious man I had ever met. And other than me spending a lot of time away from home, he had no reason to be. For one thing, I was too sly (and lucky) to let him catch me up to no good.

I couldn't wait to be alone so I could remove and hide the condoms in my purse, which I had forgotten to do after my last date a couple of days ago.

Chapter 4
Joan

Reed wobbled up off the bed with a groan. Not only did he sound like he was in pain, he looked like it too. And so was I. My head was throbbing on both sides, and not because of all the alcohol I had drunk.

It was hard to decide which one of us was the most miserable.

If Reed ever found out about my affairs, he would probably kill me, and then himself. A chill ran up my spine every time I thought about that. But the chill was not cold enough for me to change my ways. I was not about to become the meek, stay-at-home little housewife my husband wanted.

He had known me well enough before we got married to realize that shrinking violet characteristics were not in my DNA. I had been a free spirit since the day I was born, and I was going to be one until the day I died. I figured that as long as I stayed under the radar and nobody knew about my Inter-

33

net sex life, why the hell shouldn't I enjoy myself while I still could?

I had never tried to control Reed, so I was not about to let him stop me from being myself. How did I know he wasn't having affairs behind my back or involved in some other kind of shady activity? Even though I had no proof that he was anything but what he appeared to be, just the *thought* that he probably had a few deep, dark secrets himself was enough to justify my actions.

"Whatever you have to say, say it and get it over with and stop looking at me like I'm crazy," I snapped.

"Were there any men drinking with you and Lola?" Reed looked me straight in the eye as he twiddled his thumbs and tapped his foot on the floor.

"There were no men drinking with us this time."

He gulped and took a couple of steps backward. "What do you mean by 'this time,' Joan Riley? What about other times?"

I got so close up in his face, I could smell the onions he'd eaten with his lunch. I could tell from his wince that the tequila on my breath was twice as potent as the onions. "Look, I'm not your daughter; I'm your wife."

"I wish you'd act more like my wife," he

said sharply. "I'm in a position that most black men can only dream about. It doesn't look good for *my* wife to be out in public drinking like a sailor and spinning around town like a loose wheel."

"I get the picture, Reed. Now, if you don't mind, let's change the subject," I said with a heavy sigh.

We stared at each other for a few seconds. The inside of my mouth tasted stale and foul, the way it always did after I'd had a few drinks. I held my breath to keep from belching, but one flew out of my mouth anyway. I moaned and massaged the side of my head. "I . . . I don't feel so good right now," I whimpered.

"You want an aspirin?" Reed asked, giving me a sympathetic look. One good thing I could say about my husband was that no matter how angry I made him, he usually ended up purring like a kitten after our arguments, no matter which one of us had started it. "How about some green tea?"

I shook my head. "I'll be okay after I use the bathroom."

"Do you want to go out to dinner? I know you don't like to cook on weekends." He followed as I headed toward the bathroom adjacent to our bedroom.

"Uh, no, thanks. You can go pick up some

35

Chinese takeout," I suggested. Reed followed me all the way into the bathroom. "I'm going to take a bubble bath while you're gone."

"You want me to go now?" He glanced at the Rolex I'd given to him for his birthday last year.

"Uh-huh. We're out of wine, so can you go by the liquor store too?" I didn't even wait for him to answer before I turned on the water in the bathtub.

"Yes, baby," he mumbled, backing out the door. I was pleased that he didn't sound or look so pitiful now. "I'll go as soon as I freshen up."

I waited a couple of minutes and then I retrieved my purse off the bed. As soon as I heard the shower running in the guest bathroom across the hall, I went back into the bathroom and locked the door. I turned off the water in the bathtub and sat down on the commode, then crossed my legs.

I fished my cell phone out of my purse so I could check my messages. There were the usual mundane texts and voice mails from Mama and a few other members of my rowdy family. They all complained about something, asked for money, or both. Lola had left a voice mail message. She told me to call her back whenever I could. But only one name on my caller ID really made me smile: Dr. Ezra Spoor. His screen name was "DrFeelGood." He had called me up at one p.m., shortly after Lola had picked me up. I had turned off my cell phone by then. The other callers could wait, but I decided to return the good doctor's call right away. I was so anxious to talk to him, I punched in the wrong number twice before I got it right.

"It's Joan," I whispered as soon as the deep, cultured voice on the other end of the line answered. "How's the sexiest plastic surgeon in Palm Beach doing?"

CHAPTER 5
JOAN

"Hello, precious. I'm doing just awesome. I've been thinking about you almost every day since our last rendezvous."

"I'm happy to hear that. I've been thinking about you too. I'm surprised you called again so soon. But I'm glad you did," I said in my sweetest tone of voice.

"I arrived in San Jose this morning to speak at another one of those damn boring medical conferences today. Thank God it's over."

"I wish I'd known you were coming this way."

"So do I. My unpredictable bride had planned to accompany me, but she cancelled at the very last minute. I called and left you a message right after I checked into my hotel. I had hoped to hear from you before now. You see, I really need to see someone soon. A few seconds before you called, I was about to turn on my laptop and log into the club's site to see if there was another woman in your area who'd be interested in having a good time with me tonight. . . ."

Because being in a sex club was all about casual sex, I had no right to get "jealous," but I did from time to time. I got jealous when my dates talked about the "good times" they had enjoyed with other club members. I got jealous when one cancelled a date with me, and it didn't matter what the reason was. I even got jealous when a man I wanted to hook up with chose another woman over me.

"I'm sorry I interrupted you. Would you rather see someone else?" I asked dryly.

"Oh, no! I was hoping you'd be available to see me. That's why I called you up when I did. I would have called yesterday or even a few days ago, but I didn't know I was going to have free time after my presentation. And I didn't know that my wife was going to cancel on me just as we were about to leave for the airport. As luck would have it, the last session of the conference ended a lot sooner than I expected, so I have some time to kill before I return to Florida tomorrow night."

"Well, I couldn't get alone to call you back until now."

"I see. So what's-his-name is keeping tabs on you?"

"As always. Nothing has changed on my end. If anything, my husband has gotten worse — if that's possible."

"Joan, you are a smart woman. A smart, young woman who should be in a much healthier relationship. Why in the world do you stay with that loser?"

Loser? Reed was a lot of things, but a loser was not one of them. At least not by my definition. He was a very successful dentist, and a lot of people respected and admired him. He was outgoing with everyone he interacted with in public. Every year most of his patients sent him Christmas cards, and a few even gave him gifts. He'd even been interviewed by one of the many national medical journals he subscribed to. Last year, two local elementary schools had him speak to their students about the importance of good dental hygiene. Because of Reed, I had security, a wonderful son, and a beautiful home. I knew that most women would be happy as pie to have what I had. But behind closed doors, I also had a distant, moody, and controlling husband who knew that I was miserable.

Even with all the good things I had because of Reed, I still wanted more. And from the way things were going, all I had now was all I was going to get out of my marriage. As far as I was concerned, if anybody was a loser, it was me.

Before I started searching for sex partners on the Internet, I had never cheated on Reed. But one night when he climaxed before he even entered me — spilling his semen all over my thigh — I bit the bullet and decided to take some serious action. I was determined to get my body the attention it deserved. As soon as he started snoring that night, I slid out of bed and tiptoed to the library, where we kept one of our computers. I immediately logged on to Google and searched for dating sites. I came across some interesting ones and was quite impressed. The main thing I realized was that the "one size fits all" rule didn't apply. I didn't waste my time checking out the sites that catered exclusively to Christians, gays, overweight people, senior citizens, or any other category I didn't fit into. I was interested solely in connecting with men who only wanted to have sex.

Less than a week after I'd started my search, I hooked up with a couple of cool dudes. I had fun, and the sex was acceptable, but I needed something more substantial.

When I eventually stumbled across Discreet Encounters, I knew I'd hit the mother lode. Most of their club members sounded more open-minded and sophisticated than the ones on the other dating sites I'd explored. They were interested in having sexual encounters with other members, nothing more. And it was easy to find potentially compatible partners. All a member had to do was click on the home page search box and enter the preferred age range, gender, and ethnicity of the person whom the member wanted to connect with.

I immediately became very popular with the male members of Discreet Encounters. Some of them were so awesome, I felt guilty about having so much fun while poor Lola was sitting around twiddling her thumbs and sleeping with duds. I eventually told her my "dirty little secret" for two reasons. One, she was so uptight, she was getting more and more frustrated with her lackluster love life. The other reason was, sometimes I needed her to cover for me when I went on dates. With Reed breathing down my neck, in person and by telephone, sometimes it was difficult for me to get away for two or three hours a few times a month. Even though I spent a lot of time shopping, visiting family, and participating in other miscellaneous pastimes, I still needed to use Lola as an alibi to explain my rapidly increasing absences to Reed.

Lola had reluctantly joined Discreet Encounters. At first, she'd compared it to prostitution! I eventually got her to understand the difference between prostitution and organized sex clubs. "Prostitutes get paid; sex club members get laid. Case closed," I told her. Now she was going on as many dates as I was! And she often used me as an alibi so she could keep her new social activity from her stepmother.

Internet dating was doing wonders for my morale and even more for my body.

I had already seen Ezra's profile when he contacted me for the first time six months ago. We had enjoyed each other so much on our first date, I allowed him to become one of my "regular" dates, and that was one of the things I had promised myself I wouldn't do with any of the club members. That was a promise I had not been able to keep. So many hot dudes wanted to see me more than once, I couldn't help myself. But I had not added any new regulars since Ezra. Not only did I meet up with him in hotel rooms for a two- or three-hour romp, he often called me up just to chat. No matter what the subject was, I managed to slip in a few comments about how unhappy I was with Reed. I kept telling myself that I needed to be more careful about how much personal information I shared with my lovers in the future. Even though I no longer loved my husband, at least not in a romantic way, I still had feelings for him. I didn't want to hurt him, and I didn't want other people to say things about him that would make me feel guilty and act defensive. But, other than myself and Lola, my lovers were the only people I allowed to talk trash about Reed. After all, he cared more about me than any other man I knew, and I appreciated that.

"My husband is not a loser," I defended, feeling confused and frustrated. "He . . . he's really a good person, in some ways."

"Whatever you say," Ezra said with a chuckle. "So are my four ex-wives," he added, chuckling some more. "And while we're on the subject of losers, that's what they all call me." His last remark even made me laugh. It didn't take long for me to bounce back, but I wasn't sure what to say next, so I remained silent for a few seconds.

"Joan, are you still with me?"

"Yes, I'm still here. I was thinking about what you just said about my husband."

"My dear, I am really sorry. In the future, I promise to think before I speak. After all, you do have a history and a child with the gentleman. It's not so hard for me to understand why you stay with him. I'm sure that if I had not dumped my first wife, she'd still be with me, even though we had no children together and she knew about my extracurricular activities with other women. Why she stayed with me as long as she did baffles me to this day."

The main reason I stayed with Reed was because I didn't want him to kill himself, and he'd assured me that he would do just that if I left him. Of all the men I'd been with on the side, none of them knew the real reason I stayed in an unhappy marriage. The "relationships" I had with other men were only supposed to be about sex, not therapy sessions for me. It was hard at times, but I usually managed to stay more focused on the sex than my marital problems — especially when my partner was a hottie like Ezra. He was one of the most charming men I'd ever met. He was also one of my best lovers. I'd had four dates with him in the last two months.

"Listen, I'm sitting in this hotel room with a bottle of your favorite champagne and my Johnson got as hard as Chinese algebra as soon as I heard your voice. Can you come out and play with Mr. Johnson tonight?"

Ezra said in a mock pleading tone.

I answered immediately. "Most definitely."

I was not used to the attention I got from this man, and I enjoyed every minute of it. Last month he had to attend a seminar in L.A. Afterward, he boarded a private jet, flew up to the Bay Area, and booked a suite just so we could spend a couple of hours together before he returned to Florida.

"Sweetheart, you just made my day!" he hollered.

"I just made mine, too."

"What I'm about to say next may sound corny, but I'm going to say it anyway." Ezra cleared his throat. "I think about you a lot, Joan; my marvelous, sexy, beautiful Hot-Chocolate. And that's such a fitting screen name. You have some of the most amazing skills, and I'm sure you know what I mean. . . ."

"Thanks," I said meekly. "You have some amazing skills, also, and I'm sure you know what I mean, too, *DrFeelGood.*" We both laughed. "Those mysterious pills you gave me to put in Reed's drink last month worked better than I thought. He was out — *way* out — for over ten hours. He could have slept through a hurricane."

"I hope that means you can stay the whole night tonight."

"Uh-huh. I'll put an extra pill in his drink this time so he'll still be knocked out for a few more hours even after I get back home."

"Joan, I can't wait to see you again. I can't say it enough; you're the most exciting woman I've ever known. Not only have you done wonders for my morale, you've done wonders for my health. Because of you and your talk about healthy living, I exercise regularly now and I watch what I eat. As a matter of fact, according to my physician, I am almost as fit as I was twenty years ago. You make me feel like a college boy again. If only I'd met you before you met your husband."

"You tell me all this every time we talk," I reminded. We laughed again.

Despite the good mood I was in now, I couldn't stop thinking about Lola and all the mushy things she'd said about Calvin Ramsey this afternoon. Even though he was only a truck driver, I hoped that he was also the dreamboat she'd been looking for.

CHAPTER 6
CALVIN

When Lola and I finally met in person for the first time the Saturday before the Super Bowl, I wish I could have killed her that day. There was no doubt in my mind that of all the women I had to murder, she deserved it the most. Not just because she resembled my ex-wife Glinda — the two-timing bitch who had caused me to go on a killing spree. But also because Lola was the most annoying, shallow, oversexed heifer I had ever encountered. Even her laugh, which sounded like the screech of a magpie, made me cringe.

I had to hold my breath and suppress my anger a few times just to keep from lunging at her while she sat across from me in that coffee shop sipping coffee. The whole time, she "inspected" me as if I were a piece of meat to be bought by the pound. Patience used to be one of my good qualities, so I had no trouble restraining myself with her that day. But I couldn't wait to wrap my hands around her pretty little throat and squeeze the life out of her.

You would have thought that Lola's coffee had been spiked with booze the way she'd sat across from me batting her eyelashes. She practically drooled as she babbled all kinds of silly shit about reality TV shows, her stepmother, her job in a fucking grocery store, and even shopping. It was obvious that she thought I was her Prince Charming, with a white stallion waiting outside for us to ride off into the sunset. I always found women to be so goddamn gullible and unrealistic! Well, this "Prince Charming" was actually *every woman's nightmare.*

That Lola. She was a real piece of work, and I had my work cut out for me. She was on my mind in such a profound way, I could still hear her voice and smell the stench of that unholy, floral-scented perfume she wore. And to think, she had the nerve to attempt to come off like she was so demure and respectable.

She had come to our meeting dressed in such prim and proper clothing, had I not known any better I'd have sworn she was a Sunday school teacher or some preacher's daughter. But those women did a lot of dirty things too. It was no wonder so many men were frustrated, confused, and angry when it came to romance. With so many of the "good" girls actually being the "bad" girls in disguise these days, a man looking for a decent woman to marry didn't stand a chance.

I wondered what Lola's family and friends would think of her if they knew she was nothing more than a sex machine, picking up men online, and knowing her, no telling where else. She had eagerly admitted that she liked to drink in bars and at parties. I wondered how many fuck partners she had picked up at those places. I could still see that smile on her face. Well, she wouldn't be smiling by the time I got through with her!

She was good for laughs, being so superficial and giddy. If there was life after death, she'd be good entertainment for Glinda and the rest of those no-good bitches I'd killed. It was a thought that made me laugh every time it entered my mind.

There was one thing I never laughed about, and it not only scared me, it made me very nervous: ghosts. A lot of the people I knew believed in them. Two of my coworkers swore that their late parents' spirits had visited them more than once. Despite all of the documentaries I had seen on TV and reports I had heard from credible sources, I was still somewhat skeptical. But something very peculiar and spooky was happening in my life that I couldn't figure out or ignore. Five nights ago, I heard a strange noise coming from the other side of my bedroom wall. My bedroom was right next to the garage, where the sound was coming from. It sounded as if somebody was moaning. It was so loud, it woke me up.

I was buck naked in bed because, at my request, one of my random female associates had made a booty call. I'd put her in a cab and sent her home a couple of hours earlier because I liked to sleep alone in my house.

I'd sat up and clicked on the lamp on my nightstand. This was not the first time I'd heard strange sounds coming from my garage. The first time, which was last month, I'd heard something crash to the floor. Naturally, I thought an intruder had entered my residence. My ranch-style three-bedroom house was located in a quiet, middle-class, well-maintained neighborhood in San Jose, just a few blocks from the police station. However, we had our share of burglaries.

Last year on two separate occasions while I was out for the evening, some asshole broke into my house. The first time the crook helped himself to my laptop, my cell phone, and a few other small items.

The second thief stole my new laptop, a fifth of cognac, and a leather jacket. Since I'd installed cameras outside, like several of my neighbors, I hadn't had any more problems. At least not with burglars. And to be even more on the safe side, I kept a loaded Glock semiautomatic pistol in the top drawer of my nightstand. I had a license for it, and so far, except for target practice, I had never fired it.

The world had become a very dangerous place, even for a dangerous man like me. I was just as likely to die violently in America, in my own home, as I had been when I was stationed in Afghanistan. I didn't care what I had to do to protect myself. Hopefully, I'd get the bad guy — or the bad girl — before they got me.

I eased open the drawer and removed the Glock. Even with all of this fire power at my disposal, my hand was still shaking. And for more than one reason. First, I feared that I'd shoot and miss the motherfucker who'd been bold enough to break into my place. Another fear was that I'd end up shooting myself instead of the intruder. But one thing was for sure: I would shoot first and ask questions later.

Without turning on any other lights, I moved closer to the wall and put my ear against it. I listened for a few minutes. The "moaning" suddenly stopped. I waited a few seconds and told myself that it had been the wind.

I heard the moaning again last night. I knew for sure that it was not the wind, because this time it sounded more human. I also knew that an intruder had not come into my house and started moaning, because those bastards tried to be as quiet as possible during their break-ins. And it certainly had not come from one of the three dead women I stored in the freezer in my garage. At least that was what I hoped. I had always been a reasonable, no-nonsense type of person, so it didn't take much for me to convince myself that I had imagined what I'd heard.

I owned a Bible, but I rarely cracked it open. It had belonged to my grandmother on my late father's side. It was quite shabby now. Some of the pages were dog-eared, some were falling out, and every single one had turned yellow. But Scotch tape and staples kept it from falling completely apart. I kept it mainly for sentimental reasons. Grandma Daisy had scribbled births, deaths, and other important events in our family in the records section. Other than my house and enough money to pay for a management training course, the Bible was the only thing she had left to me when she died.

Like the devout Christian people thought I was, I had always displayed the "good book" on an end table in my living room. Right after the moans stopped last night, I tumbled out of bed, padded to the living room, and retrieved it. I put it in the night-stand drawer right next to my Glock. With such an arsenal, I was confident that I had nothing to worry about.

A few minutes later, after a shot of bour-bon and a hasty prayer, I returned to bed and slept like a baby.

When I got up this morning, I decided that I was not going to waste any more time thinking about the strange sounds. If and when the situation developed into some-thing more ominous, I'd deal with it then. I'd even get Reverend Fisher to come out and do a blessing. In the meantime, I wanted to sharpen my focus on Lola and how I was going to fuck the living hell out of her when we finally decided to hook up in a hotel room. She was more than enough to keep my mind occupied for hours at a time every day. The only other thing I thought about more than the sex I had coming from her was the fact that she was going to be my most memorable victim.

CHAPTER 7
LOLA

Joan and I would have stayed in the bar longer if she had been able to. But with Reed being such a suspicious crybaby, she'd had no choice but to leave just when we had begun to really enjoy ourselves. I was glad we left before it got dark. Crime in Northern California had become so bad in the last couple of years, I didn't like to go out at night unless I was with a man. Murder was bad enough. But even more disturbing was when a woman turned up missing and was never found or heard from again. Like the three missing black women featured in a recent local newspaper article. I shuddered every time I thought about that story. The most unsettling thing about it was that all three of the missing (and presumed dead) women resembled me. . . .

I was back in my bedroom now, stretched out on my bed staring up at the ceiling. All kinds of thoughts were moving back and forth in my mind. Joan was in almost all of them. Before Reed entered her life and sent her on a one-way trip to the doldrums, I'd envied her. She had been the most well-adjusted, happy-go-lucky girl I knew. I had not seen her half as happy since she married Reed. She reminded me of a poor little rich girl who had everything money could buy, except peace of mind.

Despite Joan's bad marriage, I was still anxious to have a husband of my own. I didn't expect a perfect man, and certainly not a perfect marriage, but that didn't make me want it any less.

All I needed to do was find a man who wanted to marry me.

I couldn't wait to see where my "relationship" with Calvin was going — if it was going anywhere at all. I still couldn't determine if he was as into me as I was into him. For all I knew, he could have been the type of man who came off looking like he was interested in a woman whether he was or not. I'd met a few others who'd seemed too good to be true. They had led me on and lied about how much they "liked" me, but never called me again.

I recalled my first meeting with Calvin in the coffee shop last Saturday, the day before the Super Bowl. I hoped that by replaying part of our conversation in my head, I'd get a better idea of where his head was. One, if he was only interested in a sexual encounter, the sooner I knew that, the better. Two, if he wanted to develop a relationship with me, the sooner I knew that, the better too. Running in and out of hotel rooms with men passing through town was still exciting, but from my past experiences, I knew that it was just a matter of time before I got bored with that activity.

The truth of the matter was, I had been looking for my soul mate since I was a teenager. I didn't want to waste too much more of my time in relationships that had no future. I joined the sex club Joan introduced me to mainly because I was sick of going on dates with men who not only bored me to death and spent very little money on me but also left me sexually unfulfilled. As a member of Discreet Encounters, fun and sex were only a mouse click away.

I still wasn't sure Calvin even planned to see me again for another coffee break, or anything else. From the way he had eyeballed me in the coffee shop, like he couldn't wait to get his hands on me, I thought I almost had him in the bag, so to speak. But I wasn't so sure of that by the time we got up to leave. He gave me a hug, a quick peck on the cheek, and a pat on my shoulder. Then he was gone. He'd rushed out of the coffee shop as if it was on fire.

I'd felt so slighted and unattractive, I couldn't wait to be on my way. Normally, when I drove on Highway I-880, which was busy as hell all the time, I stayed in the fast lane. Like almost every other motorist in the Bay Area, I was always anxious to get to my destination. Even when that place was the gloomy house I shared with my nosy, meddlesome stepmother. I knew that Bertha would be sitting by the door waiting on me like a spider, so I stayed in the slow lane all the way back to South Bay City.

Just as I had predicted, Bertha was standing in the doorway in one of her outlandish, floor-length dusters, wiping her hands on her apron when I parked in the driveway. I had taken my time getting out of my Jetta. And by the time I stumbled up onto the porch, Bertha had moved to the living room and sat down on the couch. She was fanning her face with the tail of her apron when I entered the room.

"I thought you were going shopping at the mall to look for some lamps?" she'd said, looking at my empty hands with her eyebrows raised.

"Um, I did, but I didn't see any lamps or anything else I liked enough to buy." Along with being as manipulative and nosy as she was, Bertha was one of the most gullible women I knew. I had been telling her tall tales since I was a child, and she had bought everything I said hook, line, and sinker. I'd even created a fictitious invalid named Liza Mae Ford. This unfortunate woman, one of my former classmates who'd been injured in an auto accident, had no family, so she asked me to come to her house to help her out on an as-needed basis. It was the most creative story I'd ever come up with. Joan even got some mileage out of it too. Bertha and Reed never pressured us to meet "Liza Mae," so we continued to use her as one of our excuses when we needed to get out of the house for a few hours. Bogus trips to the mall were good-enough excuses, but how many trips to the mall could a normal woman make in a week and come home with one or two items, or no purchases at all? We also used legitimate reasons to be away from home, such as movies and having lunch or drinks with somebody.

"Where else did you go? To check up on that woman in the wheelchair?" Bertha had asked with her brow furrowed. She was the only person I knew who had jet-black hair on her head, which was dyed, of course, and gray eyebrows.

"Not today. I just went to visit her two days ago, and Joan went to help her out two nights in a row last week, so Liza Mae's doing great."

"Oh, I was just asking because you were gone such a long time. . . ."

From the look on Bertha's face, I knew she was not going to let up on this subject until I told her where else I had been. I was thirty-two-years old, but the way she kept tabs on me, you would have thought I was still a girl. Almost every time that I returned from being out, she had to know where I'd been, who I'd been with, and what we had done.

"I, uh, I met a friend for coffee." I'd moved slowly toward the staircase so I could go upstairs and hole up in my bedroom.

Of all the subjects my stepmother and I discussed, the one I avoided as much as I could was men. It was no secret that she didn't want me to put romance ahead of her in my life. Her fear was that I'd abandon her for a man. It was also no secret that her forty-four-year-old twins, Libby and Marshall, had no desire to move her into their homes and take care of her, so it was easy for me to understand why she had put so

61

much of the burden on me. She and Daddy, that is. I blamed him for the predicament I was in just as much as I blamed her.

I could still picture the hopeless look on his face as he lay dying when he made me promise that I would take care of Bertha. Incredibly, at the tender age of fourteen, I'd agreed to that monumental promise. And it was one that was getting harder and harder for me to keep.

"Who?" Bertha had asked, rising from the couch with a grimace on her heavily lined face. She stood in the middle of the living-room floor for a few seconds, wringing her gnarled hands. Before I knew it, she started following me as I headed upstairs. "Do I know this friend?"

"No, you've never met him."

"Him? Him who?"

"His name is Calvin Ramsey. He's a truck driver, and he lives in San Jose."

I couldn't believe I was revealing so much information about a man to Bertha. I usually didn't anymore, unless I'd been drinking. And I couldn't believe I had the nerve to be talking about a man I wasn't even sure I'd hear from again, let alone see. But there was something about that truck driver that had me acting like a love-struck teenager. Maybe he didn't want to have a relationship with me, but maybe he did. No matter what happened or didn't happen between us, I planned to play it cool and take things slowly. I didn't want Calvin to think that I was too aggressive or desperate. However, even as levelheaded as I was, I had developed a mild obsession about this man. I was afraid that it would get even worse and I'd lose my perspective and start acting like a fool, just as some of the women Joan and I pitied. When that thought entered my mind, I *almost* wished that Calvin had never sent that first message to my club in-box.

"Oh." Bertha had followed me into my room. "Um, I hope you don't let him take advantage of you the way some of your other boyfriends did. . . ."

Her comment had startled me. With an incredulous look on my face, I whirled around so fast and hard, the bones in my neck made a cracking noise.

"He's just a friend, Bertha. And, for your information, I don't let men take advantage of me. I don't know why you come up with these crazy opinions. Besides, whatever I do is my business. After all these years, you ought to know that."

Bertha had looked so sad and small standing there blinking and rubbing her chest. I felt sorry for her. And that was not easy, because she was one of the sources of my aggravation.

It had been almost nineteen years since Daddy married Bertha Mays, Mama's best friend. He had told everybody that his romantic relationship with Bertha had not started until after Mama passed, but I knew better. I used to see them getting busy while my mother was upstairs knocking on death's door.

Once Mama was gone, Bertha sopped Daddy up like she was a sponge. Before I knew it, they were married and Daddy and I had moved into Bertha's big, fancy house in the same neighborhood I had grown up in.

In a way, I was glad that Daddy and I had Bertha, for his sake more than mine. But even back then, I already had plans for my future. I wanted to do something meaningful. Mama and Bertha had taught at the same elementary school I had attended. My plan was to either teach or become a nurse. I couldn't decide which profession was more honorable, so it didn't matter which one I pursued. Somewhere along the line I hoped to meet and marry my soul mate, have several children, and live happily ever after.

Well, things didn't work out in my favor.

It didn't take long for me to realize that "happily ever after" was something that happened only in fairy tales. Shortly after Daddy married Bertha, he was diagnosed with liver cancer. It was so aggressive, he died within a few months. But that was not the worst part. Before Daddy died, Bertha assured him that she would continue to take care of me. I had expected that, since I had no other family to speak of and because Bertha was a caring woman. She went out of her way to make other people happy. What I had not been prepared for was my being the main person Bertha counted on to take care of her until she died. And, according to her doctor, she had *decades* longer to live.

Bertha was so afraid of growing old alone or in a nursing home, she clung to me like lint on a cheap bedspread. Her own children spent very little time with her, and when they did they treated her like shit. They were nice to her only when they needed money from her, and that was several times a month.

When I was in my teens, Bertha would often track me and my dates down and join us. When boys came to visit me at the house, she'd sit in the same room with us and dominate the conversation. She'd even ruined one promising relationship by sending an anonymous note to the boy's mother, claiming I slept around, that I'd given another boy an STD, and all kinds of other shit. None of it was true. When I mentioned it to her, she insisted that a jealous female had sent the note. To this day I was convinced that she was the jealous female.

So here I was now, still living under Bertha's thumb. My dream to become a teacher or a nurse was still just a dream. On top of all that, I was not even in a serious relationship with a man and hadn't been for years. And it was all because of my commitment to Bertha. Most of the men I'd been with didn't stay with me long once they found out she was part of the equation.

I had a feeling things were finally going to go my way, and all because of Calvin Ramsey.

"Where did you meet this Calvin Ramsey," Bertha had asked, interrupting my thoughts.

"Huh? Oh, I met him at the mall," I'd lied.

If Bertha ever found out I had joined an online sex club, she would probably have a heart attack. A few years ago, if somebody had told me that I would fall in love with a man I met through a sex club, I probably would have had a heart attack myself.

CHAPTER 8
LOLA

"Lola Mae, you picked up a man at the mall? Have you lost your mind, girl?" Bertha had asked, looking quite disturbed by now. From the grimace on her face, I thought she was about to have a seizure. "It was bad enough when you were picking up men in bars. Now I can worry about you day and night. I sure hope I don't read about you in the newspaper, missing like those three other young, black women who folks are still talking about."

"Aren't you overreacting?"

"No, I'm not overreacting," she said gently and with tears in her eyes. "What in the world were you thinking? What's the point of you watching *Dr. Phil* and *Oprah three or four times* every week and not paying attention to what they say about picking up strangers in public?"

"I didn't 'pick up' anybody, Bertha. A nice man asked me for directions to Macy's today and then he asked me to have coffee with him."

"I am surprised to hear that after all you've been taught, you let a strange man pick you up in a predator's playground like a mall," Bertha had said, giving me an incredulous look and shaking her head. "That's as bad as plucking somebody out of one of those Internet chitchat rooms. *Tsk, tsk, tsk.*"

One thing was for sure: If I eventually developed a relationship with Calvin, or any other man I met online, I would rather tell Bertha that I'd met him on the street. Most of her generation would never embrace today's technology. She was the only person I knew who used the computer only to Google coupons and recipes.

"He was shopping for some curtains for his house." One thing I had learned over the years about lying was that the more "innocent" you made a situation sound, the more believable it was.

"He has his own house, or does he live with his mama and sleep on her couch?"

"It's his house and he lives alone. Um, a few years ago, his wife ran off with another man. His mama passed several years ago," I'd said, easily recalling every piece of information Calvin had told me.

"How many children does he have?"

"None yet. His wife didn't want any." The words were rolling off my tongue like pebbles. I was glad Calvin had told me as much about himself as he had. "And he goes to church."

"So?"

"I thought you wanted me to find a church man."

"I did for a while. That was before I realized that the church is where a lot of women find Satan. . . ."

Bertha's comments never ceased to amaze me. The ones that had just popped out of her mouth caused a sharp pain to shoot through my chest. She had been married twice, so I knew she had to have a man herself. However, she had not dated any other men since Daddy died. She was in her late sixties, but there were several old dudes in her church and in our own neighborhood who had attempted to woo her. She could have grown old with one of them! But she was not interested. It seemed as if the only person she wanted to grow old with was me.

I rolled my eyes. Before I could respond, Bertha clapped her hands and gave me a curious smile. "Good news! I thawed out the last of those chitlins you brought home from work last week. We'll have a nice dinner. Complete with turnip greens and yams. And you can tell me more about this Calvin man."

"That's nice, Bertha," I'd muttered, flopping down on my bed. "I'll make the corn bread."

"Pffft!" she responded, waving her arms in the air. "You don't have to worry about that! Guess who's coming to dinner?" Before I could guess, Bertha announced, "Libby is coming to dinner, and she's going to bring a pan of corn bread."

I gulped and then held my breath. I didn't breathe again until Bertha left my room, which was a few seconds later. The last thing I'd wanted to do on a Saturday evening was have dinner with a bitch like Libby.

That was last week, and it had been a painful dinner with Libby sitting directly across the table from me, grazing like a cow, guzzling beer straight out of the can, and complaining about us having chitlins for the fourth time in less than a month. The only good thing about that dinner was that Bertha had not mentioned what I'd told her about the man I'd met in the mall and joined for coffee.

Here I was today, sitting on my bed scolding myself for jumping the gun with Calvin. I hadn't heard a word from him, and after all I'd told Bertha last Saturday, I felt like a damn fool now. She had not mentioned his name since. If she never brought him up again, I wouldn't either, unless I heard from him.

I removed my cell phone from my purse and hit speed dial for Joan's number. She answered right away. "Hey, girl. I need to talk," I began.

"Uh-oh. You finally heard from your truck driver and he told you he's not interested after all?"

"No, I haven't heard from him."

"Now that you've had a little time to think about what we discussed today, do you still think Calvin seemed as interested in you in person as he did in his e-mails?"

"Well, the more I think about how nice and attentive he was in the coffee shop, the more I think he is interested in seeing me again. He listened very patiently and with a lot of attention while I rambled on about TV shows and shopping — things that would bore the average man."

"Then I wonder what the problem is with him."

"What makes you think there's a prob-lem?"

"There is a reason why he hasn't contacted you again. I mean, he knows he doesn't have to commit to anything, other than the sex, so something else must be up."

I silently agreed with Joan, but I took my time responding. "Maybe I'm wrong and he's just not interested!" I snapped, not meaning to come off sounding so blunt.

"Not interested in sleeping with you?"

"I don't know. I couldn't tell if sex was even on his mind."

"Girl, the man joined Discreet Encounters, so sex is definitely on his mind. He could get busy with a woman every night of the week if he wanted to."

"I know that, but . . . well, he gave me the impression that having sex with *me* was not a priority. When I told him I wanted to see him again, he said, 'I'll make sure that happens,' but he didn't sound that eager. I've gained a few pounds since I took that picture I posted on the club's website. Maybe he thought I was too big. . . ."

"Lola, you're a size 8. If any man thinks you're too big he's crazy, and you do not need to be fooling around with a maniac." Joan laughed first. I laughed a second later.

"If Reed's not being too obnoxious, I might come over after Bertha goes to bed tonight so we can continue discussing this."

72

"Not tonight," Joan said quickly. Then she lowered her voice to a whisper. "I have a date and I'll be leaving in a few minutes."

"Oh? Who with? You didn't mention anything about having a date tonight when we were having drinks today." I felt slighted, but I didn't want to make a big deal out of it.

"Remember DrFeelGood?"

"Oh yes. The plastic surgeon from Palm Beach who has all those celebrity patients. After your first date with him, you couldn't stop talking about him."

"Uh-huh. He's back in town again already. He called and left a message while I was with you this afternoon. Anyway, he's sitting in his hotel room with a hard-on that's got my name on it."

"Well, excuse me! I'll let you go so you can go take care of that hard-on. I want a full report tomorrow. Where are you going to tell Reed you're going?"

"Honey, I've got that covered. He wouldn't know if the house was on fire."

"Oh. You drugged him again with those pills you got from DrFeelGood?"

"Yup!" Joan chuckled. "Hey, if you ever want to use them on Bertha, just let me know."

"I just might do that. She's as big a

problem as she ever was."

"You think you've got problems? Reed keeps badgering me to go with him to that sleazy adult toy store on Brandon Street so we can pick up a few items to put the spark back into our sex life."

"What spark? From what you've told me about Reed, there was never a spark to begin with. If anything, I thought you were trying to wean him. Anyway, you're getting enough sex from men in the club for three women. Putting a spark in your dead-dick husband is the last thing you need to do if you ever hope to make him lose interest in you enough for you to get that divorce."

"I know, I know. But until I get to that point, I'll do just enough to keep him off my back." Joan exhaled and sucked on her teeth. "I'd love to keep talking, but I need to get to that hotel lickety-split because my pussy is on fire."

There were times when my girl was so explicit, it made me flinch. But that was the kind of woman she was. I wished that I could be more like her. "Joan." I hesitated.

"What?"

"Have fun."

"I always do!"

CHAPTER 9
JOAN

It was Monday morning, just before dawn. Ezra and I were both awake, lying in silence after a night of incredible sex. He rolled over in bed and roughly pulled me into his arms again. We made love for the fourth time since I'd sashayed into his hotel suite a few minutes past eight last night.

It had been a long night filled with the kind of rip-roaring good sex I lived for. I couldn't remember the last time I climaxed five times with the same man during the same session.

The posh hotel suite was cluttered with empty champagne bottles, leftovers from our midnight seafood snack, and used condoms. The bed was in such disarray, it looked like somebody had been murdered in it. The pillow that Ezra had used to elevate my butt was now lodged between my legs.

Around seven a.m. I wiggled out of his

viselike embrace and scrambled out of bed. With a disgruntled snort he threw back the covers, kicked one of the king-size pillows to the floor, sat bolt upright, and folded his arms. There was a pout on his face. On a man his age, which was fifty, it looked downright ridiculous. He was spoiled, so naturally he pouted when he didn't get his way. I had to remind myself that Ezra was the only son of a pampered Jewish socialite from Boston and a Dutch billionaire from Amsterdam. People had catered to him all his life.

"You know I don't like to eat alone," Ezra reminded. "Will you stay long enough to have breakfast with me?"

"You know I would if I could. If Reed wakes up before I get back home, I'll never hear the end of it." I gave Ezra the most endearing look I could manage. "Next time we'll plan better."

He sighed. Then he took his time looking me up and down as I stood naked by the side of the bed. "I didn't want to mention it, but you're getting a little fluffy around the middle, my dear." I didn't know if the remark was a serious criticism or just a light-hearted, random observation. No matter which one it was, it made my chest tighten and my head swim. "You know I could tighten up or smooth out any part you'd like. Free of charge, of course."

I sucked in my gut and gave Ezra a pensive look. "Do you really mean that?" I asked, cursing myself for gobbling up chitlins and peach cobbler at Lola's house three times last month. "Can I get breast implants, too, pretty please?"

"Absolutely! And any size you want. Making people look good is what I do best, and I sure as hell get paid well enough to do it. A woman's appearance is very important to me."

He sure was particular about how other people looked. It was a good thing he was so skilled in bed, or no woman in her right mind would want to sleep with him. The main reason I'd accepted his first date request was because every single review of his performance on the club's blog had rated him five out of five stars.

Despite his plain looks, chronic bad breath, and hairy body, I adored Ezra. He did something no other man had ever done for me. He made me have orgasms so intense, they vibrated all the way down to my toes! And, because of his work and all the famous people he socialized with and performed surgery on, he was an interesting person to talk to. If I agreed to let him remodel my body, the surgeries and recovery process could really put a strain on my time, which I was already pushing to the limit.

"Let me think about it," I said.

"Well, you'd better not take too much time to 'think about it.' I have back-to-back appointments on my calendar for the next few months. It'll be hard to squeeze you in somewhere, so the sooner you let me know, the easier it'll be for me to make the arrangements. I'll have you flown by private jet from here to Palm Beach, and I can book you into the hotel of your choice, where you can take as much time as necessary to recover. Then we'll mosey on over to Worth Avenue, which is a stone's throw from my office, and I'll purchase you a whole new wardrobe to go with your new body. And, whenever you can get away for two or three weeks, we'll spend some time lounging at my beach house in Costa Rica."

"Damn," I mouthed. "You'd be willing to do all that for me for *free*?"

Ezra nodded and gave me a smug look. "That and more."

"Damn," I said again.

When I got back to South Bay City, I parked the shiny, blue Buick that Reed had purchased for my birthday last year on the street in front of our building. I glanced at my watch as I entered the lobby. I realized I'd been gone for almost ten hours.

I entered the condo as quietly as possible. On any other Monday morning Reed would have been up long before now. I was happy to see that the living-room drapes were still closed, and the place was as silent as a tomb. I shuffled closer to the hallway and then started moving toward the master bedroom. I silently prayed that the knockout drops I'd put in Reed's wine last night had not worn off. But I already had a list of believable lies in the front of my mind in case I had to use one.

I stopped in front of the door, held my breath, and listened. I could hear him inside snoring like an ox. I eased open the door, tiptoed across the floor to my closet, and grabbed one of my bathrobes.

I almost jumped out of my skin when Reed mumbled some gibberish and gritted his teeth. I stood stock-still and held my breath until his snoring resumed a few seconds later. Then I went into the bathroom across the hall. I closed and locked the door and changed from the slacks and blouse I'd worn to the hotel into my bathrobe. Next I removed an unopened pack of condoms from my purse. I slid them into the same large baggie under the sink where I kept my tampons, douche powder, butt spray, and all the other feminine products that made Reed flinch so much that I never had to worry about him snooping around in this area.

I emptied my bladder, flushed the toilet, and took a deep breath as I headed back to the bedroom. When I opened the door, I cleared my throat and let out a loud cough. Reed spewed some more gibberish and flopped around a little, but he didn't open his eyes.

I looked at him for about a minute before I strolled over to the bed and sat down on his side. I ran my fingers along the side of his face and pinched his nose. His eyes flew open, and he sat bolt upright, flailing his arms as if they were wings on a dying chicken.

"What — what the hell . . ." he began. With his eyes looking as big as saucers, he looked at the clock on the nightstand and gasped. "Baby, I must have really been drunk last night, huh? I don't remember a damn thing after we finished that fried rice and that bottle of wine."

"You were really tired last night, honey. You drank most of the wine. From now on, you get only one glass when we eat Chinese food," I scolded, offering him a warm smile to sweeten the pot. "You could barely walk on your own. I had to practically drag you to the bedroom, and don't get on my case about putting you to bed in your clothes. After hauling your drunken ass from the living room, I was too worn out to undress you too."

Reed gave me an apologetic look and shook his head. "You poor thing. I'm sorry. I'll make it up to you."

"Make what up to me?"

"The way you were teasing me by sucking on those egg rolls last night and giving me one lusty look after another, I could tell you wanted to do some sucking on me. And you know I *always* want to do the same thing to you," he said hoarsely, rubbing the side of my arm. "Don't worry; we have a couple of hours before Mother brings Junior home, so we can get as buck wild and loud as we want to!" Reed sat up straighter, squeezed my breast, and gave me a long, sloppy kiss. I moaned. "I hear you, baby," he yelled. He leaned his head back and looked directly into my eyes. "You're going to be moaning a whole lot louder than that when I get my hands on you! I'm going to take a shower, have a cup of coffee, and then I'm going to make love to you like I've never made love to you before!"

"Ooh . . . wee. I . . . I c-can't w-wait," I stammered, slowly and dryly. He was too dense to notice my indifference.

"I am a lucky man to have such a beautiful, sexy wife all to myself." Reed pulled me into his arms and gave me another sloppy kiss. His morning breath was as foul as mule shit. What he said next made me want to run out of the room screaming. "Joan, marrying you was the best thing I ever did in my life, and I'm sure I'll still think that forty, fifty years from now. You're my most prized possession, and I will *never* let you go. . . ."

CHAPTER 10
CALVIN

It had been two weeks since I'd met Lola Poole in person. I was glad Valentine's Day was going to end in a few hours. Like Groundhog Day, it was one of the stupidest "holidays" on the calendar. As far as I was concerned, lovers were supposed to show affection to each other every day of the year. Lola had casually mentioned it during our coffee break, which I had taken as a hint that she wanted to spend it with me. Well, I didn't have time for anything that foolish. Especially with a woman I was planning to kill. I had told her some bullshit story about me having to work today. She had given me her cell phone number, so I'd felt obligated to give mine to her as well. Since that day, I'd repeatedly replayed some of the things she'd babbled about. Her mama had been a schoolteacher, her daddy had driven a city bus, blah, blah, blah. What made her think I would care about all that mundane shit, I

83

wondered. I made appropriate comments to everything she said, and I shared a lot of information about myself. But only enough to impress her, which was not hard to do. This woman was an all-day sucker. Now that I'd seen her in the flesh, I couldn't stop thinking about her pending murder. And I still occasionally thought about the moans that I thought I'd heard coming from my garage. I hadn't heard them since last week. But from that night on, each time I got into my bed, I slept on the side next to the night-stand that contained my Bible and my gun.

I slept like a baby almost every night; even when I was on an interstate haul and had to check into a cheap truck stop motel. When a place looked too seedy and a bunch of lowlifes and hookers were on the premises, I stretched out in the cab of my rig. As well as I slept, I occasionally had dreams that I couldn't remember the next day. Since Lola was on my mind so much now, I was pretty sure that she'd been in some of those dreams. I was certain that if there was such a thing as a "dream girl," she was mine. It didn't matter to me that she was an immature ditz. During our coffee shop conversation, she'd told me how much she enjoyed watching some of the same TV shows I watched, like *60 Minutes, 48 Hours,* and most of the documentaries featured on the National Geographic channel. In the next breath she told me her favorite programs were *The Real Housewives of Atlanta, Golden Girls* reruns, and *Family Feud*! I could not imagine what a woman Lola's age got out of watching straight-up, moronic crap like that. A pretty woman with scrambled eggs for brains could cause a man a lot of headaches and heartaches. One as idiotic as Lola Poole would be better off dead no matter what!

Like a lot of scatterbrained women, Lola had power she probably didn't even know she had. She was so sexy, I got an instant erection when I was within two feet of her, just like I had when I met Glinda for the first time, almost nine years ago. It was amazing how two women could have the same impact on me. Well, for one thing, they were carbon copies of each other. Even more so than I'd originally thought. Not only was Lola Glinda's physical clone, she had some of the same mannerisms. I'd almost fainted when Lola laughed with a cute snort the same way Glinda used to. And Lola drank her coffee through a straw — one of Glinda's habits that used to amuse me. Lola's life was now in my hands. And I was ecstatic. I wanted to savor every moment of the euphoria that was so potent I could almost taste it. Otherwise, I would have killed her already. The ball was in my court. I would determine when and how she died — unless some other maniac did her in first.

The day I met Lola, the effect she already had on me doubled. So did my homicidal urges. By the time I got home after our meeting, I was seething with anger. I immediately turned on my computer and went straight to the club's website. I spent fifteen minutes reading the reviews about her and staring at the picture that she'd included with her profile. That was basically all I did for the next two weeks. Even when I was on the road. I always took my laptop with me, and I stopped for rest or food only at places that had free Wi-Fi, because I couldn't go a day without looking at that bitch's face, reading the reviews about her nasty ass, and fantasizing about her dead body. Each time I thought of something new to add to the plan, like mutilating her face with a box cutter and removing her toes and teeth with a pair of pliers. I even thought about dismembering her. The thought of putting her severed head in a bucket and marinating it with my own urine amused me. No matter what I ultimately decided to do to that goddamn woman, it was going to be a pleasure.

Because of Lola, I temporarily lost interest in all other females. For the next two weeks, I avoided them all. When I went to my local grocery store a few days ago, I waited around until a male cashier was available before I paid for my purchases. I refused to cash a check at my bank the day after that because all of the tellers were female. I didn't even want to see or talk to Sylvia Bruce, my longtime lady friend.

Like a lot of women, Sylvia saw everything through rose-colored glasses when it came to romance. She was no raving beauty, but she was attractive enough with her medium-length brown hair, Cabbage Patch–looking face, and petite body. She was about as gullible, docile, and naïve as they came. As far as she was concerned, I was the "perfect" lover. And it was no wonder. I gave Sylvia enough attention to keep her happy, I was generous to her, and I usually treated her with a decent amount of respect. However, I couldn't be *too* good to her, because I didn't want her to think that I had even a drop of wimp blood in my body. No matter how weak or strong a woman was, she wanted a strong man.

I even told Sylvia on a regular basis that I loved her. I had her in the bottom of my hip pocket and she didn't even know it. All she was to me was a front — somebody who made me look good to the rest of the world. I planned to keep her around for as long as I needed her. Hell, there was even a chance that I'd marry her and start a family. I knew that with a wife like Sylvia, I could continue doing everything I wanted. And the main thing was, I *had* to spend time with other women. What straight man didn't? It was unrealistic for anybody in their right mind to believe that a dude could be faithful to one woman. That didn't even happen in the Bible.

After my two-week "hiatus," I decided it was time to check in with Sylvia.

"Calvin? Where have you been for the past couple of weeks? I haven't heard from you since the day before the Super Bowl! I've been worried sick about you," she told me this evening when I responded to the numerous voice mail messages she'd left on my landline and my cell phone. Even though I couldn't see her, I knew there was a "woe-is-me" look on her face from the weary tone of her voice. "I was so frantic, I called up one of your neighbors. I had him check to see if you'd been attacked in your house or something and was lying in a hospital. I was glad to hear from him that that was not the case. I was beginning to think you'd decided not to see me anymore, but I would have preferred to hear it from you."

I read Sylvia like a book, so I knew she'd be upset with me because of my unexplained absence. I also knew that she'd still be glad to see me again no matter how long I stayed away.

"I've been real busy with a lot of personal issues," I said, speaking more harshly than I intended. I immediately softened my voice. "I just needed some time alone to clear my head, that's all. Baby, I'm so sorry, and I'll make it up to you. I've missed you. . . ."

"I've missed you too. I picked up some of those His and Her steaks a couple of weeks ago that you wanted me to cook for our dinner after the game. They're still in the freezer. Are you going to be home this evening?"

"Yeah, I'll be home."

"Did you watch the Super Bowl?"

"No, I missed it." I'd drunk so much booze that evening after my meeting with Lola, I had passed out and slept for twenty-four hours. That was the only reason I'd missed the game. And, had it not been for Lola, I wouldn't have been drinking like a fish in the first place.

Sylvia gasped. "Oh my God! You really

must have been out of it if you missed the Holy Grail of football games. You've never missed it."

"I know. But the dude next door recorded it, so I'll still get to watch it. Baby, um, I'm sorry I haven't been in touch lately. In addition to work issues, I had to deal with another nasty family situation about the house."

Sylvia let out a loud sigh of disgust. "Damn those people! I wish they would get off your back and stop trying to make you sell your house and split the money with them. And that's a damn shame. That's *your* house. Your grandmother left it to you in her will, and they should respect that."

"You know what they say about relatives. They can be your best friends or your worst enemies."

"Tell me about it. Me and my used-to-be favorite cousin Pam, we haven't spoken in ten years. All on account of me dating her ex." Sylvia suddenly began to speak in a meek tone of voice. "Um, if you don't . . . um . . . mind telling me, exactly where were you when I tried to reach you at seven this morning? I figured that with today being a Sunday, you'd still be in bed. I called your cell phone and your home phone. I even sent a text message." Sylvia paused and sucked in some air. I could hear the pain in her voice, and it made me feel like shit. "I was so concerned, I even called your boss this morning to make sure you hadn't been in an accident. A couple of days ago, there was a TV news report about a driver who was hauling some produce up from Mexico, fell asleep at the wheel, and drove over a cliff. He died on impact."

"In the first place, I always stop and check into a motel as soon as I get drowsy. And in the second place, I wasn't scheduled to work this weekend, baby, and wouldn't have been able to do so if I had." I decided to tell Sylvia part of the truth. "I've been drinking a lot these past couple of weeks, and missing a lot of work that I'll have to make up. I was blacking out left and right. I blacked out again four days ago and I didn't wake up until the next morning — on my living-room floor."

"What made you go off the deep end?"

"My cousin Willis and that battle-axe he's married to stormed my house again the day before the game. They had been doing cocaine for days, so they got all up in my face about how they needed the money from the sale of the house so they could get a new roof put on theirs. After I chased them off, I went for a drive to clear my head, sweetheart."

"Calvin, you never drink and drive —"

"I didn't do any really heavy drinking until about five days ago, and I did it in my own home," I said quickly.

"You poor thing, you. I feel so sorry for you having to deal with those obnoxious relatives of yours. No wonder you don't have much to do with most of the folks in your family."

There was a good reason why I didn't associate with some of my family members. They didn't associate with me was a more accurate way of putting it, though. I had embarrassed and upset them by marrying the town slut. Shortly after my discharge from the military almost five years ago, Glinda left me for another man and then she mysteriously "disappeared." A lot of folks, including her family, thought she was dead. Most of my relatives were still angry with me for marrying her in the first place and had little or nothing to do with me now. Glinda had had a fling with my older sister Vickie's philandering husband, so she avoided me. Other than my older brother Ronald, my uncle Ed in Chicago, my co-workers, a few buddies I'd served with in the Marines, and Sylvia, I didn't socialize with a lot of people.

"Before my drinking got out of control yesterday, I drove around for a while. While I was sitting at a red light, I saw that driver from Berkeley that I filled in for a couple of months ago. You remember Joe Lurie, don't you? I took you to a Juneteenth cookout at his house last summer." I didn't give Sylvia time to respond. "His wife had told him that morning that she wanted a divorce, so he was in pretty bad shape. He had me follow him back to his house. We talked, drank, and played cards for hours. I didn't feel like driving, so I spent last night at his place. That's where I was when you called this morning." It was such a blatant lie. Last night I'd spent two hours drinking in my living room while I stared off and on at Lola's picture on my computer monitor again. I was trying to come up with more ways to make her suffer. I got so creative; I considered pouring sulfuric acid over her entire body — while she was still alive — to obliterate her completely. I didn't stay on that notion for long. I had been saving a spot in my freezer for her too long to change that part of my plan.

"You spent last night at Joe's house? Hmmm. Isn't he one of the men you suspected your ex was fooling around with while you were in Afghanistan?"

"Huh? Oh, uh, yeah. That was one of the rumors going around. I don't know if it was true or not. I confronted Glinda about Joe, and she denied being involved with him. I asked him about it, and he denied it too."

"Honey, I hate to say this, but I truly believe that Glinda really is dead. I know they never found her body, and they don't have any evidence that she's dead, but I have a gut feeling that she's gone. From the rumors I've heard, she was heavy into cocaine, and everybody knows there is no happy ending to a story when drugs are involved. Maybe she overdosed in some-body's house and they didn't want to get in trouble so they disposed of her body in some remote place where it'll never be found."

"Yes, she was into drugs. And she was hanging out with some very dangerous people, so there is no telling what happened to her. . . ."

"I ran into her cousin Nita the other day. She's nothing like Glinda, but she's still kind of strange."

"Strange in what way?"

"She lives with some guy from Haiti who calls himself a psychic. I don't believe in that baloney but she told me that he told her somebody murdered Glinda. He claims her body is in a very strange, very *cold* place."

"Hmmm. Well, I don't believe in any mumbo jumbo coming from a witch doctor, but I have a very strong feeling that Glinda is dead too. They found the body of the dude she'd been fooling around with in one of the most dangerous areas in Mexico. Dead bodies are dumped there on a regular basis. She's probably down there somewhere too. What's left of her, that is. She probably pissed off one of those drug-dealing pig farmers and he used her for fertilizer."

"I can certainly believe that," Sylvia said in a low voice. "Just talking about that woman gives me a chill. Well, I hope they find her remains someday so you can give her a proper burial."

"I sure hope so too. No matter what Glinda did, she was still a human being and my wife, and I still loved her. I'd hate to spend the rest of my life wondering what happened to her," I responded with my voice cracking.

"Baby, I can hear the pain in your voice. I am so sorry for bringing up painful memories."

"Don't worry about it, honey. I'm fine." I sniffed. I decided it was time to toss Sylvia a very big bone. "Sweetheart, I'd like to take you to Brazil for your birthday in June."

"You would?" she gasped. "Oh, Calvin! That would be my dream come true. I've always wanted to visit the country my mother's family came from."

"June is a long way off, but in the meantime, I'm going to work overtime on our relationship. I even bought a new suit to wear to your supervisor's wedding next month."

"You didn't forget about that? I was so afraid I was going to have to go to Felice's wedding with my cross-eyed cousin, Alonzo. I . . . I'm so happy, I think I'm going to cry."

"So am I," I said.

We both laughed.

"When will I see you again, Calvin?"

"I still have a slight headache from all the drinking and the mess with my cousin, so I'd really like to get some rest tonight. If it's not too inconvenient, can I come over tomorrow evening around six?"

"You can come over at any time you want!"

"Then six it is."

After my conversation with Sylvia, I took a hot shower, slid into my pajamas, and mixed myself a large glass of rum and Coke. It was seven p.m. when I stretched out on my living-room couch to watch an episode of *Law and Order* that I had recorded.

As soon as I got a good buzz, my mind began to wander. I wondered how many other criminals enjoyed watching crime shows on TV as much as I did. I also wondered if they learned how to be better criminals by doing so. I sure had. Even though cops were generally dumb as hell, they had gradually come up with all kinds of ways to solve crimes over the years. Had I not known about DNA, forensics, and all the rest of that shit I'd learned from TV, I'd have been caught a long time ago.

When *Law and Order* ended, I decided to do some chores that I had been putting off. I did my laundry and ran the vacuum over my living-room and bedroom carpets. Then I checked the online schedule for my next run. I was glad to see that I had two back-to-back runs from Portland, Oregon, to the San Fernando Valley next week. I was ready for a fresh kill. It had been too long since the last one. I had a mission to continue, and I was not about to let anything get in my way. Meeting Lola had been the shot in the arm I'd needed to get myself back on track.

My plan was to let another week or two go by before I communicated with her again, unless she contacted me first. That was just what happened.

CHAPTER 11
JOAN

Despite the fact that Reed and I had been together for almost fifteen years, there were times when it felt as if I was married to a stranger. He was not the man I thought he was when we first met. Had I known what he was really like before I married him, I would have dropped him like a bad habit. He was a neat freak of epic proportions. A single crumb on the kitchen counter could set him off. Everything in our home had to be arranged to please him. One time he actually took a ruler and measured the distance between the framed photographs I had hung on the walls. He was insecure and paranoid, and he whined and pouted like a baby almost every single day. He was an only child, and his stuffy parents were a major thorn in my side. I cringed every time they visited us. They had their own keys, and sometimes they even dropped in when Reed and I were out. I was horrified the first time I came home from a shopping trip and found my mother-in-law wallowing in my bathtub with bubble bath up to her three chins like she was Queen of England. My father-in-law didn't come around that often, but when he did he was as annoying as his wife. If all that was not enough to drive a woman like me crazy, Reed was a major flop in the bedroom. I spent a fortune on batteries for the vibrators I owned, which I used to finish the jobs he started.

Leaving him was not an option. At least not yet. In addition to his threats to commit suicide, my family made it clear to me that no woman in her right mind would leave a man who had as much to offer as Reed. Especially a black woman from the hood. Besides, he was a cash cow to most of my relatives. Reed's parents didn't offer much support or sympathy either. Even though he had attempted suicide once, they still refused to believe he was serious. No matter how many times I tried to get them to be more proactive in this situation, each time they told me that I was "overreacting" and that as long as I treated Reed the way I was supposed to, everything would be fine. Once I even offered to contact intervention professionals I'd heard about, and it only made him angry. "Woman, if you even think that I'd be willing to sit down face-to-face and talk to a bunch of meddling strangers about my problem, you're crazier than I thought! Putting my business out there like that would really push me over the edge!" he warned.

Two days after our latest confrontation, he drove to San Francisco to attend a conference and would be gone most of the day. I called up Mama and told her to set a plate at the dinner table for me.

It was always a treat to be with my family. Every time I visited, I got so much attention, you would have thought that I'd just come home from an extended leave. But that was not the case. I went to my mother's house at least once a week.

Five minutes after everybody in the house had sat down to feast on the oxtails and rice that Mama had prepared, I kicked off the conversation. As soon as I spoke the first sentence, all eyes were on me. "I wish I'd never met Reed Riley. It's getting harder and harder to live under the same roof with him." I was not surprised to hear gasps and see stunned looks on every face at the table. I knew I was going to get a tongue-lashing from them, but I didn't care. I had been keeping my feelings from them long enough.

Mama was horrified. Her mouth dropped

open so wide, I could see the fillings in her molars. "What's wrong with you, girl? Your home is a palace compared to this dump we live in. Y'all got a swimming pool, a fitness center, and doctors and lawyers and businessmen for neighbors."

"That's not all I care about. It's still not enough for me, anyway," I insisted.

"Not enough? Are you crazy? What else do you want, Joan — gold?" my stepfather Elmo hollered with an incredulous look on his face. "You can eat steak and lobster and drink champagne every day if you want to. This is the third time this week we've had oxtails and rice and Kool-Aid," he added as he made a sweeping gesture over the table. "And your poor, sweet mama uses coupons every time she goes to the market. I bet Reed ain't never even set foot in the Food-4-Less or the grocery store outlets like us regular folks do."

Reed had never set foot in a discount store. Last week when he went to an auto supply store to purchase new seat covers for his Lexus, he refused to park in any of the vacant parking spaces in the strip mall because they were too close to Walmart. He had personalized license plates — DRRRDDS — so a lot of people recognized his vehicle. He didn't want any of them to see his car and assume he was shopping in a Walmart! He parked three blocks away.

"Reed didn't grow up the way I did," I defended. "And if he can afford to shop in high-end stores, why not?"

"That's all the more reason why *you* shouldn't still be shopping in no discount store," Mama pointed out.

"I shop in the expensive stores too," I declared, holding up my arm so they could see the diamond bracelet on my wrist. I was sure that it had cost more than every piece of jewelry Mama owned put together. The beige suede dress I had on had set me back nine hundred dollars. "But I still like to take advantage of a good bargain." I was wearing a bra I had purchased at Target for eight dollars.

"Well, you know what they say. You can take a person out of the hood, but you can't take the hood out of the person," my step-father snickered. His comment made all of us laugh. Then Elmo suddenly got quiet. With his eyes squinted, he gave me a critical look. "Joan, you got it made in the shade. Most rich black men are as old as Methuselah and they look like baboons. They're probably stingy as hell too. And they marry white or Asian women. Not only do you have a youngish, rich black man,

Reed's generous with his money and he's good-looking!"

"I'm still not happy," I insisted, looking across the dinner table at my forty-two-year-old sister, Elaine. Since she had divorced her husband when I was still in high school and had her share of problems with other men now, I expected some sympathy from her.

Instead of showing me some support, Elaine stared at me with a blank expression on her face and started talking in a low, detached voice. "I curse the day I left my husband. I hear he just bought a house, furniture, and a new car for his wife. And they just had their third baby. If I had had more sense and patience, all of that would be mine. Here I am almost forty-three years old, still living with my mama, and I don't have a new husband or any kids of my own in sight."

I turned to Too Sweet. She had never been married and had not had sex in over twenty years. The only thing left on her bucket list was a husband. She was the family fool, so she was flighty, irresponsible, and unpredictable. A person never knew what to expect from her. She owed me a few favors, so I thought she'd be in my corner. "Too Sweet, you saw how Reed complained about a few specks of dust on the furniture last month when you came over to have dinner with us. And you heard how he was complaining about the roast beef I'd cooked that day."

Too Sweet reared back in her seat and tilted her head to the side. She still had a wad of food in her jaw, but she started talking anyway. "Well, I ain't taking sides, but there was a lot of dust on the furniture and you did burn the roast beef. I had to take some Pepto-Bismol to settle my stomach and get that nasty taste out of my mouth." I didn't like what my cousin said in her husky voice, but she did display a hint of sympathy by touching my shoulder and giving me a warm smile. "I pray for you every night, Joan. To you, Reed Riley might not be the best husband in the world, but I bet a dollar to a donut you wouldn't want to trade places with me." Too Sweet swallowed the food in her mouth and reached for another piece of corn bread. Then she added, "Get yourself together, girl. If you was to lose Reed and end up back in the hood, then you'd have something to be bitching and moaning about."

"Amen, amen, amen," Mama chanted, glancing at my stepfather. Elmo made fairly good money as a mechanic but not enough to please Mama. She complained almost every day about still having to work as a security guard at the local women's detention facility. I never bothered to remind her that if she'd stop trying to live a champagne lifestyle on a beer budget, she'd be okay. Even though she purchased groceries at the outlets, she had to have a high-definition TV in her bedroom, the living room, and the den. She had to shop in the high-end stores at least once a month, and she had to spend money on lavish parties to entertain our whole family — which was very large — and half of the neighborhood on a regular basis.

"You should have stayed single like your girl Lola," Elaine said with a dry chuckle. "She don't have a husband and she's happy as can be."

"For your information, Lola is anxious to get married. Lately, that's all she talks about," I said.

"Well, if Lola wants to get married, get a house of her own, and have kids, she'd better hurry up. She ain't getting no younger. And you can tell her I said so," Too Sweet said with a smirk. "Is she even dating anybody right now?"

"Uh, yeah. She's going out with a few guys, but there's one I think she's really got a thing for," I announced. "He's a real good-looking truck driver who lives in San Jose."

"Uh-oh. What's wrong with him?" Mama wanted to know. "Lola has never had much luck with men, and that's why she's still single. If this truck driver is serious about her, he must not have much going for him." Mama stopped talking and frowned at her baby brother as he entered the kitchen, yawning. Uncle Billy was fifty, recently divorced, and between jobs. He'd moved in last month and had promised Mama and Elmo that he'd be on his own within six months. "Only God knows where the *good* men are hiding these days," Mama added, still looking at my uncle. His wife had dumped him because he was lazy and couldn't hold a job longer than a few months. He wasn't the first relative to end up on our doorstep with a tale of woe. Mama and Elmo didn't know how to say no when somebody in the family needed help. And, despite the fact that they thought so highly of Reed, I knew that if I wanted to come back home, they'd welcome me with open arms. But as long as Reed held me hostage with his suicide threats, I was not moving back home or anywhere else.

CHAPTER 12
CALVIN

I got up Sunday morning around nine so I could go to the market and pick up a few groceries. I planned to spend the rest of the weekend kicking back and having a few drinks. Right after I took a quick shower and got dressed, I turned on my laptop and checked my e-mail messages. I was not surprised to see one from Lola. I rolled my eyes, let out a sigh of disgust, and read it.

Hello Calvin. I hope you are having a good day. I just wanted to say hello and tell you again how much I enjoyed meeting you. I REALLY enjoyed your company! Lola . . .

☺

I had her pegged right. She sounded like a giddy schoolgirl who hadn't been fucked in years. I was almost afraid to imagine what she'd be like between the sheets. As frisky as she was, she'd probably fuck me off the bed. The thought of me tumbling to the floor in the middle of an orgasm made me chuckle.

I wanted to see her again and get a "relationship" going so I could pursue the mission I was determined to complete. The way she'd gazed at me and after hearing some of the corny shit she'd said when we were having coffee, I could tell she couldn't wait to get me into bed. And I was looking forward to it. She had a luscious little body, and it would be a damn shame to kill her before I fucked her and let all that pussy go to waste. But since the mission I had arranged was so elaborate, I had to stick to my original plan and take my time getting to know her before the big day — Lola's *last* day — arrived.

Although the rest of my plan was set, I wasn't sure how I was going to do the bitch in. I didn't want to shoot her. That would be too quick. But I could picture the look of terror in her eyes if she saw the barrel of my Glock aimed at her face. No matter what method I used, I wanted her to suffer. I didn't want to beat or stab her to death. That would be too messy. I had strangled all the others, but since Lola was so special, I wanted her to die in a unique way. Pushing her off a cliff after I'd beaten the dog shit out of her sounded like fun until I realized I'd have a hard time retrieving her body so I could stuff her into the freezer. If I did decide to strangle her, I'd make it as painful and slow as possible. With my hands around her throat and my eyes looking into hers as she gasped for breath, the process would be up close and personal. Picturing that excited me.

I scratched my chin and pursed my lips. One thing was for sure: Somewhere along the way I'd let Lola know *why* she'd been chosen. So many murder victims die and never know why. I'd even show her a picture of Glinda. It was the least I could do, because under different circumstances I might have fallen in love with Lola and maybe even married her!

I told myself that she had it coming. She had put herself in danger by being such a slut, hopping in and out of bed with Internet strangers. Was the woman insane too? Had I not taken on the role of executioner, some other Internet dude probably would have eventually killed her anyway. And she'd only have herself to blame for it. For one thing, nuts were everywhere, especially on social media. For all I knew, she could already be on another killer's hit list! She would not be hard to find. Right next to her picture, her online profile on the club's website listed her full name and her place of employment. She had posted the same information on Facebook, Twitter, and Instagram! And if that wasn't enough to make her a sitting duck, her name, telephone number, and home address were even listed in the damn telephone book! It was unlikely that another killer would do her in before I could do the deed, so I put that notion aside.

Just as I was about to reply to Lola's corny e-mail message, my cell phone vibrated in my pants pocket. I was not one to spend much time yakking on the telephone, especially on a Saturday morning. I was tempted to let the call go to voice mail, but I'm glad I didn't. It was my uncle Ed calling from Chicago. He was my mother's only living brother and the only family member who had not objected to my marrying Glinda, even though the institution of marriage brought up some painful memories for him. At the age of thirty-five Uncle Ed had married a young woman; she died suddenly in the third month of her first pregnancy. My uncle had always been a good-looking dude, so there had never been a shortage of women in his life. But he didn't meet another one he cared enough about to marry until he was sixty-four, more than twenty years ago. She was in her fifties, had four grown children, and had already been married three times. Everything was going well until that bitch jilted him on their wedding day. He was so devastated, he never proposed to another woman. The day he saw the woman who had jilted him on the arm of another man, he quit his job, sold his house, and a week later he moved to Chicago.

I was always very close to Uncle Ed. I called him up fairly often, and I wrote to him at least once a month. His letters to me were so sad and full of emotion, sometimes I cried while reading one. When I realized how lonesome he was, I begged my mother to let me go live with him for a while, and she reluctantly agreed to do so. I was seventeen at the time. As much as I loved my uncle, I missed California and the rest of my family, so I moved back to San Jose when I was twenty.

I plopped down onto the side of my bed and quickly answered my phone. "Uncle Ed, my man! It's so good to hear from you. I was going to call you in a day or so," I exclaimed. My uncle was so old school, he made telephone calls only when he had to, so I knew he was not calling me up just to say hello. My chest tightened. Like most men his age who drank too much and ate everything he shouldn't, he had a laundry list of health issues. "Are you okay?" I asked.

"I've had better days." Uncle Ed paused and belched a few times. "Excuse me. I just had another pain in my bosom. If it ain't my prostate condition sending me back and forth to the doctor, problems with my diabetes, or my arthritis, it's something else."

"Oh? Things are that bad?"

"Uh-huh. Well, this time it's something else and it's real serious, so I won't waste your time or mine beating around the bush."

"Oh?" I said again as I held my breath.

"Remember that pain my daddy had in his gut?"

"Yeah," I said in a low voice. My grandfather had died of stomach cancer twenty-five years ago.

"I'm having that same pain in my gut. I swallowed some barley soup yesterday evening, and this morning it came back out of me from *both* ends."

"I see. Have you been to a doctor lately?"

"Lately? *Pffft!* I been going to see a doctor almost every week since last year. And for what? Most of them quacks spend more time playing golf than healing folks! That jackass I used to go to told me I had gas.

That's what I believed for months even though all he did was give me a prescription. The more of them nasty-tasting horse pills I swallowed, the worse I felt. I finally went to a new doctor a couple of weeks ago. Three days after my first visit to his office, he took it upon hisself to call me at home at night to tell me the real deal: I got one of the most aggressive cases of stomach cancer he's ever seen. Just hearing that, I got so weak and confused I got off the phone and took to my bed and cried like a baby. I had to get sloppy drunk just so I could get some sleep.

"Then, as if Dr. Goldstein hadn't already gone beyond the call of duty for me, the next morning he called and told me to come see him immediately. He was rescheduling somebody else's appointment just so he could tend to me. I was too sick to get out the bed, so he sent his nurse to pick me up and bring me to his office. That's when I seen the X-rays and whatnot. He sent me straight to the hospital that same day. Had I been going to Dr. Goldstein all along, I probably wouldn't be in the mess I'm in now."

I responded with hesitation, practically whispering, "What mess is that?"

"It don't look like I'm going to be around

long. Dr. Goldstein said that if I had come to him from the get-go instead of that play doctor I been going to for years, I'd have another few years to live. Instead, I might be around only a few more weeks now, months if I'm lucky. I wanted to see you again real soon in case my mind goes before the rest of my body."

"It's *that* serious?" I croaked. A huge lump formed in my throat, and I could feel the bile wreaking havoc on my insides.

"Uh-huh. I never did get along with your siblings or too many of the other idiots in our family. You always knew that. But you and me always had something special. I hope you can come see me right away. I would hate to leave without seeing you one more time."

"It's *that* serious?" I asked again, my voice cracking this time.

"Yup," Uncle Ed chirped. I couldn't understand why he was not in a more somber mood.

"I . . . I am so sorry," I fumbled. "Life has been so unfair to you."

"Sure enough. But if you think I'm still pissed off about that heifer leaving me at the altar, I ain't. I had a lot of fun with other ladies. Shit. I had me some of the best nookie in the world. And I've had a real good and long life." My uncle paused and released a mighty belch. "I'm sitting here right now guzzling my sixth beer in the last two hours. And before that, I gobbled up a box of Cracker Jacks, some hog head cheese, a baloney sandwich slathered in mayonnaise and mustard, and I done smoked three whole packs of Marlboros since last night — all the things I had stopped doing for my health. Well, a lot of good denying myself a few pleasures done for me!"

I remained silent because I was trying to come up with something to say that didn't sound patronizing or insincere. Before I could find the right words, Uncle Ed continued.

"Calvin, I'm eighty-seven years old. I should have been dead a long time ago." My uncle surprised me with a hearty laugh, and I was glad that he was still able to do so. I hoped that I would be as "jovial" when I got close to the end of the line. But at the moment, laughing was one thing I didn't know when I'd be able to do again.

"I . . . I'm glad you're still alive and kicking," I said.

"Still alive, yeah. Kicking? I ain't done that in a long time. Now listen to me, boy; I don't have much, but I want you to have everything I leave behind. There's twenty-two thousand bucks in my bank and a few stocks and bonds worth another eight thousand. Do something nice for yourself with it. Pay off your bills, treat yourself to a nice car, and if you have enough left over, take a real long vacation to one of them countries where the local pussy is real good and real cheap — say a place like Asia or one of them islands in the Caribbean. Don't be a fool like I was and let the money sit in the bank for a rainy day. People don't realize it, but every day is a "rainy day," so they need to enjoy whatever they got while they still can. I took out an insurance policy years ago to cover my funeral and burial, but I don't want none of that. I don't want a bunch of hypocrites gazing at my dead body, saying shit they don't mean. I done been to enough funerals to know that most people hate the whole procedure anyway. Cremation is what I want. I'm planning my "going-away party," so to speak, and I want you to come help me get everything in order. I never ask you for anything, but this is the one thing I hope you can do for me."

"Uncle Ed, nothing in this world is going to keep me from coming to be with you. I'll make my travel plans as soon as I get off the telephone. Other than me, who else knows you're . . . ?"

Uncle Ed cut me off. "Just Dr. Goldstein, my sweet nurse, a few of my neighbors, and that lawyer I hired to make out my will. Oh! And I told your bow-legged cousin, Catherine, just before she took off to go live in France with that Frenchman she met in college. I called her up day before yesterday. She wanted to come, but she's about to have a baby any day, so I told her to stay put. Anyway, that's all the family I want to know. Because I stood by you when you married that hoochie-coochie woman, the rest of the family treated me like shit, so to hell with them."

My uncle rambled on for twenty more minutes about all the good times he and I had shared. By the time we ended our conversation, I was crying so hard you would have thought that I was dying too.

CHAPTER 13
CALVIN

After I composed myself, I went online and made my travel arrangements.

Then I dialed my boss's cell phone number. Monty Sims was one of the coolest dudes I knew. Some of my coworkers, the Hispanics and other African Americans, called him a racist behind his back because he spent more time socializing with other white truckers. But Monty had always treated me with respect, and we got along just fine. I spent a weekend in his house last year when his daughter got married.

Monty was very understanding when I informed him that I had to go out of town right away and the reason. "I promise I will work double time when I return."

"Cal, don't you worry about a thing. Just go on to Chicago and do what you have to do," Monty told me. "And take as much time off as you need."

After I hung up, I gave Sylvia a call and

told her everything Uncle Ed had told me.

"I wish I could go with you," she sobbed. "I'm sorry I never got to meet your uncle. Let me know if you need me to do anything while you're gone. With all the recent burglaries in your neighborhood, maybe it'd be a good idea for somebody to be on the premises at night. I can stay at your house and keep an eye on things for you, or I can get one of my brothers to do it."

"Oh, that won't be necessary," I said quickly. There was no way in the world I was going to have somebody roaming around in my house when I couldn't be there to keep an eye on them. The possibility that they would get nosy enough to snoop around in my garage and come across the freezer with the three corpses sent a shiver up my spine. I recently decided that after I took care of Lola and put her in the freezer, I'd find a more permanent location for the makeshift casket. The strongest possibility was that I'd haul it down to the border and bribe some Mexican thugs to take it to the desert and either torch it or bury it. There were so many other bodies buried in the Mexican desert, a few more wouldn't matter.

"If you change your mind, just let me know," Sylva told me between more sobs.

She was the kind of woman who boo-hooed at the drop of a hat, so I could understand her being so upset about a man she'd never even met. "Do you want me to at least collect and hold your mail? And it's not a good idea to let your newspapers pile up in front of your house. That's a dead give-away to burglars that a resident is not home."

"Don't worry about any of that either. I can go online and have the post office hold my mail, and I'll have the newspaper delivery temporarily stopped too."

"Calvin, I love you. I am so pleased and impressed to know that you care so much about people that you are not wasting any time going to be with your uncle. That Glinda woman you married, she didn't know what a good man she had, did she?"

"I guess she didn't," I said gruffly. "But I'm so much better off without her. And, as long as I have you in my corner, I'm happy. Now if you don't mind, I need to get off this phone and start packing."

I didn't realize it was raining like hell until I heard some thunder. I parted the drapes in my bedroom just in time to see the flash of lightning that followed. When I was a young boy I used to love nasty weather like this, especially if it happened at night and I was in bed. The sound of rain on the win-

121

dow and roof was soothing to me. I hated bad weather now because it made my job dangerous and even more tedious. This unexpected break in my routine was going to do wonders for my morale.

After I packed my suitcase, I sat down at the desk in the corner of my living room where I kept my desktop computer. I read Lola's e-mail again and then I proceeded to check the rest of my messages, which included a bunch of outlandish ads and requests from other female club members who wanted to hook up with me. I was not a vain dude, but most of the women who browsed my profile on the Discreet Encounters website wanted to be with me. I accommodated as many as I could, but only if they were worthy of my attention.

My newest admirers included a middle-aged blonde who lived in Baltimore, a buck-toothed redhead in the L.A. area who sounded like a washed-up Valley girl, and a female executive in Dallas. They all had top-notch, high-tech jobs and would be traveling to nearby Silicon Valley soon to attend meetings and other events. They all wanted to "have some fun" with me. I got turned off when non-black women went on and on about how curious they were about black men in the bedroom. I usually didn't respond to the ones who broke it down like that. Tonight, all three of the women who had notified me were curious to see what it was like to fuck a black man. I sent replies to each one. I explained that I had a personal matter I needed to resolve, so I needed to take a rain check. Just as I expected, less than five minutes later the blonde in Baltimore fired off another message to me. She informed me that if she didn't hear from me by the end of the month, I'd hear from her again.

As much as I loved my dear uncle, his bad news could not have come at a better time. It was the perfect excuse for me not to have contacted Lola since our coffee shop date. Otherwise, I would have to have come up with a good lie to tell her that would explain my two weeks of silence. This way, I only had to tell part of a lie.

My plan was to make it sound like the situation with Uncle Ed had been going on for a while. It didn't take me long to come up with a reply to her e-mail.

Hello, Lola,
I apologize for not communicating with you before now but I am currently involved in a serious family situation. My elderly uncle Ed, who lives in Chi-

cago, is dying. He and I are very close, and I love him dearly. He called me the day after my coffee date with you and told me the bad news. A few hours later, I was on a plane. I want to spend as much time with him as possible while I still can. I've been busy trying to put his affairs in order and assist him in every other way. These matters are very stressful and time-consuming. I haven't been thinking clearly, so I've been out of touch with a lot of people. I returned to California yesterday and his nurse called me up a few hours after I got home to tell me that he'd taken a turn for the worse. Now his days are literally numbered. I will be returning to Chicago tomorrow for the last time.

I will talk to you soon and hope to see you soon. And I enjoyed meeting you, too.

Regards,
Calvin

I was glad I had only slightly altered the truth. If Lola was a righteous woman, she'd feel sorry enough for me to put things on hold until I got back to her. I felt unbearably sad about my uncle, but my life still had to go on.

Less than three minutes after I hit the send button, Lola sent me another e-mail. I didn't like to judge people, but her message was rife with misspelled words and unnecessary symbols. No wonder she was stuck in a dead-end job in that Mickey Mouse grocery store.

Hello again Calvin!@
It was so nice to see a message in my in-box from you. I'm hoppy to know you didn't forget about me!@&#%. I am so sorry to here about your uncle. Unfortunately, we all have to go sooner or later. As you know, I lost both my parents wen I was very young so I know what grief feels like. Take care of yourself and your uncle's business. If you want to see me when you return from Chicago, let me know. Lola XOXOX

I was glad that she had not included another one of those silly smiley face symbols at the end of her message this time. The ones she did include were annoying enough. I shook my head and closed her message. I played part of it over and over in my head until I went to bed. *We all have to go sooner or later* were the words that stood out the most. She was right! I couldn't have said it better myself! *Bitch, you're going to go sooner rather than later. . . .*

CHAPTER 14
LOLA

I looked at the message that I'd sent to Calvin and cringed when I saw the clumsy sentences and typos. When I'd started typing it, I was so excited I couldn't think straight and hit a few keys by mistake. It looked like something a third grader had composed! And I'd been so anxious to send him a prompt reply I had not taken the time to proofread it first. Well, it was too late now.

During the few moments I had spent reading Calvin's message and sending him a reply, I'd received a message from Joan. She asked me to call her either later today or sometime tomorrow. I had promised Bertha that I'd drive to her church and a few other places and give her a perm before it got too late, so I decided to wait until tomorrow and call Joan when I got to work.

Monday morning between nine and eleven, I ducked into the restroom several times and tried to reach Joan on her cell phone. Each call went straight to voice mail.

A few minutes before I clocked out to go home that evening, I called her cell phone again, and she still didn't answer. I assumed she was busy doing chores, on an extended shopping trip, or on a date and had turned her cell phone off. I reluctantly called her landline. I was so disappointed when her mother-in-law answered.

It wasn't that I disliked Reed's mother, but she was one lady who could really give you a run for your money. Joan called her all kinds of colorful names behind her back — dragon lady, battle-axe, and bad news bear were just a few. Mrs. Riley was one of those snobby, old black women who looked down on black women on my level. Her idea of a "good time" was hanging out with her friends at garden parties and political events. Just from the things Joan had told me about her and from the few conversations I'd had with Mrs. Riley, she couldn't understand why *all* black folks were not doing as well as her family. Reed's father, a retired dentist, was not nearly as bad as his wife. Except to play golf and visit his doctor, he rarely left the house, so Joan saw him only every now and then. He was mild-mannered and dull but fairly pleasant enough. The few times I'd been in his presence I could tell that he was just as uncomfortable around folks from the hood as his wife. And every now and then he said something stupid to Joan. "My son could have married a girl with more education and class than you, but he loves you, so you'll do, I guess." She told me that her father-in-law had made that insensitive remark out of the blue last Thanksgiving in the middle of the lavish dinner his wife had prepared for their family and a bunch of their snobby friends. Joan and Reed had laughed it off, but the other guests gasped and traded horrified looks with one another. I couldn't figure out how Reed had ended up with such an outgoing personality and been brave enough to marry a ghetto princess.

"Hello, Mrs. Riley," I greeted with my voice cracking. "This is Lola."

"Oh." Her indifference didn't even faze me.

"Is Joan available?"

"No, she's not here."

"Uh, will she be back soon?"

"Only God knows. She left here a few minutes ago. She's *supposed* to be on her way to a book club meeting in Oakland. I don't remember the last time I saw her crack open a decent book. But then again, I can understand why she reads that loathsome mess she does read. . . ." Joan and I both had similar tastes when it came to books. Our favorites included Mary B. Morrison, Trice Hickman, ReShonda Tate Billingsley, Victoria Christopher Murray, and most of the other popular African American authors. The Riley family read the stale classics that we'd been forced to read in high school, and a lot of nonfiction riffraff that could bore a person like me to tears.

"The book club! Oh — that's right! I forgot she told me about that," I exclaimed. Joan had some explaining to do. Her joining a book club was news to me. If she had to lie to her mother-in-law about where she was going, there was only one reason: She had a date. "When she gets back, please have her give me a call. Bye, Mrs. Riley. Have a blessed day."

"Lola, every day I wake up is a blessed day. I don't need you to tell me that. Goodbye." Nothing this old lady said surprised me. I was glad to end this awkward conversation. I made a mental note that for all my future calls to Joan's landline, I'd block my telephone number. If Mrs. Riley or Reed answered, I'd just hang up.

I put my phone into my purse and waltzed out of the restroom and over to the meat counter. I picked out a large package of smoked turkey necks, a bucket of the dreaded chitlins, and a few other items that Bertha had requested. A few minutes later, I clocked out and began the five-block walk home.

My mind was in a tizzy. I was glad I had heard from Calvin, and I was anxious to let Joan know that he *did* want to see me again after all. I was just as anxious to scold her over not telling me about the date she was on and the "book club" thing. How did she expect me to keep covering for her if she didn't keep me in the loop when she was up to no good? I rarely went on a date without her knowing about it!

Joan's mother-in-law was number one on my list when it came to "bad news bears," but my stepsister, Libby, tied that spot with her. I groaned when I spotted her car parked in front of the house when I reached my block. If I happened to be home when she came, she usually ignored me or said something unflattering about me. She usually stayed just long enough to tell her mother her latest tale of woe that always involved her needing money. In a typical month, the total amount of money Bertha "loaned" to Libby and Marshall was more than all of our other expenses combined. Bertha's children had no shame whatsoever.

They had been bleeding her dry as long as I could remember.

I was tempted to walk around the neighborhood until Libby left. But the grocery bag was heavy and my feet were on fire from standing all day. I dragged myself up onto the front porch like I was about to face a firing squad. When I opened the door, I was glad to see that Libby was on her way out. Her appearance was as outlandish as ever. The long, flat weave hanging off her head resembled a beaver's tail. It was pathetic to see a lumpy woman like her in outfits like the brown jumpsuit she had on. With the red Windbreaker she wore over it, she looked like Winnie-the-Pooh.

"Hey, Lola!" she greeted with a fake smile. Then she looked me up and down with a curious expression on her pie-shaped mug, which had way too much makeup on it. "Girl, the buttons on your blouse look like they are going to pop any minute. I guess that diet you told me you started last month isn't working, huh?" This was a strange comment coming from a woman who outweighed me by at least thirty pounds. But almost everything about me that came out of Libby's mouth was strange.

"I only stayed on it a week," I replied.

"I hope you find one you can stick to

someday," she sneered. Then her eyes rolled up to my hair. "And another thing, you need to go back to wearing braids so your face won't look so pudgy. Well, gotta run! It was nice to see you. Bye!" She tapped the top of my head with her hand before she scurried off the porch.

I shook my head and stumbled into the house. I could hear Bertha banging pots and pans together in the kitchen. She didn't even look up from the sink when I entered and dropped the heavy grocery bag onto the table with a loud thud.

"Libby should lay off those sweets, or she'll be borrowing money from you again to get another liposuction procedure," I commented.

"Libby is big-boned. Just like me and most of the women in my family," Bertha said in an exhausted voice. She still had not turned around to face me.

"How much did she borrow this time?" I asked. I walked over to Bertha and put my hands on her shoulders. The look on her face was so sad. I cared about her, so when she was sad I experienced the same emotion, but not this time. Because of Calvin, I was on cloud nine. I was not about to let Libby's rude remarks, or anything else, burst my bubble.

"Just a grand," Bertha murmured.

"You gave her 'just a grand' two weeks ago. And Marshall came to get a grand three days ago," I wailed.

I had no idea how much money Bertha had, but she was a long way from the poor house. In addition to her divorce settlement, her monthly pension, and Social Security checks, Daddy had made her the only beneficiary on his life insurance policy. She never told me how much it was, but she had given me five thousand dollars as a present when I graduated. And, according to the neighborhood gossips, forty-five years ago when Bertha's only brother died in a helicopter crash while he was stationed in Vietnam, she received a huge settlement from the army, and most of it was still sitting in her bank. No matter how much she had, I resented the fact that her children were grabbing it with both hands.

"Lola, it's only money. My babies need it more than I do. Besides, I am not going to live forever and I can't take it with me."

"Bertha, I know it's none of my business, but Libby and Marshall are coming to get money twice as often — and twice as much — as before."

"So what, Lola? That's my business."

"I know it is, but I care about you. I don't

like people taking advantage of you —
especially your own children."

Bertha dropped her head and looked at
the floor for a few seconds. When she looked
back up at me, I was not surprised to see
tears in her tortured eyes.

"Lola, I don't know what I would do if I
didn't have you," she mumbled. "I know
I've depended on you a lot since your daddy
died. I appreciate the fact that you continue
to honor the promise you made to him that
you would take care of me for the rest of
my life."

A lump formed in my throat. That
wretched "promise" was my least favorite
subject. Before I could say anything else,
Bertha said the last thing I expected to hear
from her. "You know, a woman your age
should have a love life."

The comment was unexpected and bi-
zarre. It made me so lightheaded you could
have knocked me over with a feather. I
didn't know how to respond. "Huh?" I
croaked.

"You're pretty and you're smart. And for
the life of me, I can't figure out why you
haven't had a *real* boyfriend in years."

CHAPTER 15
LOLA

Bertha's memory was not as sharp as it used to be. Two or three times a week she misplaced her keys, went out of the house without her false teeth, and she even forgot the names of people we'd known for years. Apparently, she also "forgot" how often she had sabotaged my relationships with men.

"A real boyfriend? What do you mean by that?" I asked dumbly.

"Well, I'm an old woman now, but I remember what it was like to be young. I've noticed that you haven't had much of a social life in quite a while. You were pretty fast when you were younger. But you've slowed down so much in the past couple of years, it doesn't seem, uh, natural." Bertha dipped her head and peered at me with her eyes blinking rapidly. "You're not, uh, I mean, you still like *men,* don't you?" I didn't know how to interpret the look of pity on her face. In all the years I'd known her, this was one of the most peculiar conversations we'd ever had.

I couldn't decide if she was asking me if I was a lesbian or not. I promptly answered her odd question. "Yes, I still like men. But it's been a long time since I met one I really liked." I paused because I was stunned by her insinuation. "You're wrong if you think I suddenly turned into a lesbian."

"Well, I'm glad to hear that. With you not showing much interest in men lately, I guess I got a little confused," Bertha said, giving me an apologetic look.

I had to hold my breath to keep from laughing. Last month I hooked up with three club members. And last night I finalized my plans to spend time with a businessman from Connecticut in a few days. Since I couldn't bring any of my club member dates to the house, Bertha didn't have a clue about my very active social life with men. It was no wonder she thought I had "slowed down so much." Unless my dates took place on a Saturday or Sunday during the day, I went out only at night, after she had gone to bed.

"I know that some man, like that truck driver you met at the mall and had coffee with, is going to sweep you off your feet one of these days." Bertha paused, sniffed, and gave me a pleading look. Then she continued talking in a weak, hollow voice that almost brought tears to my eyes. "I just hope you don't let any man come between us. . . ."

I knew her well enough to know that she was fishing for another major, life-altering "promise" from me. I was still in a mild state of shock because of the one I'd made to Daddy, so there was no way I was going to make another one if I could help it. To this day, I still couldn't believe that I'd been coerced into making a commitment that had become more and more difficult for me to keep. I hadn't even told Joan, but I had told myself that the next time I fell in love with a man who wanted to marry me, I was not even going to tell Bertha about it until the wedding plans had been finalized. That way, she would have no choice but to go along with whatever my new husband and I offered if she was determined to continue clinging to me. Ironically, I hoped that my future husband would accept Bertha as an extension of me so she wouldn't have to live alone, go into a nursing home, or fall back on her useless children. As morbid a thought as it was, I reminded myself periodically that Bertha was not going to live forever. . . .

I gave her a tight smile, but I remained silent.

She blinked her eyes a few more times and continued. "When you get married, I can rent out the house. You, me, and your husband can move into an apartment for a while — unless he's got his own house. I've lived in this house since my first marriage, and I know a change of scenery would do me a world of good."

Bertha never ceased to amaze me. Very few things she said surprised me anymore. "It could be a whole lot of years before I get married. But if you need a change of scenery and want to live among people your age, you can move into that new senior citizen complex on Grimly Street. My bosses just moved there, and they love it." I couldn't wait to see her reaction.

She gulped, and her mouth dropped open so wide, it looked like a manhole. She looked so terrified, you would have thought she'd just been handed a death sentence. And, in a way, I guess that's exactly what it was as far as she was concerned. "With the rapists and other criminals breaking in on senior citizens every time I turn around, I know you don't think I would want to live in a place all by myself! If a crazed maniac kicked my door down one night, I wouldn't have a chance in hell. *Are you telling me you don't want me to live with you when you get married?*"

"No, I am not saying that. You know I'm going to always have your back. But the way my love life is going, I may be old enough to move into a senior citizens place myself before somebody marries me." I was dead serious, but I forced myself to laugh. The irony of my last statement was that it was true. Even though I had men coming out of my ears, I was no closer to marriage than I was ten years ago. Or was I?

"What about that truck driver? I could tell by the way your eyes lit up when you first told me about him, that he might become special to you."

"Uh, I have to get to know Calvin better first. His first marriage ended in divorce, so I don't know how he feels about getting married again. Anyway, he gave me the impression that he likes being single for now." This was a smart comment to make in case my relationship with Calvin didn't go beyond a bed in a hotel room — if that.

"Humph. I guess you can't expect too much from a man who is brazen enough to walk up to a strange woman in a mall and get friendly enough with her to buy her a cup of coffee, right?"

Bertha's comment was ridiculous, but I agreed with her anyway. "Uh-huh." But I wasn't going to form any opinions about Calvin until he gave me a reason to. He wanted to see me again, at least once. And that was all that mattered to me.

CHAPTER 16
JOAN

I hated last-minute dates. Especially when I had not planned to see anybody for a while. The comments and reviews about me on the Discreet Encounters website were so spectacular that I was more popular than ever.

Because I had to plan my trysts around Reed, I had to turn down a lot of men — and a few women. Even though my profile made it clear that I was 100 percent heterosexual, bisexual female club members sent me messages left and right requesting dates! I had nothing against gay people, but I had no desire to make love to another female. If anything, I planned to reduce the number of dates I went on, not because I was getting bored but because Reed was increasingly giving me suspicious looks and asking more nosy questions than ever before.

When John Walden (his screen name was "LongJohn"), a long-time member and a favorite whom I had dated several times, called me on my cell phone a few minutes ago, I was happy to hear from him. He was a prominent Phoenix attorney and a great lover, but I made it a point of not getting too attached to any of the club members. I didn't want them to get too attached to me either.

I had never been involved in a fatal attraction, but I had read a few horror stories on the club's blog about members who had. One of my partners told me that he had been stalked by a former supermodel who had fallen in love with him after just one date. He was lucky, because the woman left him alone a couple of months later when she fell for another club member.

I knew John liked me a lot, and I liked him. He was a very intriguing man. His family was originally from Jamaica, but they'd moved to England when John was a baby. He moved from London to New York when he was thirty and met and married a woman from Phoenix. A year into their marriage, they moved to Arizona so she could be closer to her family. John was the kind of man I wish I had married. He was considerate, generous, funny, handsome, and rich. But Reed was all of those things too. I didn't see his dark side until after I married him.

I had just taken an hour-long bubble bath and washed my hair when John's call came in Monday afternoon a few minutes before three. It was a good time, because Reed was still at his office. I had a towel wrapped around my hair when I entered the living room and plopped down on the couch. Before I could pick up the remote to turn on the TV and get comfortable, my cell phone rang. I was tempted to let the call go to voice mail until I saw John's name on my caller ID. I wasted no time snatching the phone off the coffee table and answering.

"Joan, it's John," he said in a low voice. He had a deep baritone voice and a slight English accent. That combination sounded so damn sexy to me. Just listening to him talk turned me on. I assumed he was practically whispering because he was calling from home and his Italian bride of fifteen years was lurking about. That was one thing I had in common with almost all of my dates: a nosy mate.

"I know," I said in a loud voice. "It's good to hear from you again, and so soon. Where are you, and why are you whispering?"

John responded in a voice that was more like a boom. "I'm in California, and I was whispering because I'm so used to doing it when I call you from my office or from

144

home. Anyway, one of the partners in my firm is handling a real estate deal in Frisco for one of our most important clients. Unfortunately, my colleague's son was involved in a serious auto accident a couple of days ago, so he had to cancel his trip. He didn't want to let the client down, so he asked me to fill in for him. So here I am, dying to get my hands on your tight little body! I hope you're up for it."

I gulped. Sex with John was always a satisfying experience. There was nothing he wouldn't do for me in bed, and vice versa. "Of course I'm up for it. How long are you going to be out here?"

"I arrived late yesterday and met with the client this morning. We wrapped up everything sooner than we expected, so now I have the rest of today free."

"Well, I'm glad to hear from you. When do you want to see me?"

"ASAP, goddamnit!" John let out a long, loud laugh. "I know this is short notice, and I would have called before now, but I had a lot of things going on. I hope I can see you because . . . uh . . . there's an important issue I'd like to discuss with you."

John's last sentence made my heart skip a beat. I couldn't imagine what important issue he had to discuss with me. The first

145

thought that came to my mind was that it was something related to sex. I always used condoms with my partners, so I knew it had nothing to do with an STD. "Oh. What's wrong?"

"Nothing is wrong, luv. As a matter of fact, everything is very right."

"John, what are you talking about?"

"It's not something I want to discuss over the telephone. Is there any way possible you can meet me at the Hilton around five?"

I gasped. "No way! It's almost a two-hour drive from here to San Francisco, and it's already pretty late in the day," I pointed out. "My husband will be home soon and he'll be all over me, so it'll be hard for me to get out of the house this evening."

"I've checked out of my hotel in Frisco. I took a chance on you being available, so I rented a car and I'm already in your neck of the woods. I have a suite in the downtown San Jose Hilton."

"Hmmm. Well, in that case, I guess I can make it by five if I leave soon." My period had ended a few hours ago. Every month right after my cycle, I got as horny and frisky as a bull. I stayed like that for at least two or three days. But because Reed was such a dud, I got even more frustrated in the bedroom during that time. John had a lot of stamina for a man in his late forties, so he was just what I needed. One of his erections lasted longer than all of Reed's put together in a month! I wanted to see John again as much as he wanted to see me. I didn't want him to know that though, so I forced myself not to sound too eager. "Can you give me a hint about the 'important issue' you want to discuss?"

"Joan, I know you're not happy. You're never going to be happy as long as you remain married to what's-his-face."

"So?" One of my biggest flaws was my loose lips after a few drinks. I often revealed way too much information to whomever I was with, especially if they shared personal information with me. In John's case, during one of our previous dates, he told me how unhappy he was in his marriage. He claimed his wife had "retired" from sex. According to him, she'd decided years ago that she'd had enough. She'd admitted that she had never enjoyed sex in the first place. He also claimed that his wife "encouraged" him to find pleasure with other women — as long as he was discreet. Once I found out that John was also trapped in a miserable marriage, I wasted no time telling him about my situation with Reed. The only thing I left out was the part about his threats to commit suicide if I left him and that he'd already attempted it once.

CHAPTER 17
JOAN

John loudly interrupted my thoughts. "So why don't we do something about it?"

"We? What can 'we' do about my unhappy marriage? That's my problem."

"Joan, I didn't want to get into this over the phone, but I want you to be with me."

"Be with you? Can you be a little more specific?"

"I own several properties in Phoenix that I am sure you and your son would like very much. They are all located in quiet, safe neighborhoods with great schools. The one I have in mind for you is a three-bedroom town house in a gated area in one of the most magnificent locations in the city."

I gasped again. "You want me to leave my husband and move to Phoenix to be your backstreet woman?"

Several moments of silence passed before John answered. "Well, yes. But 'backstreet' is such an outdated word. I haven't heard it decades."

"You're asking me to be your *mistress?*"

"I guess that's what I'm asking. You'd never have to work, and I'd make sure you'd never have to worry about money as long as you stay in the relationship. I'll even put it in writing."

I was flabbergasted! The idea of *me* being a rich man's mistress sounded as incredulous as me being a poor man's sugar mama. This was the last thing I ever expected to hear from John, or any other man. I gulped and shook my head. I didn't know what to say next.

"Joan, say something, please. Your silence is making me nervous."

"John, you haven't even known me that long," I said evenly. "What if you stop liking me when you really get to know me *after* I've left my husband and moved to Phoenix?"

"I'm willing to take the risk if you are. Besides, I know all I need to know about you."

"What about the club?"

"What about it?"

"If I take you up on your offer, are you going to keep dating other club members?"

"I have dated only three other members since my first date with you and that was only because I was traveling to locations on the other side of the country or even farther away. If I had you to myself exclusively, I wouldn't want to be with anyone else."

"Huh?" I was stunned and flattered. But I found it hard to believe that such a prominent man wanted a woman with my ordinary background to be his mistress. John spoke Spanish, French, and Italian fluently. He went to operas and art museums and listened to Mozart. He read books written by highbrow authors like Alex Haley and Toni Morrison. The contrast between us was about as wide as the Pacific Ocean. However, most of that was also true of Reed, and he was willing to kill himself over me. Damn! I didn't know what it was about me that was that good! "Do you really mean that?"

"Don't sound so surprised. You know how devastatingly attractive and sexy you are. You're the most phenomenal woman I've ever known."

I could feel my head swelling, but I made myself stay cool. "Yeah, right," I said with a touch of sarcasm. I could think of a lot of words to describe myself, but "phenomenal" was not one of them.

"Joan, believe me. You're everything a man wants in a woman. Hasn't any other man l you this?"

, I've heard all this from other men."

first night I met Reed, he told me that
was "everything a man wants in a woman."
And look where I was!

"You don't believe me?"

"Well . . . I . . . I —" I blubbered, sounding more like an idiot than a devastatingly
attractive, phenomenal, and sexy woman. I
stopped spewing gibberish long enough to
compose myself. "I believe you think that
I'm everything *you* want in a woman. But I
can't just pack up and move to another
state."

"Joan, I am a rich man. I'm offering you a
brand-new start. You can have a privileged
life with me. And that's really what you need
and deserve."

I was tempted to remind John that I
already had a privileged life and a rich man,
but I didn't because it would have contra-
dicted all the negative things I'd already told
him about my marriage.

"You're asking me to make a major change
in my life. That's something I'd have to
think about carefully, and for a long time."

"I see. Please give it some serious consid-
eration before you make your final deci-
sion."

"I'll think about it, I guess." By now my

head was swimming.

"I'll handle your divorce
course. I'll pay for your mo
and let you pick out all new
you can have the vehicle of you
our first anniversary, I'll buy
ditional residence anywhere in
so you'll always have somewhere
you want to be alone. And I'll h
time housekeeper for you. All you'
do is stay beautiful and keep m
fied. . . ."

The more John sweetened the po
more my head swam. Never in my w
dreams did I expect a man to offer me
a lavish life. Reed was successful and ger
ous, but even he couldn't offer me as mu
as John.

"You'd be willing to do all those thing
for me?"

"Those things and even more," John said,
strongly emphasizing his words.

I had resisted at first, but I still developed
feelings for him. Still, I didn't love him the
way I wanted to love the man with whom I
would ultimately spend the rest of my life
with after Reed. However, I didn't know of
any marriage where the scales were bal-
anced and the love between the two partners
was equal. The way Mama rode my step-

ɔmplaint and put-
the way he hugged
father's all the time, it was
down a hey didn't love each
and fay were happy.
obvioɔout this when I get to
otherɛd so I could gather my
"Wo go now so I can make
youmy cousin to keep an eye
thɔhe gets home from school.
arɔon as I can."
Oa text and told him to go to
ɭe after school. Then I called
ɪn Too Sweet and told her to
ɭere until I picked him up.
p and glanced at my watch. Lola
ɪt work, but I had to let her know
as up to so she could cover for me
Reed pestered her with bothersome
ɭone calls. I dialed her cell phone but
ɔall went straight to voice mail. I didn't
ɔther to leave a message.
I started to call Reed's office to let him
know I was going out for a while. I changed
my mind because I was not in the mood to
listen to him whine or question me. Since I
couldn't get in touch with Lola, I scribbled
a note to Reed and told him I had to go to
a book club meeting. I put the note where I

knew he'd see it as soon as he got home: taped to the front of the liquor cabinet.

Chapter 18
Lola

I didn't talk to Joan again until Monday night. She showed up at my house at ten-fifteen p.m. I was in the living room alone watching a *Golden Girls* rerun. Bertha had gone to bed an hour earlier.

"Thank God you're home," Joan said, out of breath. She almost knocked me down as she trotted to the living-room couch and plopped down. She had a frantic expression. She was dressed in jeans and a nightshirt, her house shoes were on the wrong feet, and her hair was in curlers.

"Halloween is a long way off. You look like a fishwife," I teased as I looked her over. I had never seen Joan looking so frumpy. She ignored my remarks. "Is somebody chasing you?" I asked, joining her on the couch.

"No, nobody's chasing me. I just left the house in a big hurry." She glanced toward the staircase, then back at me, looking even more frantic. "Can I talk to you for a few minutes?"

"Yeah. I'm the only one up. How come you didn't call to let me know you were coming over this time of night? Where the heck have you been all day? And what's this about a book club meeting you allegedly attended today? That's what your mother-in-law told me when I called before I left work this evening." I grabbed the remote off the coffee table and muted the TV.

"Mother Riley showed up just as I was about to leave. I told her I had to go to a book club meeting. Actually, I went on a date."

"I figured that. Why didn't you let me know in case Reed called me?"

"My date called me at the last minute. I had so much on my mind and so much to do, I called your number but I didn't leave a message," Joan wailed.

"Which 'date' are we talking about?"

"Remember that lawyer from Phoenix?"

"John Walden? How could I not. Had I been available when he contacted me for a date, you might never have met him. You've been with him several times, so he must be damn hot."

"Girl, the man is hotter than cayenne pepper. And just as generous as ever. He gave me a diamond necklace this time. It must have cost a fortune. I know when Reed sees it, he's going to scold me again about spending so much of *his* money. Ha! If he only knew."

"I don't think you have to worry about Reed asking you about a diamond necklace," I chided. Joan owned more jewelry and everything else than any woman I knew, and a lot of it had come from her lovers. Looking in her bedroom closet was like looking into a stockroom. There were several large shopping bags that contained clothes, shoes, and just about everything else a shopaholic woman would buy. Most of the items still had sales tags attached. Reed was so busy trying to keep up with her other activities, he rarely hassled Joan about her purchases. "But I'm sure he'll get nosy about a book club, so you need to give me all the details. I might need to use that alibi with Bertha."

Joan rolled her neck and gave me an exasperated look. "*Pffft!* What's there to know about a book club? A bunch of people get together once or twice a month for a few hours to discuss a book they've all read. I've never actually been a member of a book club, but I happened to be at my cousin Norma's house one evening a couple of months ago when she and her book club were having a meeting. And I went to one at Aunt Maggie's house last year. They're all the same."

"Well, you could have at least told me what book your bogus book club was discussing in case somebody asked me."

"Woman, puh-leeze." Joan giggled and gave me a dismissive wave. "Do you think that Reed or Bertha would ever ask the title of a book that you or I would read, or where the book club meeting took place?"

"Probably not. But the next time you go to a 'book club meeting,' I wish you would let me know too." I looked toward the staircase to make sure Bertha had not crept within earshot like she used to do when I had male company. "So, how is the good lawyer from Phoenix?"

"As amazing as ever. He . . . he wants me to move to Phoenix."

My mouth dropped open, and I stared at Joan from the corner of my eye. "He wants you to move to Phoenix? For what?"

"To be with him. He said Junior and I could live rent free in one of his properties."

"You've got to be kidding!"

"No, I'm not."

I gave Joan a thoughtful look before I brought up a subject that had been on my mind for a long time. "Can we talk about something real personal? It's okay if you don't want to."

"Why wouldn't I want to talk about it? We talk about personal shit all the time. You can say whatever is on your mind."

I didn't want to beat around the bush, so I jumped into the subject with both feet. "John is so whipped, you could spread him on a slice of bread. The same goes for Reed. He's so crazy about you, he's ready to kill himself if you leave him. DrFeelGood wants to give you breast implants and reorganize other parts of your body for free. And now you're telling me that John wants to relocate you so he can have you all to himself. I could go on and on about all the perks you get from your men. Please don't take what I'm going to say next the wrong way. Girl, you're not *that* hot. What do you do in bed to make your men act like fools?" I held my breath and hoped I hadn't offended Joan.

She gave me a pensive look. "I've been asking myself that all my life." Then she giggled and hunched her shoulders. "Whatever I'm doing in bed, I must be doing it damn good, huh?"

"Apparently! Well, if you ever figure out what it is, please let me know so I can start doing it too." I laughed, but I was serious.

I'd lost count of all the men I'd been with in some very expensive hotel suites, and I had received some nice gifts from a few. But so far not a single one had ever treated me the way most of Joan's men treated her. She beamed as I stared at her in awe. Compared to her life, mine was as dull as dishwater. Had it not been for Joan, I'd have never found out about the sex club, and I'd still be getting poor-quality sex, if I got any at all.

"John also said that he would buy me a place anywhere in America so I'd have somewhere to go when I wanted to be alone."

"Damn! I'm afraid to ask if he offered you anything else. I'm jealous enough!"

"He said he'd put me in his will and let me pick out the car of my choice."

"That's a hell of a tempting offer, or maybe I should call it an 'indecent proposal' like in that old Demi Moore movie. Now I'm really sorry I was not available when he tried to get a date with me. Too bad you can't take him up on it."

"I don't know about that —"

"What's wrong with you?" I interrupted. "If you think Reed will kill himself if you leave him and just move back in with your mama, what do you think he'll do if you leave him and move to Phoenix to be some rich man's mistress?"

Joan shook her head. "I don't want to think about that right now. It's giving me a headache." She stopped talking and checked her watch. "I can't stay long. I'm supposed to be at Walgreens picking up some Advil for the headache I told Reed I suddenly got when he hinted about us having sex tonight. YUCK!" Joan grimaced and shook her head again. "I do not want that man to stick his dick in me too soon after John did such a thorough job on me. I want to savor the feeling as long as I can."

"Oh, come on, girl. Is Reed really that *bad* in bed?"

"He is to me. Shit. I get more pleasure from my gynecological exams."

Joan's comment was funny, but she didn't laugh. I did, though. Her eyes darkened, so I stopped and gave her the most sympathetic look I could manage. "I'm sorry. I didn't mean to laugh," I said sheepishly.

"Lola, you don't know how miserable I am with Reed. I'm trying so hard to be happy with him, but nothing is working. And I don't care what he says or how nice he is to me — that doesn't help much. What I don't understand is why he won't let me go so he can find a woman who really wants to be with him." Joan was not the crying type. I had known her most of my life, and I could count on one hand the number of times I'd seen her in tears, and those few times had involved funerals. I could barely believe my eyes now as huge tears rolled down the sides of her face like fat raindrops.

"You want something to drink?" I asked. I was just about to go to the kitchen and get her a paper towel to wipe her face when she pulled a handkerchief out of her purse.

"No, don't bother with that, Lola. I'll be fine." Joan choked on her words and mopped her cheeks and nose at the same time. "I'm sorry. You know I don't like getting all emotional in front of people, not even you." She sniffled and let out a weak chuckle.

"I know you're in pain, and it's probably a good thing for you to show your emotions. We all need to have a good cry every now and then. I'm too embarrassed to tell you how many times I've sat in my room and boo-hooed up a storm about one thing or another."

"Yeah, I know." Joan sniffled some more and shuddered as she returned her handkerchief to her purse. "Even after the wonderful afternoon I spent with John today, I'm still miserable as hell. I don't know how much longer I can live under the same roof with Reed!"

"But you've been miserable for years. You should be used to him by now. At least he's not beating you or having affairs with other women. You get to have fun with other men and you do pretty much everything else you please."

"No, Reed doesn't beat me or cheat on me. Yes, I get to have fun with other men, but I have to do it behind closed doors. I can't even go out to a movie or shopping at a mall with any of the men I fool around with. When they take me to dinner, it's always a restaurant in whatever hotel we're hooking up in. And even then, we have to request a booth or a table in a secluded area in case somebody I know wanders in."

"Well, as long as you stay with Reed, you'll have to keep making some sacrifices, I guess. And the one thing you have to keep in mind is that no man is perfect. I'll bet even Michelle Obama has a bunch of complaints about Barack. I'm sure she's been close to enough men to know that there's something wrong with all of them, so what's the point of trading a skillet for a frying pan? Besides, what if . . ." I paused and thought carefully about what I wanted to say next. I didn't want to make Joan feel any worse, but since she was already about as low as she could get, I said what was on my mind. "What if you do leave Reed and he . . . you know?"

"What if he kills himself?"

"Yeah. Are you still worried about that?"

Joan nodded. "It's on my mind almost every day, especially when I think about leaving him. His suicide would haunt me for the rest of my life." When she pulled her handkerchief out of her purse again, I thought she was going to cry some more, but she didn't. She just blew her nose again. By now it looked like a big, red cherry.

"So there is no way you're going to move to Phoenix, huh? And what about your family? You know you could never be happy living too far away from that crew."

"That's so true. Oh, I just don't know what to do with myself! I don't want to hurt Reed, and I don't want to hurt my family."

"I hope you don't want to hurt me either. I don't know what I'd do if you moved away," I admitted. "Especially for a man!"

"Lola, lately you've been talking about finding a husband yourself a lot more than usual. Now let me ask you something personal. And you don't have to answer if you don't want to." Joan paused long enough for me to panic. Every muscle in my body tightened, and I had to breathe through my mouth. "If something really serious develops between you and that truck driver and he decides to relocate and wants you to go with him, would you go?"

It was a fairly tame question, so I began to breathe normally again. But it was also a hard question for me to answer. I responded with the most reasonable answer I could think of. "Like you said I was doing a while back, you're getting way ahead of things. I haven't even slept with Calvin yet. By the way, I e-mailed him like I told you I would."

"And? Does he want to see you again?"

"Yup!" Just the thought of knowing that Calvin wanted to see me again made me tingle with excitement. "He's in Chicago right now visiting a sick uncle. As a matter of fact, his uncle is dying. Calvin didn't mention him having a wife or any children, so I guess that's why he has to get things in order for him. He went to see him right after our coffee date, and not long after he returned to California, his uncle took a turn for the worse, so he had to turn around and go back to Chicago."

Joan gave me a dry look. "A sick uncle, huh? That could be just a smoke screen, you know."

"What do you mean by that?"

"How do you know he's telling the truth? He could be off somewhere with another woman just to throw you off."

"Why would he need to 'throw' me off? If he doesn't want to see me, I'm sure he'd find a better way to let me know. But he said he wants to see me again and when he gets back to California he's going to get in touch with me."

"Well, I sure hope he does. And I hope you get some nookie from this dude real soon, before your pussy explodes." Joan laughed. I did too. I was glad that she was in a better mood now.

I was in a much better mood myself.

CHAPTER 19
CALVIN

I was in the last place on earth I wanted to be: Chicago. It was my least favorite city in the whole country. To me, it was a cold-blooded, angry place filled with cold-blooded, angry people of all races.

During one of my visits several years ago, I'd been mugged and beaten to within an inch of my life by two thugs who had mistaken me for another dude. The only reason they had let me live was because I'd talked them into checking my ID.

There was a lot of crime in San Jose, but innocent young kids were getting shot to death much more frequently in Chicago. And I didn't like this city's cold weather. It was February, so there was still snow on the ground. I couldn't believe I had once lived in such a brutal place. My toes ached every time I recalled walking to school in the winter, praying that the thick socks and brogans my uncle made me wear would protect me from frostbite episodes. But I would have walked on water to spend time with Uncle Ed.

Uncle Ed had already sold the rat trap of a car he'd been driving for the past ten years, so I had picked up a rental. I arrived at his shabby, green-shingled house on the South Side a few minutes past noon on Sunday. The front door swung open and he came outside a few seconds after I parked the car in his ice-covered driveway. "I'm glad you made it! I was getting worried about you, boy!" he yelled in his raspy voice.

"I'm glad I made it too," I said, piling out. I retrieved my luggage from the trunk and proceeded to walk toward the porch. The ground was so slippery, I practically slid all the way up to the steps. I held on to the railing to keep from falling. But it was so rickety and raggedy that it was practically useless, so I fell anyway. I took a deep breath and wobbled back onto my feet.

I was happy to see a huge grin on my uncle's heavily lined, bronze-colored face as I followed him inside to his living room. He clapped me on the back and gave me a bear hug. As cold as it was, Uncle Ed was barefooted and he had on a thin, ratty housecoat. His long, balding head looked like a dried-up coconut. He looked terrible. I'd seen corpses that looked more alive. He used to be quite obese, but now he was a bag of bones. I was tempted to comment on his appearance. But my uncle was a smart man. He had to know just how wretched he looked.

"Driving a car is real risky here this time of year, so I had to take my time," I explained, setting my suitcase down on the floor. "How have you been?"

"Well, for a dying man I guess I'm doing as well as can be expected. I was up all night puking my guts out."

"I'm glad I could come right away," I said as I looked around the cluttered room. It had been a year and a half since my last visit, but it looked like nothing had been moved or cleaned. The only thing Uncle Ed had added to the mess was a naked ironing board. It stood in a corner with car parts on top of it. Every ashtray I could see was overflowing with cigarette butts and stale wads of chewing gum. A cleaning woman supposedly came to the house three times a week. She must have been one lazy bitch, because fast-food containers, empty beer cans, and old newspapers were all over the place.

Uncle Ed also had a hospice nurse who checked in on him every other day. He had refused to move into a nursing home or an assisted-living facility. Being the proud man he was, he insisted on staying in his own house as long as he could.

"I don't feel much like cooking these days, but I can boil up some beans and fry some catfish if you want to eat something," he told me, nodding toward the kitchen.

"I'm fine for now. I grabbed a sandwich before I left the airport. But you don't have to cook at all today. We can have something delivered."

"Oh, don't worry about me!" Uncle Ed hollered, waving his hand in the air. He motioned me to the couch, and we sat down at the same time. "I don't eat much no more nohow. And when I do, I usually order something and have it brought to me. But the pizza and other delivery folks don't like to come out here too often, and never at night. The last time I had a pizza delivered, them young devils that used to live next door jumped on that poor woman. They robbed her and made her suck dick until the cops showed up."

"That's a damn shame," I said, shaking my head. "I don't know what this world is coming to when a person can't even do his or her job and not have to worry about getting assaulted or killed. That poor

171

woman. . . ."

"On the subject of a 'poor woman,' you ever find out what happened to your wife? She's been gone about four or five years now, eh?"

"Uh, yeah, something like that. And, no, I haven't heard anything about where she went or what happened to her," I replied with a lump in my throat.

"She's probably dead."

"Um . . . yeah. A lot of people think she is. Nobody has heard from her, there's been no activity on her credit cards, which she used almost every day, and she hasn't used her ATM card or her cell phone."

"Hmmm. That sounds like a dead woman to me. It's a crying shame she died so young, but she lived longer than a lot of folks. Anyway, I hope you took out some life insurance on her. When they do find her, she'll have to be laid to rest, and a decent funeral will set you back several thousand bucks. You know how black folks like to go all out when it comes to a de-ceased loved one's funeral — a roomful of flowers, music, fancy outfits, enough food to feed an army, and whatnot. From what you told me about Glinda's family, they all sound just as trifling as she was, so don't expect them broke asses to help with the final expenses."

"Glinda and I both have generous insurance policies," I said solemnly.

"I'm glad to hear that. Well, if she don't turn up soon, I think you'll have to wait seven years from the last day somebody seen her before you can have her declared dead. You can't collect that insurance money until then. I know a real good private detective. He helped my last lady friend locate her brother that she hadn't seen since they was little bitty kids and sent to different foster homes. I can get in touch with him and put him on the case. If Glinda ain't dead or if she ain't been kidnapped by aliens and took off to another planet, he'll find her. He found the missing daughter of a man that used to live next door to me. She disappeared without a trace about a month ago. Come to find out, she'd been beaten so bad by some thug she had moved in with, she'd lost her memory. Somebody saw her wandering down a dark road and she didn't know her own name or nothing else, so they dumped her off in one of them asylums. She didn't look nothing like herself. My friend tracked her down and verified who she was by having them run her fingerprints. I doubt if your wife is locked up somewhere with a case of amnesia, but you never know."

"Glinda and I were separated when she disappeared. If she is still alive, I'm sure she doesn't want to be found. At least not by me."

"But if she's dead, don't you want to know that so you can collect that insurance money?"

"I try not to think about her, and I don't need that insurance money. If she's still alive, I wish her well. If she's dead, I hope she's at peace." I put a somber expression on my face.

Uncle Ed gave me a sympathetic look and rubbed my back. "What went wrong? I know everybody kept saying she was a loose-booty and all, but what woman ain't? And the same is true of most men. Even me."

"I don't know what all went wrong in my marriage. Glinda just didn't want to stay married to me. I guess I wasn't man enough for her," I admitted. It was not hard for me to sound and look pitiful, because I really was. Despite all the time that had passed and the fact that I'd made Glinda pay for her betrayal, I still experienced some sadness when I thought about her. I had never loved a woman the way I loved her. My bouts of sadness never lasted more than a few moments, but my bouts of rage were

174

much more frequent and lasted a lot longer.

"Humph! I'm glad I never got married again. If a wife of mine had fooled around on me the way Glinda done you, I would have wrung her neck! I bet if you'd whooped her ass a few times, that would have stopped her from making a fool out of you!"

"I used to think about doing that before she took off, but I'm glad I didn't. I am not a violent man, especially when it comes to women," I muttered. I had to press my lips together to keep from smiling.

Chapter 20
Calvin

As weak as my uncle was, he insisted on boiling some beans and frying some catfish fillets around six p.m. I made some corn bread and we enjoyed a very pleasant dinner.

We stayed up past midnight reminiscing about the good old times. Uncle Ed was alert and lively. He recalled things I had done in my teens that I no longer remembered. After a cup of hot tea and a handful of pills, he dozed off on the couch. I literally had to carry him upstairs to his bedroom, which looked like a tornado had hit it. He had two more bedrooms, and they were even more cluttered. I searched around until I found some clean blankets so I could sleep on the living-room couch. I was anxious for morning to arrive so I could resume my conversation with Uncle Ed. I figured that as long as I kept him talking, he wouldn't die.

I was wrong.

Despite the howling wind, the loud mufflers on a couple of neighbors' vehicles, and the noisy electric space heater in the living room, I slept well. I didn't open my eyes on Monday morning until a few minutes after nine. I drank a cup of instant generic coffee and then I took a shower. Uncle Ed hadn't come downstairs by ten, so I went up to his room to check on him. He was on the floor in a fetal position. During the night he had either fallen or crawled out of bed. It was over for him. His lifeless eyes were wide open and looked so sad that mine pooled with tears.

Dead people made me nervous. I didn't like being around them, no matter who they were or how they'd died. Not counting Glinda's sudden departure, I had never been in a situation like this before, so I didn't know the calling hierarchy. I honestly didn't know who to notify first. Uncle Ed had told me the night before where to find his DO NOT RESUSCITATE document so that there would be no attempts to revive him. But he was dead, and if anybody knew death when they saw it, it was me. I sat down on the living-room couch and called the hospice nurse who had been coming to the house since his diagnosis. She immediately took over. "First things first. I'll round up Dr. Goldstein and we'll come out and make it official. Then I'll have a hearse sent out right away," she told me. That was a big relief, but I still felt uneasy. I needed to talk to somebody, so I dialed the number to the drugstore where Sylvia worked.

One of the other pharmacists answered. He told me Sylvia had not come in yet. That was when I remembered I was in a different time zone. It was two hours earlier in San Jose than it was in Chicago, so it was only a few minutes past eight in California. I called Sylvia at home, and she answered right away.

After our greeting, I told her in a weak tone of voice, "My uncle is gone."

"What? You just got there!"

"And not a minute too soon. He died before I got up this morning. I'm so glad I got here in time for us to share some of our favorite memories. I'm so thankful for that."

"That poor thing. I was hoping he'd last a couple of months longer so you'd have more time to spend with him. And I wish you had let me come with you." Sylvia exhaled loudly. "How long will you be in Chicago?"

"I'm not sure. He'll be cremated as soon as I can arrange that, and I'll notify a few folks on a list he gave me just to let them know he's gone. Most of them are on their last legs themselves. He told me that his last lady friend is in a nursing home and has Alzheimer's, so she probably doesn't even remember who she is, let alone Uncle Ed." Somehow I managed to chuckle. Sylvia didn't chuckle, so I got serious again. "I want to keep things moving so I won't have to stay here long. As soon as I can" — I paused and looked at my watch — "I'll get in touch with the lawyer who did his will. Then I'm going to go through his stuff and decide what goes to Goodwill and what to throw out."

"I can still take off work and join you if you want me to," Sylvia offered.

"I don't want you to do that," I said quickly.

"Calvin, I miss you, baby. I can't wait to see you again. I know the last few years have been rough on you. After the holy hell you went through in Afghanistan and Glinda shitting all over you and taking off the way she did, I'm surprised you're not in the nuthouse. Baby, you are such a good man and you deserve good things. I want to do whatever I can to make you happy."

"I appreciate hearing that, honey."

"When you get back to California, let's pack up and go somewhere for a few days.

Since we're going to Brazil in June, Hawaii would be nice. My time-share in Honolulu is available, so we wouldn't have to pay for a hotel. And I have so many mileage points on my credit card, we'd only have to pay for one plane ticket."

I had no idea what I had done to deserve a good woman like Sylvia. It didn't matter that she was not nearly as gorgeous as Glinda and she didn't excite me the way Glinda had. Despite all the praise I gave to her in the bedroom, she needed to hone her lovemaking skills, because she was just average. I cared for her, but the affection I felt was more pity than passion.

"That sounds like a great idea, Sylvia. We'll talk more about that when I get home. Since I had to leave so suddenly, I left a lot of things undone at work and at home, so I'll be kind of busy for a few days when I get back. But we'll spend some time together as soon as I'm available again."

"That's fine. If there's anything I can do to help you get back on track as soon as possible, just let me know."

"I'll do that." I hung up and remained on the couch staring at the telephone in my hand for a few seconds.

Yes, I would get back on track as soon as possible. Just to make sure things were still going in my favor, I decided to give Lola a call. I wanted to hear her voice. Since I didn't know when the nurse and the doctor were going to arrive, I wanted to keep myself busy so I wouldn't have to think about being alone in a house with a dead man's body. I guess you could say that death brought out the beast in me, because I was ready for some hands-on action again. Even though the clock was ticking for Lola, another woman was going to die first.

Chapter 21
Lola

Every night before I went to bed I set my alarm clock, but I usually woke up before it went off. For me, sleep was more of an escape than a necessity. I had not had a full night's uninterrupted sleep since my mother's funeral.

I tried not to think about her lifeless body in her yellow dress as she lay on display in the front of the church, but it was hard not to. Especially since a woman at the funeral told me that it looked like me lying in that casket. Unfortunately, it was true. I had thought that too before she told me.

A few years after Mama's passing, during one of my frequent visits to Joan's house, she snapped a picture of me stretched out on her bed. When she showed the picture to me, I almost fainted. Lying on that bed in a yellow blouse with my eyes closed, I looked like a dead girl. That was the day I stopped wearing anything yellow. Every wall in

Bertha's house was a dreary shade of yellow. I couldn't do anything about that. But I avoided looking at them as much as I could.

Tuesday morning I woke up at five forty a.m. I turned off my alarm so it wouldn't go off at six. I remained in bed, lying on my side until I got tired of looking at the yellow wall across from me. I could hear voices downstairs, but I couldn't make out what was being said. I got up and padded across the floor to put my ear against the door. I heard something that disturbed me almost as much as the gruesome walls: Marshall's voice.

"Mama, I'm forty-four years old. You need to stop telling me how to spend my money!" he complained in a loud, gruff voice.

"Son, if you can't manage your money and need to keep taking mine, I have a right to tell you how to spend your money," Bertha shot back, sounding unusually firm. Most of the time she was very docile when she dealt with Libby and Marshall.

I glanced at the clock on my nightstand again. I had to take a shower and get dressed, but I decided to skip breakfast. I didn't want to start off my day sitting at the table across from Marshall. I planned to grab a croissant and some coffee from the

Starbucks along the route I walked to work.

I started praying that Marshall would be gone by the time I got downstairs. Well, half an hour later when I had no choice but to get moving, I dragged my feet down the hall toward the stairs. He was standing at the bottom of the landing, as if he'd been waiting for me.

"Hey there, Lola! Good morning to you!" he yelled out the side of his mouth as soon as his eyes met mine. Even with a smile on his pudgy face, he was still unattractive.

"Good morning to you, too, Marshall." I forced myself to smile. I moved down the steps so slowly, you would have thought I had one leg. By the time I stopped in front of him, both of my legs felt as if they were about to buckle.

"Girl, I thought you'd never get your butt out of that bed and come down here." He blinked and smiled some more, revealing large, cigarette-stained teeth and thick, chapped lips. "Can you do me a big favor?"

"It depends on what it is," I said, my voice cracking and my stomach churning.

"I know it's out of your way, but can you give me a ride back to my place on your way to work?" Cornrows on a cool, young hip-hopping dude were okay. On an obese, middle-aged oaf like Marshall, they looked downright ridiculous. And his looked like they hadn't been groomed in weeks.

"Where's your car?" I asked. I didn't like to stand too close to Marshall. His presence irritated the hell out of me. And not only that, he almost always had a musty body odor.

"It's parked outside with a dead battery," he complained. "I called Triple A, but they won't get here for an hour and I need to get home. I'm starting my new job today at that construction site on Filbert Avenue, and I can't be late. And you know how suspicious June gets when I don't get back home when I'm supposed to."

"Can't you call your wife and tell her your battery died so she can come pick you up? I don't have much gas, and my signal lights went out yesterday," I said. "And anyway, I walk to work every day."

I didn't hate Marshall. Like with Libby, I pitied him so I felt sorry for him too. However, he still annoyed the hell out of me. If he suddenly fell into a bottomless pit and never returned, I wouldn't miss him. I'd experienced several unpleasant moments with him when I was a child. Back then, I had thought of him as a borderline boogeyman. He'd even exposed himself to me and Joan one Halloween night when we'd

185

knocked on Bertha's door for some tricks or treats. I shuddered when I thought of what he might have done to me with his shriveled-up dick back then if he'd had the chance. After all the years that Marshall had been in my life, I had never been alone with him. I didn't want that to change today. I was so looking forward to being with sexy, handsome Calvin, I got lightheaded and hot between my thighs just thinking about it. I didn't even want to be in the same car with Marshall, because I was afraid the experience would interrupt my euphoria.

"Okay. Then just give me your key and I'll drive myself," he countered.

"I don't know, Marshall. . . ."

"What's the problem? If you don't drive that jalopy to work, it'll just sit in the driveway! I didn't know you were this stingy!"

"That's not the reason. See, my insurance —"

Marshall quickly cut me off before I could finish my sentence. He turned on me like a pit bull. "Girl, don't trip! I ain't going to wreck that piece of shit you drive! I'll just be driving a couple of miles, not to Mexico," he roared, with spit squirting out both sides of his mouth.

Bertha suddenly shuffled into the living

room. She stopped and stood between Marshall and me with her hands on her hips.

"Son, I'll give you the money to take a cab," she said with a heavy sigh. She looked as frustrated as I felt.

"Thank you, Mama. I can always count on you." Marshall smirked with his beady black eyes glaring at me. "Lola, I'll remember this when you need a favor from me."

I'd known Marshall since I was in elementary school and I had never asked him for a favor.

"Bertha, you don't have to waste money on a cab," I said calmly. I strutted across the floor and retrieved my car key off the magazine stand by the door, where I usually left it. When I handed it to Marshall, he snatched it so fast, he almost took my hand off with it. But at least he thanked me.

He gave Bertha a long, hard hug and a peck on her forehead. He shot me a smug look before he skittered out the door like a clumsy squirrel.

"That was real nice of you, Lola," Bertha told me, rubbing my arm. "I wish I had five more children like you."

I loved receiving compliments, even from Bertha. I felt better by the time I left to go to work, but not just because of what Bertha

had said. It was because of Calvin, and what
I hoped to do when I got my hands on
him. . . .

CHAPTER 22
LOLA

When I was at work, I kept my cell phone in the pocket of the new maroon-colored smocks that employees of Cottright's had to wear while on the job. Around two-thirty p.m., when my phone vibrated, I was busy waiting on a fussy female customer. She was a regular who *always* found something to complain about when she came to the store, so I knew I couldn't check to see who was calling.

"I seen some hella big flies buzzing around the produce," the customer informed me with a smirk.

"Thank you, Mrs. Cunningham. I'll make sure it's taken care of," I replied, struggling to keep the fake smile on my face.

"And there's a great big puddle of water on the floor in front of the meat counter," she added.

"Thank you again, ma'am. I'll make sure it gets taken care of too." I breathed a sigh of relief when Mrs. Cunningham snatched her change out of my hand before I could even count it and pranced toward the exit. There were two more customers behind her. They all had dozens of items in their shopping carts and impatient looks on their faces, so I knew it would be a while before I could check to see who had called me.

Half an hour later, when I took my afternoon break, I rushed to the employee restroom and took out my phone. I was stunned to see Calvin Ramsey's name and cell phone number on the caller ID. He had called *twice*! His first call had come in before I'd left the house. My heart was beating like a drum when I punched in his number. I was glad he answered right away.

"Calvin, I've been so busy, I couldn't call you back until now," I began. "How is everything?"

"Well, my uncle passed sometime before I got up yesterday morning. Other than that, everything is fine." He sounded so sad.

"I'm sorry to hear that," I told him in the saddest tone of voice I could offer. "I hope he didn't suffer much."

"He had already done most of his suffering before I got back here. But he was in good spirits for a man in his situation. We laughed and joked and even had a few beers."

"At least he won't ever have to suffer again. I'm glad to hear that he handled things in such a dignified manner."

"He was a very dignified man, and I will miss him dearly. Look, uh, I still have some things to attend to here, so I'm not sure when I'll be returning to California. I just wanted to check in with you. I didn't want you to think I'd forgotten about you. . . ."

Hearing those words made me want to dance a jig. Instead of behaving like a giddy schoolgirl, I managed to restrain myself. I swallowed hard and said in a very reserved tone of voice, "I'm glad to hear that."

I didn't care what Joan said. Now I was almost convinced that Calvin wanted more from me than a quick romp in a hotel bed. But did he? Of all the club members who had contacted me so far, he was the only one who had *not* asked to set up a sexual encounter! If it was because he wanted more than that from me, it was a good thing. If it was because he was only mildly interested in me, it was a bad thing. My last thought was depressing, so I immediately put it out of my mind.

But since Calvin wasn't having sex with me, was he having sex with other club members? Common sense told me he was not just sitting around twiddling his thumbs and masturbating when there were so many other women in the club practically screaming for sex. Only people who were very sexually active joined sex clubs. He must have read my mind.

"Lola, you are a beautiful woman and you have an amazing body. I think it's time for us to get real close, if you know what I mean."

I gulped so hard, my throat hurt. "It's about time," I wanted to yell. Instead I said as gently as I could, "I do know what you mean. Um, when do you want to get together? And where?"

"I'll call you a day or two before I leave Chicago. We can discuss that then. I've been thinking about you a lot, and I am anxious to be with you. I'm sorry our schedules haven't allowed us to take our relationship to the next level before now. But that's water under the bridge. My schedule is a lot more flexible now."

"Mine is too," I said quickly.

"In the meantime, I hope you will keep yourself, uh, busy until we can get together. I'm sure you're still a very popular club member, right?"

"Uh-huh," I muttered. "I get a lot of attention." Before I could continue, somebody started banging on the restroom door, so I flushed the toilet. "Calvin, I hate to cut this call short, but things are real hectic around here. We have a lot of things on sale today, so we're very busy. And you know how crazy some folks can get in a grocery store when there's a sale going on. Last month two ladies punched each other out over the last ham we had on sale that day." I didn't laugh, but I was glad that Calvin did.

"I understand, Lola. I'm glad we were able to chat this long. I'll let you get back to work."

When I got home that evening, I was surprised and pleased to see that Marshall had returned my car. When I found out he had filled up my gas tank, fixed my signal lights, and washed and polished my beloved Jetta, it made me want to do more to try to have a decent relationship with him. Then I'd only have to deal with Libby's bad attitude. His unexpected and kind gesture, and the fact that I had spoken to Calvin, put me in an even better mood.

After dinner, I went to my room and plopped down onto my bed. I spent a long time trying to imagine what it was going to be like to finally make love with Calvin.

A lot of questions were floating around in

my head. There was one that I tried not to think about, but I couldn't help myself: *What if he's a lousy lover?* A month before I joined Discreet Encounters, I had a disastrous encounter with a man I'd met in a nightclub. He had been such a lousy lover, I ended the relationship. *If Calvin is a flop in bed, will I want to see him again?* I asked myself.

I did know that if my upcoming rendezvous with him turned out to be a disappointment, I still had a lot of prospects to fall back on.

CHAPTER 23
JOAN

There was nothing I enjoyed more than visiting my rowdy, fun-loving family. For one thing, the house I had grown up in was full of life. No matter the time, day or night, somebody had something going on.

I hadn't planned to visit this particular Tuesday afternoon a few minutes after four, and I wouldn't have if I'd known that my big sister, Elaine, was hosting a party in the living room selling erotic products to a bunch of housewives. I arrived just as the party was about to end. I was not a prude (and I had my own sex toys to prove it), but some of the items she had on display surprised me. There were vibrators so huge, they looked like large sausages; two-headed dildos; black condoms; fruit-flavored lubricant, and a few items I couldn't identify.

I was glad that Mama and Elmo had both taken off work so they could visit some of Elmo's relatives in Oakland for the whole day. They weren't prudes either, but I didn't think they'd approve of Elaine selling sex products in the same living room where there was a huge velvet picture of Jesus walking on water.

I was doubly glad that Junior had not come into the house with me. I'd picked him up from school half an hour earlier. As soon as I'd parked my car, he bolted down the block to go hang out with some of his friends.

Wild-eyed women were oohing and aahing like kids in a candy store. One frowsy redhead grabbed her bag of goodies and giggled all the way out the door. The last guest to leave was Mrs. Paxton, a fussy old woman in her late seventies. She was married to a man who had just turned fifty and she liked to brag to anybody who'd listen that they had a very active sex life. Mr. Paxton used Viagra, and since there was nothing yet comparable for women, Mrs. Paxton needed a little help every now and then.

My day had started off with a bang, and I was still in a good mood. At ten a.m., I'd received a call from "DaddyLongLegs," one of my favorite Wall Street hookups from New York. He was back in town and wanted to see me. I was so anxious to see him, I'd driven like a bat out of hell and made it to his hotel in half the time it normally took. Because of all the pleasure I'd enjoyed for two hours, I still had a blissful look on my face when I sat down next to Elaine on the couch.

"You sure are doing a lot of grinning these days," she teased as she jabbed my side with her elbow. She had sold almost everything, so she looked rather pleased. Elaine had provided four pitchers of margaritas for her guests. I had to drive home, so I poured myself just half a glass. It was just as well, because that was about all that was left anyway.

"That's because I have a lot to grin about these days today," I quipped. "And by the way, you'd better not let Mama or Elmo catch you having one of your sex toy parties in this house, you nasty buzzard."

"Don't worry. I never leave any evidence lying around." Elaine stopped talking and gave me a smug look. "You still like to hate on me, I see," she teased. She crossed her shapely legs and raked her fingers through her curly brown hair, which was all hers — not a weave like her real haters hoped it was. Some people (including her) thought she was the most attractive female in my family because of her beautiful, caramel-colored skin and her big, brown Diana Ross eyes. Twenty years ago, she'd lived in L.A. and worked as a swimsuit model. She'd also partied with Hugh Hefner and his crew at the Playboy Mansion. Other than Lola and me, Elaine was the only other woman I knew who thought about sex more than the average woman. She was currently juggling dates with a musician, a cop, and a bartender.

"No, I'm not a hater. Seeing all those funny-looking items you're selling . . ." I paused and nodded toward the two dildos left on the coffee table. "It makes me feel kind of strange."

"Humph! There is nothing 'strange' about sex enhancements. You should know by now that some women need a little help in that area. If a man can't get the job done, what's a woman to do? Shit. We have just as much right to enjoy sex as men."

"I know that. But the best 'prop' is still a man."

Elaine jabbed my side again and winked. "And I guess you'd know?"

"Well, yeah. . . ."

"Well, excuuuuse me. I'm about to fire that bozo cop I've been seeing. He just turned forty-five and looks it and acts it. Nowadays he can't light my fire with a blowtorch. It's a good thing I still have my two spares." Elaine rolled her neck so dramatically, I was surprised she didn't get whiplash. "I guess you don't need any of the unique new toys available these days," she added with a snicker. "Or any spares. . . ."

"I guess I don't," I said with a smirk.

"Oh well. No wonder Reed treats you like a queen. I'll bet he's the kind of man who has always dipped his stick two or three times a night, every night." She turned her head to the side and gave me a curious look.

"Uh-huh," I said weakly. If Elaine only knew! Reed had never "dipped his stick" two or three times a night, or even a week. Our sex life was down to one day a week maybe, and sometimes not even that!

What made me want to scream was the fact that Reed thought he was a red-hot lover. And from what he'd told me, all of his former girlfriends had raved about his bedroom skills. I had become so frustrated with his mediocre performance, it was a wonder I wasn't climbing our bedroom walls. Lola told me that I should talk to him about it, and if that didn't help I needed to make an appointment for us to talk to a sex therapist together. Something that drastic was absolutely out of the question. I'd read a lot of magazine articles and seen enough TV shows on the subject, so I was well aware that even casually *hinting* to a man that he was lousy in bed could make matters even worse. In a movie I'd watched just last week, a woman told her husband that he didn't satisfy her in bed. He got so depressed and self-conscious, he eventually couldn't perform at all. Reed was in bad-enough shape with his mood swings and fascination with suicide. Just thinking about how much worse he'd be if he became impotent too made me shudder.

CHAPTER 24
JOAN

I was so deep in thought, I didn't realize Elaine had gathered up what was left of her erotic products and moved to another part of the house. I didn't even hear Mama enter the room.

"Girl, you gone deaf or what?" she barked.

"Huh? Mama, are you talking to me?" I hollered, almost jumping out of my skin.

"You the only one in this room, ain't you?"

"I'm sorry, Mama. I was thinking about something. I guess I didn't hear you come in."

"I guess you didn't. Anyway, Reed just called. He said he's been calling your cell phone for hours."

"Yeah, I know. I didn't answer because I was just about to go home," I said, rising from the couch. I didn't know my son had come in, but now I could hear him fussing with Too Sweet in the kitchen. "Junior, come on, baby! Let's go home!" I yelled toward the doorway. Within seconds, he galloped into the room. The older he got, the more he looked like Reed. He was exceptionally smart and ambitious for a fourteen-year-old. He loved to watch educational TV shows, and he loved to read. He even read some of the boring medical publications Reed subscribed to. Junior had already decided that he wanted to be a dentist like his father and his grandfather. People often told him how handsome he was and that he was going to make some lucky girl a good husband.

"Can I stay here all night?" Junior asked with the same pleading look that I saw so often on his father's face. "It's boring at our house!"

"Let the boy stay. He's got plenty of clothes here, so Too Sweet can get him off to school tomorrow morning," Mama said before I could answer my son. "I got a few chores he can help me take care of. He can go out there and straighten out that mess in the garage first. Then he can clean out that litter box Elaine's too lazy to take care of. After that, he can run over to Cottright's market and pick up them chicken gizzards, Gatorade, and turnip greens that Too Sweet wants to cook for dinner tonight."

Junior turned to me with a horrified expression.

"Uh, some other time would be better," I said. I was already walking fast toward the door. "Reed's mother is in town visiting friends, and she'll probably pay us a visit this evening too. She'll be real disappointed if Junior's not around for her to fawn over. Come on, baby." With a look of relief, my son followed me as we rushed out to my car.

"Whew! I thought I was going to have to do all kinds of stupid stuff for Grandma," Junior said as he buckled his seat belt. "And I wish she'd get a real computer. The one she's got don't even have speakers and it's hella slow."

"Be glad your grandma's even got a computer for you to play games on. When she was your age, the only tech items they had were typewriters."

"What in the world is a typewriter?"

"It's a boxy little device with keys that have the letters of the alphabet on them. It's what people used before computers came out. They didn't even have the Internet back then either."

"Dang, Mama. How did people get on Facebook back in those days?"

I laughed. "Facebook, Twitter, Instagram, cell phones, DVRs, and many other electronics we take for granted now have only been around for a few years. Some of them weren't even around when I was your age."

I had to stop for a red light, so I had a few moments to look at Junior. He looked totally confused. "Mama, I feel so sorry for you old folks."

I gasped. "You think I'm old?" I asked, glancing into my rearview mirror to check for wrinkles and other signs of age. Of course I didn't see any, but I was still concerned about my son referring to me as old.

"Yup. You'll be thirty-three this year." The serious look on Junior's face now made me sad. "But don't worry, you still have a pretty face. If something ever happens to Daddy, I'm sure another man will marry you. That is, as long as you're still pretty and not too old and fat by then."

Junior's comments gave me chest pains. I was glad he remained silent for the rest of the way home.

Reed appeared extremely exasperated, his arms folded, when I entered our living room. "Woman, what's the point of you having a cell phone if you don't answer it for hours at a time?" he hollered.

I clutched the strap of my purse tighter. I knew there would be a real war if Reed insisted on checking my cell phone caller ID history, especially today. I had not deleted LongJohn's or DaddyLongLegs's numbers yet. "What's the matter this time?" I asked with one of my frequent and heavy sighs.

"Where have you been all day?" he asked with his lips snapping over each word.

I motioned for Junior to go to his room. When he was out of earshot, I turned to Reed with my hands on my hips. "I was out shopping," I said hotly, with a neck roll. When I realized how suspicious it looked for me to come home from an extended shopping spree empty-handed *again,* I added, "I didn't see anything I wanted to buy."

"That's been happening a lot lately."

"So what?"

"So what did you really do today? What do you do all the other times you go 'shopping' and come home with nothing to show for it? I know you're up to something."

"Don't you start that shit again! I'm not in the mood for it!" I yelled while I rubbed the side of my head. Then I started rolling my neck some more and wagging my finger in Reed's face, two gestures he hated. He referred to such behavior as "ghetto queen foolishness."

"Joan, how many times do I have to remind you that you no longer live in the ghetto? Why do you have to act so 'black' when we have serious conversations?"

"In case you forgot, *we* are black. And how many times do I have to remind you that the neighborhood I grew up in is not 'in the ghetto'!" I boomed. "And don't try to change the subject. Let's stick to what we were just discussing." I was talking so hard and fast, I had to pause so I could catch my breath. "I'm getting damn tired of you accusing me of being 'up to something' every time I turn around! I'm your wife, not your prisoner or your child. You don't need to know what I'm doing or where I'm at all the time! Or who I'm with!" I glared at Reed and stomped out of the room with my purse. When I got into the guest bathroom, I locked the door, pulled out my cell phone, and called up Lola. I was about to hang up when she finally answered on the fifth ring.

"Sorry it took me so long to answer, but I couldn't find my phone again," she explained. "Dummy me. I'd dropped it by mistake into my dirty clothes hamper."

"Shut up and listen and don't ask any questions. Just answer yes or no. Can you meet me at the Black Hawk bar ASAP?"

Lola replied without hesitation. "Yes. I'm on my way."

"Good. If you get there before I do, grab a booth or a table toward the back so we can have some privacy."

CHAPTER 25
JOAN

I was not sure if Reed's mother was going to pay us a visit this evening, and if she did I was not in the mood to deal with her. One of the reasons I had managed not to go completely off on her all these years was because I made myself as scarce as I could when she visited.

I didn't even tell Reed that I was going back out, because there would have been another showdown. I waited until he went into the kitchen and had been there for about five minutes before I bolted out the front door.

When I got to the bar, Lola was hunched over a glass of wine in the booth the farthest away from the entrance. The only bad thing about this particular booth was that it was the one closest to the restrooms; you could hear each time a patron flushed the toilet. The Black Hawk was rather seedy, but the drinks were good and cheap, and it was close to home. I was glad to see that Lola had already ordered a glass of wine for me too.

"Uh-oh. I recognize that look on your face," she began as soon as I slid into the booth. I plopped down so hard, the table shook. "What's the matter this time?"

I had to take a long drink before I could respond. "Reed got on my last nerve again."

"Is that all? When is he not on your last nerve?"

"This evening it seemed more irritating than usual. I had to get out of the house." I exhaled and forced a smile to my burning face. "Now that that's out of the way, let's talk about you. And please tell me something good."

Lola took a deep breath, blinked a couple of times, and then reared back in her seat. From the sparkle in her eyes, I knew that I was about to hear something juicy. "I talked to Calvin today," she announced in an excited tone.

I couldn't think of anything more appealing than the glow of a woman in love. I had never seen it on Lola's face until now. She looked almost fluorescent! But I was not too happy about her falling "in love" with a man she'd met online through a sex club — especially after I'd warned her not to! As much as I enjoyed my membership, I was convinced that a relationship that began in such an unconventional manner didn't have a chance of becoming serious and long term. However, in spite of my feelings, I refused to allow myself to share them with Lola, especially since I'd already made her think that I was in her corner. For all I knew, when she and Calvin finally had sex, they might not even enjoy it and then go their separate ways and never speak to each other again. At the end of the day, the main thing I really cared about was my girl being happy. And if experiencing one intimate encounter with Calvin was enough to do the trick — even if just for the duration of that one date — I was all for it.

"Oh? He's back from Chicago?" For some reason I was glad to hear that Lola had communicated with Calvin. By now I was real curious to see what was going to happen.

"No. He left me a couple of voice mail messages and I called him back this afternoon. He's not sure when he's going to be back in California, but he finally told me he's ready to hook up with me."

"You mean he's ready to do what he should have already done by now?" I had not meant to sound so sarcastic, but the words and the bitterness had slid out on their own before I could catch myself. I was miserable enough because of my own love life. I didn't want Lola to think I was sabotaging hers just so we'd both be miserable. The glow was still on her face, so I assumed she had not detected any resentment in my tone. And that really wasn't what it was. I was only responding the way a true friend was supposed to, I told myself. "And while we're on the subject, I don't understand how come you didn't initiate something with him yourself. You know how the club works. You have sex with somebody and get it over with and then you move on to the next person. Maybe if *you* had hurried things along and told him point-blank the first time you communicated with him that you wanted to fuck his brains out, you wouldn't be obsessing about him now."

"Duh! What's wrong with you, girl? You know me better than that. I have never initiated a hookup with one of the club members. I don't think I'll ever be bold enough to contact one and ask him if he wants to sleep with me. Shit. If I did and he turned me down, my ego would never recover."

"News flash," I said with a look of mock amazement. "I'll remind you again: You belong to a *sex* club. You don't have to be

211

'bold' to contact a club member you want to sleep with. So what if one turns you down? I'm sure that even some of the hottest club members have been turned down before."

I could tell from her exasperated look that I was making her uncomfortable, but I didn't care. She did the same thing to me often enough.

"It doesn't matter. I still don't think I'm ready to be that forward. Besides, didn't I already tell you that I liked Calvin so much from the get-go that I didn't want to rush into anything with him? After our first chat, I knew that I didn't want to just have sex with him and move on to the next man. I wanted to get to know him. And I'm happy to tell you that he felt the same way about me right after our first chat."

"He told you that?"

"Uh, something like that."

I hunched my shoulders and took another long drink before I responded. "Well, all I can say is, I hope he'll be worth the wait. Too bad I didn't think that with Reed."

"Did something happen today?"

"Same old shit." I sniffed and blinked forcefully a couple of times. "I'm trying so hard, Lola."

"I know you are. You don't have to convince me of anything. I just hope things work out for you. And I hope Reed comes to his senses and forgets about committing suicide."

I shook my head. "I don't think he's ever going to forget about that. Not as long as he thinks it'll keep me with him." I blinked some more and gave Lola a hopeless look. "A couple of days ago he left his computer on. Would you believe he's been Googling insurance companies that don't have a suicide clause?"

"Huh?"

"Some companies won't pay out if the policyholder commits suicide."

"I didn't know that."

"But there are some who will pay out a year or two after the suicide. Those were the ones he'd highlighted."

"At least you know he's thinking about you and Junior."

"That man would never leave me and his son high and dry. Even without a huge insurance payout, Junior and I will still be in good shape if something happens to Reed. He told me how hard his parents tried to get him to make me sign a prenuptial agreement, but he didn't. The condo, an apartment building he owns in Berkeley, all the money he's got in four bank accounts, and everything else he has will be mine. But I have to be honest — I don't think I'd enjoy any of that if he does, you know . . ."

"Kill himself? I know I wouldn't enjoy any money I got because somebody died by suicide. Joan, I feel so sorry for you."

"Don't feel sorry for me," I snarled, and gave Lola a dismissive wave. I was even able to follow that statement with a dry laugh.

"Do you still try to talk to his parents about his threats?"

"*Pffft!* Not anymore. They are in such denial, they refuse to believe he's serious. And when I told Reed I wanted to contact intervention professionals so they could get involved, he wasn't too happy about that. He assured me that if I did involve strangers, *that* would really send him off the deep end, Lola." I sucked in some air and looked her in the eyes. "Enough of that dreary talk. Let's talk about Calvin some more! You've been lusting after him long enough, so I'm glad it looks like you might get him into bed after all."

"I'm not 'lusting'!" Lola boomed. "I just want to find out if he's as good as he looks."

"That's the same thing, *you nasty HO!*"

We both laughed long and loud.

Chapter 26
Lola

The story about the three missing women seemed like it was never going to go away. Yesterday's newspaper printed a letter to the editor from one of the women's relatives. She expressed how sad, angry, and frustrated the family had become. A few minutes later, when I'd put on my makeup at the mirror on my dresser, my reflection made me cringe. I was looking at the face of the three missing women: Each one looked like me. Even though I was as superstitious as ever, I told myself that I wasted too much time worrying about ominous things. My fear that I would die if I ever wore yellow clothing was bad enough. I'd put the three women out of my mind and finished applying my makeup. I decided it was more important for me to focus on positive things.

I was ecstatic because things seemed to be moving in the right direction with Calvin.

But I didn't want to get too excited too soon, and I had a good reason: my past. Mine was too complicated to ignore. Whenever something positive happened in my life, something negative usually followed. I had so many examples, I had lost count.

While Joan continued to rattle on about Reed, Calvin, and a few other subjects, my mind wandered. I recalled incidents from my distant past, as well as more recent ones. Once when I scored an A plus on a math test in my senior year of high school, the classmate who had shared his cheat sheet with me blabbed to the wrong person, and that person ratted us both out. We had to take a different test, which we didn't get time to study for, and we both failed it.

When Mama died and Daddy married Bertha, I thought I was going to be happy living in her big house with two orange trees in the backyard and a bedroom almost twice the size of my old one. But Libby and Marshall came around often enough to make my life a living hell.

I pushed those thoughts to the back of my mind and focused more on recent events.

The first Saturday in January, while Bertha and I had been shopping at one of our favorite malls, we ran into one of my former classmates, Elbert Porter. Although a lot of people called him a nerd, he didn't look or act like one to me. He was not goofy and didn't wear Coke bottle glasses, but he was super intelligent, meek, and overly polite. He was six feet tall, he had a well-developed body, a nice smile and jet black hair that he wore in shoulder-length, well-maintained dreadlocks. Elbert had joined the army a week after we graduated. After his honorable discharge, he married the only girl he'd ever dated, moved her in with him and his mother, and less than a year later the marriage was over. Nowadays he directed the choir at the church that Bertha attended two or three Sundays a month, and I attended sporadically.

Elbert was the youngest of five children and everybody knew how devoted he was to his widowed mother, Alma. Especially Bertha. Alma had accompanied him to the mall that Saturday. As a matter of fact, you rarely saw one without the other. His siblings had been trying to force Alma to move into a nursing home for months, but he had made it clear that that would never happen as long as he was alive. When one of Bertha's friends came to the house and told us what Elbert had said, Bertha's response was, "That boy is going to make some woman a good husband."

"If you two ladies aren't in a hurry, please join Mama and me for lunch at the Hometown Buffet," Elbert had said, shifting his weight nervously from one foot to the other. We were in front of the Dollar Tree store Bertha and I had just left. I had been trying to lose a few pounds for weeks, so I'd been avoiding buffets. I couldn't control myself when it came to restaurants that offered an "all you can eat for one price" deal. Before I could open my mouth, Bertha had not only accepted the invitation but invited Elbert and his mother to join us for dinner the next day after church.

The day after that dinner, which had been as boring as the lunch, Bertha had told me, "It's a shame you can't get a man like Elbert. Alma is blessed to have such a devoted child. I hope his next wife appreciates him *and* Alma more than his first wife did. . . ." A few days later, Elbert and his mother started coming to the house unannounced. What had started out as an innocent encounter quickly morphed into another burden for me to bear. Before I realized what I'd gotten myself into, I was "dating" Elbert. From that day on, whenever Bertha was in his presence she beamed like a lighthouse. Running into him and Alma at the mall that Saturday afternoon had made her day. It was a positive thing for her, another negative thing for me.

I only spent time with Elbert when I had nothing better to do. The places we usually went to included movies, restaurants, church events, and the bingo hall. One Saturday afternoon a couple of weeks ago, when I returned home from a date with a club member, Elbert and Alma were sitting in the living room with Bertha. All three were sipping tea and watching *Joel Osteen.* Bertha looked like she was in ecstasy. I was too, for that matter. The man I'd just been with had covered my most intimate body parts with whipped cream and licked it all off. I was also amused. After all the men I'd socialized with over the years, Bertha had finally "accepted" one. The fact that Elbert was a devout Christian, didn't believe in sex before marriage, and managed a meat market (and gave Bertha free meat) had a lot to do with that. But his devotion to his mother was the main reason. Bertha didn't follow me when I went out with Elbert the way she had when I was dating boys in high school. For one thing, she was older and her health had declined considerably. She was no longer spry and energetic, and almost every night she was in bed by eight. I think that was the only reason she didn't follow me and Elbert when we went out.

I'd poured myself a cup of tea and joined the "party" in the living room. I sat down on the couch next to Elbert. I was surprised when he shyly put his arm around my shoulder and whispered in my ear how "relaxed" I looked to him. When Joel Osteen's show ended, he took us all to the bingo hall.

I liked Elbert; he was convenient and a great buffer between Bertha and me. At least with him in the picture, she was in a good mood more often. She even became quite close to his mother. One evening the three of them went out to dinner and the bingo hall without me. But I knew that things had not really changed that much. I was still trapped in an impossible situation: Bertha still wanted to control my future. She still wanted to *be* my future. Even though I continued to go out with Elbert sporadically, my relationship with him had gone as far as I was going to allow it. But it didn't matter to Bertha if I spent time with him several times a week or less frequently. She was happy just knowing I was seeing him at all. In the meantime, I was going to continue looking for my real soul mate. Had it not been for Joan and all the fun I was having as a member of Discreet Encounters,

I would have lost my mind by now.

"Lola, I wish you'd get that blank expression off your face and pay more attention to me," Joan said, snapping her fingers. It took me a moment to realize I was still sitting in a booth drinking with her in the Black Hawk bar.

"Huh?"

"Huh, my ass. For the last couple of minutes, you looked like somebody under a hypnotic spell. Talk to me, girl."

"Oh! I'm listening to you," I fumbled. I would never tell Joan I'd been thinking about Elbert. She was shocked and amused last month when I told her I was going out with him. Even though he was good looking, the way she'd carried on about his dull personality and lame social life, you would have thought he was Forrest Gump.

Joan and I stayed in the bar for two hours. When I returned home, Bertha was hanging up the telephone as I entered the kitchen. She glanced at me and shook her head. I was familiar with her somber look. It always meant bad news.

"Did somebody die?" I asked as I approached her. Most of Bertha's friends had already passed, and at least half a dozen were close to it. The way she complained about her health, she was convinced that her days were numbered. She had been "dying" for decades.

"Nobody died, sugar," she croaked. "Praise the Lord for that."

"Who were you just talking to on the phone? You look upset, so they must have given you some real bad news." I put my arm around Bertha's shoulder. She drove me nuts, but I still cared about her. Since I had lost touch with the few blood relatives I had left, she was the closest thing I had to family. That was one of the reasons I was so anxious to get married and start my family — so that I'd have somebody when she passed away.

"That was my son-in-law," she muttered.

Libby's husband, Jeffrey, was one of the nicest people I knew and everybody liked him, especially the women. With his sexy bald head, almond-shaped eyes, and well-built body, it was no wonder. He was hopelessly in love with Libby, so he went out of his way to please her. He was very nice to me. Had it not been for him, I would have stopped talking to Libby a long time ago.

"What did Jeffrey say?" I asked.

"He and Libby are having some renovations done on their house. Why, I don't know. Their house is not even that old, so I can't imagine why they want to make drastic changes already."

I wasn't sure where this conversation was going, but I had a good idea. Something told me that Libby had put Jeffrey up to asking Bertha for the money to pay for their renovations.

"They want you to help them pay for it, right?" I said as I rubbed her shoulder.

Bertha slowly turned her head to the side and rasped, "That's part of it."

I couldn't imagine what the other "part" was. I didn't have to wait long to find out.

Bertha's explanation made my blood run cold. "They can't stay in the house while the work is being done, so they'll be moving in with us for a while."

My chest suddenly felt as if it were about to explode.

CHAPTER 27
LOLA

What Bertha just told me was so hellish, it made my head swim. For a few moments, I thought I was going to pass out. *"A while?"* I croaked.

"Well, a few weeks at least. Maybe even a few months. I don't know how long the remodeling is going to take."

It didn't matter if Libby and her family stayed with us for a few weeks or a few months. Had it been only one day, it would have still seemed like an eternity to me. If somebody had told me that the world was going to end tomorrow, I would not have been more frightened. Of all the people on the planet, Libby was the last one I wanted to live under the same roof with. Her brother, Marshall, was close behind her in that position. When his wife kicked him out last year, he moved in with us. He stayed only a few days, but during that brief period I thought I would go crazy.

"I . . . I don't know what to say," I said, my voice barely above a whisper.

"There is nothing for you to say. This is *my* house and whatever I say goes. You have no authority here. You're just a stepchild."

I remained silent because I still didn't know what to say next. Especially after Bertha's last comment. She had told me several times that I was more like a daughter to her than Libby, and I'd felt like I was. But because of what she'd just said, I felt more like a stepchild and an outsider than ever before.

"Libby and her family need a place to stay, and as long as I have a place to stay, they will too. Case closed," Bertha said, giving me a guarded look.

"I'm sure we'll all get along just fine," I muttered.

"I sure hope so. I know you and Libby have a few issues, but for my sake and yours, please help me make this situation as painless as possible."

"I will, Bertha."

I had no idea how I was going to survive this unexpected development. I planned to enjoy whatever time I had left before Libby and her crew moved in. From my past experiences with her, I predicted that she and I would be locking horns almost every day until they left. But it got worse. What Bertha said next made me want to holler.

"They'll be coming in a day or so," she told me with her voice trembling. Despite how she was trying to make light of it, I knew she was not too happy about this turn of events either. "We'll have to straighten up the house before they get here. You know how fussy Libby is when it comes to housekeeping. She keeps her house so clean, you could eat off the floors."

For the first time in my life, I prayed for an earthquake. I wanted the ground to open up and suck me in. And just when I thought things were really looking up for me. In spite of my distress, I was still able to think about Calvin. Now more than ever, I needed somebody to rescue me. . . .

"They're moving here in *a day or so*?" Not only did I let out a loud gasp, but I stretched my eyes open as wide as I could without my eyeballs rolling out of their sockets. I was glad I was not in front of a mirror, because I did not want to see what kind of expression was on my face. Bertha had to notice how upset the news was making me, but she didn't acknowledge it. She continued talking and behaving as if we were discussing what to cook for dinner.

"Maybe with Libby back home again, she

and I can work on our relationship." She had a hopeful look.

I didn't want to comment on her last statement. My mother and I had been very close and I had treated her with respect until the day she died. I hoped that the relationship between Bertha and her daughter would get better someday. Realistically, I knew it would not.

My relationship with Libby had always been bad, but it had gotten even worse a few months after she'd given birth to Kevin. Because of some flimsy gossip, she'd accused me of sleeping with Jeffrey. She'd physically attacked me, and I'd punched the daylights out of her. Jeffrey had shown up just in time to keep us from doing some serious damage to each other.

After he convinced Libby that we were not having an affair, she "apologized" and we'd "made up." Now, we just tolerated one another.

However, every now and then she was nice to me. Two years ago when she found out I liked to read *Ebony* magazine, she gave me a two-year subscription for Christmas. The year before that, she and Marshall sent Bertha and me to Vegas to celebrate Thanksgiving. I found out later that they had financed the trip with money they'd borrowed from Bertha, though. The bottom line was, things were never going to be peachy keen between her children and me. I was going to do my best to make things run as smoothly as possible until Libby and her family moved back into their own house. And it was going to be my biggest challenge so far.

Had I not been so looking forward to getting together with Calvin, I probably would have experienced a major meltdown right in front of Bertha.

CHAPTER 28
JOAN

Whenever Reed was on the premises, I usually went into one of our bathrooms or to the ground floor pool area to make a call on my cell phone.

It was a typical Sunday afternoon, the last week in February. It was a few minutes past two in the afternoon and I needed to take a breather. I headed toward the front door with my purse in my hand. Reed entered the living room in time to see me with my hand on the doorknob.

"Going somewhere, Joan?" he asked gruffly.

"Oh, my period is about to come on, so I'm feeling kind of edgy. I thought I'd go down to the pool for a little while."

Reed scratched his neck and shot me a curious look. "Hmmm. I was just thinking about doing that same thing myself. Let me put on my trunks and grab a towel and I'll join you. I'll swim a few laps with you."

"I'm not going to get in the water. I just want to lounge and relax for a little while."

"Well, that sounds good too! Do you want me to grab a couple bottles of water?"

"No, that's okay," I muttered.

I spent the next hour stretched out on a deck chair in a baggy denim jumpsuit looking at the side of Reed's head and forcing myself to converse with him about one mundane subject after another. He had not put on his trunks, so he had no intentions of getting in the water either. He was boring the hell out of me until he shared some funny stories about a few of his regular patients, something he rarely did. It was good to see him in a pleasant mood. "It was bad enough that Mr. Richmond fell asleep in the middle of his root canal, but my nurse was not happy about him passing gas a few times before he woke up." Reed laughed, and I laughed along with him. I even gave him an affectionate pat on his thigh. This was the side of him that I actually liked but rarely saw. I knew that if he humored me more, things would be a lot better between us. "If you think that's funny, listen to this. Last week a new patient, who also happens to be a midget, asked my six-foot-tall receptionist for a date. And the week before that, a woman who had had her teeth cleaned a few days earlier stormed my office and demanded another cleaning because the exotic sake she'd had with her lunch had turned her teeth purple, so she couldn't go to the job interview she had scheduled for that afternoon. My schedule was full, so I skipped my lunch to accommodate her. To show her appreciation, she stopped by my office after her job interview and gave me a bottle of the same shit that had stained her teeth!" This time we howled like hyenas. I laughed so hard, tears pooled in my eyes.

"You should write a book about your experiences someday," I suggested.

"I have another story I've been meaning to tell you. A woman came in one Monday morning because she'd gotten drunk the Saturday night before and she lost her dentures."

"How did that happen?" I asked.

"She and her date were cruising down some back street on the East Side when she had to lean out the window and throw up. Her teeth went out the window too. She said it was so dark, her honey, who was as drunk as she was, refused to stop and help her locate her choppers. When she went back by herself the next day, somebody had run over them. I had to force myself not to laugh when she showed up in my office that Monday morning with her smashed-up teeth in a baggie. I felt so sorry for her, I told her I'd replace them free of charge."

"That poor woman! Honey, that was so nice of you to give her new teeth for free. No wonder you have so many loyal patients." I sat up and looked around. "I'm going to go get us some water after all," I said, already rising. "Would you like something to nibble on too?"

"Every day." Reed licked his lips and winked. Then he patted my crotch. "I'll do my nibbling tonight when we go to bed. And that's a promise. . . ." I didn't respond to his lewd "promise." I shuddered, but I managed to stay calm.

A lot of our neighbors were Reed's patients, so they lit up whenever they saw him. We waved to a grinning young Chinese American couple who lived on the third floor. They had just wandered in and sat down on the opposite side of the pool. "Invite the Wongs to have dinner with us next week," Reed told me in a low voice. Then he started talking fast, as if somebody had just pushed a button that controlled his mouth. "Oh! I almost forgot. The Millers reminded me last night that we owe them a dinner too, so look at your calendar and see what days work for us. Cook something real elaborate. A duck with all the trimmings sounds good. Trot down to that Asian market at the corner and pick up some organic veggies. I'm sure you can find a nice, plump duck there too. Have that florist on Jersey Street send over a pretty floral arrangement to set on the dinner table. Do the same thing for the Wongs, but cook something different because they are real fussy and two of my first patients, so I need to keep them happy. Ah! A lasagna made from scratch should do the trick. Plan both dinners for next week, but not on the same day. The Millers can't stand the Wongs."

By the time Reed turned off his motor mouth, I was ready to scream. Hosting two separate dinners in the same week was going to impact my dating schedule as well as my miscellaneous online activity. I had recently begun to spend hours at a time reading comments and reviews and chatting with other club members in our private chat rooms. I scheduled most of my weekday, in-person encounters for as early in the day as possible. It gave me plenty of time to go on a date and still beat Reed home. Three weeks ago, after two back-to-back dates in the same day, I'd come home sore from my head all the way down to my toes. I had to soak my body in Epsom salts to soothe the pain between my thighs. But it was a small price to pay for all the fun I was having.

"Um, yeah. That'll be a lot of work, but I'll try to do my best."

"You *will* do your best."

"Maybe I can get Too Sweet to come over and help me cook."

Reed looked at me as if I had turned into a tree. "Joan, do you honestly think I'd allow an unsophisticated mammy reject like Too Sweet prepare a meal for the Wongs and the Millers — or anybody else I know? I wouldn't even let her prepare the food to go into a *hog trough* for a hog I didn't like. Old-school black sisters like her cook the hell out of veggies and they —"

"You've made your point, Reed!" I hollered with my hand up to his face. He didn't know how close I was to slapping the daylights out of him, but I refused to get "ghetto" in front of the Wongs. I lowered my voice almost to a whisper and continued. "And I don't want to keep warning you about trashing my family. I could say a whole lot of shit about your folks."

"Now, now, honey. Let's stay focused on the dinners I want you to prepare."

"And if you feel that way about the way *we* black women cook, why do you ask me to cook a pot of greens two or three times a month? Last Thursday when I cooked mustard greens for dinner, you gobbled up *three* helpings."

"True, but I paid dearly for it. I had gas and cramps for two days," Reed chortled. "Baby, you can keep cooking greens for me as long as it makes you happy. But I refuse to let you subject my friends and patients to that kind of culinary abuse. Now, if you think you need help, call up one of those agencies and have them send somebody over. And make sure it's somebody who can stay and do all the serving and clean up afterward."

"If I'm going to do all that cooking and can't have Too Sweet help me, I'd rather do it by myself. And I can do all the serving and cleaning up by myself too. I don't want a stranger in my kitchen." I exhaled and gave Reed a thoughtful look. "Well, I guess I'll go on and get those bottles of water."

Reed looked at my purse in my hand, and I clutched it tighter. I knew that if I left it behind, he would remove my cell phone and check my calls. "You're coming right back, so how come you're taking your purse with you?" he asked.

"Huh? Oh. I need to put a few tampons in it in case I need them."

"Okay, baby. Don't take too long. Bring some chips and dip with you."

As soon as I got back upstairs, I went into the guest bathroom and locked the door. I took my cell phone out of my purse and dialed Lola's number, but she didn't answer. Because I'd spent so much time on my outside activities in the past few days, I decided to stay close to home today. It was painful, and had Junior not been in his room playing video games, I would have jumped into my car and gone to the mall or Mama's house for a couple of hours. I wanted to log in to the club's website and see if I could arrange another date for one day next week. But I couldn't take that chance today as long as Reed was around.

One of the many good things I liked about Discreet Encounters was that none of the men I'd contacted had ever turned me down for a date. Unlike Lola, I was bold enough to initiate an encounter. Another good thing was, even though I'd been the initiator in a few cases, none of the men had allowed me to pay for the hotel room. That had always been one of the club's rules: The initiator was responsible for all the expenses, even airfare if the hookup involved some traveling. Usually, when I did the "soliciting," I e-mailed visitors who had already checked into a local hotel, or ones who were scheduled to come to the Bay Area.

There were times when I had to remind myself not to get too greedy. But the bottom line was, I enjoyed sex — *good* sex. And when the urge to get some hit me, I didn't sit around and wait for it to come to me. I went after it.

When I left the bathroom less than a minute later and went into the living room, Reed was slumped on the couch with Junior. The remote was in Reed's hand. He had not turned on the TV and that all-too-familiar look of despair was back on his face. I had my purse in one hand, my cell phone in the other.

"I guess you forgot I was downstairs, huh?" Reed mumbled, frowning at the phone in my hand like it was a piece of shit.

"I just left you a few minutes ago, and I had to use the bathroom," I replied.

"Who did you call?" He nodded toward my cell phone.

"I didn't call anybody and nobody called me. But I'm expecting a call from Mama. I just checked to see if she'd called. I'm sorry."

"You sure are sorry," he snarled.

"Mama, can I order some Chinese takeout

237

for dinner?" Junior piped in. My son was totally oblivious to the tension between Reed and me. I made it a point to never show too much of my frustration in front of him.

"Yes, son. Go ahead and do that," I said quickly and cheerfully. "Make sure you get some egg rolls for your daddy." Reed was staring at the wall, and he looked like he was in mourning. And just a few minutes earlier, he had been laughing and joking with me. I didn't know what to do or say to bring him out of the doldrums, so I didn't even try.

I returned to the bathroom and tried to reach Lola again. She still didn't answer her cell phone, so I tried her landline. She didn't answer it either. When I returned to the living room, Reed didn't even look in my direction. I ignored him and went into our bedroom.

I stretched out on the bed, and for the next hour I stared at the ceiling and replayed a conversation I'd had with John on the telephone yesterday. He had asked me to move to Phoenix again. That was not going to happen, but it made me feel good about myself to know that a man like him was so anxious to have me all to himself. And his proposition couldn't have come at a better time. I didn't feel as confident about myself as I had in my early twenties. Now that I was in my thirties, I had all the same concerns about my looks as other women my age. I examined my entire body thoroughly in the full-length mirror behind my bedroom door at least once a month. I didn't have any noticeable lines on my face, or any gray hair, but my breasts were not as perky as they used to be. One thing was for sure, I was not going to grow old gracefully. I was going to approach it kicking and screaming the way celebrities did. I would do whatever it took to look good for as long as possible. If I didn't take DrFeelGood up on his offer to perform all the free surgery I wanted, I'd use Reed's money to do it. My appearance was very important if I wanted to continue having a good time.

When I got up and headed back to the living room, Junior was on the couch with a large plate of shrimp fried rice and egg rolls on the coffee table in front of him. I gave him a sideways glance and shook my head as he stuffed food into his greasy mouth. I plucked an egg roll off his plate and headed toward the kitchen to see if Reed was in a better mood. If he was, I thought it would be a good idea to invite him to go to the movies with me.

He was sitting at the table with his back to the door. There was a full plate in front of him. He hadn't even removed his chopsticks out of the wrapper. It took me a second to realize he was talking to somebody on the telephone.

I stopped dead in my tracks when I heard what he was saying. "I don't want to live without my wife." He choked on a sob and then he sniffled. *What the hell is going on with this crybaby now,* I wondered. I stepped back, hid by the side of the door, and listened. I was dying to hear who he was talking to. What he said next made my flesh crawl. "Thank you, ma'am. I never thought I'd be calling Suicide Prevention, but I'm glad I did. You've been very helpful. The way things are going now, I'm sure I'll be calling again. . . ."

CHAPTER 29
LOLA

The news about Libby and her family moving in with us was so disturbing, I had to figure out something to do to keep myself from going crazy. I was so wound up, I couldn't even think straight. I went to my room and tried to read the latest issue of *People* magazine. I couldn't concentrate on any of the articles long enough for them to make any sense to me. I tried to watch a couple of TV programs, but I couldn't concentrate on them either. I needed to talk to somebody about my latest crisis. I dialed Joan's number, but she didn't answer.

I was reluctant to go online and log on to the Discreet Encounters live chat. Since sex was the club's main objective, I knew none of my fellow club members would be interested in chatting with me about my domestic problems. I got up from my desk and started pacing. After only a few minutes, my chest felt so tight, I had trouble breathing. I had to open a window so I could get some fresh air. It dawned on me that I should get out of the house for a while.

I had heard Bertha go into her room several hours ago. I waited another ten minutes before I tiptoed out into the hallway. Before I even got within five feet of her door, I could hear her snoring.

If this was not a case where I needed a drink, I didn't know what was. Unfortunately, a liter of generic beer was the only alcohol in the house. That shit tasted like Alka-Seltzer, and even though it might have helped the throbbing headache I had suddenly developed, I needed something much more potent. I padded down the stairs with my car key in my hand. I rushed out the door to my car and I didn't stop driving until I reached the first bar I saw.

I parked in front of the Green Rose, a dive bar eight blocks down our street. Their closing time was two a.m. It was already one thirty, but half an hour would be enough time for me to get drunk.

I was glad the four male patrons inside were already with other women so I didn't have to worry about anybody trying to hit on me. I had time for just one drink anyway. Instead of my usual glass of white wine or a Cadillac margarita, I ordered a double shot of Jack Daniels. As soon as I gulped it down, I got a strong buzz.

After I paid my tab and began to stagger toward the exit, the bartender offered to call a cab for me. I declined his offer. When I got outside, the cool night air blew some sense into my head. Instead of attempting to drive myself home and possibly having an accident and getting arrested, I decided to give Joan another call. If she answered, I'd ask her to rescue me. She didn't answer her cell phone, so I dialed the landline. To my everlasting horror, Reed answered. If I had blocked my number, I would have just hung up without saying a word.

"Yeah," he mumbled, sounding as grumpy as ever.

"Reed, this is Lola." I hiccupped. "I'd like to speak to Joan." I hiccupped again.

"What's wrong with you, girl? Do you know what time it is? And it sounds like you're hella drunk! Shee-it!" Reed was such an educated man, but there were times when he sounded like a typical homeboy from the hood.

"I know," I slurred. "But I really need to talk to her. It's important."

"Well, unless it's a matter of life or death, it's not important enough for me to wake her up. Now, is that the case?"

"Not really," I mumbled.

"Then it can wait until tomorrow. I'll tell Joan you called." Just as I was about to speak again, he hung up.

I had three choices: walk around in the night air until I sobered up, call a cab, or drive myself home and risk getting stopped by the cops. I had never been arrested. If that ever happened, the last thing I wanted to be hauled in for was drunk driving. I decided to call a cab.

When I got home, I couldn't get to sleep, so I turned my computer on and fiddled around on the Internet for about an hour until I could no longer stay awake.

At seven in the morning, I called my work and told my boss I had severe menstrual cramps and would be a few hours late. Mr. Cottright, like so many other men, didn't like to discuss female body issues. He mumbled some gibberish under his breath, and then he told me to take the whole day off.

Every few minutes I glanced at the clock on my nightstand. A few minutes after eight, I dialed Joan's cell phone again. I breathed a sigh of relief when she answered on the first ring.

"I was just about to call you. Reed told me you called a few hours ago," she said as soon as she heard my voice. "You don't sound good at all."

"You got that right. I received some bad news last night," I blurted.

Joan took her time responding. "Don't tell me, let me guess." She cleared her throat. "Calvin doesn't want to see you again after all, huh?"

"No, that's not it. He still wants to see me and I want to see him more than ever now. I'm going to count on you, and hopefully him, to help keep me from going crazy these next few weeks, or months."

"Look, whatever it is, tell me now. I've got the usual mess on my hands over here. And I'd be willing to bet that my mess is bigger than yours."

"I don't know about that."

"Reed's about to take his bath and he wants me to wash his back."

"What's so bad about that?"

"I'm never going to wean this man by doing shit like washing his back."

"True. But you should have never stooped that low in the first place. Next thing you know, he'll be asking you to wash his butt. Anyway, back to the reason I called." My head was aching, bile was rising in my throat, and my tongue felt as if it were about to melt as I continued. "The most dreadful

245

thing is about to happen to me since my daddy died."

"Oh shit! Honey, what is it?"

"Libby and Jeffrey are having some home improvements done on their house. Bertha told me they'll be staying with us for a while. Kevin, their teenager from hell too."

I heard Joan let out a loud breath before she spoke again. "Girl, I'm going to pray for you."

"I'm going to need more than prayers to survive living with Libby. I'd even be willing to use black magic if I knew a good witch doctor."

"Oh shit again. How long of 'a while' do you think they'll be staying?"

"A few weeks at least. Maybe even months. I don't know yet."

"Fuck me! Well, there's nothing you can do about it, I guess. I feel for you, though. You know I'll do whatever I can to help you get through this."

"Thanks, Joan. I appreciate hearing that. I won't be going in to work today, so if you can get away, I can meet you for lunch. When I couldn't get in touch with you last night, I ended up at the Green Rose bar. That's how upset I was when Bertha told me. I got too tipsy to drive, so I had to take a cab home."

"You're really taking this shit hard!"

"Oh yeah. Can you drive me back over there to pick up my car? That is, if you can get away from Reed. He was real nasty to me when I called to see if you could come pick me up from the bar."

Joan sucked on her teeth before she responded. "Well, you know how he is. And he's getting worse by the day. Last Sunday, I overheard him on the telephone talking to somebody at suicide prevention."

"What? Oh my God. Listen, you stay home and don't worry about me. I can take the bus or a cab to go pick up my car. If old Mr. Fernandez next door is home, I'll ask him to take me."

"Thanks, Lola. Otherwise, you know I'd help you out. But . . . well, things are pretty tense over here. I don't know how much more I can take." Joan blew out some air and a groan. "I'm going to check my club in-box. I could sure use some outside male attention."

"Joan, let things cool down first. Maybe you shouldn't set up another date for a while. Reed's probably not as gullible as you think he is. You could be asking for trouble."

"Don't you start! You and I are roommates in the same glass house, baby. You could be asking for trouble too."

"Now, don't get mad at me. I am not trying to tell you what to do with your life, but I don't have a husband to answer to. And as far as my clients, um, I mean 'hookups' go, none of them have asked me to move to their city to be their mistress. LongJohn has asked you more than once, which means he's serious. What if he gets mad at you one day when you're with him because you keep turning him down? There is no telling what he might do. You watch all the true crime shows on TV and you read the newspaper, so you know that people snap when they get mad enough. They do all kinds of violent shit to other people. How would you explain a black eye or a bunch of black and blue bruises to Reed?"

"Honey, getting my ass kicked by a date is the last thing I'm worried about!" Joan hollered. "Especially by a pussycat like John. No matter how many times I turn down his proposal to move to Phoenix, he just shrugs it off. He told me that he still wants to see me again, and again, even if I never take him up on his offer." Joan paused and began to speak in a more gentle tone. "He makes me feel so special and relaxed when I'm with him. John is . . . well, he's just what I need right now. I hope he can pay me another visit again real soon. Let me shut up. I'm beginning to sound like you, going on and on about that truck driver," she chuckled.

I ignored her last comment. "Look, I checked out John's profile and picture right after the first time you told me about him last year. I even Googled him, so I know he's got a lot going for him. He's . . . um . . . fairly good-looking but he's no Mr. Universe. What is it about him that's got *you* acting like a fool? Is it his money and the fact that he's so crazy about you, or is he that damn good between the sheets?"

"He's good in bed, but I've had better. He works hard to please me and he stays *hard* . . . if you know what I mean. With Reed, I'm lucky if he can keep an erection for a full minute. Until John says or does something I don't like, I'm going to see him whenever he comes to town and wants to see me."

"Whatever," I mumbled. One thing I knew for sure was that Joan was a woman who lived by her own rules most of the time. I couldn't remember the last time she'd taken any advice from me. "I still think you should slow down for a while."

"Slow down? Slow down, my pussy! I wish *you* would stop talking that holier than thou bullshit with me! Not when you're planning to meet up with that mysterious Calvin Ramsey when he gets back into town."

"What do you mean by 'mysterious'?" Joan didn't respond right away, and that made me feel defensive. "I wish you'd stop taking potshots at Calvin. At least he's not married like John, and he's not putting pressure on me to move closer to him."

"Honey, Calvin's not doing much of anything where you're concerned."

"Exactly what is it you're trying to say, Joan?"

"I . . . I don't know. I just have a gut feeling about Calvin. I can't put my finger on it, but there is something strange about this dude. He sounds too good to be true."

"Thanks for telling me now. If you think he's mysterious and too good to be true, why did you encourage me to hook up with him?" I was talking so fast, my words sounded like one long sentence. I began to speak in a slow, even tone of voice. "And all you know about the man is what I've told you, so what makes you think there's something strange about him?"

"Like I just said, it's a gut feeling I have about him." A long moment of silence passed before Joan continued. "Look, don't pay any attention to me. I'm talking off the top of my head. I'm not Dr. Phil, and my own life is a major mess, so who'd take advice from me?" I was glad to hear Joan chuckle some more. "If you still want to check Calvin out and try to have a real relationship with him, go for it."

"I am going for it. If I have to put up with Libby, I'm going to need all the distractions I can get. If I think Calvin is 'mysterious' or 'strange' when I get busy with him, you'll be the first to know."

CHAPTER 30
LOLA

Libby and her family arrived on Saturday around six in the evening. I peeked out my bedroom window and watched as Jeffrey started removing things from Libby's Camry and his Bronco onto the sidewalk. By the time I got up enough nerve to go downstairs fifteen minutes later, a lot of stuff had already been brought into the house and dumped onto the living-room floor.

Jeffrey and Bertha were the only ones bringing their belongings into the house. Libby was sprawled on the living-room couch texting. The look on her face was so serious, you would have thought she was performing surgery. When she glanced up and saw me, she frowned. "Look what the cat dragged in. I was wondering when you were going to come down and help get the rest of our stuff unloaded." Her voice was just as shrill and annoying as ever. "I can't do too much on account of I just picked a splinter out of my hand and it's still too sore for me to lift anything."

"I smell something stinky every time I come in this house!" Kevin hollered, entering from the kitchen and looking directly at me. It was amazing how much he looked and acted like Libby. He was fourteen, but most of the time he behaved like a toddler. "I ain't going to like bringing my friends over here!"

I hadn't been in the living room a full minute, but my head already felt like it was about to burst. I was glad I had some Advil, a large bottle of wine, and a Bible in my room, because I was going to need all three. I was going to do whatever else it took to survive what I thought of as a "home invasion."

The front door was standing open. Bertha was outside on the sidewalk with a bulging shopping bag in each hand.

"I was taking a nap," I told Libby.

"Well, if you don't mind, there are a few more things to bring in," she snapped.

Without a word, I shuffled out the front door and stopped right next to Bertha. She looked as if she was tired enough to pass out. She gave me a pleading look and handed me one of the shopping bags.

For the next twenty minutes, I helped Jeffrey and Bertha bring in more shopping bags and boxes. We carried everything upstairs to the room that Jeffrey and Libby were going to use. Marshall had occupied it before he moved into his own place with his wife. Kevin was going to share Bertha's room and sleep on the floor in his sleeping bag.

Libby and Kevin, both on the couch now clutching their smartphones as if they were diamonds, didn't lift a finger to help bring the rest of their stuff into the house. That really pissed me off, but for Bertha's sake I held my tongue.

I brought in the last shopping bag, which contained Libby's numerous bottles of perfume and bubble bath, and dropped it onto the floor with a thud. She scrambled off the couch and marched up to me wagging her finger in my face.

"What's wrong with you, Lola?" she shouted, furrowing her brows. "Have you lost your goddamn mind?"

"What are you talking about?" I asked, too tired to show my anger. The palms of my hands and arms were aching from hauling so many shopping bags into the house. My feet felt like they were rooted to the floor.

Libby glared at me. "There's at least five hundred bucks worth of smell goods in that shopping bag you just dropped to the floor like it was a sack of garbage!"

"Then why didn't you get up off your backside and help us bring the stuff in?" I asked, glaring back at her with my hands on my hips. By now I didn't care if I made Bertha mad by standing up to Libby.

"Girls, be nice now," Jeffrey said, entering the house with a box full of Kevin's video games. "I don't feel like playing referee today." He laughed even though I knew he was just as frustrated as I was. He kicked the door shut.

A few moments later, Bertha came back downstairs, huffing and puffing and sweating as if she had just run a marathon. "I'm glad we finally got everything in," she mumbled, wiping her forehead with the back of her hand. "I haven't worked this hard in years."

"And I sure do appreciate it, Mama," Libby said. She actually sounded sincere and grateful. "I wish I could have helped. Lola, you're welcome to use some of my bubble bath whenever you want."

I couldn't remember the last time she offered me something nice. I whirled around so fast to look at her, I heard the bones in my neck pop. "Thank . . . you," I mumbled. She was actually smiling at me.

A sheepish grin covered Jeffrey's face, and he winked at me. I was glad Libby had returned her attention to her smartphone and didn't see that. Jeffrey set the box on the floor and then he walked up to Libby and kissed her cheek.

"When do we eat? And I don't want no chitlins!" Kevin hollered. Not only had he inherited Libby's looks and dumpy body, he was just as mean-spirited as she was.

We were all standing in the middle of the living-room floor, looking like sheep without a shepherd. "Dinner will be ready in a few minutes," Bertha announced. She was flustered, but I didn't feel too sorry for her. No matter what she'd said, I knew she didn't want Libby and her family staying with us any more than I did. If she had said no, Libby and Jeffrey had other options. They had a lot of friends, and Jeffrey had family all over town whom they could have moved in with. "Lola, you want to help me set the table? We're having smothered chicken and mashed potatoes. And good news! I made some of those sweet rolls you like so much, especially for you."

"I can help you set the table, but I'll be eating out this evening," I stated. "Just leave me a few rolls to eat later tonight or tomorrow." I had not been able to sleep much last night. Just before midnight I'd piled out of bed and turned my computer on. All I had planned on doing was spending a few minutes in a chat room until I got sleepy. I got bored with that real quick, so I logged on to AOL to check my regular e-mail. In addition to the usual junk, I received an ad for penis enlargement pills. I couldn't understand why shit like that didn't go directly into my spam folder where it belonged. But I didn't have time to worry about that. I logged out of AOL and signed in to the Discreet Encounters website. The only new message in my club in-box was from a college professor at Florida State. He was in town for his twenty-fifth class reunion. I Googled him first to make sure he was who he said he was. And then I read the reviews other members had posted about him. Every woman had given him either four or five stars. I had called him up at nine o'clock this morning and arranged an encounter for eight-thirty tonight.

"You going out with that Elbert Porter again," Bertha asked with a smile.

"Elbert? You're still going out with him?" Jeffrey asked, also with a smile. "I'm so glad to hear that! You two make a nice couple."

"Humph. I always thought he was a fag," Libby sneered. I ignored her comment, but that didn't shut her up. "His ex-wife told my Zumba instructor that she found a gay porn magazine in his sock drawer."

"I still see Elbert every now and then, but I'm going to go visit Liza Mae Ford tonight. We'll be ordering some takeout for dinner. Her home care nurse had a family emergency and had to cancel her visit," I said. My ruse about the invalid who needed my assistance was not only getting old, but I had used it so many times I had almost begun to believe this woman existed. I made a mental note to start mentioning in front of everybody in the house that I was going to join a book club. Like Joan, I could use that bogus excuse at least a couple of times a month. I finally turned to Libby and added, "And for your information, I know for a fact that Elbert is not gay."

"Humph! I guess you got physical proof, huh?" she babbled.

"I don't need 'physical' proof." It was hard to keep my voice at a normal volume. "Even if Elbert is gay, I still enjoy his company."

"Isn't Liza Mae the woman who was the victim in a hit-and-run accident a few years ago?" Jeffrey asked in his usual calm, soft-spoken voice. I was so glad he steered the conversation away from Elbert. It was always nice to have him around when Libby was on the premises. Had he not been such a good "referee," there was no telling what might have transpired between Libby and me this time.

"Uh-huh," I mumbled.

"Who the hell is Liza Mae?" Libby asked harshly, looking from me to Bertha to Jeffrey and back.

"A woman I went to school with. A drunk driver hit her a few years ago, and she's been disabled ever since," I replied.

"Since when do you know anything about caring for disabled people? You ought to leave that to a trained professional. You know how clumsy you are. If you drop this woman and she breaks a few bones, or you give her the wrong medicine, we'll read about you in the newspaper. You ought to know by now that it doesn't pay to be a Good Samaritan. I heard about a man who carried his drunk friend out of a bar and dropped him and broke his hip. The friend sued —"

"Libby, please. Let's not turn a positive situation into a negative one." I could have hugged Jeffrey for cutting Libby off. "I admire Lola for being so thoughtful and willing to help her friend. You should admire her too." Jeffrey looked at Bertha. "Mama, I am so proud of you for raising Lola to be such a caring person."

The room got quiet and stayed that way until I spoke again. "Thank you, Jeffrey. I really appreciate hearing somebody say that."

I had never heard Jeffrey, or anybody else, compliment Bertha on how well she'd raised Libby and Marshall. I was certain that thought had crossed other people's minds. Even Libby's. I rolled my eyes to the side and gazed at her. She looked so sad, I wanted to say something to make her feel better. But it was hard to come up with something positive to say about Libby.

"Thank you, son. Lola was real easy to raise," Bertha said, beaming like a lightbulb. The smile that suddenly appeared on her face stretched from one side to the other. She was looking at Jeffrey as if she wanted to kiss his feet. Then she turned to me. "Lola, Liza Mae is so lucky to have a friend like you." I almost felt guilty about her and Jeffrey making such a fuss on something that was based on a lie.

"Is this Liza Mae a great big fat woman?" Libby wanted to know. "Most folks confined to wheelchairs get real heavy after a while."

"Um, yes, she is. She's gained over a

hundred pounds since the accident," I replied.

"Well, you just be careful, Lola. A lot of things could go wrong in a situation such as this." Libby's tone was much softer now, and her words really touched me. This was a good time for me to say something nice to her, but before I could, she started talking again. "Not only could you end up with a lawsuit on your hands, you could fall and get seriously hurt trying to do whatever it is you do for this fat woman." For a moment, I actually thought she had finally begun to care about me. I was wrong. "I wish you would spend more time looking after Mama. I don't know what we'd do with her if something happened to you. . . ."

I didn't look at Bertha to see her reaction, but I heard her gasp as I continued. "Your mother is not an invalid. She doesn't need that much looking after. And nothing is going to happen to me," I insisted. I had said and heard all I could stand on this subject. I looked at my watch and let out a yelp. "I'm going to be late! I hate to rush off, but I need to take a shower so I can be on my way."

I didn't wait around for anybody to respond. But as soon as I turned my back and headed toward the steps to go upstairs, I heard them all start talking at the same time. I was glad the subject was no longer Liza Mae. Libby was complaining about how "gummy" the yellow walls looked. Kevin was yelling about how hungry he was and how musty the house smelled. Jeffrey was repeatedly thanking Bertha for letting them move in with us. And Bertha was gushing about how happy she was to have them. I shook my head and rushed into my room to keep from throwing up.

When I left to go on my date, everybody was in the living room hollering at the contestants on *Family Feud*. They were all so engrossed in it, nobody noticed when I eased out the front door.

Bertha stored so much junk in her garage, there was no room for my car. I always parked in the driveway. Libby had blocked my Jetta with her car. I didn't want to deal with her anymore tonight, so I started walking down the street and flagged down the first cab I saw.

The fare and the tip to the hotel in San Jose set me back thirty dollars. I hoped that Professor Darrin McMann would make the date worth my time and money. Other members had posted a lot of excellent reviews about him, so that was a positive sign.

When he opened the door to his suite wearing only a pair of tight Speedo shorts, he didn't say a word. He just smiled and nodded, closed the door, then pulled me into his arms and gave me a passionate kiss. I was already turned on, but the kiss was so good, it made me tingle. His dark brown hair was thin, and he had a few wrinkles on his slightly handsome face. He was a little plump around his middle, and his arms were flabby. But I could tell from the hard bulge between his legs pressing against me that at least one part of his body was in pretty good shape. He clamped his hand around my wrist and led me toward the huge bed in the middle of the room.

"My, my, my. And you're so pretty!" Darrin whispered in my ear as he patted my crotch. "This is what every man deserves."

"Thank you," I said, as we eased down on the bed. "I was glad to see your message last night."

"I'm glad you saw it too. There were a few other young ladies in your area that appealed to me tonight, but you were my first choice."

I was pleased to see a huge bottle of champagne on top of the dresser. "Do you mind if I have a drink so I can loosen up a bit? Today was pretty tense."

"Of course!" Darrin made a sweeping gesture with his hand toward the dresser. "The wine will help, but I promise you'll be nice and loose by the time you leave this room!" He looked at his watch and whistled. "I hope you don't mind if we put off dinner until after we'd gotten *cozy*. . . ."

"That'll be fine. I'm not that hungry anyway." My stomach felt as if it had been empty for days. I hadn't eaten anything since the Big Mac I'd gobbled up for lunch. Now I wished I had grabbed a few of those rolls Bertha had baked for me and eaten them in the cab.

"My wife's appetite for sex is not what it used to be. And the lady friend I've been seeing on the side for years wasn't available to see me before I left Florida, so I'm hornier than I care to be right now," Darrin told me. He cleared his throat and a very serious look crossed his face. "I want you to know that it's a true delight for me to be with you tonight. The reviews on the club's board about you are spectacular."

"Um, thank you," I said shyly. "I've been on a lot of dates with club members. That's the extent of my sex life for now."

"Hmmm. Well, I don't plan on staying in the club too much longer. As soon as I can work out a good settlement with my soon-to-be ex-wife, I'm going to marry my lady friend. She wants me to retire and buy a house for us in Miami. She keeps me on a fairly short leash, so if I do retire, I won't be able to get away as often as I do now. By the way, BrownSugar — you don't mind if I call you that, do you? I think it's such a cute screen name. And, if you don't mind me saying so, Lola doesn't really suit you."

"You can call me whatever you want. What would you like for me to call you?"

Darrin gave me an amused look before he laughed. He started removing my clothes and talking at the same time. "When I joined Discreet Encounters two years ago, my screen name was COCKaDoodleDo. The first club member I had a rendezvous with advised me to change it to BIGDaddy. She felt it was more appropriate and certainly more attractive."

"It does sound more attractive," I eagerly agreed.

"And certainly more appropriate. In a few moments, I'm going to show you why."

CHAPTER 31
JOAN

Sunday morning got off to a good start for me. I had just turned on the bedroom desktop computer, which I kept on a stand next to the dresser. I needed to order a few things from Amazon and check my e-mail messages. Before I could even enter my username and password, I heard somebody slam the living-room door. It was a few minutes past eleven. Reed had left at ten-thirty to go get a haircut, so I knew it wasn't him. And Junior was at Mama's house. I cringed because I already knew who had dropped in uninvited: my mother-in-law.

I cussed under my breath and turned off my computer. I could already feel a major headache coming on, so I opened the bottle of Advil I kept on the nightstand and swallowed a couple.

"ANYBODY HOME?" Mother Riley roared. "JOAN! JOAN! UU-UUHHH, JOAN!" My mother-in-law had a fairly pleasant voice when she spoke in a normal volume, but today she sounded like a carnival barker. "JOAN, I'M HERE!" Of all the people in the world I didn't want to talk to or see on a Sunday morning, she was the main one.

I took several deep breaths and scurried out of the bedroom. The way my stomach was flipping and flopping, I felt like I was about to face a firing squad. I was glad I wasn't still in my bathrobe, because Mother Riley would certainly complain about that. By the time I got to the living room, she had already parked her big butt on the couch and kicked off her shoes. Bunions on each of her long, flat feet stuck out like elbows.

There was an exasperated expression on her face. She blew out a loud breath and shook her head. "In the first place, with all the shopping you do, why do you wear pants so often?" she grumbled. "And with the generous allowance Reed gives to you, you ought to dress the way the other women in his social circle dress. Pants, especially as tight as the ones you have on now, make a woman look cheap. You don't live in the ghetto anymore, Joan."

These pants, which I had plucked off a clearance rack in an upscale boutique, had cost over six hundred dollars. Michelle Obama, Hillary Clinton, and Oprah had worn the same brand in some recent magazine articles. "I'm going to change into a dress later today," I said. "Reed went to get a haircut," I continued, wringing my hands, wishing it was my mother-in-law's neck I was wringing.

Mother Riley always dressed to the nines. Today she wore a green tweed suit with gold buttons. The red scarf she had looped around her thick neck resembled a noose. Her tight, black velvet hat reminded me of a stocking cap. She looked like a cross between a Christmas tree and a plump elf. She sniffed and shifted in her seat. Then she put her feet up on the coffee table and crossed them at the ankles, as if she was at home. "I know where my baby is, young lady. Reed calls me two or three times a day to let me know where he'll be in case I need to get in touch with him. He called me on my cell phone a few minutes ago." She stopped talking and stared at me with a weary look. "I wanted to talk to you without him being present." She patted the spot on the couch next to her. "Maybe you should sit down for this."

I shook my head. "I'd rather stand for whatever it is you have to talk to me about,"

I said firmly. Even though my mother-in-law drove me to distraction, I always tried to treat her with respect. However, there were times when I stood my ground and challenged her in some way. "Whatever you have to say, please say it now so we can get it over with."

Mother Riley's eyes got big and she removed her feet from the coffee table. There was a wounded look on her face, but then a couple of seconds later she shot me a hot look. "Joan, you know I don't like it when you sass me. Where I come from, young people don't sass their elders."

"I'm sorry if it sounded like I was sassing you. I didn't mean to."

"Well, it sounded like it to me. I guess you can't help yourself, though." She shifted in her seat again and returned her feet to the coffee table. Most of the time, I didn't even like being in the same room with Mother Riley, so I was not about to join her on the couch. My legs felt heavy, and I wanted to sit down. But I had more control on my feet. And the thing I wanted to control the most was my temper. A lot of other women would have cussed out a mother-in-law like mine a long time ago. And some of the ones from my hood would have banned her from visiting them and maybe even kicked her ass. I was not crude enough to go that far, but she was pushing me in that direction.

"I don't like to get in your business," she went on, pausing to roll her eyes around the room. From her pinched look, I thought she was gearing up to criticize my housekeeping skills again. Then she looked back at me with her eyes narrowed. "I noticed how depressed my baby sounded when I talked to him this morning."

"Well, I don't know why your 'baby' is depressed."

"There is no easy way to say this, so I won't beat around the bush. I'm going to tell it like it is. Please don't tell Reed what we talked about."

I took a deep breath and held it for a few seconds. "What are we talking about?"

"When Reed was a little boy, he was often very unhappy. I know a lot of it had to do with the fact that he never had any siblings to interact with. I assumed that marriage would give him something to hope for. . . ."

"What are you trying to tell me?" It took a lot of effort for me to hide my impatience.

"He wants more children."

"I am aware of that." Reed had told me several times over the years that he wanted at least two more children. And each time

I'd told him I wasn't ready. It had been about three years since he'd brought up the subject. But he knew how hard I tried to please his mother, so I wondered if he'd put her up to approaching me. "We've discussed it."

"Well?"

"Well what?"

"Is there some reason why you haven't had another child after all these years?"

"Excuse me?"

"I've discussed it with Mr. Reed several times, and he suspects there is a medical reason." Mother Riley gave me a pitiful look. "Is that it, dearie?"

"A medical reason? Well, yeah. It's something like that," I said with a smirk.

"Something like what?" Her eyes, which were already big, got even bigger.

"Something like birth control pills."

"Oh my God!" she shrieked.

"I started taking them right after Junior was born, and I've been on them ever since. Reed knows I'm not ready to have another baby. I've told him that more than once. One is enough for now."

"Why not?" Mother Riley started fanning her face with her clutch purse. "The boy is practically grown!" she hollered.

"The boy is fourteen!" I hollered back.

"Joan, you are in your thirties. Before you know it, you'll be in your forties. What if you wake up one day in your fifties and wish you had had more children? It'll be too late then. I'm sure your mother is anxious to have another grandchild. After all, she did have *seven* children of her own."

"All my mother cares about is me being happy. I am happy with just one child."

"Joan, this is not about just you and what you want. Why are you being so selfish?"

I could have gotten a lot of mileage out of that comment, but I decided to let it slide. The conversation was already ugly enough. "Mother Riley, raising a child is hard work. I love my son, but like I just said, he's enough for now. When and if I decide to have more children, I'll do so way before I get too old." I paused long enough to catch my breath, which felt hot and tasted sour. "And for your information, the number of children Reed and I have is our business."

"My grandchildren are my business!"

There was so much profanity trying to get out of my mouth, I had to press my lips together to hold it in. "What . . . ever," was the best response I could come up with, because I knew that if I started cussing, I wouldn't stop.

"Joan, what do you think marriage is for?"

I couldn't figure out why Mother Riley asked me this question, because she answered it herself. "It's to make a home for a man and raise his children. Reed probably would not have married you in the first place if you hadn't got yourself pregnant. . . ."

"If you think I got pregnant on purpose so Reed would marry me, you're wrong. I didn't have to marry him."

"Well, if you didn't want to raise a family, why did you marry my son?"

"I married your son because I thought I loved him," I said with my voice cracking.

Mother Riley yelped and covered her mouth with her hand. She glared at me for a few seconds before she continued. "You *thought* you loved him? Well, do you love him now? Girl, Reed loves you, and you should be thanking your lucky stars every day. If he hadn't come along, you'd be with some low-income snaggle-puss like the rest of the women in your family."

"Now, don't even go there!" I shouted with one hand in the air and the other on my hip. "You can trash me all you want, but please leave my family out of this. They've never done or said anything mean about you."

"Humph! Well, I'm your family now, Joan.

I was not happy that Reed settled for you, but I've learned to live with it. You still have a lot of good years left, but Reed is ten years older than you. The least you can do is give him more children like he wants and deserves before he gets too old to enjoy them."

I didn't know why I was wasting my time debating with a woman whose mind was about as nimble as a slab of concrete. It wouldn't have done any good for me to leave the room. The last time I did that, she followed me and we spent ten more minutes yelling at one another in the kitchen. She'd started the conversation this time, but I was going to finish it. "I wish you wouldn't twist things. I never said I didn't want to raise a family. All I said was one child is enough for me, for now. Junior is a handful. Anyway, you had only one child."

"I also had to have a hysterectomy six months after I gave birth to Reed. Had I not, I would have had several more children. I'm surprised and disappointed to hear that you think one child is enough."

"Well, it is — for now," I insisted again. "I barely have time to myself these days."

"Maybe if you slowed down and spent less time roaming around with that footloose Lola woman, shopping, and going to book club meetings, you'd have a lot more time.

Oh! Speaking of Lola, I've been meaning to tell you something I found out about her! She's getting quite a reputation these days, and I don't mean a good one."

It was hard for me to get the next sentence out of my mouth. "What do you mean?"

"I think that woman is up to some serious hanky-panky. You being her so-called best friend, her antics could make you look worse than you already do, if folks find out. . . ."

"As long as Lola is not breaking the law, I don't think there's anything she can do that would make me look bad. What did you find out about her?"

"When I was at a luncheon with my flower garden club members at the Hyatt hotel in downtown San Jose last month, I saw her prancing out of the elevator with a man in an expensive-looking suit. It was a Saturday and the middle of the day."

"So?"

"Uh-huh. 'So' is right! There was no telling what she'd been up to. That man, who looked like a foreigner to me, was all over her and she was all over him. She was dressed like a floozy, like she is every time I see her."

CHAPTER 32
JOAN

A person had to be damn careful and lucky if they didn't want to get caught in an embarrassing or suspicious situation these days. The world was smaller than I thought, because I was stunned to hear that Mother Riley had been in the same hotel on the same day that Lola was there with one of her dates.

I was glad it wasn't me she had seen in that hotel with a man. I made a mental note to start altering my appearance for my future dates. I wouldn't use anything as elaborate as a wig and a floppy hat, just some dark glasses and a scarf on my head.

"So what? Lola is a single woman. She has a lot of men friends."

"I'm sure she does. She has her own place, so why would she be holing up with one in a hotel? I'll bet that man she was with has a wife. But then again, after the way Lola's daddy flaunted his affairs in her mother's face, Lola's behavior must seem normal to her."

"She lives in her stepmother's house. She has too much respect for Bertha to be bringing men home to . . . uh . . . have relations with."

"Well, at least Lola's taste is not all in her mouth. The man I saw her with was quite handsome. And from the way he was carrying himself, he had a lot of class. But like I just said, I'll bet he's married and that was the reason he couldn't take Lola to his place — in the middle of a Saturday afternoon."

I didn't know what to say next, so I remained silent, hoping it would prompt Mother Riley to change the subject or leave.

"Are you still coming to our barbecue next weekend? Or will you be too busy like you were the last time?"

"We'll be there," I confirmed.

"Reverend Sharpe and his wife will be joining us, so I advise that you wear something suitable." After a raspy sigh, Mother Riley looked at her watch and shrieked, "My goodness! Look what time it is!" She slid her feet back into her shoes. With a groan she wobbled up off the couch, fanning her face as she walked toward me. "I hate to run, but I'm having lunch with Maybelline Hanson today, and she hates it when I'm

277

late. I had planned to come talk to you afterward, but it's so hard to catch you at home. I wish I had a dollar for all the times you were out and about when I came by." An extremely serious look suddenly crossed Mother Riley's face. "I want you to think real hard about what we talked about — you having more children, I mean. We'll discuss it again in the near future." She took a deep breath and patted my shoulder. "You have a nice day, honey."

"I'm sure I will," I responded, each word dripping with sarcasm.

Immediately after Mother Riley waddled back out the door, I snatched up the telephone by the couch and punched in Lola's cell number.

"Where did you go last night?" I asked when she answered on the third ring.

"How did you know I went out last night?"

"You didn't answer your cell phone when I called, so I tried the landline and Libby picked up. She told me you went to visit Liza Mae."

"Oh. I would have called you, but I was in a hurry to get out of the house."

"What's up?"

"Libby is already on my nerves big time and they've been here only one day. My head was throbbing from the inside out last night, and I had to go somewhere because I didn't want to lose what's left of my sanity."

"Where did you go and who were you really with last night?"

"I was with a real nice gentleman from Florida. He's a professor at Florida State. He grew up in San Jose and he's in town now to attend his twenty-fifth high school reunion. I swear, his request for a date couldn't have come at a better time. When I got to his suite at the Hyatt, he had a bottle of champagne ready."

"How was he?"

"Well, even with all the rave reviews other members gave him and the long, thick equipment between his thighs, he was just average to me. He was so nice and he had such a great sense of humor, I enjoyed his company. But I'd rather not see him again."

"And you shouldn't. Don't waste your time on a bad fuck. We've both had enough of that. Speaking of the Hyatt in San Jose, my mother-in-law saw you there last month. She just left here."

"No wonder you sound so tense."

"I am tense. That woman really gets under my skin. I thought that I'd get used to her, but she irritates me now just as much as she did before Reed and I got married."

"So what did she have to say about me?"

"She thinks the man she saw you with is married."

"He is. So what?" Lola laughed. "It's none of her business. What was the lady dragon doing in the Hyatt hotel?"

"She was having lunch with her flower garden club."

"Well, it won't be the last time I go to a hotel room to hook up with a man. And I hope she didn't spook you."

"She didn't. If she, or anybody else, ever spots me in a hotel with a man, I'll say I was there having lunch with a friend from out of town who was a guest in the hotel." I laughed. "If we can make people believe that bullshit Liza Mae ruse, we can make them believe anything." The words were rolling out of my mouth so fast I had to clear my throat. "Would you believe Mother Riley had the nerve to call me selfish because I told her I didn't want another child yet?"

"What's it to her? She had only one child."

"She had a hysterectomy shortly after she had Reed. She claims she wanted several more."

"Oh. Well, if having a lot of kids was such a big deal to her, she could have adopted some."

"Tell me about it." I let out a loud breath.

"Have you heard from Calvin again yet?"

"No, I haven't. But I hope he doesn't forget about me. The more I look at his picture on his profile page, the more I want to see him."

Chapter 33
Joan

I was glad our condo was so big. There were a lot of places I could go when I didn't want to be in Reed's presence. We had three bedrooms, three bathrooms, a game room, a library, and a huge living room that was connected to the dining area.

Saturday morning I prepared a lavish breakfast. As usual, Reed and Junior took their good old time coming to the breakfast table. And when they did, fifteen minutes after I'd told them everything was ready, I had already eaten. I was still in the kitchen reorganizing the canned goods in the cabinets, putting everything in alphabetical order, which was what Reed expected and monitored a few times each week.

Right after scarfing down a Spanish omelet with a side of fresh fruit, Junior skittered back to his bedroom to chat online with a girl he'd been pursuing for a few weeks. I had eaten all of my New York steak, lobster, and poached eggs, but Reed had put only a dent in the same items on his plate. When I started washing the dishes, he left the kitchen without looking at me or saying a word, and went into the living room.

I planned to do some reading in the library before I tackled the laundry and a few other chores. Before I could make it past the living room, Reed got off the couch and started following me with his cell phone in his hand. "Mother just called. She wants to know what time we'll be arriving for the barbecue," he told me.

I stopped in my tracks and looked at my watch. I whirled around so fast to face Reed, my hair flopped forward. "Huh? Is the barbecue *today*?" I yelped as I tucked a strand of hair behind my ear.

He looked at me like I was crazy. "Joan, we just talked about this last night. How could you forget so soon?"

"I thought the barbecue was next Saturday," I said, blinking.

"Today is just a little backyard get-together with a few close friends. Next Saturday, Mother and Father are hosting a formal dinner party at the country club to celebrate their forty-fifth wedding anniversary. They're having the barbecue today because Reverend Sharpe and his wife are leaving for a three-week cruise to Hawaii in a couple of days. You said you might not go to the country club next week because your book club is having their monthly meeting at the same time."

"Oh, yeah," I said, slapping the side of my head. "I guess I forgot. Well, I can go to the barbecue today. But I'll have to skip the country club party next week because I had already made plans to attend my book club meeting. . . ."

"I don't expect you to change your plans for next week, Joan. Now, if you're going with Junior and me today, you need to start getting ready. I told Mother we'd be there by noon," Reed said harshly. Then his voice got real low. "I hope you won't disappoint Mother again by not coming with us."

"I'll start getting ready right away." I hurried to my bedroom closet to find something suitable to wear. It was March and the temperature was in the mid-seventies, which meant it was not warm enough for me to wear the outfit I usually wore to outdoor barbecues — shorts and a halter top. I grabbed the first pair of jeans and sweatshirt I saw.

We arrived at my in-laws' house in Monterey a few minutes before noon. After we greeted the other dozen guests on the spacious backyard patio, Reed ducked into the house. He returned a few minutes later wearing a bibbed apron and grinning from ear to ear. My silver-haired father-in-law, who was still quite handsome despite his wrinkled face, a lazy eye, and a pot belly, stepped aside and let Reed take over the grill.

A couple of the female guests complimented me on my figure and hair, and one even told me she had come to the barbecue only because she heard I'd be attending. I was actually enjoying myself. Everybody was having such a good time, it was hard for me not to. And out of respect for Reverend Sharpe, I retired the sullen look I'd had at home.

Reed was in his element. Every time I looked in his direction, he winked and blew me a kiss. Just as I was about to fix myself a plate, Mother Riley beckoned for me to follow her back into the house.

As much as I loved my in-laws' sprawling, cream-colored Spanish-style house, which was located on a street lined with palm trees in a gated community, I rarely enjoyed my visits. For one thing, Mother Riley was a show-off. She liked to brag about her antique furniture and imported carpets and how much money she spent on every item she purchased. Today was an exception. So far, she had not done any bragging.

A few seconds after we entered the kitchen, she lit into me. "Joan, of all the clothes you must have by now, why are you dressed like that?"

I gave her a puzzled look and a shrug. "Dressed like what?"

"Like a . . . like one of those cheap wenches from the projects!"

I experienced the same kind of brain freeze that I experienced when I drank a Slurpee too fast. I shuddered and shook my head. "What are you talking about? There is nothing cheap or wenchy about a sweatshirt and a pair of jeans. Reed is wearing a sweatshirt and jeans too!"

Mother Riley glanced out the window, then back at me. "A man can wear a loin-cloth and nobody would care. You're a woman, a married woman. The clothes you have on were made for a much smaller woman. Just look at you. That sweatshirt is hugging your bosom like a straitjacket." There was a grimace on her face as she gazed at my chest and shook her head. "Your breasts are jutting out all over the place. And I would think that you'd want to hide that bubble butt of yours in something more loose fitting, like a skirt or a muumuu like the one I have on. Didn't you see the lewd look on Reverend Sharpe's face when you hugged him? And when you walked by him a few minutes ago in those skin-tight jeans with your rump jiggling like Jell-O, I thought his eyes were going to pop out of his head. The man's a preacher!"

"The man's a man, Mother Riley."

"And what's that supposed to mean?"

"You know what it means."

"Shame on you, Joan! I know you come from a crude environment, but I am appalled to hear you imply that a man of the cloth is having ungodly thoughts about another man's wife. You have stooped really low this time, but I guess you can't help yourself. From what I've heard about how loosey-goosey you were when you were a teenager, I'm sure you were not a virgin when you latched on to my son."

"No, I wasn't a virgin, but Reed wasn't either," I pointed out. "And from what I've heard, he was one of the biggest man-whores in town before he met me."

"Young lady, that's my son you're talking about! Shame on you!" I hadn't seen my mother-in-law shed a tear since the day I married her son. She screwed up her face and started boo-hooing like a baby. And I felt like shit. When Reed walked into the kitchen a few seconds later, I had my arms around Mother Riley, patting her on the back and telling her how sorry I was for upsetting her again.

"What's going on in here? What did you do to Mother, Joan?" Reed asked, rushing across the floor. He looked like an idiot wearing that bibbed apron with KISS THE COOK in big, bold, black letters across the front.

"I was just telling Joan how happy I am that she was able to make it to the barbecue," Mother Riley choked.

"Oh?" Reed glanced from me to her with a skeptical look on his face. "So those are tears of joy, huh?"

"Yes, son." Mother Riley sniffed, dabbed at her eyes with the tip of her finger, blinked a few times, and forced a smile. Then she pranced over to the counter and lifted a large tray of dinner rolls. "I'd better take these outside right now," she said as she slowly backed out of the kitchen door.

Reed looked at me and hunched his shoulders. "Well, honey, you've made Mother very happy today and I can't thank you enough. However, I still think you need to spend more time with her."

"Reed, I don't have a lot of time on my hands. I have a very busy life."

"Tell me about it. But it's what's keeping you busy that's the problem. It's bad enough you spend so much time with your hard-partying family and Lola. Not to mention what's her name — that woman in a wheelchair. You shop for hours at a time, several times a week. Now you've joined a book club!"

"Well, I'd rather be doing all of that than spending time with your mother."

Reed's eyes got big and his jaw dropped open so wide his mouth looked like a Big Dipper.

"The only thing you're not doing is sleeping with other men! Or have you crossed that bridge already?"

"Oh, please! How many more times are you going to bring up this subject? I have never cheated on you and I never will. Don't you know that by now?"

Reed folded his arms and got within inches of my face. "Look me in the eye and tell me you would never cheat on me!"

I held my breath and blinked first. Then I looked him in the eye and said, "I've never cheated on you and I never will." I put so much emphasis on my words and I sounded so convincing, I almost believed the lie myself.

He looked into my eyes for what seemed

like an eternity. "Are you sure about that?"

"Of course I'm sure."

"Joan, please don't lie to me."

"And that's another thing. I've *never* lied to you." Had I been Pinocchio, my nose would have grown halfway across the room. I pictured that, and it made me snicker.

"Oh, so this is funny to you?"

"No, it's not funny. I just thought of something funny. Did you notice those baggy shorts Sister Wilson is wearing today?"

"See there? You can't even keep your mind focused on me when I'm talking to you."

"Reed, I would never cheat on you or leave you for another man. I know how serious you are about us breaking up. Especially after your, uh, accident with those pills."

"Accident, my ass. I tried to kill myself. The thought of you being with another man drove me to do it. If I ever find out you're cheating on me, I won't be responsible for my actions."

CHAPTER 34
JOAN

"Reed, I don't know what else I can do or say to make you believe me. And no matter what I do say, you're going to believe what you want to believe anyway." I folded my arms and leaned against the counter.

He placed his hands on his hips, pressed his lips together, and blinked a few times. "I know how much you like sex, Joan. And I know how easy you are. You had sex with me just a few hours after I met you."

"A lot of women have sex on the first night they meet a man they like."

"I don't give a damn what 'a lot of women' do."

"What is your point?"

"You didn't waste any time jumping into bed with me. You were so frisky, you almost wore me out."

"That was because I really liked you, Reed."

"I guess you did! What will happen if you

meet another man you really like? Will you have sex with him too? Your own sister told me about all the boys you fooled around with when you were in high school."

I looked around the room and then toward the doorway that led to the patio. All we needed was for Mother Riley, or her dirty-minded preacher, to walk in and hear us discussing our sex life. "Are you ever going to let me forget what I was like when I was a *teenager*?"

Reed wiped his forehead, even though there was no sweat on it. "Despite all your flaws, I still love you, Joan." Then he looked at me in a way that he or no other man ever looked at me before. He tilted his head to the side, winked, and smiled, then kissed the tip of his finger and pressed it against my lips. I was so touched, my heart began to beat like mad. "You are so sexy, I get hotter than hell just thinking about you when we're not together." Reed leaned closer to me and started whispering. "Some days I sneak into my office restroom and masturbate with a picture of you in my hand. I can't wait to get you back home. We're going to fuck like porn stars."

"Reed, please stop talking nasty. You're embarrassing me." I was pleased to hear that he found me so appealing. I was tempted to wrap my arms around him and cover his lips with mine. But I couldn't. Our marriage was beyond repair and I didn't want to confuse him, or give him false hope. I lowered my head and stared at the floor. He lifted my chin and kissed me.

The look of love suddenly left his face. His pupils looked like drops of pitch-black ink, which was scary because his eyes were brown. In the next breath he said the last thing I wanted to hear. "I've told you many times before, but I'll tell you again; I will not go on if you ever leave me. . . ."

I shook my head and stomped my foot so hard the pans hanging from the ceiling rattled. "Oh, please! Here we go again!" I snapped.

"I mean it, Joan. My life is in your hands." Reed shook his finger in my face and gave me a stern look. "And I won't use pills the next time! I'll take myself out in the worst possible bloody way and I'll do it right in front of you so you'll never forget what you made me do!"

I covered my ears but I could still hear his ominous words. I shuddered and gave him an exasperated look. "I've heard enough of your insane foolishness. I'm going back outside."

"Just remember what I told you."

One thing I never wanted to do was get violent with Reed. But he was pushing me in that direction. About three weeks ago, I dreamt I tried to cut off his dick with a *dull* knife so I could inflict as much pain as possible. That dream haunted me for days. The last thing I wanted to do was cause him even more pain, physical or mental. In the meantime, I had no choice but to continue going on about my business as usual.

Instead of going back outside, I brushed past him and rushed into the nearest bathroom. The only reason I didn't have myself a good cry was because when I did, my eyes got red and puffy. I stared in the mirror above the sink and asked myself, "How much longer are you going to allow yourself to be so miserable?" This was a question I had been asking myself for years, and I still couldn't answer it.

I managed to get through the rest of the afternoon with a smile on my face. But only because I gulped down two bottles of beer and two glasses of wine. I had to be tipsy in order to take Mother Riley aside and apologize for upsetting her earlier. She was pleased and receptive. She even gave me a big hug. "Joan, let's just forget about that little incident in the kitchen," she told me as she rubbed my back. "My son is happy

with you, and that's all that really matters."
I had to blink very hard to hold back my
tears. "Maybe someday you'll be the kind of
daughter-in-law I've always dreamed about.
But until then, I have to accept you the way
you are."

Right after I heard Mother Riley's last
statement, I told Reed that I was ready to
leave. Even though she gave me another hug
and thanked us for coming, she did so with
a smirk on her face. I was glad Reed was
aware of her behavior. He mentioned it right
after we piled into his Lexus and headed
home. He started talking in a steely tone of
voice. "I noticed how annoyed Mother
looked every time she looked in your direction. She even rolled her eyes at you a
couple of times."

"Huh? Well, I'm surprised to hear that she
was doing that."

"I was surprised too because you two had
had such a nice little encounter in the
kitchen earlier. Somebody must have said
something nasty to her, because I noticed
that she also looked at a few other people
the same way. Maybe she had a little too
much to drink."

"Maybe she did," I mumbled.

"But at least you two are getting along
better now. I hope things keep moving in

that direction."

"They will," I said. And I really meant it. Mother Riley's birthday was coming up next month, and I planned to do something special for her. I was determined to improve our relationship.

"And another thing, I want you to be more people-friendly when we go out in public together."

"What? What do you mean by that? I thought I was 'people-friendly' today."

"Except for Mother and Sister Sharpe, you practically ignored most of the other women at the barbecue. Just before we left, Stella Wharton made a comment to me about how 'aloof' you were with her and how giddy and flirtatious you were with the men — especially her husband."

My mouth flew open and I whirled around to look at Reed. "Oh hell no! Don't you dare go there! You know me better than that! I would never be that loose and disrespectful in public." Reed kept his eyes on the road. My eyes were on the side of his face, which I wanted to slap with both hands. "Can we discuss this later?" I said in a low voice, motioning my head toward Junior slumped in the backseat, bobbing his head to whatever he was listening to on his precious headphones.

"We'll do that!" Reed boomed.

It was a tense ride the rest of the way home. Reed didn't say another word, and I didn't either. I closed my eyes and played possum.

When we made it back home, I made a beeline for the library. Reed went to the living room. Before I could select something to read, I heard him marching down the hallway to our bedroom. I decided not to read, but I still wanted to sit in the library for a while.

Now that my buzz had worn off, I replayed some of the things my mother-in-law had said to me in her kitchen and I got agitated, not just at her but Reed too. If that wasn't enough to ruffle my feathers, I recalled a comment my father-in-law had made at the barbecue: "Joan, I'm glad to see that you're a little more polished than you were when I first met you." For a man who always had so little to say, and who was practically a recluse, I was surprised that he'd noticed anything at all about me. I was just as surprised to hear that he thought I was "more polished." As far as I was concerned, I was basically the same person I'd always been, and always would be.

I stayed in the library until it was Junior's bedtime.

I made sure he was tucked in before I went to the living room and dropped down onto the couch. There was something about being miserable that made me feel so tired, and I was about as tired as I could be. I could no longer feel the alcohol I'd consumed at the barbecue, and I was glad. I needed to be completely lucid because when I joined Reed in the bedroom I knew he was going to resume the conversation he'd started in the car. And I didn't plan on doing that for a while.

Before I could reach for the remote on the coffee table, I noticed several magazines scattered next to it. Most of them were medical journals, recent issues of *Sports Illustrated,* and various other publications. I was about to organize them into a neat stack when the one on top caught my eye. It was a local magazine. I cautiously turned to a page that Reed had dog-eared. "I don't believe that man," I said under my breath. I squinted and read the article's title, which he had underlined with a red Sharpie:

<u>When Suicide Is the Only Solution</u>

It was a four-page piece, but I was in no mood to read the whole thing. I didn't want to know why some people thought suicide was the only solution to their problems. There was a picture of a sad-faced middle-aged woman below the title. She was the mother of a young man who had taken his life a few months ago when he found out he was dying of leukemia.

Tears flooded my eyes. I did not condone suicide. But it made more sense for a person who had no hope to do it than a man whose only reason was he didn't want to live if his wife left him! I still didn't want to read the whole article, but I glanced at a few sentences that reported the huge number of suicides in Northern California. The author had done a lot of research and had even broken the numbers down by age, ethnicity, and profession. According to him, most of the people who had chosen suicide were white males between the ages of thirty and seventy-five. Black men in the same age group were a close second.

I had seen enough. I knew that Reed was bad off, so I didn't need a magazine article to convince me. And I knew he'd purposely left the magazine out in the open for me to see. I didn't know why he thought it was still necessary to keep "reminding" me that he was suicidal, because he had made his point a long time ago. Now I was convinced that he had staged that call to Suicide

Prevention for my benefit.

I was so tired, physically and mentally, it was difficult for me to move. I wobbled up from the couch and padded to our bedroom. When I clicked on the light, I was surprised to see that Reed was still awake. He was on his back, staring up at the ceiling.

"Reed, honey, are you all right?" I asked gently as I moved toward the bed. "I'm really worried about you." He looked so pitiful lying there, I felt guilty about having that dream about cutting off his dick with a dull knife. As far as I was concerned, he was already only a piece of a man.

"Could have fooled me," he whined.

I stood stock-still for a few tense moments and breathed through my mouth. I sat down on his side of the bed and placed my hand on his shoulder, giving it a gentle squeeze.

"You know I care about you," I said with my voice faltering. "I just wish . . ." I paused. "I wish you would stop scaring me with talk about . . . well, you know. I saw that magazine article you made sure I'd see."

He sat bolt upright and looked at me as if I had just sprouted a beard. He glared at me as if he wanted to kill me. I had never seen such a hostile look on his face, and it frightened me.

"Reed, why the hell are you looking —"

He interrupted me with words that shot out of his mouth like bullets. "You say you care about me? Then I suggest you treat me more like a husband than a dog, Joan," he barked.

His remark caught me completely off guard, especially after what he'd said to me in his parents' kitchen earlier. I had no idea what had made him turn on a dime. "I thought I was treating you like a husband," I hollered. "I don't know what you want me to do!"

"You don't? Well, let me tell you a few things, Joan Riley." Reed cleared his throat and continued, speaking in a husky, angry tone of voice. "One thing you can do is show me more affection. The last half hour of the barbecue you practically ignored me, and it's been bothering me ever since. And there's another thing that's been bothering me. The last time we made love, you were like a bump on a log. You didn't move a muscle until we finished, and then you leaped off the bed like a frog! Sometimes when I kiss you, it feels like I'm putting my lips on a goddamn rubber blow-up doll. I don't remember the last time you gave me a blow job! Or, even a hand job!"

There were times when I found it hard to believe that Reed was an educated man. What he had just said sounded like some of the shit I used to hear from my hood boyfriends in high school.

"Is this conversation just about our sex life?"

"This conversation is about our married life."

"What do you want me to say?"

"I don't want you to say another damn thing!"

I gave him a dry look and then I let out such a hard, loud snort I was surprised that sparks and smoke didn't shoot out of my nostrils. "Fine. I won't. This conversation is over, and I think I'll sleep in the guest room tonight." I stood up.

Reed's next move happened so fast, it took me a few seconds to realize what he was doing. He leaped to the floor, grabbed me by my arms, and threw me down on the bed. Without a word, he piled on top of me and ripped off my clothes.

Then he did something I never thought he would do: He forced himself on me.

CHAPTER 35
CALVIN

I was so happy to be back on California ground, I was tempted to kiss it when I got off the plane in San Jose.

It had been a rough flight — lots of turbulence and screaming babies. Taking a nap had been impossible, so I'd just sat slumped in my seat with all kinds of thoughts. On my mind the most was Lola Poole and how anxious I was to get my hands on her throat. And since she was such a hottie, I planned to fuck her at least a couple of times before she took her last breath. I couldn't ignore that restless beast within me too much longer, especially since I'd logged in to the Internet during the flight and gazed at Lola's profile again. I was filled with so much white-hot anger, I thought my blood was going to melt my veins. How much more could I take? How much longer could I wait to kill the bitch? A month, two months, a year? I scolded myself for even thinking I would wait longer than a few more weeks.

The sooner I completed my mission, the better. Maybe that beast in my belly would die or be satisfied enough and I could move forward and actually live like a *normal* man. The next phase of my life would be crime-free — I hoped — and include a wife and two or three children.

I didn't know yet if I was going to marry Sylvia. I knew she was crazy about me, but I wasn't sure I was crazy enough about her to spend the rest of my life with her. She was too much of a pushover, for one thing. And she was not the brightest woman I'd been involved with romantically. Sex with her was a comical event. I did all the hard work and all she did was wiggle like a worm on a hook and holler. She always managed to climax, and she raved about my bedroom skills, so I never complained about her mediocre performance. Oral sex with her was absolutely out of the question. She thought it was too "nasty" and refused to even consider it. And there were other things about her that I didn't like. She hated sports and the fact that my job took me away from home for days at a time. I couldn't stand her siblings, her parents, her dog, her coworkers, her neighbors, and most of her friends. If I did marry her, we would have to do most of our socializing with my friends, or be alone. I had no doubt that if I proposed to Sylvia, she'd accept in a heartbeat. If I married her, the most important thing was, I'd always be the one calling the shots. That was how well I knew her.

I decided to wait a few days before I contacted Sylvia to let her know I was back in town. With all the time I'd spent thinking about Lola since my trip to Chicago, my mind was so scrambled I wouldn't have been good company to Sylvia anyway. As important as she was to me, I had another important woman to call on first. I didn't know her name yet, or what she looked like. But I was anxious to find out.

I was not exactly sure when I was going back to work. When I notified my boss and told him I had returned to California — but I was also still stressed out — he told me again that I could take off as much time as I wanted. No matter when I decided to return to work, I couldn't count on picking up a female hitch-hiker to help ease my frustrations. I couldn't wait another day anyway. I had to go hunting for a new victim *tonight.*

After I left the airport I took the rental car

shuttle to Avis and picked up a car to drive myself home, and to use later. I didn't want to go hunting in my Jeep. I had had it thoroughly detailed before my trip to Chicago. I was in no mood to sop up some nasty bitch's blood, sweat, tears, or any other DNA shit off my seat covers tonight.

I had planned to go home, change clothes, drink a few shots of tequila, and get one of my knitted caps to hide part of my face. But during the drive on the crowded freeway, I changed my mind. I didn't want any of my nosy neighbors to know I had made it back home yet. Robert what's-his-name, the busybody who lived next door, would be at my door in no time.

I cruised down my street to make sure nothing looked out of place at my residence. Everything appeared to be in order, so I drove back in the direction I had come from. A few turns and about fifteen minutes later, I entered a run-down, low-rent area where some of the most ferocious people in San Jose lived. They robbed, beat, and killed one another on a regular basis. Last year, somebody stabbed a disabled man to death, robbed him, and took off with his wheelchair.

A man had to be horny as hell, a fool, or both to drive into this neighborhood at night to pick up a woman. I felt like both. I was glad to see that there were a lot of other horny fools looking for sex on this particular night. That meant all of the prettiest women would be so busy they would have to turn down dates, but it also meant nobody would be paying too much attention to me and who I picked up. And it didn't take long.

Her name was Adele, but she told me to call her "Miss Honey." I couldn't take my eyes off her face. This random woman had only a slight resemblance to Glinda/Lola, but it was close enough. I was so anxious to do what I had come to do, I settled for just a twenty-dollar blow job. But I had a rage going on inside me, so I didn't even let her finish doing that.

She put up one hell of a fight, but she still lost. I wondered why a female stupid enough to trust a stranger died with such a surprised look on her face.

CHAPTER 36
LOLA

Sunday morning, I rolled out of bed around eight. I was anxious to get dressed and go downstairs to eat a plate of the grits and bacon I could smell Bertha cooking.

Jeffrey and Kevin had left before dawn to go fishing, so it was just Bertha, Libby, and me at the breakfast table. Libby and I had very little to talk about, so most of the conversation was between her and Bertha.

After Libby talked trash about a dress one of her friends had worn to somebody's baby shower last week, she announced that she was going to get her nails done.

"Mine need to be tuned up too," I said, looking at my own nails, noticing a few cracks and chips. "If you're going to that shop on Morgan Street, do you mind if I tag along? They take drop-ins."

"Um, I have several stops to make along the way first," Libby replied, looking uneasy. "And after I leave the shop, I'm going to go shopping. I'd rather go by myself so I can take my time. Maybe we can go together the next time."

"Oh. Well, I guess I'll go to that nail salon on Cambridge. It's just a couple of blocks from here, so I can walk." I would rather shovel shit than accompany my stepsister to a nail salon, or anywhere else for that matter. But I was still trying as hard as I could to get along with Libby. I brought her favorite wine and food home from the market, and I offered to take Kevin to the movies and do other things with him so she could have some time to herself. Unfortunately, no matter how hard I tried, it didn't do much good. She'd be nice to me for a short time, but it didn't take long for her to be her same old mean-spirited self again.

Libby left the house first. A couple of hours later, one of Bertha's friends picked her up so they could go have lunch. I went back upstairs to my bedroom and started flipping through the most recent issue of *Ebony* magazine. I was still trying to decide which article to read first when my cell phone rang. I was hoping it was Calvin, but when I saw Joan's name on the caller ID, I was just as pleased.

"Hey you," I began.

"Lola, I was forced to have sex last night,"

she said in a steely tone of voice.

"OH MY GOD!" I sat up on my bed, gripping my phone with both hands. "Are you okay? Did you call the police?"

"There was no need to. I'm fine," Joan said with a sigh.

"Joan, you have to call the police and you have to report it to the club's management people."

"Tell the club's management people? W-Why would I do that?"

"The rapist was a man you met on the Discreet Encounters website, right?"

"Lola, none of those men would have to rape me. I joined the club for the same reason they joined."

"Then who did it?" I was frantic, and I couldn't understand why Joan was sounding so cool and calm.

"Reed did it."

"What? Joan, he's your husband. I don't think you can call it rape."

"He forced himself on me. Last time I checked, forcing somebody to have sex was still called rape."

"Tell me what happened."

"I don't want to go into the details right now, but on the way home from Monterey yesterday, Reed started talking all kinds of crazy shit again. He said I was aloof to the other women at the barbecue and was flirting with their husbands. He warned me that we'd finish our conversation later. When we got home, I made myself scarce because I wanted to put off talking to him as long as I could. I holed up in the library first, and after I heard him go to our bedroom, I went to the living room." She had to pause and take a couple of deep breaths before she could continue. "Anyway, he had left a magazine on the coffee table where he knew I would see it right away. It had a long article about suicides in Northern California. He'd even dog-eared the page to make sure I'd turn to it when I picked up the magazine. After spending the afternoon at my in-laws' barbecue — which was not as agonizing as I thought it would be — I was not interested in reading about suicides. I glanced at a few paragraphs before I joined Reed in the bedroom. We started talking and one thing led to another. Before I knew it, he was on me like a cheap suit. He raped me."

"I can't believe what I'm hearing!" I hollered. "I know the man has a few screws loose, but I never thought he'd physically hurt you. Did you try to fight him off?"

"Girl, I just laid there like I always do when we have sex. I knew it wouldn't last long. It was over in no time. Thirty seconds, if that. After he finished hissing like a damn cobra and yip-yipping like a rowdy-ass cowboy, he rolled off me."

"You should have called me to come pick you up! I don't care if Reed is your husband, he can't victimize you like that!"

"He was more of a victim than I was. Once he was done with me, he started apologizing like crazy. But I went upside his head with that ceramic elephant I picked up at the last flea market we went to. He didn't even try to defend himself. He just cried like a baby and cowered like a punk-ass bitch."

"I thought Reed was a macho man. I can't even picture him crying and cowering. Where is he now?"

"He's in the bathroom putting more medication on his wounds. I wonder how he's going to explain the knot on his forehead and the scratches on his face to everybody, especially his parents and his staff."

"Joan, I am so sorry you had to go through that."

"*Pffft!* Don't be sorry for *me.* If you want to feel sorry for somebody, send Reed a get-well card." Joan laughed. "I told him I'd report him to the cops if he ever does it again. If he does, I wouldn't call the cops because he'd probably get away with it and I'd be the one looking like a fool. But my threat shook him up enough. He swore he'd never do it again, so as far as I'm concerned, this case is closed. Now let me tell you the real reason I called."

"You mean you didn't call to tell me about the rape?"

"Yeah, I did, but that's not the only thing I called to talk to you about. Reed feels just awful about what he did and now he wants to make up for it."

"Why he damn sure needs to! Exactly how does he plan to do that? And I'm warning you, you'd better not let him off with a slap on the wrist or I'm going to kick your ass! I don't care if he is your husband, rape is a very serious matter and you'd make it worse by letting him get away with it! If his raping you doesn't justify a divorce —"

"Stop right there," Joan interrupted. "I'm not in the mood to talk about divorce. I already feel like shit, and that subject would make me feel even worse."

"Are you telling me you've changed your mind about divorcing him someday?"

"Lola, didn't you hear what I just said? Let's put me getting a divorce on the back burner for now."

"Okay. Then what do you want to talk about?"

"Reed wants to take me to Vegas this evening. He even mentioned getting some counseling when we get back. As much as he annoys me, I guess I have to give him credit for trying to make things work."

"I guess." I was confused, mentally and emotionally. If a man raped me, I'd be mad and miserable as hell. And I'd never get over it, even if the rapist was my husband. I wasn't exactly sure how Joan was feeling right now, but as long as she wasn't screaming and crying — and was about to go to Vegas with her rapist — I assumed she wasn't as miserable as a typical victim. I didn't go along with everything she said or did, but I was glad to hear that there was still some hope for her and Reed. I knew she'd never be truly happy with him, though.

"On a happier note, what's up with Calvin? Is he back yet?"

"Not that I know of. I — hold on. I think I hear somebody downstairs."

"I'll let you go. If I don't talk to you again before I leave for Vegas, I'll call you from down there."

After I disconnected the call, I got up and padded to my door. I cracked it open just enough to stick my head out. Libby was downstairs talking to a man whose voice I didn't recognize.

Ten minutes went by before I left my room and walked quietly toward the staircase. I eased down the steps and got the shock of my life. There was a strange man lying on the living-room couch on his back. *Libby was on top of him with her granny panties down around her ankles.* Her cellulite-covered butt was humping so fast and hard, you would have thought she was riding a mechanical bull. The man had his eyes closed and was moaning like he was in pain. I could tell they were both about to climax, so I crept back up the stairs before they noticed me.

Chapter 37
Lola

A few minutes after I got back to my room, Libby came up the stairs. And she wasn't alone. She and her mysterious male companion were laughing and joking as if they didn't have a care in the world. The two of them stomping down the hall at the same time sounded like two horses with heavy hooves.

They were walking toward my room, which was at the opposite end of the hall from the one Libby and Jeffrey shared, so I closed my door.

"It'll be much more comfortable in a bed," she told the man. "But we don't have much time."

"Sugar Pie, I don't know why you didn't want to go to a motel like we usually do. Being up in here ain't too cool," the man complained. He had a nice, deep voice. And from what I had seen of him on the couch, he had a very athletic body and he was not bad looking. But he obviously wasn't too particular when it came to women if he was willing to screw a frump like Libby.

"Oh stop being such a crybaby!" Libby crowed. Then she let out a sharp snicker. "Why should we waste good money on a motel when we can do our business here for free?" Her voice was getting closer, so I locked my door. She usually entered without knocking, and if she did that this time, I wanted to have time to compose myself first.

While I stood by the door listening, with my heart beating a mile a minute, she said something to the man that made me want to laugh my head off. *"Baby, I'm going to put something on you a doctor can't take off."* I could not believe Libby's nerve! Was she stone crazy? She had a handsome, hardworking husband who adored her! Why would she risk losing him by having an affair? I immediately reminded myself that Joan also had a handsome, successful husband and she had lovers coming out of her ears. Was it possible that Jeffrey was as big a dud in bed as Reed? One thing was for sure: I would never find out.

"Yum, yum," the man said in a loud voice. "Ooh-wee, girl. I can't wait!"

"It wouldn't be right for us to do it in the same bed I sleep in with my husband. I respect him too much to stoop that low. And you know how holy my mama is. It would be sacrilegious for us to fuck in her bed. Lola's such a slut, it only makes sense for us to use her bed. Knowing her, she probably screws her punks in her room every time Mama leaves the house. And another thing, my stepsister is a straight-up slob. Her room is the only one in this house where you might ever see a roach or a gnat. If it's the mess it usually is, and smells like rotting fish, just close your eyes and hold your nose."

Libby was bringing a strange man to my bed so she could have sex with him! That was one thing. But the remark that really got my goat was her calling me a slob. My room was as neat as a pin and pleasant-smelling today and every day. And as far as roaches and gnats, I had never seen any in Bertha's house.

They must have stopped walking, because they would have made it to my room by now. "You mean Lola, the woman I see roaming around with that tight-ass Joan Riley from time to time?" the man asked.

"That's her. Lola is just as skanky as Joan, maybe even more so. And let me tell you, you wouldn't believe how mean Lola is to me and my brother," Libby said hotly.

"Oh, Marshall told me all about how she uses your mama. Humph! If I was you or Marshall, I'd evict that bitch before she gets even worse. Your mama is too nice to do it on her own."

"Honey, we're working on that!" Libby boomed. "Just wait —" She stopped talking and attempted to open my door. I was so glad I had locked it. "What the hell — I'm sorry, baby. I didn't know that heifer locked her room when she left the house. I'm going to talk to my mama about this!"

"Yes? Who is it?" I yelled.

Even with the door closed, I could still hear Libby mumbling cuss words under her breath. She cleared her throat and said, "Uh . . . Lola, it's Libby." I was amazed at how sweet and gentle her voice sounded now.

"Uh-huh. Just a minute." After a deep breath, I took my time shuffling over to the door. I cracked it open just enough to see Libby's face. "I was taking a nap," I lied, faking a yawn. "What's going on?" I looked over her shoulder at the man who appeared to be in his mid- to late thirties. There was an embarrassed look on his face. Now that he was closer, I could see that he was better looking than I thought. He had really light skin, hazel eyes, a cleft in his chin, and a buzz haircut.

"What are you doing here?" Libby asked. She was looking at me as if I had just sprouted horns.

"Well, it is my room," I said, giving her an incredulous look.

"Lola, didn't you say you were going to the nail salon this morning?" Libby blinked hard. She was so flustered, she could barely stand still.

"I was, but I changed my mind at the last minute. I decided to wait a little while and then go to the gym and walk on the treadmill." I was blinking just as hard as she was. "What are you doing here, Libby? I thought you were going to the nail salon and then shopping."

"Huh? Oh!" She waved her hands and rolled her eyes. "Some dimwit didn't write my appointment down. You know how slow and ignorant some of those people are in that place. When I got there, they already had four other walk-ins sitting around waiting. You know I'm not a patient woman."

"Oh, yes, I do know," I said dryly. I looked into Libby's eyes with so much intensity, sweat suddenly appeared on her face. I wondered how she felt now that she'd been busted. It was hard for me to keep a straight face when I asked the next question. "Was there something in my room you needed?"

"No, I . . . uh . . . I thought I heard a commotion up here, so I was checking every room upstairs to make sure nobody had broken into the house."

I opened my door all the way.

I had to hold my breath to keep from laughing or making a sarcastic remark. I didn't want Libby to know how busted she was. "I'm going to get my gym bag and leave in a few minutes," I said. I glanced over her shoulder again at the man behind her. Libby's plum-colored lipstick was all over his face.

"Oh! My bad. Where are my manners? Lola, this is Greg. He's an old friend. I ran into him at the corner store and he invited me to have lunch." That was all she said about the man I'd seen her having sex with a few minutes ago.

"Hello, Greg. Nice to meet you," I said as graciously as I could. He didn't say a word. All I got from him was a nod, a weak smile, and another embarrassed look.

Libby started talking so fast, her words shot out of her mouth like fireworks. "I had to come home first though to change into more comfortable shoes. I might go jogging after we eat lunch." I looked down and saw that she had on a pair of her Nikes, some of the most "comfortable" shoes in the world to run in.

"Yeah . . . sure," I muttered, giving her a sideways glance. I could tell she didn't appreciate the way I was looking at her, because a menacing scowl appeared on her face so fast it looked like she had put on a mask. "Uh, I hate to cut this conversation short, but I need to get a move on." They started walking backward toward the stairs. "I'll be at the gym for at least a couple of hours." Before I shut my door, I gave Libby a smug look and said, "You two have fun now. . . ."

CHAPTER 38
JOAN

Reed had cried so much since last night, his eyes were red and swollen. He looked so terrible, he didn't want to spend too much time in public. He didn't even want his parents to see what a mess he was. He suggested we postpone our jaunt to Vegas and have a "date night" instead.

Had he not decided to put Vegas on hold, I would have come up with an excuse not to go anyway. Sin City was the ultimate party town and I loved going down there and getting loose with Lola or some of my family members. But when I went with Reed, it was another story. If he lost money at the tables, he got so upset he drank like a fish. When we went to the shows on the strip, which were very expensive because we always requested front-row seats, he spent most of the time dozing or texting. The last time he and I visited Vegas, we spent most of our time holed up in our hotel suite watching TV and having thirty-second episodes of dull sex. And in between all that, he called his answering service every hour on the hour. I could have had more fun with a monk.

Sunday evening we decided to drive to San Francisco and have dinner at a popular restaurant that attracted A-list celebrities like Clint Eastwood and Sean Penn.

I wore my new white silk dress that I'd been saving for a special occasion, and Reed wore the navy blue suit he'd worn to a colleague's wedding last month. Because he was so self-conscious about his red, swollen eyes, he wore a pair of the darkest glasses he owned. People stared at us because we looked like a celebrity couple.

We both ordered filet mignon, and our server promptly filled our wineglasses with the restaurant's best champagne.

"Joan, I hope you can forgive me for my behavior last night. I never thought I'd force myself on a woman — especially my beautiful, young wife," he told me with his voice cracking. He reached both of his hands across our candlelit table and squeezed mine. "I'm so sorry I hurt you, baby."

"Reed, how many more times do I have to tell you to forget about what happened? I already have. And for your information, you didn't 'hurt' me," I assured him. Right after those words left my mouth, a brilliant idea zoomed into my head. If he was so remorseful about "raping" me, and was doing and saying everything he could think of to show me how sorry he was, I was going to use this situation to my advantage and milk it bone dry.

"Um, maybe if I went away for a few days on my own, I'd feel better," I cooed.

To my surprise, he perked up. He even smiled, which he had not done since he'd attacked me. "That's not a bad idea, honey. I have a patient who checks into one of those spas in the wine country when she's in a funk. She gets mud baths, massages, and all kinds of other shit you women get off on. Mother recently started going to one herself. It's done wonders for her. Just last month, she spent four days relaxing at a place in Santa Rosa. During that whole time, she was totally unreachable. Even Father couldn't track her down. When she came home, she was a new woman." Reed paused and took a sip from his wineglass. "Haven't you noticed a change in her? She's much more serene."

His words almost made me choke on some air. Even if my mother-in-law got help from the Wizard of Oz, she would still be about as serene as a blowtorch.

"She sure is," I replied, clearing my throat to get the taste of that bitter lie off my tongue. I wondered how Reed could make such an outrageous statement and still manage to keep a straight face.

"You can — why are you giving me such a peculiar look now, Joan? Did I say something to upset you again?"

I shook my head. "You say I can go somewhere on my own? I just want to make sure it's you talking and not the alcohol."

"Baby, I've only had a few sips of my wine," he insisted, lifting his wineglass and waving it in the air. "I'm not even tipsy yet. I meant everything I just said."

I was tense, so I took a long drink. The champagne was so potent, it relaxed me right away. I shifted in my seat and crossed my legs. "Are you sure you don't mind if I go off somewhere all by myself for a few days?" I asked softly, giving Reed a skeptical look.

"Sweetheart, I want you to do whatever it takes to restore your peace of mind. I don't care what it is." He was talking, but it was another man's words coming out of his mouth.

I was so incredulous, I did a double take. My mouth wanted to drop open, but I managed to stay composed. I didn't want to look or sound too excited. The last thing I wanted Reed to do after the statement he'd just made was backtrack and change his mind. "I'm so happy you feel that way. Now if I can get Too Sweet to keep an eye on Junior, I just might go off somewhere by myself for a few days. I was still in high school when you and I got married, so I didn't get to spend a few years 'sowing my wild oats,' as they say, the way some of the girls I know did."

"True, true, and I realize that. Before I left home to go to college, I joined a couple of my friends and we spent several months roaming around Europe with backpacks, sleeping bags, and guidebooks. It was an exhilarating experience. It was refreshing for me to experience different cultures. I really got to know the real Reed Riley and at that point, I realized what I wanted in a wife, my career, and everything else." He paused and gave me a pensive look. "A change is definitely what you need, sweetie."

"Thanks, honey," I purred. "I appreciate hearing that." I uncrossed my legs because I felt more comfortable now.

"I love you, Joan. I always have and I always will."

I dipped my head and swallowed hard. I

remained silent because I didn't know what to say. One thing was for sure, I was not about to look Reed in the eye and tell him I loved him.

"Maybe if you do go away for a little while, you'll feel the same way I felt after my trip to Europe. You can spend as much money as you want, wherever you go. And I promise you, the whole time you're gone, I won't bother you. As a matter of fact, you don't even have to tell me where you're going."

"Do you mean that?" I gasped. I couldn't believe that this was the same love-struck sad sack who got severely paranoid when he couldn't locate me.

"I mean that. Just let somebody know where you're at in case a coconut falls off a tree and lands on your head and you get amnesia or something." He chuckled.

"Wherever I decide to go, I'll let Lola know," I chirped. As soon as I mentioned my girl's name, Reed's whole body jerked and he gave me a glassy-eyed, slack-jawed look. He stayed that way until I snapped my fingers in his face. "Are you okay?"

"I'm fine," he croaked, with his face looking normal now. He lifted his glass to his lips and took another drink. His body didn't jerk again, but the glassy-eyed, slack-jawed look returned to his face.

"Reed, are you sure you're okay?"

"What are you talking about?"

"As soon as I mentioned Lola's name, you looked like you were having a spasm or something."

"I was hoping to hear that you'd tell Mother where you were going. . . ."

"I'd rather tell Lola. I thought this was supposed to be about me and what I want," I said with a pout and a sniff.

He smiled suddenly. "It is, baby. Go wherever you want to go, and tell whomever you want to tell. You can even go to Europe if you want to. We can afford it."

"I don't want to go that far away from home."

"I just want you to know that the sky's the limit. I don't care if you go somewhere halfway around the world or somewhere local."

"Thank you, honey. You're so good to me."

CHAPTER 39
CALVIN

I was glad to return to work a week after I returned to the West Coast. It was a smooth predawn ride in my Jeep up to Roseville, California, where I parked my eighteen-wheeler in one of the company's satellite locations when I was not working. It was an even smoother ride to Los Angeles, where I had to deliver some toys and clothes to a high-end children's department store.

After I completed my delivery, I drove as far as Fresno before I decided to take a break around ten p.m. I pulled into a truck stop and checked into one of the three seedy motels facing the gas pumps. I was pleased to see that there were several fast-food joints in the vicinity and a lot of "lot lizards" milling about. These hookers were very popular with truckers. They were usually so busy they never spent more than a few minutes with each trick. I had to wait an hour before one was available to give me a ten-minute, twenty-dollar blow job. After she left to go take care of the dude in the room next to mine, I went to bed and slept like a baby.

Right after I got up at eight a.m., I dialed Sylvia's home telephone number. I knew she'd be getting ready for work so she wouldn't have time to talk long.

"When did you get back to California, Calvin?" Her voice was low and distant.

"Um . . . last week."

"*Last week?!* And you're just now calling me when you knew how anxious I was to see you?" In all the years that we'd been together, Sylvia had never shown any hostility toward me until now. "I was worried sick!" she screeched.

I made her suffer enough, so I overlooked her hostility this time. I decided to play the "woe is me" card. First I snorted real loud and blew my nose into a napkin, and then I began to speak in a low, weak tone of voice. "Sylvia, I just laid my uncle to rest. That was traumatic enough." I blew into the same napkin again, this time throwing in a sob. "Excuse me . . . I'm sorry, baby. Anyway, then I had to spend hours at a time with Uncle Ed's lawyer going over all kinds of estate paperwork — sign this, notarize that, and on and on. All that shit is still stressing me out. After all that, my flight back to

California was a fucking nightmare. The plane was three hours behind schedule, half a dozen babies squalled during most of the flight, and the attendants were rude. I had a severe case of the runs and spent more time in the toilet than in my fucking middle seat squeezed between two female buffalos who smelled like hell! I was a wreck by the time I got to my house. They needed me back at work as soon as possible, so I was back on the road a few hours after I got home. When I returned from my run, I was so exhausted I was almost delirious, so all I wanted to do was crawl into my bed and regroup my body and my mind." My telling little lies here and there had become so necessary, there were times when I almost believed them myself. I could barely remember the man I used to be — a righteous dude who'd rarely told lies and had been honorable in every way, all the way up to the moment I killed Glinda. . . .

"Well, I wouldn't have minded crawling in that bed with you," Sylvia said in a bleating voice. "If I had known you were sick, I could have come over and cooked you something."

"I know you would have, sweetheart. I know you're getting ready for work, so I won't keep you on the phone long. Are you busy Friday night?"

"Me busy?" she gasped. "What would I be busy doing? I've been waiting on pins and needles for you to get back so we could be together. And you know I'm never too busy for you."

"I'm happy to hear that."

Sylvia remained quiet.

"Are you still there?" I asked.

"Yeah," she said with hesitation and a loud sniff.

Her hesitation and that unnecessary sniff annoyed me. "Sylvia, if there is something on your mind, I wish you'd tell me. You know I don't like it when you beat around the bush."

"I'm just curious as to why you didn't call me as soon as you got back into town."

"I tried!"

"You tried what?"

"I tried to call you the same night I got back. I got a recorded message that said your line was out of order."

"That's news to me. I haven't had any trouble with my phone lately. Are you sure you dialed the right number?"

"I thought I did. But since I was so frazzled, it's possible I dialed somebody else's number by mistake."

"Why didn't you call my cell phone number or send me a text message?"

"Because you changed your cell phone number last week!" An anonymous caller had been making obscene calls to Sylvia and I'd encouraged her to have her number changed.

"Calvin, I've called your number several times since then, so my new number has to be stored in your phone."

"I know it is, baby. To be honest with you, I just didn't feel like talking to anybody. My uncle's passing hit me real hard, and I've had a few flashbacks from the war this week. I know I should have been in touch with you. But since I got back in town, I've been so preoccupied and down in the doldrums I just —"

"Calvin, that's all the more reason why you should have called me," Sylvia interrupted. "I know you're still grieving the loss of your uncle and I know you still have a few flashbacks from the war. I love you and I want to do all I can to help ease your pain. The next time you feel down, please call me anyway. Otherwise, I won't know what to think."

"Thank you, baby. I'll do just that. Anyway, I was scared to show up at your house without calling first. It's rude to just drop in on somebody unless they know you're coming."

"Calvin, I'm sorry you think of me as just 'somebody,' but I'm letting you know now that you can come to my house any day, any time, whether I know you're coming or not."

One of the many things I hated and would not tolerate was a woman reading me the riot act. Even though this was the first time for Sylvia.

"Listen, let's talk when you're in a better mood. I'm still stressed out, so I'm not thinking too clearly. I don't want to say something to you that I will regret —"

"I'm sorry, Calvin! I . . . I am being selfish and inconsiderate. You can call me up, or come by my house when you can. I don't know what I was thinking by being such a bitch."

"I'll see you Friday evening. How's that? Is seven okay with you?"

She hesitated again. "That's fine with me. I had planned to go over to my sister's house so she could braid my hair, but I can do that another time."

"I don't like braids," I said quickly. "They're too ethnic."

"Oh? I didn't know you felt that way. I thought men liked braids on a woman, especially black men."

"Not this black man. Braids don't look

good on every woman."

"I wish you had told me that sooner. I would have never worn braids if you had."

"Well, I'm telling you now."

"I don't like going to my sister's house that often anyway. Baby, you get some rest and take care of yourself. I'll see you tomorrow night."

As soon as I got off the phone, I turned on my laptop to check the messages on my AOL account. I didn't even bother to read all the obvious junk and mundane shit from other people. I signed off and logged on to the Discreet Encounters website. I went directly to my in-box to see if Lola had sent me more messages. She had not. I immediately pulled up her profile. I stared at her wretched picture for five full minutes before I angrily logged off.

Well, it was finally time for the second phase of my plan: sex.

I didn't want to discuss our first intimate encounter by e-mail, but it was too early in the day to call her up. I decided to wait a couple of hours and call her at work before I checked out of my motel.

When I called Lola's cell phone number a few minutes after ten, I purposely blocked my name and number. I wanted her to be surprised to hear my voice.

"Hello, Lola," I said.

"Hello," she said. "Who is this?"

"It's Calvin. You've forgotten how my voice sounds already?"

"Oh! Um, I had no idea it was you. I didn't see your name on my caller ID."

"I misplaced my cell phone, so I'm using my coworker's. He's got his programmed so it won't show his name and number."

"Where are you?"

"I'm at a rest stop in Fresno. I would have called you before now, but I had an emergency run to do to help out a sick coworker. And all kinds of other crazy shit's been going down since I got back to California from Chicago. My run is over, so I'll be heading home in a couple of hours. You suddenly popped into my mind and I didn't want to wait until I got home to call you." I coughed to clear my throat. "I've been thinking about you a lot, Lola. You were on my mind every day while I was in Chicago."

"Oh. I thought about you a lot too. I'm so glad you called, Calvin. I hope you still want to get together with me . . . someday."

"Someday is closer than you think." I laughed. "Now that my schedule and everything else in my life is under control, I'd like to see you. I don't want to spend time with any other woman in the club until I spend some time with you. If my uncle hadn't died and I hadn't had to do so many long hauls in the past couple of months, I would have made a date with you long before now."

"Oh. I'm happy to hear that. Uh, when?" She was actually panting.

"How about tomorrow?"

"Tomorrow?"

"Yes, unless you have other plans."

"I don't have any other plans!" she practically roared. She must have realized how ridiculous she sounded, because a second later her voice dropped almost to a whisper. "Tomorrow is good. Where do you want me to meet you?"

"Do you have a favorite hotel in your area? I'll reserve a room for us as soon as I get off the phone."

"We have a few nice hotels in South Bay City, but I'd rather go to one in San Jose if that's okay with you."

"How about the downtown Hyatt? It's a really nice hotel, and it's in a convenient location. It's a favorite spot among club members. I've had several hookups there."

"Me too," she admitted. "What time?"

"Is eight p.m. a good time for you?"

"I'd rather get together a lot earlier. Tuesday is not so busy at my work, so I know I can take off early. And I'm not too crazy about driving alone at night. My car is not reliable, and I don't want to get stranded on the freeway, or anywhere else. It's pretty dangerous out there these days, especially for black women. I recently read in the newspaper that somebody killed another one of us and left her in an alley in one of the roughest neighborhoods in San Jose."

"I read about that. What a shame. As my grandmother used to say, 'When you live by the sword, you die by the sword.' "

"What do you mean? *Did you know the dead woman?*"

"Oh, no, I didn't know her. The paper did say she had been working the streets for a couple of years. That's a very high-risk activity. I'm sure she ran into all kinds of nutcases. She could have been one herself, for all we know. Yep. Live fast, die young. Granny used to say that a lot too."

"I agree with that. Why don't we firm up our plans by noon tomorrow?"

"I'll call or text you again then."

"And, Calvin . . ." she said sweetly. I was surprised when she abruptly stopped talking.

"Yes, what is it?"

"I'm sure I won't disappoint you." For

Lola to be such a small woman, she sure had a big voice when she wanted to get a point across. She sounded like a female drill sergeant. "I can promise you that much!" she boomed.

"I'm sure you won't either. I've read the glowing reviews about you on the club's review board."

"I wasn't going to tell you, but I read the reviews about you too. We have the same number of five-star ratings."

We both laughed.

CHAPTER 40
JOAN

"Guess what?" I said as soon as I met up with Lola. We'd decided to have lunch at a deli near her work two days after my dinner date with Reed. "I'm going to Phoenix this Thursday," I said before she had time to answer my question.

We occupied a table for two in a corner near the kitchen. We had both selected roast beef sandwiches and orange juice. I was not hungry, but I was going to make myself eat because Lola was treating. The deli was as crowded as usual with people we both knew. Each time before we spoke, we glanced around to make sure nobody was close enough to hear our conversation. Like the beauty shop and nail salons Lola and I patronized, this deli was a cesspool of gossip. I had heard some of the most intimate details of other people's lives sitting in this place. If people knew half the shit that Lola and I were involved in, the gossip about us would reach epic proportions.

I had originally invited her to meet me for drinks after she got off work today, but she'd declined. She told me that she had something real juicy to tell me and it couldn't wait until the end of the day. Apparently it wasn't that juicy, because when I asked her a few minutes ago, she told me she'd tell me in a few minutes. That was the reason I'd jump-started the conversation about my upcoming trip to Phoenix.

Lola had just bitten off a piece of her sandwich and didn't respond until she stopped chewing. "You're going to Phoenix? What are you going there for? I — Oh my God!" She slapped her forehead with the palm of her hand and gave me an incredulous look. "Isn't that where your love-struck lawyer lives?"

I bobbed my head like a rooster. "Yup!"

"You're going to Phoenix to be with him?" I couldn't tell if Lola was asking me a question or making a statement.

"I talked to John Walden last night and told him I wanted to come down there for a few days. He got very excited. Reed is trying so hard to make up for forcing me to have sex with him, he told me I could take a little break and go somewhere nice to spend some time by myself. I didn't ask

John to send for me or book me a room. But he insisted on doing it anyway. Right now he's the only man I know who can make me feel really relaxed."

From the flabbergasted look on Lola's face, you would have thought that I was speaking Greek. "Girl, I'm surprised at you!" she practically roared.

"Why?"

"Joan, there must be at least four or five men coming this way in the next few days that you can make a date with. You just told me two days ago that DrFeelGood has another conference to attend out here next week. Why are you going all the way to Phoenix just for sex?"

"What makes you think I'm going to Phoenix just for sex?"

She gasped. "Girl, this is Lola you're talking to. I *know* you. Why else would *you* be going out of town to spend time with one of the club's members?"

"John is more to me now than just 'one of the club's members.' " I could tell from Lola's body language and the various looks she kept giving me that I was exasperating her, but I didn't care. She was exasperating me too.

"Woman, have you lost your mind? You've repeatedly turned down his offer to move there to be his mistress and I'm sure he's not happy about that."

"So?"

"So? Joan, it is one thing for you to hook up with John when he comes to California. But it's another thing for you to set foot on his turf. That's a whole different ball game."

"What in the world are you trying to say?" I wasn't paying enough attention to the volume of my voice. I was talking loud and people had started looking at us, so I started whispering. "What difference does it make where John and I hook up?"

Lola started whispering too. "Going down there to fuck up a storm with this man might give him the wrong idea. Shit. You don't even know him that well."

"Listen to the pot calling the kettle black! I know way more about John than you know about that truck driver! And you're so hot and horny for that motherfucker it's a damn shame."

"That's different. John lived in Europe for years before he moved to the States. He and Calvin have had different cultural experiences. They are so unlike each other, you'd think they came from different planets. Men with European backgrounds have been known to do some crazy shit to women who piss them off," she blubbered.

"Different, my ass. You can't pick up a newspaper and not read about an American man doing something crazy to his woman, and anybody else that gets in his way. You talk about me not knowing John that well. At least I know where he works and lives. I Googled him one night right after our first date. His name, page after page of the high-profile cases he's won, pictures of him with the other partners in his law firm, his wife and kids, pictures of him with politicians and other high-end associates were all over my monitor. He's one of the most prominent men in the state of Arizona. Do you need to hear more?"

"I've heard enough."

"So don't tell me I don't know John Walden that well."

"Um, Reed is also very prominent and you *thought* you knew —"

I leaned forward and wagged my finger in Lola's face. "You leave my husband out of this conversation or you'll be sorry!" I warned.

"Okay, okay," she replied, holding up her hands. "You don't need to get all uptight with me. I'm on your side." It pleased me to see her smile. "I'm glad you're going away for a few days, and I know you'll have a wonderful time. I just don't want you to get yourself in trouble."

I rolled my eyes and let out a long, loud breath. "Stop! Let's change the subject right now."

"That's fine with me." Lola exhaled and gave me a dry look. "You started it."

"Well, I'm ending it now." I gritted my teeth and continued. "Now, what's the juicy news you have to tell me?"

There was a faraway look in her eyes and she remained silent.

"Lola, you said you had something to tell me that couldn't wait until you got off work. Do I have to guess what it is, or are you going to tell me before your lunch hour is over?"

She glanced at her watch and shrugged. "I'll tell you in a few minutes. I just want to think about it a little more first. I'm not sure I should even tell you. . . ."

"If you're not sure you should be telling me, maybe you shouldn't."

"I will tell you, but let me finish my lunch first. What I have to tell you is not something I want to discuss on a half-empty stomach. Oh, did you see today's newspaper? Macy's is having a big sale."

"Macy's is always having a big sale. And I'm glad you brought up the newspaper." I took a sip of my orange juice and pushed my plate to the side. I couldn't eat or drink another thing. "Did you read about that young black woman they found strangled to death in an alley in San Jose the other day?"

"Yeah, I sure did. Poor thing."

"That was a nice picture of her in the newspaper. She was so pretty. And she reminds me of you. . . ."

CHAPTER 41
LOLA

I knew Joan was tuning up her mouth to make more comments on the subject of another missing woman who resembled me, so I took it and ran. "You know, Bertha told me that same thing when she saw the newspaper article. She made a joke about me possibly having half sisters all over town because of the way Daddy got around." I stopped talking. A curious look appeared on Joan's face, so I continued. "She even mentioned that big newspaper article from last year about those three black women who disappeared and are still missing."

"The same three women who look a lot like you."

"A lot of women look like me. As a matter of fact, everybody looks like somebody else. You've been going around since we were teenagers bragging about how much you look like Halle Berry."

"Lola, you should take this more seriously."

"I am! But I refuse to let my imagination run wild the way you are on this subject. Look, they never found those other three women. Nobody even knows if they're dead or stretched out on a beach in Costa Rica drinking piña coladas. At least they found the body of this latest woman so her family can give her a proper burial. You would think that by now prostitutes would stop working the streets and get their tricks off craigslist or one of those other sites that the smart hookers use. Picking up strange men off the street, the woman they found in that alley is lucky she lived as long as she did."

"Yeah, you're right, I guess." Joan cleared her throat and glanced at her watch. "I have an appointment to get my nails done and I need to swing by Macy's on my way home." She cocked her head and looked at me out of the corner of her eye. "If you don't tell me why you wanted me to meet you for lunch, it'll have to wait until I get back from Phoenix on Sunday," she warned.

"You can't tell anybody what I'm about to tell you now."

"Since when do you have to warn me about keeping my mouth shut? As long as we've known one another, I've never blabbed anything juicy that you shared with me."

"Libby is having an affair," I blurted.

Joan's eyes got as big as golf balls. "Lola, are you telling me that your loathsome stepsister is fooling around with another man?"

"That's exactly what I'm telling you."

"What man, other than Jeffrey, would be desperate enough to want her with her plain, dumpy, mean self?"

"At least one other man does. And, believe it or not, he's even better looking than Jeffrey."

"Yikes!" Joan laughed. "That conniving bitch! Who does she think she is — *me*? Either she's using witchcraft, or she's blackmailing this man. I'll be goddamned. I don't know what this world is coming to."

"I could make a whole lot of trouble for her if I wanted to." I snickered. "I could even send Jeffrey an anonymous note."

Joan shook her head. "Uh-uh. Don't do that. That's something Libby would do to somebody, and you're nothing like her. How do you know for sure she's having an affair? It could be a rumor like the one that went around years ago about you sleeping with her husband. You of all people should know you can't believe everything you hear."

"Uh-uh. This is no rumor. I saw her with my own eyes."

"What? You caught her? Have you been following her around?"

"I didn't have to follow her. She had the nerve to bring the dude to the house Sunday! She didn't know I was still in my room."

I couldn't stop thinking about what I had witnessed. When Libby's lover left the house, which was less than a minute after she'd been busted, she came back to my room. She hadn't knocked, and when she barged in she had one of the most frightened looks on her face I'd ever seen. Her thick brows were furrowed, her nostrils were twitching, and her lips were trembling. I had just stuffed some clean workout clothes into my gym bag and had it, my purse, and my car key in my hand.

"Lola, I know you're about to leave the house, but can you hold up for a few minutes? I need to talk to you."

"I guess so," I'd said with a shrug.

"Um . . . I'm telling you now, you'd better not blab my business to anybody," she warned, and shook her finger in my face. She hadn't shut the door. Instead she'd stood in front of it with her hand on the knob, shifting her weight from one foot to

351

the other. "What I do is between me and my husband."

"Libby, I don't care what you do," I said casually. "But don't expect me to cover for you."

"Cover for me? What makes you think I'd ask you to 'cover' for me?"

"Gossip travels faster than the speed of light in this town. Other people might already know what you've been up to. If Jeffrey hears any rumors and asks me if I know what's going on, I won't lie for you."

"Who asked you to? The thing is, what Jeffrey doesn't know won't hurt him. He won't know what I did if you don't tell him. Greg has a wife and kids, so I know he won't tell anybody. Besides, you have nothing to gain by ratting me out." Libby had given me a pleading look. This was one of the signs she rarely displayed that told me she was human. "Um, do me a favor and keep this to yourself. If he asks if you knew about Greg and me, I hope you'll dummy up. . . ."

I shrugged. "He probably won't ask me, so don't worry." I'd cocked my head and given Libby a thoughtful look. "How long have you been seeing Greg?"

"Why? What's it to you?"

"I'm just curious," I'd replied. "I didn't

think you were the cheating type."

Libby's jaw dropped. "I'm not 'the cheating type'! Girl, you need to stop watching those cheesy movies on the Lifetime channel. They are putting all kinds of ridiculous ideas in your head. I just had a weak moment, that's all. And anyway, you were supposed to be at the nail salon."

"So were you," I'd pointed out.

"Well, I'm going there now." Libby turned to leave, then she turned back around and gave me another pleading look. "You scratch my back, I'll scratch yours."

"Meaning what?"

"Look, I know you don't like me, but you can at least be civil to me. I mean, woman to woman, females in the same family need to stick together. If there's something you want to do that you shouldn't be doing, I'll cover for you."

"*You* cover for *me?*" I'd wanted to laugh. I didn't, because I knew that it would upset Libby even more. And she would probably spend even more time running her mouth. All I wanted was for her to leave me alone. "Libby, with all due respect, I doubt very seriously if I'd ever need you to cover for me."

By the time I finished telling Joan everything that Libby and I had said to each other, she was laughing so hard she had tears in her eyes. "So what are you going to do with this information? I know you're not the blabbing type, so other than me, who can you share this juicy story with?"

"That's the next part of what I wanted to share with you," I gushed. I cleared my throat, sat up straighter in my seat, and puffed out my chest. "Calvin's back. He called me up and we finally set a date to get together in a hotel in a few hours. He has some catch-up trucker work and a few personal things to attend to first, so he won't be available to see me until then. I don't know what all we'll talk about, but he's got a great sense of humor, so I think this story about Libby will give him a lot to laugh about. I've already told him about Bertha, and a little bit about Libby and Marshall. I'm sure he'd like to hear an update." An extremely gloomy look crossed Joan's face. "What's the matter? You look like a pallbearer."

"You're going to hook up with Calvin in a hotel in a few hours and you're just now telling me?"

"I didn't want to seem too anxious."

"*Pffft!* Honey, you reached that point a long time ago."

"Oh well." I shrugged. "I am very anxious

to make love with him. But I never expected him to call me out of the blue and ask to hook up on the same day. I wish he would have given me more notice. But —" I paused and gave Joan a dreamy-eyed look. "I've been waiting long enough to get my hands on that man, so I'm going to make a beeline to that hotel."

"I'm happy for you, Lola," she said. Within seconds, her normal face returned. But there was a hint of despair in her voice. "I know how long you've been itching to check out what Calvin's got between his legs."

"Well, you don't have to make it sound so crude!" I snapped. "For all you know, we might not even have sex."

"And Santa Claus has nothing to do with Christmas. Be serious! Let me remind you *again* — you met the man through a sex club."

"What about that day I met him and all we did was have coffee in a coffee shop?"

"So what? This time you're meeting him in a hotel room." Joan pressed her lips together and eyed me critically. I didn't like the way she was looking at me, but since the conversation was tense enough already, I decided not to mention it.

"Joan, sometimes you make me feel so

uncomfortable. Maybe I shouldn't have even told you about my upcoming date with Calvin."

She gave me an apologetic look. "I'm glad you told me, and I'm sorry for talking shit. I . . . I just hope you find what you've been looking for all your life. You deserve it."

"Thanks. I really appreciate your saying that."

"And I mean it. Good luck on your date with Calvin." Joan patted my shoulder and gave me a warm smile. "I want a full report afterward. I can't wait to hear if your sexy truck driver is as good as he looks."

"After all the energy and time I've spent trying to get to him, he'd better be." I laughed. Joan didn't.

CHAPTER 42
CALVIN

I had a dream about Lola a few nights ago. In it, I finally made love to her for the first time. It had been such a pleasant experience, I needed to experience it for real as soon as possible. That was the reason I asked her to see me *today*! If she was a lousy lay, I'd have to revise my time line. I'd have to kill her even sooner than I planned, because I would not want to waste more of my time having sex with a woman who couldn't satisfy me. Nothing irritated me more! I recalled a woman I'd pursued several years ago because a buddy of mine had raved about her performance in the bedroom. Sex with that same woman had not done much for me. Despite all the great reviews other club members had posted about Lola, I needed to find out for myself. If she was as good as I hoped, I'd probably stick to my original time line.

She had sounded pleased to hear my voice

and even more pleased, and surprised, that I'd finally asked her for a date so we could take our "relationship" to the next level. She surprised me by agreeing to see me on such short notice, a man who was still practically a stranger to her. It was another indication that she was a damn fool.

After I had dropped off my rig and made it back to my house, I took a shower. I saw that I had numerous messages on my cell phone and my landline, most of them from Sylvia, but I was not interested in talking to anybody until after I'd checked out Lola's goods. If she was going to disappoint me, I'd be in a bad mood when I got back home. If she was good, I'd be in a much better mood when I talked to Sylvia and everybody else who'd blown up my answering devices.

I checked into the Hyatt at four p.m. Lola showed up thirty minutes later.

"Um, I was going to call you and see if you wanted me to bring anything," she muttered as she entered the room.

I shook my head. "Baby, you brought everything I wanted you to bring," I told her, draping my arm around her shoulder. "You look as beautiful as ever."

She had on that disgusting smock she worked in, and her makeup looked a little crusty, but she was still one of the hottest women I had ever come across.

"Really? I didn't even have time to go home and change clothes or redo my makeup," she said, patting her hair. "I didn't want to get caught on the freeway in that commute traffic and get here later than I wanted to."

"Honey, the important thing is, you're here now," I said with a sniff. I led her to the bed and we sat down at the same time. She seemed nervous. "I've been looking forward to this day."

"I have too," she said, then coughed. She kept her eyes on the wall in front of her until I touched her chin and turned her face toward mine. "Oh, Calvin!" she swooned.

Before I knew it, she hauled off and kissed me and wrapped her arms around my neck. We kissed some more and groped one another for about five minutes before she pulled away. She was giggling and blinking and looking me up and down all at the same time.

"I can't stay long," she said, looking at her watch. "I'm afraid to be out alone after dark," she explained.

"I understand," I said, slowly rising off the bed. "Well, do you have time to have a drink with me? The minibar is fully stocked.

You seem a little tense, and a glass of wine will help you relax."

"Yeah. I would like something to drink."

I filled two glasses with white wine, and we sat on the bed and drank in silence. She finished first. Then she sat there sniffing and glancing at me with the empty glass still in her hand. I finished mine, set both glasses on the end table, and pulled her into my arms. She got out of that damn smock and the rest of her clothing and shoes so fast, it made my head spin. With a glazed look on her face, she stretched out on the bed and watched as I removed my clothes. Her eyes never left mine.

"I am so happy you called and asked to be with me today," she admitted.

"I'm happy too," I chirped, as I kicked off my shoes.

Even after we got as close as two human beings could get, I could tell that she was still tense. "Lola, relax and let yourself go," I whispered. "I want you to enjoy this as much as I know I'm going to."

Right after I said that, from that point on, she behaved like a tiger in heat that had just been let out of a cage during mating season. And, to my delight, she was extraordinary. We didn't make love, that word was too tame. We *fucked.* By the time I pulled out of her body and rolled off her, I was so exhausted all I wanted to do was get some rest. Now that I knew what she had to offer, I definitely didn't want this to be a one-time event, so I decided to give her as much attention as I could.

I handed her another glass of wine and pulled her into my arms again. As soon as we got comfortable on the bed, I initiated a conversation knowing that she was going to bore the hell out of me, babbling about the same stupid shit she always babbled about every time I conversed with her. I didn't think she'd ever stop rambling, so after listening to her nauseating drivel for ten minutes straight, I interrupted her.

"Lola, if you don't have any plans for Saturday, I'd like to see you again," I said.

She gasped. "You would?" I had just fucked the living hell out of this woman. I knew she could tell that I had enjoyed myself. So why did she sound so surprised that I'd want to see her again in a few days? "You mean this coming Saturday?"

"Yes." I gently caressed her arm. "If you come early enough, we can have lunch. And if you can stay as long as I'd like you to stay, we can have dinner too."

She kept her composure, but she couldn't fool me. The way her eyes lit up, it looked like she wanted to dance a jig. "I'd love to see you again on Saturday." She cleared her throat and looked in my eyes and blinked. "I'm just so happy that we finally got together." She got up off the bed and started putting her clothes back on. "I wish I could stay longer, but it's already starting to get dark."

I stood up and wrapped my arms around her so tightly, I could actually feel her heart thumping. She had all of her clothes back on except for that ridiculous smock. "Let me escort you home."

"You don't have to do that. I'm not ready for you to meet my folks," she said, giving me a hopeless look.

"I'm sorry. I'm getting way ahead of myself. What I meant to say was, I'll drive right behind you to within a couple of blocks of where you live. That way you don't have to be afraid to be out driving alone at night." I gave her the most compassionate look I could manage. "I won't let anything happen to you."

Tears pooled in her eyes. I was afraid if I said any more corny shit and she didn't leave soon, she'd start crying. "Thank you, Calvin," she added in the most demure voice a woman ever used in my presence. "I . . . I am so glad I met you."

I wanted her to be happy. I wanted her to live with the fantasy that she was making me happy all the way up to the moment I killed her. I embraced her even tighter. It was time to throw her a very big bone. "Lola, I know you don't know me that well yet, but I'd love to do something very special with you for my birthday in July."

"Oh?" There was a look on her face that words could not describe. She blinked rapidly a few times. "What would you like to do?"

"I'd like to spend an entire weekend with you. I love Frisco in the summertime, so we can check into a hotel and really enjoy ourselves. Maybe even take in a show and some sightseeing. Please say yes. It would be the best birthday present I ever had."

"Calvin, I'd love to spend a weekend with you in Frisco!" she hollered, almost choking on her words.

CHAPTER 43
JOAN

A pain shot through my chest when Reed walked into the bedroom Wednesday at six a.m. while I was packing for my upcoming mysterious getaway.

"I think your going away alone to refresh yourself is a good idea," he said as he wrapped his arms around my waist from behind. I cringed when he started nibbling on my earlobe. He'd drunk a glass of wine with the leg of lamb, asparagus, and garlic mashed potatoes I had cooked for last night's dinner, so his breath was foul enough to irritate the hell out of me.

"Uh-huh. I'm sure I'll be a new woman when I get back."

"Not too 'new,' I hope. I just want the Joan I married back."

"Yeah," I muttered. "That's what I meant."

"What do you want me to tell Mother and Father if they come by or call and ask where you are?" Reed removed his arms from around me, but he was still close enough for me to smell his breath. I was glad he had stopped slobbering on my ear.

I hunched my shoulders. "You can tell them the truth if you want. If any of my relatives get nosy, tell them the same thing. But I'll be gone only three days, so you may not even hear from any of our folks before I get back." I turned around and embraced Reed. I even gave him a quick kiss on his lips.

"Make sure you take one of the credit cards with a high limit. I don't want you to spare any expense."

"Sure, baby."

Since John had booked the hotel room in his name and paid for my airfare, I wasn't going to use one of our credit cards for those expenses. It would leave a paper trail for Reed to follow if he decided to do some snooping when our credit card statement came. I didn't want him to know I had a connection to Phoenix at all — in case I did disappear one day and move there to be with John, which was probably never going to happen. But with the way things were going in my life I was not going to rule out anything.

Lola let me borrow one of her credit cards

to use in case I wanted to make a purchase in the airport, or do some shopping in Phoenix on my own. I didn't expect John to spend every minute of my visit with me. And I didn't ask him if I could go shopping with one of his credit cards, even though he had already told me he was paying for my airfare and the hotel with a company card so his wife would never see it. I had already decided that if Reed ever asked how I'd financed my mini-vacation, I'd tell him I paid for everything with cash.

He almost fainted yesterday morning when I told him that I was going away by bus. Traveling by Greyhound was at the top of his shit list of disgusting things. "Baby, make sure you carry a can of pepper spray in your purse and take a seat near the front of the bus. Don't sit too close to anybody who doesn't speak English, keep your cell phone on, hold on tight to your purse, and take some toilet seat protectors in case you have to use the bathroom," he had told me with his face screwed up like a coin purse. "And whatever you do, don't ever tell Mother you rode on a Greyhound bus. It would traumatize her, and we'd never hear the end of it."

An hour after Reed left for his office yesterday, I drove to the bus station and purchased a round-trip ticket to Santa Rosa. When I got back home, I planted the receipt for the purchase on top of our bedroom dresser so he would see it right away when he got home.

Thursday morning, when it was time for me to be on my way, I took a cab to the Greyhound bus station. From there I took another cab to the airport. I didn't breathe a sigh of relief until I was actually on the plane.

My plan was to take a cab from the Phoenix airport to the hotel and meet up with John there. But when I reached the baggage area, I immediately saw a stone-faced chauffeur holding up a sign with my name on it.

When the town car arrived at the Ritz-Carlton hotel in Phoenix's financial district, I piled out and skittered into the lobby. I had John's room number, so I didn't have to stop at the front desk to get that information.

When I knocked on John's suite he opened the door immediately. He snatched my suitcase out of my hand and set it on the floor by the door.

"Darling, I am so happy to see you again!" he boomed. He pulled me into his arms and squeezed me so hard he almost cut off my circulation.

"I'm happy to see you too," I wheezed as I pried his arms from around me. I was happy to see John. Even though I was not willing to be his mistress, I was willing to continue seeing him as long as we enjoyed each other's company. Or until I got rid of Reed and found another man like John who was free to marry me.

He kissed me long and hard. Then we made love, long and hard.

An hour later he took a quick shower and left. He had to rush home to take his wife out because it was her birthday.

I took my time dismembering the lobster I ordered from room service for dinner. I ate less than half of it because I didn't like eating alone. I didn't like lying in that king-size bed watching TV by myself either. I had not brought a book or any magazines to read, so I had plenty of time on my hands and I didn't know what to do with it.

Unpleasant thoughts started dancing around in my head. With John gone, I felt lonely and confused. I had no idea where my life was going. I couldn't imagine still doing the same things I was doing now ten years down the road. Some of my thoughts were downright frightening. It had occurred to me, more than once, that Reed might put a private detective on my tail and find out all my business. Another thing that I couldn't stop thinking about was: What if he decided to kill himself no matter what I did, and *take me with him*? Or what if he just decided to kill me? But one thought concerned me more than the others: What if I got so depressed and fed up because of Reed that *I* committed suicide? I told myself that whatever was going to happen was going to happen. I had not even discussed these disturbing thoughts with Lola, and I didn't plan to. She was paranoid enough, so I was going to leave well enough alone. In the meantime I was going to continue having fun with John and other club members. Other than my son, my family, and Lola, my crazy sex life was one of the few joys I had these days.

My phone rang just before ten p.m. and I grabbed it on the first ring. "I just wanted to say good night, m'lady," John whispered.

"Good night," I whispered back. "What time will I see you tomorrow?"

"I'll be with a client most of the morning and then I have to attend my son's basketball game, so it won't be until later in the day. Hopefully I'll see you in time for dinner."

Even though John and I didn't have a

traditional married man/mistress relationship (at least not yet . . .), I still experienced some of the same emotions as a real mistress. I got sad when I couldn't see him when I wanted to. Every time we got together, it had to be when it was most convenient for him. I got jealous when I thought of his wife and children. He was so devoted to them; a mistress would never be anything to him but that. And he admitted that he'd had several since he got married.

"Oh," I said, sounding disappointed on purpose. One of the reasons I really liked John was because he read me like a book.

"Now, now, luv. I can tell you're disappointed. But I'll make it up to you. My wife is having dinner with some of her bridge club friends tomorrow evening, and after that she's going to Scottsdale to spend a couple of days with her sister. I'll be free for the rest of your visit."

"Oh!" I said again. This time there was no disappointment in my voice. "I'll be ready for you when you get back."

"And you'd better be naked," John said firmly.

If Reed was half the man John was, I would be the happiest woman on the planet.

I was tempted to call Lola and brag about all the fun I was having, but the last thing I wanted to do was make her jealous. I loved my girl, but I knew she envied the fact that I had a husband (even though it was only Reed) and that I was John's club favorite.

I hoped that things worked out the way Lola wanted between her and Calvin. Her ultimate goal was marriage. If she got that far with Calvin, at least she would have a husband who earned a decent living, and maybe she could stop working. If he decided he didn't even want to take the relationship to the next level, I hoped he would be man enough to let her down gently so she wouldn't take it too hard. If he didn't she would come undone, and I would have to help her pick up the pieces.

On the other hand, if Lola decided Calvin was not the man she'd been fantasizing about and didn't want to see him after their big date, she'd come undone anyway. And I'd still have to help her pick up the pieces.

CHAPTER 44
LOLA

Last night, Calvin escorted me all the way from the hotel to the corner of my street. And before he left, he got into the passenger seat of my car and spent fifteen minutes kissing and fondling me. "Lola, this has been one of the most amazing days of my life," he told me.

"I feel the same way," I panted as I nibbled on his ear.

"I have never met a woman like you," he added.

I didn't say the same thing about him, because I didn't want to sound too corny. But bells were ringing in my head. I thought I had died and gone to heaven. No man had ever been so open and passionate with me! I didn't care if he knew where I lived, but I was glad he didn't want to know, at least not yet. I didn't want to invite him to the house while Libby and her crew were still living with us. "I can't wait for Saturday to get here," I whispered in his ear. He kissed me one more time before he got out of my car.

I checked my cell phone before I continued on my way and saw that Bertha had left five messages. I dreaded going home. Libby and her family were at the bowling alley — their weekly pastime — and Bertha was sitting on the living-room couch when I shuffled into the house. "Where have you been all this time?" she asked with a worried look on her face.

"Um, I went out for drinks with my coworker to celebrate her birthday. Then we went to a movie," I lied.

"Oh. Well, the next time you're going to be a few hours late, I wish you'd call and let me know." Bertha wobbled off the couch and marched up to me. She surprised me with a hug, because she rarely showed me any affection. "I thought maybe some maniac had got his hands on you."

"You don't have to worry about that. If one ever grabs me he'll curse the day he picked me, because I will give him a hell of a run for his money."

I hurried up to my room so I could savor the good feeling I had because of Calvin. I was anxious to tell Joan what a fantastic lover he was, and that I was going to see him again on Saturday. But I couldn't wait to see the look on her face when I told her about his invitation to spend a weekend in Frisco with him on his birthday in July.

She told me last night that she would call me as soon as she checked into her hotel. But I really didn't expect to hear from her at all until she returned to California. I certainly didn't expect to hear from Reed at a quarter to nine Thursday morning, the same day she left. When I saw his name on my caller ID, my heart started pounding like a drum and my stomach turned. I hated having a conversation with Reed unless it was in Joan's presence. I had a hard time keeping up with all the lies I told him to cover her butt.

"Hello, Reed. It's so nice to hear from you," I said, struggling to keep the bile from rising in my throat.

"Hello, Lola. Have you heard from Joan? I know that you're the only person who knows exactly where she decided to go. She told me that before she left."

"No, I haven't heard from her yet. But I'm sure she made it to, uh, her destination all right."

"Hmmm. Now I'm a little worried. All I know is that she went to Santa Rosa on a Greyhound bus this morning, because I found a receipt for the round-trip ticket she purchased. It doesn't take that long to get there, so she should have arrived already. I don't know the name of her hotel. That little devil has probably already lined up a few winery tours between her mud bath appointments." I was glad when Reed chuckled. I chuckled too. Mine was so forced, it sounded hollow and fake, even to me.

"I know she's going to have a good time. I think her getting away by herself for a few days will make a big difference in her morale. She's been down in the dumps lately."

"Yeeaaaah." He stretched the word out so long it sounded like he'd suddenly developed a Southern accent. Reed was one peculiar man. I felt sorry for my girl for getting stuck with an oddball like him, but I was glad it was her and not me. "Lola, I don't know what all Joan told you about our recent spats, but I want you to know that I love her from the bottom of my heart. I get a little goofy from time to time, but all I care about is keeping Joan happy."

"I know that, Reed," I said meekly.

"I know you have no frame of reference, so you don't know how rewarding marriage is — especially when it's with the right person."

"I hope I find out soon." I was so anxious to end this call, my mouth was watering.

"By the way, I'm not in the habit of playing matchmaker that often, but I have a couple of single friends I can introduce you to."

"You don't have to do that. I know a lot of single men. I had a date Thursday with a real nice guy and I'm seeing him again this Saturday. But thanks for the offer. If I change my mind and want to take you up on it, I'll let you know."

"Well, Lola. Whoever this 'real nice guy' is, I hope he's worthy of your time."

"Thanks, Reed. Now if you don't mind, I have to go. I'm running late and I have to be at work by nine. If I hear from Joan I'll let you know. She was probably too tired after her flight."

"Her *flight*?"

"Huh? Oh! I meant her bus ride," I said as fast as I could form the words. "Traveling on a Greyhound bus can wear a person out. When my mother took me to Disneyland on one before she died, we were so tired when we got there we went straight to bed. Don't worry about Joan. Greyhound buses aren't that reliable so it could be that it was behind schedule. . . ."

"Well, just make sure you let me know

when you hear from her. Bye now."

"Bye, Reed. It was nice talking to you."

Thursday was a long, rough day. I had to deal with one difficult customer after another. Despite my bad day, I was so excited about my upcoming date with Calvin, love juice was flowing out of me like somebody had stuck a faucet up into my vagina. I had gotten so wet at one point during the day, I had to run to the restroom and plug myself up with a tampon.

And, of course, there was Libby. I didn't even want to go home. There was so much tension between us now, I avoided her as much as I could. She did the same thing. I didn't want Bertha or Jeffrey to get suspicious and start asking questions, so in front of them I forced myself to converse with Libby. No matter what I said to her, she replied with one- or two-word responses. When I got home, I was pleased to hear that Libby and her crew had gone out for the evening. On the days that Bertha served chitlins they bolted to one of their favorite restaurants. This time they had gone to Red Lobster. Just having Libby out of the house for a few hours eased some of my discomfort. But I was not going to eat any chitlins for dinner myself. Nothing gave me *long-term* gas quicker than those things, so I no longer ate any within two or three days of a date I had scheduled. I ate a ham sandwich instead. Afterward, I gave Bertha a back rub and then I went to my room and turned on my laptop.

There was a message in my club in-box from a rancher in Waco, Texas, who wanted to chat with me by Skype, with both of us in the nude. I deleted his message without responding. I was not interested in chatting with another man — especially a naked cowboy on Skype — until after I knew how things were going to work out with Calvin.

"Good morning, everybody. Libby, that new eye shadow looks good on you," I said when we all gathered at the kitchen table for breakfast around eight Friday morning.

"Ummm," was all she said. Why she followed that peculiar response with a smile baffled me. I think it was more for Bertha and Jeffrey's benefit. Bertha gave me a curious look. Jeffrey gave me a mild shrug.

Awkward silence followed and hung in the air like a black curtain. If Bertha hadn't spoken again half a minute later, I would have. "Kevin, sit up straight and say grace for us," she ordered.

"Aw, come on, Grandma. Do I have to? We ain't in church so why I got to be praying?" Kevin complained, still slouched in his seat. He had already started scarfing down his food.

"Say the blessing, son," Jeffrey ordered.

We all bowed our heads. With an exaggerated sigh of impatience and a chunk of bread in the back of his jaw, Kevin blurted out a hasty blessing. "Good bread, good meat. Lord, let us eat." I laughed along with everybody else, but I was still apprehensive. I couldn't wait to leave the house.

Just knowing that I was going to see Calvin again — twice in the same week — had kept me from going off the deep end the past couple days. He had sent me a text during the night, but I didn't see it until nine a.m., just before I opened my cash register. I read it twice.

Hello, BrownSugar. I can't wait to spend more time with you! Until I see you tomorrow, stay beautiful. Yours truly, RamRod.

I was so overjoyed I wanted to dance a jig and text him back. But I couldn't because I was at my workstation and there were customers already in the store. As usual, the other cashier who worked the same shift was late. I had to wait for Tyrone, the Cottrights' grandson, to come in before I could take my morning break and text Calvin back.

Twenty minutes before noon, Mrs. Cottright shuffled up to the check-out area. There was an exasperated look on her jowly face. She glanced at her watch and then at me. "Lola, Tyrone just called to say he won't be in today."

"Again," I replied, rolling my eyes.

"I know running the show by yourself is stressful, and I don't want you to wear yourself out. Ann Beasley, that girl who works on weekends, is on her way. Starting Monday, she'll be working weekdays, full-time. And she'll be working the same shift you work. Tyrone don't know it, but whenever he drags his tail back up in here, I'm going to hand him his walking papers. I guarantee you he'll show up at the unemployment office on time if he wants to get paid. I don't care if he is my daughter's son, that boy is useless!"

I was so excited about my upcoming date, I didn't care who covered the other register that day or any other day, or that Tyrone was going to be out of a job.

"Will Ann get here soon? I need to take a bathroom break," I said quickly and in a dry tone. I didn't even try to hide my impatience.

"She's on her way, but I'll cover the

register so you can go rest yourself for a while." Mrs. Cottright glanced at her watch again. "Just be back in ten minutes because by then I'll have a full bladder, and you know when a woman reaches my age every organ in her body has a life of its own."

When I got to the restroom, I whipped my cell phone out of my pocket. Instead of texting Calvin, I called him. My heart skipped a beat when I heard his voice.

"Hello, Lola."

I didn't know if it was my imagination or what, but his voice sounded even sexier than before. A warm tingle ran up my spine. I had to cough to clear my throat and my head. I told myself, *If this man is half as good with his dick as he was on Tuesday, I'm going to die of ecstasy.* "Um, I'm sorry I didn't respond to the text you sent. I didn't see it until I got to work this morning. And we've been so busy, this is my first break today."

"I hope we're still on for Saturday. Two p.m. is a good time for me. I know the concierge, and he told me I could check in even earlier," he said.

"Yes, we are, and two is the best time for me." I tried not to sound too excited. "Tuesday was nice, but I'll be glad when Saturday gets here so we can *really* get to know one another. It's been a long time . . .

uh . . . coming."

"*Coming?* Pun intended, I hope." Calvin laughed and I did too.

"Well, it is what it is." I suddenly felt so awkward, I didn't know what to say next. I said the first thing that came to my mind. "Is there anything you want me to bring this time?"

"Such as?"

"One of my previous dates was a little on the kinky side," I mumbled. "His screen name is 'CrazyHorse.' " I hadn't told Joan about my date with the freaky stockbroker from Tacoma, Washington. I knew if I ever did, she would tease me for days. I felt comfortable enough with Calvin to tell him though.

"Hmmm. Kinky like handcuffs and, uh, other things along those lines?"

"That and me spanking his naked ass with a wooden paddle for him being a bad boy by cheating on his wife with me. He didn't want to take a chance on the security people searching his luggage at the airport and seeing his toys, so he gave me a list of things to pick up from an adult store to bring with me."

"You paddled the dude's ass?"

"Yes, I did. Right after I put the handcuffs on him. And I kid you not, it was hard for me to keep a straight face when he told me all the things he wanted me to do to him."

"No shit? Well, I've done some outlandish shit myself, but I've never tried any of that. I'm very broad-minded and flexible though. I want you to know that I'm open to almost anything." Calvin stopped talking for a few seconds. Before I could speak again, he continued. "I'm getting excited right now."

"Me too," I admitted.

"I don't know if phone sex is considered kinky, but I'm game if you are."

"Um, as tempting as that sounds, I'd better not. I'm in the employee restroom. The door is locked, but the walls are thin. My bosses are elderly, and if they wandered close enough and heard me in here moaning and groaning, they'd probably call the paramedics first and ask questions later." We both laughed.

CHAPTER 45
CALVIN

Before I discovered Discreet Encounters, I had hooked up with a few other women that I'd met on other sites. But so far the only one I'd eliminated was that escort named Cherry. In her case, the list of potential suspects had to be a mile long. Since I'd been smart enough to use a fake name, my real name was not on that list.

The media reported so much crime, it was hard to keep up with it. I read the newspaper every day and watched the TV news when I could. According to one recent report, the investigation into Adele "Miss Honey" Beaumont's murder was "ongoing." A homeless man had stumbled across her body in that alley the day after her doomed encounter with me.

Just like I had predicted, her vicious pimp — who had already served time for brutalizing some of his other women — had been named as the prime suspect.

I made it to Sylvia's house at exactly seven Friday evening. I enjoyed the lavish dinner she had cooked: turkey wings, corn bread dressing, mustard greens, mashed potatoes, and yams. For dessert, I enjoyed an hour of raw sex.

"We need to make love more often. You almost wore me out," she whimpered as she lay in my arms in her bed.

Even though Sylvia had cried out in pain and begged me to be more gentle, I had pumped into her like it was going out of style. She had "complained" about my lovemaking before, so this was nothing new to me. Sometimes I got aggressive in bed, but I couldn't help myself. My rage had become so profound I had to take it out on *somebody*. Besides, rough sex turned me on, especially after my last conversation with Lola. I couldn't wait to get her into bed again. Instead of strangling, shooting, or beating the bitch, *fucking* her to death was another possibility. Just thinking about that excited me.

"Sylvia, baby, sometimes when I'm with you, I get so caught up in the moment I get carried away. I'm so sorry," I apologized.

"Don't worry about it, Calvin. I know you

missed me as much as I missed you. Before you go on your next run, we should get together every night. That way, when you get back in town you won't be so energetic."

"That's cool, baby."

"Why don't we get up and go to your place so you can pick up a few clothes and stay with me the whole weekend? Or I can pack a bag and go home with you and stay until you go out on your next run. My new neighbors, Jose and Rosa Garcia, are hosting a cookout tomorrow afternoon at one to celebrate their tenth wedding anniversary. I don't want to go alone, and I've told them so much about you, they're dying to meet you. Jose also served in Afghanistan, so I'm sure you two will get along like old friends."

"I'd love to meet Jose and Rosa, but at one in the afternoon? That's kind of early in the day for me to party with people I don't even know."

I eased Sylvia out of my arms and sat up. The only light was coming from the screen of the muted TV facing the bed, so the room was pretty dim. I was glad because I didn't want to see the look of disappointment on her face.

"We don't have to be there that early. I doubt if it'll start on time anyway." Sylvia paused and chuckled. "You know Mexicans are as bad as we are when it comes to doing things on time. I'm sure it'd be okay if we got there around two, or even later."

"I wish they'd planned it for later in the day. Besides, I have plans for tomorrow afternoon."

"Aw, Calvin, come on!" Sylvia hollered. She sat bolt upright with her face so close to mine I could feel her hot breath on my cheek. "Baby, you just got home a few days ago. I thought you'd want to spend as much time with me as possible."

"I do, honey, and I will. But I promised my boy Rudy that I'd go fishing with him and a couple of our buddies tomorrow. I cancelled on him last month because I had to go to Chicago. Now he's really looking forward to me going out on the water with him on that fancy new boat he just spent a fortune on."

"You know, going out on the open water on a fancy new boat sounds like a lot of fun. Would you do me a favor and ask Rudy if it's okay for me to tag along? I don't really want to go to the Garcias' cookout anyway."

"Sweetheart, there won't be any other women on board. Besides that, we're going to be drinking, talking a lot of male bullshit — that might offend you — and doing a lot of other shit you would not enjoy. Remember how you almost fainted when I tried to show you how to bait a fishhook the last time I took you fishing?"

"Yeah. I'll never forget that."

"And you were so prissy, you complained the whole time about having to hide behind a bush to use the bathroom."

"Ewww! I damn sure remember that. That was not a pleasant experience. Oh well. I'll keep my prissy ass off Rudy's boat. Are you going to be gone the whole afternoon?"

"Pretty much."

"What time do you think you'll be home?"

"I'm not sure."

"If it's not too late, maybe you can still come to the party. I'd hate for you to spend all that time on a boat with a bunch of musty, beer-guzzling men. After all you've been through lately, you need as much tender loving care as you can get."

In less than twelve hours, the next phase of my plan would take place. In addition to getting all the sex I could on our next (and possibly our last) date, I hoped to find out enough about Lola so that I could proceed with the final phase of my plan in a timely manner.

It was a good thing I knew how extensive her dating habits were. From what she'd told me, and from the club's reviews, she had been with numerous other club members — some more than once. There would be a very long list of suspects when she disappeared. Even if my name came up and some busybody cop questioned me, I had my impressive record as a marine with an honorable discharge to fall back on. I had never been arrested and I had no history of violence. Nobody would suspect me of harming somebody, especially a woman.

CHAPTER 46
JOAN

The weather in Phoenix was very mellow, but I didn't leave the hotel to do any shopping or sightseeing like I had considered before the trip. I purchased a key chain and a coffee mug for Lola in the hotel gift shop, but I couldn't buy anyone else souvenirs that were obviously from Phoenix, because I didn't want them to know where I'd been. I did buy a huge, generic box of chocolate candy for my greedy cousin, Too Sweet, to go along with the two hundred bucks she'd charged me to keep an eye on Junior until Reed got home.

I'd brought my laptop with me so I could keep up my online activity. I was pleased to see that DrFeelGood had sent me a message a couple of hours after I left California. He wanted to schedule a date for next month. I e-mailed him back and told him to let me know which dates he had in mind. I also reminded him that I was still thinking about his offer to perform free cosmetic surgery on me. I just didn't know how I was going to get away from Reed long enough without a hassle. Going away on my own for just a few days was one thing, but a couple of weeks was another. Somehow I was going to go to Palm Beach and let DrFeelGood redo my face and body!

I was pleased to see that a new club member had also left a message in my club in-box. Bryce O'Grady introduced himself, commented on the rave reviews about me, and requested a date. His screen name was "Suck&Blow." Like one of my previous partners, he was also a computer guru from Bar Harbor, Maine. He had an important meeting to attend in Silicon Valley in a couple of weeks. On his profile page he'd posted a picture of himself in a tuxedo. Not only did he look prosperous, he was quite handsome in a Vin Diesel kind of way. Even though my mighty big plate had so much on it already, I made a note to e-mail Bryce back in a day or so.

The only other e-mail I had received since I left home was from a ritzy prep school guidance counselor in Boise, Idaho. His screen name was "TrickyDick." He told me that looking at my picture had really turned him on, but he didn't want to get together with me in person. His request was too weird for words. He was very straightforward about how he was interested only in having either phone sex or a date by Skype while he masturbated. He was so homely and overweight, I would never hook up with him in a hotel, even if he changed his mind and wanted to meet me in person. Instead of ignoring him, like so many other women he'd complained about, I e-mailed him back and told him I wasn't interested. And I was nice enough not to tell him why.

To help kill some of the time I had to spend on my own, I worked out in the hotel fitness center and visited the bar a couple of times. Several men traveling alone attempted to pick me up in both places, but I declined. Even though my actions the last couple of years were not much different from those of a whore — an *unpaid* whore — I didn't want strangers to treat me like one.

Each time I returned to the luxurious suite I watched on-demand movies and game shows on the massive flat-screen TV. When I got tired of that, I read boring publications like the *Wall Street Journal* and *Newsweek,* which John had left in the room. Waiting for him to return was hard. But when he did, we made up for it. We had sex every way imaginable, even with him sitting on the commode with me in his lap.

Our last night together, he left the room around ten. But not before asking me again if I wanted to leave Reed and move to Phoenix. This time I didn't say no. Instead I told him, "Let me think about it for a while."

"Joan, I care about you. But I'm not such a young man anymore. I want to enjoy the good years I have left, and there is no woman I'd rather spend that time with more than you. Besides, there is no reason why you should stay with a man who makes you so miserable."

John and I had discussed a lot of things since the first time we got together. He had told me more than once how unhappy he was in his marriage. There were several reasons why he stayed with a woman he no longer loved. The youngest of his three children was still in high school. Another reason was because Mrs. Walden's health was so fragile. She had lupus, diabetes, and conditions I had never even heard of. She cried when they watched sad movies, fainted at the sight of blood, and couldn't wear perfume because it made her sneeze. And she was from a very prominent and wealthy family. They supported a lot of worthy causes by donating thousands of dollars at a pop. Her father socialized with some powerful media representatives who could ruin John's name if he created a scandal by leaving his sickly wife.

All I had told him about my marriage was that I had fallen out of love with my controlling husband, I was extremely miserable, and I wanted a divorce. I still didn't want to discuss Reed's fascination with suicide with too many people. Lola was the only person I had discussed it with in the past few months.

"Joan, I *have* to stay in my marriage, but you don't. Get out now while you're still young," John insisted. "Is your son the only reason you stay with what's-his-face?"

"Yes!" I said quickly. "Maybe in a few years when Junior finishes high school, he'll be able to deal with a divorce."

"I see." John paused and let out a loud breath. "I'll be attending several business meetings in California in the next few months. I hope you'll find a way to spend most of my free time with me."

"Honey, I will," I assured him, nodding my head so hard my neck hurt.

I actually cried when I left the hotel to go to the airport on Sunday morning in the same town car with the same chauffeur. The airport was so crowded and hectic there were no seats available at my gate, so I had to stand. I thought that was bad enough until they announced that my flight was going to be delayed by forty-five minutes.

After a trip to the restroom, I made a beeline for the nearest bar. Right after I placed my order for a Bloody Mary, I pulled out my cell phone and called up Lola to see if she could give me a ride home from the airport. Picking up a rental car was out of the question. I couldn't use the credit card I had borrowed from her because I'd have to show some form of identification. And I didn't want to use my credit card because it would leave a paper trail that Reed might stumble upon, and I'd have a lot of explaining to do. Especially since I'd planted that Greyhound bus ticket receipt for his benefit. I was anxious to talk to Lola anyway to see if she had met up with Calvin on Tuesday. My call went straight to voice mail, so I took a cab home.

I walked into my living room a few minutes after eleven a.m. I was surprised and pleased to see that Reed was nowhere in sight. I immediately called Too Sweet to let her know I had returned so she could bring Junior home, but he wanted to stay a few more hours. Since I was alone, and tired and sore as hell, I decided to take a brief nap.

Reed came home a few minutes before noon. I was still lying on the bed when he entered the bedroom, belching, farting, and humming our favorite Beyoncé tune, "Halo."

"Hey baby! You're home!" he slurred. He stumbled over to the bed and plopped down on my side. He started kissing up and down my neck, even though I was playing possum.

"Baby, wake up and let me love you before my damn dick falls off!" he hollered. I could hear him unzipping his pants. "Joan, wake up, wake up, *wake the fuck up*!" He pinched my cheek and smacked my butt so hard, I flinched. By the time I opened my eyes, he was completely naked. He sat on the side of the bed, slid his clammy hand under my dress, and started tugging on my panties. The expression of a sex-crazed madman was on his face.

"I . . . hello, honey," I whimpered. "I missed you." John had sexed me so thoroughly, my body was still tingling. Just the thought of the few quick and clumsy humps I was about to get from Reed now literally reduced me to tears.

"I know you're glad to be home, but don't

cry, honey. I'm with you now, and I'm going to give you what you want," Reed muttered. He began to caress my shoulder, but I kept crying. "I'm going to take real good care of this sweet little pussy!" he growled. When he pinched the lips of my vagina, I experienced a full-body spasm and started shaking like a leaf.

"Reed, I —"

"Shhh!" He cut me off so abruptly and mounted me so fast, I couldn't even resist. "Just look at you! Your body is twitching so hard you can't wait to get this good dick!" The last thing I wanted to do was have sex with him while I was still sore from my workout with John. But Reed was determined to get what he wanted. I didn't want to get raped again, so I decided to just lie there and count the seconds that it would take for him to satisfy himself. He ripped my panties off and flung them across the room, where they landed on top of my computer. "I know you've missed my good loving, but don't worry. I'm about to make up for it."

I was still crying when he finished a minute later.

CHAPTER 47
LOLA

Right after I got out of bed Saturday morning a few minutes before eight, I turned on my computer. Before I could check my e-mail, an instant message popped up on my screen. It was from Elbert!

> Good morning, Lola. I'm just checking to see what time you want me to pick you up today. Your boy, Elbert

"Pick me up for what?" I asked myself out loud. I darted across the floor to my cell phone on the nightstand so I could give Elbert a call. He must have already had his cell phone in his hand, because he answered halfway through the first ring. "Good morning, Elbert. I just read your instant message. What is it you're supposed to be picking me up for today?"

"Well . . ." he began slowly, "last week when I invited you to go to the bingo

398

tournament with me today, you said you'd love to go. Did you forget?" I could hear the disappointment creeping into his voice. "I hope you didn't, because I've really been looking forward to spending some time with you again. There will be a lot of people there, so we need to arrive before eleven if we want to sit at one of the front tables."

The difference between my feelings for Elbert and Calvin was that I thought about Elbert only when we were together in person or communicating by telephone or online chat. I thought about Calvin almost every hour of the day. "Elbert, I am so sorry. It slipped my mind and I made other plans for today." I was truly sorry. I didn't like to hurt or disappoint anybody, because I knew from experience how painful that was. Elbert was such a sweet, loyal, innocent man. He reminded me of a hamster I owned when I was a little girl. But I didn't even remember telling him that I'd see him *today*. And I was not about to pass up an afternoon of passion with the man I'd been obsessed with for so long to attend a bingo tournament with Elbert! Especially since he was about as likely to have sex with me as the pope.

"I see." His voice was so distant now, it sounded like he was talking through the opposite end of the phone.

"I hope it's not too late for you to ask somebody else to go with you. What about your mother?"

"She's on her way to the flea market with Sister Barnes from next door, and that's always an all-day affair for those two."

"Elbert, I feel terrible about this," I said, trying to sound as if I was disappointed too. "I knew I should have told Bertha to remind me about the bingo tournament." I paused because the words were flying out of my mouth so fast I lost my breath for a few seconds. "Can I take a rain check? We can do something else you like real soon."

Elbert took his time replying. "Yeah, we can do something else. What about the hot-air balloon race in Fresno next Saturday? I know you'd have a good time, because I go every year and I always enjoy myself."

I had no idea what had made me agree to go to a *bingo tournament.* Now a hot-air balloon race? I . . . could . . . not . . . believe . . . my . . . ears! "Check with me next Wednesday or Thursday. I'll let you know then."

"Okay," Elbert muttered. "Um, if I'm not being too nosy, what other plans did you make for today?"

"Huh? Oh! I'm going to Reno with a girlfriend I haven't seen in a while. We might

400

spend the night up there, so I'm not sure when I'll be back home."

"Well, I hope you have a good time. I'll call you next week."

I hung up, but I stared at the telephone in my hand for a few seconds. As a couple, Elbert and I were going nowhere in the future — except to bingo games, church events, and cheap restaurants. I decided that it was time for me to end our "relationship" so he could find a woman on his level. I didn't want to hurt him, so I planned to ease out of it gradually. In the meantime, I had a much bigger fish to fry. . . .

My date with Calvin in a few hours made me feel the way I used to feel on Christmas morning when I was a child. I was so excited I could barely stand it!

When I went downstairs a few minutes after my conversation with Elbert, Bertha had already prepared my favorite breakfast: grits, bacon, ham, eggs, and biscuits. A pot of coffee was brewing on the stove.

Jeffrey, Kevin, and Libby were already seated at the kitchen table smacking on their food and talking about watching a football game that Jeffrey had recorded. He planned to watch it tomorrow in Bertha's living room along with Libby and a bunch of their beer-guzzling friends who had missed the original showing. Bertha hated sports as much as I did. But she was going to watch the game too. She had already cooked up a huge batch of buffalo wings, made enough spinach dip to feed an army, and purchased several six-packs of Corona beer — the only brand Libby would drink. I knew that Bertha was making a mighty effort to keep her happy, but I didn't see any difference in Libby's demeanor.

"What's wrong with you, Mama? That coffee will be nothing but mud by the time you serve it!" Libby yelled. Bertha sprang up out of her seat like a Ping-Pong ball and trotted to the stove, even though Libby was closer.

"I'm sorry, sweetie," Bertha apologized, and poured coffee into Libby's cup.

"And don't you forget to make sure we have enough ranch dressing, carrot sticks, and celery to go with the wings tomorrow."

Jeffrey cleared his throat and gave Libby a critical look. "Baby, I told you that I'd take care of all that. Bertha's done more than enough already."

"Then you'd better pick up a couple more six-packs too. You remember how upset everybody got when we watched the Super Bowl at the Whitakers' house last month and ran out of beer before half time."

"Libby, don't worry about anything," Jeffrey insisted, rolling his eyes. He took a deep breath and turned to me. I had poured myself a cup of coffee and remained standing in front of the stove. "Damn, Lola. You must have had a hell of a rough night. Looks like you didn't sleep well," Jeffrey exclaimed, giving me a pitiful look. He had never said a mean word to me, so I knew he was not trying to be mean now. He was just making an observation. But if Libby had told me the same thing, I would have been offended.

"Lola always looks this way," she murmured out the side of her greasy mouth, just loud enough for me to hear.

"I didn't feel too well last night," I said, pulling out the chair next to her, and only because it was the only one available.

"You don't have to work today, so you should get some rest," Bertha told me. "You don't want to be too tired to watch that ball game with us tomorrow, sweetie."

"I feel just fine now, but I won't be watching that game tomorrow." I would rather get a whupping than sit in front of a TV and watch *any* ball game. As soon as the words left my mouth, all eyes were on me. "I'm going to meet up with one of my former classmates this afternoon," I announced. "We're going to drive up to Reno today, and we might spend the night." I didn't know how much time I was going to spend with Calvin, but I was prepared to stay as long as he wanted, even the whole night.

"I hope you'll be back home in time to drive me to my foot doctor's office before you go to work Monday morning. My appointment is for seven-thirty. You know how much I hate having to take cabs and buses," Bertha complained.

Libby's and Jeffrey's vehicles were much more comfortable and reliable than mine. But when Bertha needed to go somewhere, she usually asked me to take her.

"Mama, I can drop you off on my way to work Monday morning," Jeffrey said, giving me a wink.

It seemed like there was no way for me not to ruffle Libby's feathers. Out of the corner of my eye, I saw the hot look she shot in my direction when Jeffrey winked at me.

I was glad when she got up and left the kitchen, pulling Jeffrey away by his hand.

When Bertha and Kevin left the room, I started cleaning up.

Fifteen minutes later, when I was drying the last of the dishes, Libby returned. "Lola, why don't you use the dishwasher?" She opened the refrigerator and snatched out a bottle of Corona. She removed the cap with her teeth like a roughneck hillbilly and blew it into the trash container next to the sink. And then she took such a long pull, the bottle was half-empty when she stopped.

"I don't mind washing the dishes by hand," I said, trying to sound as nonchalant as possible. "Sometimes our dishwasher doesn't do the job completely."

"Whatever." Libby lifted her chin and stared at me with her eyes narrowed. "I hope you forgot about what you saw that day. . . ."

"You mean you and that dude?" I said with one eyebrow raised, placing a hand on my hip. I threw in a mighty neck roll for emphasis, a gesture Libby often displayed. "We don't need to talk about you having sex with that man anymore."

"*Shhh!* You want everybody in the house to hear my business?"

"You brought it up, Libby. I hadn't given it any more thought since it happened."

"Maybe not, but I know how you like to yip-yap with the neighbors and those chatty hens at the beauty shop. You haven't mentioned it to anybody yet, and you won't." I couldn't tell if Libby was making a statement or a threat.

Chapter 48
Lola

It didn't matter if Libby and I were involved in a dispute or not, the impact of our volatile relationship had begun to take a serious toll on me. Lately, just her presence was enough to make me want to move out of Bertha's house and not look back. I knew in my heart that it would come to that someday. I was almost at a point where I didn't care what happened to Bertha if I left her at the mercy of her children. With or without a husband to fall back on, I had to think about holding on to my sanity. I had lost some of my dignity years ago, but I was determined to restore it — once I had "escaped."

"Did you hear what I just said?" Libby asked with her neck rolling and her finger wagging in my face.

"I heard you. As long as you don't give me a reason to discuss it with anybody, I won't," I responded.

"I love my husband."

"Sure you do. I can tell."

"Whether you know it or not, Jeffrey and I are very happy together, so don't you even think about causing trouble between us."

"You're worried about *me* causing trouble between you and your husband? I suggest you tell that to the man you brought to the house and fucked on your mama's couch."

Libby gasped. "I don't know who you think you are messing with, but you need to watch your step, girl. I could make you very uncomfortable and you know it!"

"I could make you even more uncomfortable too. Now if you don't mind, I need to finish the dishes so I can go get ready to meet my friend."

Libby stayed in the kitchen while I finished up, and then I headed toward the staircase. Less than two minutes after I got to my room, she barged in still clutching her beer bottle, which was now almost empty. She closed the door and sat down next to me on my bed. She seemed bewildered. I had no idea what she was about to say or do this time. I was scared.

"Lola, can I talk to you? I know you're leaving in a little while, so I won't take long."

"What about?" I scooted a few inches

away from her and folded my arms. "I thought you'd said all you had to say to me about me keeping your business with Greg to myself."

"I'm through talking about that," she said as she waved her hand. "I swear, if you don't bring it up again, I won't either." For the first time, Libby seemed almost bashful. She could barely look me in the eye. She kept clearing her throat and blinking. All this was even more disturbing than her sitting next to me on my bed — something she'd never done before. "We'll be out of here by summer, and I'd like to get along with you a little better so it'll be easy for you to tolerate me, and vice versa."

By *summer*? We were only in *March*. Just the thought of spending a few more *days* living under the same roof with Libby chilled me to the bone. Several more months would be like a prolonged illness. "That's a long way off," I said with a mighty gulp.

"I know it is. I don't like it any more than you do, but it is what it is." Libby actually seemed nervous. And that made me nervous. "Uh, I'd like to talk to you about something else." She drank some of her beer and then she exhaled. I noticed a tremor in her hand, and I couldn't imagine what was causing it. "I hope you know that I don't mean all the nasty things I say to you."

I almost choked on my tongue. "Excuse me? Then why do you say so many nasty things to me?"

"It's just my nature. It's a way for me to feel like . . . uh . . . like I'm somebody."

I was curious now. I didn't think this woman had a humble or remorseful bone in her body. I wasn't so sure anymore.

I glanced at my watch.

"Don't worry about the time. It'll only take a few more minutes for me to say what's on my mind," she told me.

"Whatever it is, do you think this is a good time?"

She nodded. "Lola, I'm a real bitch to you."

I gasped and did a double take. "Oh really? Well, it took you long enough to admit it!"

"Please hear me out."

"I'm listening," I replied with my arms still folded.

"But I wasn't always a bitch. When I was in junior high and high school, I wasn't too attractive. And I was a little on the heavy side. The cute, popular girls made fun of me and the boys called me all kinds of names. The only dates I went on were with the pretty girls' rejects or the pimply faced hounds nobody else but girls like me would date."

"But you have a lot of friends now, so I assumed you'd been real popular in school."

Libby shook her head. "Only because of Jeffrey. When we got together, his friends became my friends. He was the first handsome guy to pay any attention to me. And when he did, I took him and ran. I had no idea what he saw in me, and I didn't ask. I'm forty-four years old and I look it. So far, Greg is only the second handsome man to want me. And by the way, he dumped me last night. He said you catching us must be a warning sign for him to stop cheating on his wife. He doesn't want to lose her, and I don't want to lose Jeffrey. So I'm done fooling around with other men." She stared at the floor for a few moments, and when she looked back at me I saw one of the most miserable women I'd ever seen in my life.

I had always felt sorry for Libby because she was so crude and unlikable. I figured a woman like her deserved to be pitied, not despised. I wasn't sure what I thought about her now. In a way, I wanted to hear what else she had to say. And when she did, she dropped a bombshell. "You are a very lucky woman, Lola. A woman with your looks can't even relate to what I've been through."

I had to shake my head because I wasn't sure I'd heard her right. "A woman with my looks? You . . . you think I'm pretty?" I asked, more curious than ever now. I was amazed at how cool and calm Libby was acting and sounding.

She snapped her fingers and blew out a loud *"Pffft!"* Then she said something I never thought she'd say to me. "Girl, you look like a film star. Joan does too, but don't tell her I said so. Her being the wife of a rich hunk like Reed, she already thinks her shit don't stink. So does every other female in her family. Her sister, Elaine, was a couple of years behind me in high school, but we had a few classes together. She was one of the girls who made fun of me. She was even worse when she was modeling swimsuits in L.A. and hanging out with celebrities. Every time I ran into her on the street when she came up here to visit her folks, she said something mean and nasty to me."

"I didn't know that. Joan never told me."

"She probably doesn't know. Elaine was real nice to me at Joan's wedding, so I'm sure she's forgotten how nasty she was to me when we were young. But I got the last laugh on her. I still have a husband, and she doesn't." Libby paused and gave me a pleading look. "And I want to keep my

411

husband."

"If Jeffrey ever finds out about you and Greg, it won't be from me. That's a promise."

"I'm glad to hear that. Anyway, what I'm trying to say is, I act the way I do because it makes me feel better about myself and it makes me feel special, like you must feel."

"Are you trying to tell me that you're envious of me?"

"What? Hell, no, I'm not envious of you!" Libby said hotly. Then her voice got cool and calm again. "I'm just trying to explain my behavior." She got up off the bed, still clutching her bottle. She suddenly finished what was left of her beer and let out a mild burp. "I'm too old to change, so don't get too upset when I talk trash to you the next time."

I stood up too. Had there not been such a sneer on Libby's face, I would have given her a hug.

"That's that. And I'm glad to get it over with," she said with a triumphant look. "Now, I hope you and your friend have a good time in Reno this weekend."

"I'm sure we will," I predicted. Now I wasn't so sure I was going to tell Calvin about Libby having an affair. If I did, I'd have to tell him about this conversation too.

She started backing toward the door, but I stayed in the same spot. "Thanks, Libby."

"Thanks for what?"

"For being so honest with me."

"Don't thank me. I did this more for my benefit than yours, and so you wouldn't rat me out about Greg." She gave me a sheepish grin and I just shook my head. "Like I just said, I'm too old to change my ways."

"Well, at least the next time you say something mean to me, I won't take it so hard."

"Whatever." Libby looked around the room and then back at me. "Anyway, there are always a lot of women in Reno younger and better looking than you. But I hope you and your friend meet some hot dudes up there. Marshall told me he thinks the only thing wrong with you is, you've never been properly laid. . . ."

It seemed as if the old Libby was back. My response to her comment was a mild shrug. When she realized she was not going to get a rise out of me, she plucked the latest issue of *Today's Black Woman* magazine off my dresser and pranced back out the door.

And that was that.

Since Calvin had come into my life, some things didn't irritate me as much as they used to. Even Libby. I knew I had jumped the gun, by thinking of him as my soul mate, but I had convinced myself that he was.

Everybody was in the living room when I went back downstairs. It was one p.m. and I was about to leave to go meet Calvin.

I still got a little apprehensive each time I went to a hotel to meet a date, especially when it was a man I really liked. My legs felt like jelly when I walked into the hotel lobby. I didn't know if it was because I was nervous or excited. Even though the people at the front desk didn't know me from Queen of Sheba, I didn't want them to think I was a hooker. That was the reason I always dressed conservatively, especially if it involved a hotel I visited regularly. For my date with Calvin, I decided to wear a simple white blouse with black cuffs and a knee-length black skirt with a wide white stripe on each side. Unless a date had a shoe fetish — like a TV producer from New York who'd told me a couple of months ago to wear the highest, sharpest stilettos I owned — I enhanced my prim and proper appearance with the same low-heeled black pumps I wore when I went out with Elbert.

"Dang, Lola! You look hella cool. Even your hair," Kevin acknowledged in a loud voice with a toothpick hanging off his lip.

He sat cross-legged on the floor, fiddling with his smartphone. I had pinned my hair back with a black and white barrette on each side of my head. I was surprised when Kevin gave me a smile, because he rarely did. I was not surprised by what he said next. "But with all that black and white you got on, you look like a penguin with long legs." Being compared to one of the oddest-looking creatures on the planet really poked a hole in my ego, but I didn't let it show. I gave Kevin an exasperated look and a dismissive wave, but I sucked in my stomach and laughed along with him, Libby, and Bertha. Jeffrey shook his head and frowned at Kevin.

"I hope you packed some clothes that are a little more stylish and attractive," Libby added when she stopped laughing. "The men in Reno are going to think you're an old maid librarian."

"What men?" Bertha asked. She looked at me like I had just stolen her purse. "What about Elbert? He's bringing me a rump roast from his market to cook for dinner this evening, and I know he'll ask about you... ."

I was amazed that after all the years I'd been with Bertha and all the men I'd dated (that she knew about), the one she "approved" of the most was Elbert Porter. He was a good cover for me, but he was just as boring and dull as ever. And the only time we kissed after one of our ho-hum dates, which was a couple of weeks ago, I'd kissed him. That was one night I'd never forget, and every time I thought about it, I laughed. He had walked me to the door and just given me one of his hasty, weak one-armed hugs. Without warning, I'd hauled off and kissed him long and hard. "Goodness gracious! What's gotten into you, Lola?" Elbert wailed, sliding his tongue across his lips. Then he skittered off the porch like a scared mouse. He called me the next day and made me promise I'd never behave like "a woman who'd just been released from prison" again. It was impossible for me to get mad at Elbert. He was just that lame. I laughed about his comment off and on for days. Some of the things he said and did were so amusing, I enjoyed spending time with him just for the comic relief.

"What's so funny? What are you laughing at, Lola?" Libby asked, interrupting my thoughts.

"Oh, nothing. I just thought of something funny that happened at work the other day," I replied, clearing my throat. I turned to Bertha and added, "I talked to Elbert this

416

morning. He knows I'm going to be busy today."

"Did you ask him to go to Reno with you?" she wanted to know. Despite her age, I thought Bertha knew better than to ask such a dumb question.

Libby and I gasped at the same time. And then she gave Bertha an incredulous look. I shook my head in disbelief.

"No, I didn't ask Elbert to go with us. My friend and I are only going to see a show, have a few drinks, and gamble a little," I replied. "We just want to spend some time together without having men breathing down our necks. And anyway, Elbert doesn't drink or gamble." After my last statement, I left the house in such a hurry I forgot to put my cell phone in my purse. I had planned to call the hotel to get Calvin's room number. When I stopped to get gas, I called from a pay phone. The hotel operator gave me the room number and then immediately patched me through to him. He answered right away.

"Calvin, it's Lola," I announced, trying to sound demure and aloof at the same time. I still didn't want him to know how anxious I was to be with him.

"Lola?" He paused. "Did you change your mind?" He sounded disappointed.

"Oh, no!" I said quickly. "I just called to let you know I'm on my way."

"I'm glad to hear that." He sounded relieved, but his voice was hollow and distant.

When I got to his room, hoping he was ready for me, I stood outside in front of the door and twiddled my thumbs for a few seconds, and then I knocked.

My heart started beating a mile a minute when he slowly opened the door. The fact that he was buck naked told me he was ready for me.

CHAPTER 49
CALVIN

According to her online profile, Lola was a size 6. That was a goddamn lie. And that was another thing about women that annoyed me. Unless they were the size of a piano, why did they have to lie about how big or heavy they were? Lola was at least a size 8. But her body was firm and the pounds were in all the right places.

"Lola, you don't know how happy I am to see you again!" I hollered.

"I'm happy to see you again too, Calvin." There was a dazed look on her face when I took her purse and overnight case out of her hands and set them on the dresser on the other side of the room. She looked even more dazed when I sprinted back across the floor and scooped her up into my arms. I stumbled and almost dropped her as I carried her to the king-size bed and gently laid her down on her back.

"That was a nice welcome. I wish every

man would greet me the same way." The way she was gushing, you would have thought that she had just reached nirvana. For the next few seconds, she giggled like a hyena.

I sat down next to her and massaged her knee. We chatted for five minutes about a few mundane things. Finally, I told her in a voice so low and gravelly it sounded more like a growl, "You look absolutely gorgeous. I'm glad you can stay a lot longer this time."

"I don't have to work tomorrow, so I can even stay all night if you want me to."

"Um . . . I wish. I have to get back to work tomorrow morning and I have several things I need to take care of before I get on the road, so I can't spend the night here. The room is paid for and check-out time is not until noon, so you're welcome to stay if you'd like."

"Thanks, but it wouldn't be the same here without you. I hope we can spend the whole night together the next time. . . ."

I nodded. "We'll do that, Lola."

She touched my lips with the tip of her finger. "As for today, I'm sure we'll both have a good time."

I wasn't sure about Lola, but I was going to have a good time. Women lied so much about sex, it was impossible to tell if they enjoyed it or not. But I didn't care. Especially if it was with a woman who I was going to kill anyway. Almost every time I made love to Sylvia, she told me I was the best lover she'd ever had. But that wasn't saying much. She claimed that I was only the fourth man she'd ever slept with. She'd wasted the previous ten years before me with a man who had promised to marry her someday. And he probably would have if he hadn't died of a brain aneurism two months before I met her.

Without taking my eyes off Lola's face, I stood up and placed my hands on my hips. Her eyes went straight to my crotch. She gazed at my rock-hard dick like she wanted to gnaw on it until her jaws locked, and that would have suited me just fine. "Would you like a drink? Something to eat?" I nodded toward the dresser where I had set a bottle of champagne that I had brought with me.

"I'm not really that hungry, and I don't want to drink before we . . . uh . . . I'll have something to drink in a little while."

"You're a beautiful woman, Lola," I said, giving her the biggest smile I could manage. "I want you to know right now that you don't have to do anything you don't want to do. Just tell me what *you* want."

She gave me a deadpan look, so I had no

idea what she was thinking. I didn't have to wait long to find out. "Well, we're on the same page, so I'm not going to beat around the bush, Calvin. You know why I'm here, so let's get busy." I had been with dozens of women, and except for the hookers I had never been with one as bold as Lola. I pitied the man who married her. Then I remembered — she was not going to live long enough to get married.

Since I was already naked, I didn't have to waste any time taking off my clothes. She was out of hers in record time. I removed a condom from the package I'd placed on the nightstand and promptly slid it on.

"I like a man who comes prepared," she cooed. "If we need more protection, I have some in my purse."

"That's good to know. I like a woman who comes prepared."

I was admiring the way she was admiring my generous equipment, with her eyes glistening and her mouth hanging open like a female dog in heat.

"I was so glad on Tuesday when I saw that Mother Nature had not been stingy with you," she told me with awe on her face. Her mug was now as disgusting to me as a sheep's ass. "You're packing a whole lot of meat. . . ."

"Think you can 'handle' this a little longer than the last time?" I asked. I gently stroked my dick and then wagged it in her direction. I was so hot for this woman, I was already in a cold sweat and I could feel my stomach knotting up.

"It'll be a challenge. But I love challenges." She smiled.

"I'll be gentle anyway. I don't want to hurt you or have you limping out of here like somebody shoved a baseball bat up your . . . you know." I almost laughed out loud as I thought back to a night when a horny, foul-smelling, hitchhiking bitch with an ass as wide and flat as the side of a barn insulted the size of my dick! I couldn't recall her exact words, but she had said something about seeing "more meat on a hot dog bun." I couldn't even remember if I'd enjoyed having sex with her in the cab of my eighteen-wheeler during one of my interstate runs. But I could remember how exhilarated I had felt when I choked the life out of her and left her body on the ground in a wooded area. That husky blond wench — a poor man's version of Paris Hilton — must have provided an elaborate buffet for the snakes, flies, and other creatures to gnaw on.

I shook off that disgusting memory and

returned my full attention to Lola. The sight of such a luscious woman was so intoxicating, I felt light-headed for a couple of seconds. She was like an elaborate buffet too, and I wanted to devour everything on her menu. If I could have, I would have literally eaten her alive, munching on her dainty toes first and then working my way up to her plump, juicy lips. I knew other women in their thirties who had already begun to age. But Lola hadn't. Her body was as fit as a teenage girl, and her skin was flawless. I hadn't really noticed all that on Tuesday, but I noticed it this time. Everything else about her was just the way I liked it. The best word to describe her was: perfect. My most perfect project. Lola didn't just look like Glinda, she smelled like her and moved like her.

Without another word, I climbed on top of her, plunged into her, and started grinding. She wrapped her legs around my waist, and within seconds she was bucking and rearing like a spooked stallion. Had I closed my eyes, I could have sworn that Glinda was in bed with me.

Lola got so loud when she climaxed she almost brought down the house. I covered her mouth with my hand, just like I used to do with Glinda. When she stopped yipping and started moaning, I froze. *It sounded like the same ghostly moaning noises I'd heard coming from my garage!*

Lola stopped moaning and froze too. "Is something wrong?" she asked, panting in my ear.

"No, baby," I managed. And then I began to pound into her again.

Even though I was as deep inside her vile body as I could go, it was Glinda who was deep inside me. She would be until I erased everything from my life that reminded me of her. I couldn't stop reliving the pain she'd caused me. Killing her had been the biggest thrill of my life. I kept recalling some of the events that had occurred the night I became a monster. A monster that was now out of control . . .

I had never seen a woman more beautiful than Glinda. The memories of our last encounter rarely left my mind. She had come to the house to get some more of her stuff that fatal night and to brag about the man she had been sleeping with while I was in the military. No matter how hard I tried to talk her out of leaving, she refused to listen. She taunted me, told me how much she hated me and what a lousy fuck I was. I had married her because she'd told me she was pregnant with my child. She admitted that she had used me because the other man she'd been seeing behind my back was married. The pregnancy turned out to be a false alarm, but she told me she wanted to stay married to me anyway just so she could collect my military benefits. She'd laughed when she said that. I had never physically harmed a woman until that night. Glinda's betrayal had turned me into a killing machine and now I couldn't stop.

The look on Lola's face made me pump into her as hard as I could. A woman who was not as sexually active as Lola was would have experienced a hell of a lot of pain. Knowing her and all the traffic that had traveled between her legs, she was used to it. With my mouth hanging open and my spit dripping onto her shoulder, I stared at her face as she closed her eyes, clenched her teeth, and writhed beneath me like a fish on a hook. The more I looked at that face, the more she looked like Glinda. I was glad she had closed her eyes so she couldn't see the mounting anger in mine. I got so caught up in the moment, my trembling, sweaty hands moved toward her neck. The only thing that saved her was the fact that she climaxed just in time and opened her eyes. "Oh, Calvin!" she screamed, and that was what brought me out of the trance I had drifted into.

While she continued to grind against me, begging for more, I closed my eyes and pumped into her even harder. I couldn't believe how deeply I'd pushed myself into her body. Only a woman in a coma couldn't feel the pain I was inflicting on her.

CHAPTER 50
CALVIN

"Calvin, slow down! Take it easy! You're hurting me!" Lola yelled, beating a tattoo on my back with her fists.

I slowed down my movements, and a few moments later I pulled my dick out but I stayed on top of her. I lifted myself up a few inches so I could see her face better. She looked like a deer caught in high-beam headlights. Sweat was dripping off me, splashing onto her like raindrops.

"I am so sorry, Lola," I apologized, still straddling her. "You feel so damn good inside, I got carried away." I gave her a tender look and rubbed the side of her arm.

"Oh, don't worry about it. I . . . I'm okay," she whimpered, gasping to catch her breath. "I was just as caught up in the moment as you were. I hope you don't have too much trouble explaining the scratches and bruises on your back to anyone." Her unexpected giggle put me at ease, but it also annoyed the hell out of me. She must have read my mind, because she stopped giggling and her face became serious. "Calvin, do you mind if I ask you a personal question?" The tone of her voice was so soft and meek now. She didn't seem like the same woman who'd been squealing like a stuck pig and flopping around like a seal beneath me a few minutes ago.

Her large, almond-shaped, brown eyes sparkled like jewels as she gazed at me. Her being such a whore, I wondered if she looked at every man the same way. Especially the ones she allowed to sample her luscious body.

"Sure." I was still on top of her, but at least I had stopped showering her with my sweat.

"Are you currently in a serious relationship?"

I remained as cool as I could, but the rate of my heart doubled as I tuned up my mouth to tell another lie. "No, I'm not in a serious relationship with anyone at the moment."

"Oh. I was just wondering," she mumbled. There was a skeptical look on her face. "I'm surprised to hear that a man like you is not seriously involved with someone."

"Are you?" The question must have startled her, because her body stiffened and she blinked a few times.

"I go out every now and then with a man I went to high school with. I was supposed to go to a bingo tournament with him today."

"Oh? You cancelled a date with him to be with me?"

"Not exactly. I forgot all about my date with him until he sent an instant message this morning asking me what time I wanted him to pick me up today."

"You could have cancelled on me, you know. As much as I wanted to be with you today, I don't want to interfere with anything else you have going on. Was dude mad?"

"Not really. He's so mild-mannered, it would take a lot to make him mad. There's a hot-air balloon race coming up in Fresno that he wants to take me to. I'll probably go because he is a really sweet guy and I don't like to disappoint people."

"Hmmm. Well, you haven't disappointed me." I gave her a quick peck on her forehead.

"I'm glad to hear that." She giggled *again*, and that annoying shit was about to drive me crazy!

"Are you in love with him?" Had I been

an actor, I would have collected numerous awards by now. That's how good I was. It was amazing how I was able to hide my disgust and continue speaking in my normal tone of voice when I really wanted to yell my head off and bite hers off.

"Him who?"

"The dude who wanted to take you to the bingo hall."

"No, I'm not. We're more like brother and sister. I've known him for years and he's kissed me only one time. Actually, I kissed him. He's such a devout Christian he doesn't smoke, have sex, drink, or gossip. He won't even take me to R-rated movies. One time I slipped and said a cuss word in front of him and he almost jumped out of his skin."

I lifted myself higher and gave her an incredulous look. "Now I find that hard to believe. You're a very passionate woman. Why would you be in a relationship like that?"

She shrugged. "It's a long story."

"I have long ears."

We chuckled at the same time. I was glad she was in a humorous mood. The more I gained her confidence, the easier it would be to lure her to her *final* destination.

"My stepmother likes him and he's convenient. He's so polite and nerdy it's funny, but everybody likes him. Whenever I need an escort to a social event, or if I don't want to go to dinner or a movie on my own, Elbert — that's his name — is always happy to take me."

"Well then. I guess we're in the same boat. I do see a woman from time to time, but only because she's convenient. I guess she and your mild-mannered boo are in the same boat." I laughed. When she didn't laugh along with me, I stopped. "Why do you care if I'm involved with someone?"

She shrugged. "I got pretty carried away a few minutes ago, clawing your back like a panther and beating on it like a bongo drummer. I was concerned that you might have to explain the scratches and bruises to someone, when — I mean if you make love again before your back heals."

I laughed again. I rarely laughed this much when I was with a woman. "If I do make love to another woman before my back heals, I'll keep my undershirt on," I said as I caressed my chin. "Lola, I know I was pretty rough with you and I hope I didn't scare you."

"Scare me? *Pffft!* That kinky dude with the handcuffs and paddle who I mentioned to you, if some of the things he did didn't scare me, nothing will. And, if you really want to know, I did some pretty scary things to him with that paddle."

"Can I ask you a real personal question?"

"Yeah." I detected some reluctance in her tone.

"Why did you join a sex club?"

"For the same reason everybody else joins, I guess. I like sex. I used to think about the morality issue, but I don't anymore. I mean, a woman having sex with strangers left and right sounds so . . . *trashy*. And I was raised by Christians."

"Lola, there is nothing trashy about consenting adults having sex with multiple partners. Look at it this way. Technically, it's something that millions — maybe even *billions* — of adults are doing today on some level anyway. Besides, it's been going on since biblical days."

"I know. When I reminded myself of that, I forgot all about the morality thing." She chuckled.

"What's funny?"

"My daddy was a Christian, and he cheated on my mother on a regular basis. He even moved one of his girlfriends in with us."

"Damn! Your mother must have been a very understanding woman to allow that!"

"She was, I guess. But she was so used to his affairs she didn't care what he did as long as he took care of us. Why did you ask me why I joined Discreet Encounters?"

"Well, you seem like the kind of woman who ought to be in a kitchen baking cookies and burping babies."

She gently slapped the side of my head and gave me a mock exasperated look. "Calvin, the same women who bake cookies and burp babies still need sex. I saw a movie once about these soccer moms who spent their afternoons working as escorts."

"Have you ever worked as an escort?" My chest tightened and I braced myself.

"Heavens, no! I was reluctant to join Discreet Encounters because, well, at first I thought of it as glorified prostitution."

I breathed a deep sigh of relief. Had she told me that she had sold her body the way Glinda had, I probably would have snapped. All hell would have broken loose if I'd found out she was that big of a slut! Both our lives would be over today. She would end up in the morgue, and I would end up in jail. She was disgusting! I *had* to get rid of this nasty bitch sooner than I planned to! The thought of her roaming the earth another few weeks was more than I could stand. Even though I'd decided to let her live until next month, that expiration date was subject to change. It all depended on my mood, my work schedule, and the cooperation of the beast inside me that continued to control my actions.

"There is nothing illegal about adults having consensual sex. We all have needs, and I like the idea of making love to beautiful women with no strings attached," I told her. I couldn't wait to hear her response.

"Oh. Was that the only reason you joined Discreet Encounters?"

I nodded. "I guess so."

"Do any of your friends know?"

I gave her a stony-faced look. "My friends are pretty cool, but they are not as broad-minded as I am."

"Almost every club member I've been with so far is either married or in a relationship."

"Well, like I just told you, I have a lady friend, but she's somewhat shy in the bedroom. We've been together for several years and I've never even seen her completely naked. Other than that, I enjoy her company. She's a career woman, and she is not interested in ever being a mother. I want to be a father someday, so my relationship with her has gone as far as it can go." I sniffed. "If I wanted to see you again, would it matter if I had a wife?"

"If it doesn't bother you, it doesn't bother me." Lola gave me a pensive look. "I don't like to talk about myself with too many people, but when I was a teenager, I thought I'd be married and have a couple of kids by the time I was twenty-five. Here I am in my thirties and I'm not even close."

"Have you ever been close?"

"Just once. His name was Maurice Hamilton. He was also a marine, like you. Do you remember what I told you about the commitment I made to my stepmother?"

I nodded. "You promised her and your daddy on his death bed that you would take care of her for the rest of her life. How could I forget something like that? I'm glad you shared that with me."

"She was the reason Maurice and I broke up. She *hated* him and she made sure he knew it. It got to him eventually and he couldn't stand the pressure, so he broke up with me. Bertha's interference turned out to be a blessing in disguise. As it turned out, he was into drugs and beating up on women." She paused and suddenly looked a little sad. I stroked her face and nodded, and she continued, talking slowly with a mechanical tone. She almost sounded like a robot. "My stepmother is a good person and

she means well — and I care about her —
but living with her is getting harder and
harder for me."

"Oh? What do you mean?"

"In addition to her clinging to me like a
vine and controlling my life, her children
treat me like a, well, they treat me like an
ugly stepsister."

I chuckled. "You are a stepsister, but not
an ugly one, that's for sure. Cinderella had
the ugly stepsister, *two* if I remember that
fairy tale correctly." I chuckled again and so
did she. It was obvious that she thought I
was thoroughly interested in everything she
had to say. And my sense of humor was like
icing on the cake. I decided to throw in a
little compassion. "Thanks for sharing so
much with me, Lola. Most of the women
I've been with were reluctant to be as
forthcoming as you about their personal
lives. I'm a people person, so I try to have a
good interpersonal relationship with everybody I come in contact with."

Lola stared blankly for a few seconds. And
then she smiled. "Thanks, Calvin. I don't
reveal a lot of my business to most people,
but it's so easy to talk to you. I hope I'm
not boring you."

"I'm a good listener, and it takes a lot to
bore me," I said firmly. I motioned with my

hand for her to continue, even though every word sliding out her mouth was making my ears ring with irritation.

"Anyway, my stepsister and her family recently moved in with us while their house is being renovated."

For the next hour, Lola bombarded me with more details about her home life and how miserable she was because of it. I laughed long and loud when she told me about catching her stepsister with a dude and the clumsy way the stepsister tried to offset her nasty behavior toward her. She also told me about all the lies she told her family about her social activities.

I listened with interest, and even as disgusting as she was, I admired the way her juicy lips moved each time she spoke.

Tears pooled in her eyes when she told me she was afraid of the color yellow. She had a spooky premonition that she'd die if she wore something yellow, because her mother had been laid to rest in a yellow dress. Some goofy bitch had told her at the funeral that it looked like she was the one lying in the casket. This piece of information intrigued me. Glinda's favorite color had been yellow. She'd worn a yellow blouse the day I met her. Right after we got married, she covered almost every window in our house with yellow curtains. And I'd wrapped her body in a yellow blanket the night I killed her. She was still wrapped in that yellow blanket. . . .

"I even created a fictitious invalid named Liza Mae Ford, who my stepmother thinks I'm with sometimes when I have a night-time date with a club member."

"Where did you tell your family you were going today?"

"I told them that I was going up to Reno with a girlfriend."

"It sounds like you're very creative." I laughed. "So no one knows about me?"

"Just my best friend. I tell her everything because her home life is even more miser-able than mine. She's married, but she's been in the club longer than me. She's the one who talked me into joining so I don't have to worry about her blabbing my busi-ness."

"What's her name?"

"Joan."

I held up my hand and shook my head. "No, I mean her screen name. I've been with a few sisters in the club, and I'm curi-ous to know if she's one."

"Online she calls herself HotChocolate, but you've never been with her. She only dates men who live in other states, or other countries. She's got this notion that if a member lives too close and gets too attached to her, and flips out, she'd have a fatal attraction stalking situation on her hands." Lola shook her head and rolled her eyes. I held my breath because it looked like she was going to burn my ears with another giggle. Thank God she didn't.

"Are you concerned about stalkers?" I asked.

"Not really. If a person is determined to stalk somebody, they won't let distance stop them. A couple of months ago, I saw a TV program about the man who was so obsessed with John Lennon, he traveled from Hawaii to New York to kill him. On that same show, they did a segment about an actress who was in the movie *Raging Bull* with Robert De Niro and later on one of those old TV shows. Theresa something."

"Theresa Saldana. I've read several articles about that case over the years."

"The man who tracked her down and stabbed her came from Scotland. But as far as I'm concerned, the person who lives next door can do as much damage to you as somebody who comes from the other side of the planet. It's up to us to stay alert."

"Running into a psycho was one of my concerns when I joined Discreet Encounters," I admitted.

"I hear you. There are a lot of nuts running around these days, Calvin. People are killing people for some of the most ridiculous reasons."

"Tell me about it."

"I read the paper and watch all those crime shows on the Investigation Discovery channel. Most criminals don't look like Charles Manson. They look like you and me!"

"They sure do. . . ."

Chapter 51
Lola

I felt much more comfortable with Calvin this time. I liked everything about him — so far. I felt like I could talk to him about anything. But I had no idea what made me ask the next question. "Do you ever wonder what's going through a person's head when they're killing somebody?"

Several seconds passed before he responded. "That's an interesting and morbid question. Why do you ask?"

"I wonder what a killer is thinking while he or she is stabbing or shooting somebody. At the rate murders are happening in this state alone, how can a person not think about it on a regular basis? About ten years ago, a woman who lived on my block was murdered. She was walking home from work one night and some maniac raped, robbed, and stabbed her to death two blocks from her house. Nobody was arrested for that crime. I wonder if her killer ever feels sorry about what he did, and all the pain he caused that woman's family and friends."

"That is something to think about, I guess."

"I know you didn't have a choice in the war, but I'm sure you didn't like taking any lives, even if they were the enemy."

"I sure didn't. It was very traumatic." Calvin paused for a few seconds, and then he began to speak in a very cold and controlled manner. It was as though he was reading cue cards. "Before I got deployed to Afghanistan, I'd never even hurt a fly. Life is too precious."

"I feel the same way. I don't even believe in abortions, the death penalty, or even mercy killings. People are going around shooting innocent people in schools, workplaces, movie theaters, killing family members for insurance money, and cutting up bodies and burying them like it's going out of style! The only way I'd ever kill or hurt another human being would be if I got caught up in a self-defense situation."

"I don't think a sweet woman like you needs to be concerned about that." Calvin gave me a thoughtful look. "Maybe we should get off this morbid subject and talk about something more pleasant."

"I totally agree with you, and I apologize

for bringing it up," I said quickly.

"Lola, I don't know about you, but I wouldn't mind having some steak and lobster."

"I am hungry now, so I wouldn't mind having some too." There was a smile on my face that was so extreme, it made my cheeks ache.

Room service was so busy, it took over an hour for them to deliver our orders. After scarfing down my steak and only part of the lobster, I had three glasses of champagne, which was something I'd rarely done on a date. One glass was usually my limit. When I joined Discreet Encounters, I promised myself that I'd never get drunk and let my guard down when I was with a date. For Calvin, I was willing to make an exception. I was so relaxed and tipsy, I could not keep my eyes open.

After several minutes had passed, Calvin nudged my shoulder as we lay in bed with CNN broadcasting the usual disturbing news. "Are you okay, Lola?"

"Huh?" I lifted my head off his chest and sat bolt upright, looking around the room. It took a few seconds for me to realize where I was and who I was with. There was an amused look on Calvin's face. I silently prayed that I had not done something embarrassing during my brief snooze, like blasting a few farts or drooling on his chest.

"I know I gave you a hell of a workout, so why don't you relax for a little while."

"Uh, what time is it?" I asked.

Calvin glanced at his watch. "Five minutes to six. Unfortunately, I have to get going soon."

His last sentence really got my attention. I didn't want him to leave soon, or ever. I loved everything about this man! I was so into him, my mind went haywire. All kinds of thoughts began to swim around in my head. I skipped over his marriage proposal to me, our brief engagement, and the lavish wedding we would have so I could focus on a name for our first child! But I didn't entertain these outrageous thoughts too long. I was *way* ahead of myself. My mind shifted back to the present moment and the reality of my situation. With reluctance, I reminded myself that Calvin and I belonged to a *sex club* and that was all today's encounter was supposed to be about.

Or was it?

The only way for me to find out was to ask him, but I had to have another drink first.

CHAPTER 52
CALVIN

"I hope you don't think I'm a lush," Lola mumbled. And then the greedy bitch poured herself another glass of champagne. "I don't even like alcohol that much."

"I don't think you're a lush, and all I care about is you being happy while you're with me."

She took a mighty swallow from her wineglass before she started asking me more stupid questions. "Have you ever dated the same club member more than once?" she asked shyly, which she was anything but. When it came to sex, Lola was one of the boldest women I'd ever encountered. And one of the loudest. She'd started yip-yipping and gasping almost from the minute I entered her and had kept it up until I'd satisfied her.

"Not yet," I admitted. "But I've attempted to. There was this super-fine redhead I hooked up with during one of my stopovers near San Diego. I wanted to see her a second time, and hopefully on a regular basis after that. But when I contacted her for an encore, she told me that another club member she'd seen several times had asked her to marry him. She was in her forties and had never been married, so she wasted no time accepting his proposal."

"Oh? So there are people in this club who actually marry other members?"

"It's quite common. One of the first club women I was with was married to another member. Happily married, I might add. They had an extremely 'open' relationship. They had threesomes, foursomes, and straight-up orgies with other Discreet Encounters members, as well as members of other clubs."

"Did you have a threesome or something with that woman and her husband?"

"I was with her only that one time," I said with a shrug and a frown. "I didn't really like her that much, and she was a little too wild in bed for me."

Lola's eyes got big. "Really?"

"She was so off the charts, she scared me. See, she was into biting and other aggressive shit."

Lola dropped her head. "Like me?"

"Puh-leeze!" I laughed, mainly to keep the

conversation light. "Those baby taps you laid on my back don't count." I rose from the bed and backed all the way to the dresser where I had dropped my clothes, then started getting dressed. "Listen." I paused. I had to think hard for a few seconds so I could choose the right words. "I am so glad we finally got together, Lola." I exhaled and gave her one of the most engaging smiles I could manage. "You were everything I hoped you'd be and then some. Especially today."

The surprised look on her face confused me. She was a great lover, and I was sure that I was not the first man to compliment her. "Thank you," she mumbled, dropping her head. I didn't know if her sudden shy demeanor was for her benefit or mine. One thing I did know was that she was a stone freak and a sex machine and I had pushed all the right buttons. I didn't have to be a mind reader to know what she was thinking: She was ready, willing, and able to do whatever she thought I wanted. She probably would have sucked the corns on my toes if I asked her.

"Lola, I know you're very busy with other members, but would it be possible for us to get together on a regular basis?" I already knew her answer. I could tell by the way her eyes lit up like a fluorescent light. Then her mouth dropped open. She looked as if she wanted to swallow me whole. I gave her a woeful look anyway. I wanted her to believe that I was as ditzy as she was. A woman as stupid, naïve, and love-struck as Lola wouldn't know any better.

"Yes, I'd like that," she chirped. "I would like that very much, Calvin."

I decided to say something noncommittal so she wouldn't get too carried away and do something stupid, like stalk me. "I'll be in touch." I slid my tongue across my bottom lip and rubbed the back of my head. "I just don't know when. I have a lot of hours I'd like to make up at work to offset the times I took off to go to Chicago."

"I see," she muttered. She cleared her throat and continued, speaking in a low, mechanical tone. "I'm going to be real busy myself over the next few weeks." She was obviously trying to sound as if it didn't matter one way or the other if she heard from me again.

I sat down at the foot of the bed with my back to her and began to put on my socks and shoes. "I'll give you a call in a week or so. In the meantime, I hope you don't run into somebody who'll make you not want to see me again." That comment made her perk back up. I could feel her crawling up behind me, so I turned around to face her. She leaned forward and gave me a hungry little kiss on my forehead. Then she stared into my eyes as if she were trying to see clean through me. I had never seen such desperation in my life. This woman was a real piece of work. She was enough to drive a normal man stark raving mad. No wonder she was over thirty and still single!

"I'm sure I won't," she purred, batting her lashes. "I don't, uh, date as much as I used to. . . ."

I gave her a peck on the tip of her nose and then I stood up and buttoned my shirt. "Well, a beautiful woman like you should not be spending too much time sitting at home alone — or with that stepmother and your wicked stepsister. You're a woman who needs a lot of attention, and you deserve it. Have as much fun as possible while you still can." I had to hold my breath to keep from laughing some more. There was no way Lola could know the real meaning of my words. I wanted this bitch to enjoy the time she had left, which was only a few more weeks at best. "And don't let those colorful customers you wait on at the grocery store get to you. Remember, it's just a job. And somebody has to do it. That's what I tell myself every time I climb into that eighteen-wheel contraption I'm practically married to."

A curious look crossed her face. "I thought you liked being a long-haul truck driver."

"I do," I said with a sigh as I folded my arms. My eyes were on her, but my mind was on the door and how soon I could open it and bolt. "But it can be real monotonous and lonely. Sometimes I go fifty or sixty miles at a stretch without seeing another human being on the road. Especially in farm country like Fresno and Bakersfield."

"That would drive me insane. I know it can be dangerous, but have you ever thought about picking up a hitchhiker every now and then? At least you'd have somebody to talk to. And if you deal only with female hitch-hikers, you probably wouldn't have to worry about them doing something stupid or violent to you like you would with a man."

"I've thought about doing just that. But like you said, it's dangerous. One of my coworkers gave a ride to a teenage chick along Interstate 5 a few weeks ago, and she robbed him at gunpoint."

"Oh well. Then don't give rides to strangers — male or female. I'd hate to read about you in the newspaper. It was foolish of me to suggest it." Lola had an anxious look on her face, which made me think she wanted to keep talking. But I had said all I wanted to say for now, and I had heard all I wanted to hear.

"Listen, baby, I really do hate to leave. The room is paid for, so you can stay the night if you want. My credit card is on file, so you can order more room service, watch an on-demand movie, do whatever at my expense."

"Thank you. I think I will spend the night. My folks don't expect me home until tomorrow anyway."

"Now, give me a kiss before I leave," I demanded, licking my lips and rubbing the palms of my hands together.

Lola had that deer caught in headlights look again. I strolled back toward her with my arms outstretched and my lips puckered. I probably looked like a love-struck idiot, because I sure felt like one. She jumped off the bed and shot across the floor and into my arms like a bat out of hell. We embraced in such a vigorous way, it felt as though we had suddenly become conjoined twins. Then she pressed her lips against mine so hard, mine went numb. It was the kiss of death . . . for her. BITCH! BITCH! BITCH!

CHAPTER 53
CALVIN

This was one Saturday that I would never forget. I had been with dozens of beautiful and sexy women, but not a single one had satisfied me the way Lola had. She had been so passionate and insatiable, I could barely stand it! I tried to imagine what my dick would say if it could talk. Spending so much more intimate time with her than on our previous date had done more for my morale than I thought it would.

I had already begun to feel like a changed man, and I was only going to get better, thanks to Lola. I had to fuck her at least one more time before I killed her.

My late wife was the last and only woman who had made me feel *almost* as good as Lola had. There were times when I wished I could communicate with that slut one more time. I would ask Glinda if all the pain she had caused me was worth losing her life over. I would never know, and I didn't give a damn. Fulfilling my needs was all that mattered to me now.

I wanted to finish my business with Lola more than ever now. I was afraid that if I didn't do it soon, my plans might fall apart. A tramp of her magnitude could meet another dude she liked more and move away and I couldn't find her! There was no telling what all else I'd do if that happened. I had visions of myself with an assault rifle in each hand entering a beauty parlor or a nail salon and blowing away as many bitches as I could.

I was holding in so much rage, there were times when my body felt as if it had swollen to twice its normal size. If I had already disposed of Lola, maybe the beast in my belly might not have grown so large. Some days I felt as if I'd been stuffed with sawdust. The thought almost made me laugh.

I had actually been quite amused by the stories Lola shared with me about her stepmother and stepsiblings. They sounded like three of the most fucked-up and annoying jackasses on the planet! Lola had tears in her eyes when she told me how that Bertha hag had sabotaged so many of her relationships with men. She seethed with anger and literally gnashed her teeth when she told me how mean Libby and Marshall were to her most of the time. Her problems would be all over in less than a month. She would never have to deal with those three miserable assholes again, or anybody else.

I made it to Sylvia's neighborhood just as that damn cookout she had made such a fuss about was about to end. I had a couple of beers, talked shit with some of her neighbors, and told some very tall tales about the bogus fishing trip I had told Sylvia I was going on with my buddies.

Most of Sylvia's neighbors were silly and boring. The host, Jose Garcia, was a grinning, pudgy character in dingy blue jeans and a plaid shirt. Dude liked sports as much as me, so he was pretty cool. I enjoyed conversing with him. His moon-faced, no-neck wife, Rosa, rambled on and on about one thing after another, from a diet she had just ruined to all the reality TV shows she was addicted to. By the time she finished babbling, I had a headache on both sides of my head. Less than a minute later, a middle-aged, bug-eyed, muumuu-wearing woman — whose ethnicity I could not determine — took me aside and grilled me like a cheese sandwich. She wanted to know everything about me, from my military experience to my job.

I'd eaten lunch with Lola, so I couldn't eat much. I had to force myself to gobble up two chicken legs, a small plate of rice and beans, and a few tortillas.

Sylvia, decked out in a floor-length flowered dress that looked more like a couch cover, skittered around the patio like a hamster as she chatted with the remaining guests. I thought she'd never want to leave. Finally, when I couldn't stand the agonizing boredom any longer, I told the Garcias that I had a headache so my lady friend and I needed to be on our way. We left immediately.

"Calvin, were there any females on that boat with you and your buddies?" Sylvia had the nerve to ask as we strolled toward the cute little beige stucco house she owned in the same block.

"What?" I stopped in my tracks and gave her a look that was so incredulous, she shuddered. We stood at the edge of her driveway, where I had parked my Jeep behind her Altima. "Why are you asking me such a ridiculous question?"

"Because there's a woman's scent on you and it's not mine," she whimpered. "You smell like a rose garden. . . ."

I had showered after my romp with Lola. But we had embraced long and hard prior to my departure. The last thing on my mind at the time was her loud-smelling perfume marinating my flesh after I'd washed. It didn't take but a few moments for me to compose myself, gather my thoughts, and offer Sylvia a believable lie.

"Oh! I went to high school with the woman who works at the fish and tackle place where we bought our bait. She used to go out with one of my cousins. She was so glad to see me, she gave me a bear hug. She was always heavy-handed when it came to splashing on perfume." I slid my arm around Sylvia's waist. "Honey, I am surprised and disappointed to hear you even suggest that I might have spent the day with another woman. You're worth *five* women to me."

Before I'd arrived at the Garcia's cookout, I had stopped by my house. I called the hotel to let Lola know again how much I had enjoyed her company. She got extremely excited when I told her I definitely wanted to see her again. For the next couple of minutes she spewed such a long stream of "You made me feel so good" gibberish, my ears throbbed as if somebody had mauled them. I wanted to bite my telephone just to shut her up. I was certain that if I'd told her to go jump off the Golden Gate Bridge, she would have asked, "Which side?" Women were so easy to manipulate. Lola was making things so easy for me! And since she was such a special project, I decided she deserved "special treatment." Her murder had to be much more creative than the others. In addition to strangling her, I needed to do something elaborate first. I considered putting her in chains, locking her in my guest bedroom closet, and torturing the shit out of her for a few years like that Puerto Rican weirdo did to those three girls in Cleveland two years ago. I didn't entertain that thought for long, because it sounded like too much work and a big risk. I inhaled and glanced at the ground before I resumed my end of the conversation with Sylvia.

"Maybe I should go on to my place and give you some time to think," I suggested with a mild grunt.

"What do I need to be thinking about, Calvin?" she asked sharply. The menacing look on her face stunned me. And then she did something that almost made me grab her by the throat. She poked my chest with her finger as she berated me. "Look, I was not born yesterday, so don't play with me. I've been in serious relationships with other men, so I can tell when something is not right. I care about you and I want to be with you, but if you do decide you would rather be with someone else, just let me know. I am not going to be made a fool of!"

Somehow I managed to keep my voice fairly low. A few of the Garcias' guests were walking nearby and I didn't want to give them something else to yip-yap about. "Wait a minute now. Where is this coming from? What the hell is going on? Are *you* trying to ease out of our relationship and think this is a good way to do it?"

"No, I am not trying to 'ease out of our relationship,' so please don't even go there."

I put my hands on Sylvia's shoulders and looked into her eyes. She gave me a hopeful look, and I continued talking. "Sweetheart, I hope we're going to be together for a very long time." I let out a sigh that was so profound, it made my chest hurt and I winced. "This is so . . . painful," I whimpered. I closed my eyes, swayed from side to side for a couple of seconds, and then I moaned. "Aaarrggh . . ."

"What's the matter? You look terrible!" she gasped. She grabbed my hand and squeezed. Then she felt my forehead. "Baby, are you okay?"

"I . . . I just had a . . . a f-flashback of the w-war," I stammered. When I opened my eyes, I couldn't believe the expression of sympathy on Sylvia's face. "Stress brings it on."

"Oh, baby. I'm so sorry. I didn't mean to upset you."

"I'm fine," I insisted. I rubbed my chest, took several deep breaths, and placed my hands back on Sylvia's shoulders. "Just bear with me, sweetie." A thought suddenly exploded in my mind like a hand grenade. I decided that by the end of next week I would finalize my plans for Lola. I would choose when, where, and how I was going to kill her. When it was over, I could begin the transformation that would change me back to the law-abiding, honorable man I was before Glinda destroyed my peace of mind, integrity, and common sense. I *knew* that I would be completely restored! The exhilaration was so intoxicating it felt like I was about to slip into a trance.

"Calvin, you look strange all of a sudden," Sylvia told me. "Honey, I'm worried about you. Are you having another flashback?"

"No, I'm not." I shook my head and forced a chuckle. "I was just thinking about how amazing you are and how much I love you. I guess it all overwhelmed me."

"Really? You think that much of me?"

"If God made a better woman than you, He kept her for Himself."

"Ahh, honey." Sylvia rubbed my shoulder and caressed my chin. "That's such a sweet thing for you to say," she cooed.

She was overjoyed, but I was even more so because I was still thinking about Lola and my final plans for her. I said in the most sincere and loving tone I could drum up, "Baby, um, I have a very important question to ask you, one I never thought I'd ask another woman." I paused and blinked a couple of times. Words could not describe the tense look on Sylvia's face. She looked as if she wanted to stick her fingers into my mouth and pull the question out herself.

"Don't stop talking *now*! What do you want to ask me, Calvin? Don't stand here keeping me in suspense!"

"I was going to ask you over a romantic dinner next weekend." I finally offered up a huge smile too. "But I can't wait any longer." I paused again.

Lately I'd been thinking that if I'd met Sylvia before Glinda, my life would be less complicated. And a lot of females would still be alive. Sylvia was not perfect, but she was perfect for me. She was more attractive now than when I'd met her. And she seemed smarter too. But at the same time, she was still gullible. What man wouldn't want her in his life?

I sucked in some air and took her hands in mine. Then I kissed the tips of her fingers. "Do you really love me?" I asked in a whisper.

The tense look was no longer on Sylvia's face. Now she looked bewildered. She parted her lips and whispered back, "Is that all you wanted to ask me? You know I love you."

I grinned sheepishly and shook my head. "You're the only woman I will ever love, and now I'm ready to do something about it." I didn't give her time to let the words sink in. I looked into her eyes and with a straight face I asked, *"Sylvia Bruce, will you marry me?"*

CHAPTER 54
JOAN

"I was worried about you, Lola," I said when I met her for dinner Sunday evening at the Denny's closest to us — one of the many places Reed refused to take me to because he felt it was beneath him. She sat across from me in a booth near the entrance.

As usual, the restaurant was crowded with mostly blue-collar workers, cranky babies, and bored-looking servers. We had already placed our orders.

"Well, I was worried about you too. We haven't talked since you got back from Phoenix," she told me, toying with her silverware. She let out a loud breath and looked at me with her head tilted to the side. "How was it? Did LongJohn make you another indecent proposal?"

"I wish you wouldn't call him that. The man's name is John," I complained.

"The man's screen name is *LongJohn*," she shot back, wagging her fork in my face.

"That's what he calls himself."

I held my breath and leaned forward to keep our conversation private, even though I didn't see anybody I knew. "He was amazing, and yes, he did ask me again if I want to move to Phoenix. And I told him no, again. Now" — I exhaled and leaned back — "you know I'm dying to hear about your rendezvous with Calvin on Tuesday." A faraway look immediately appeared on Lola's face.

"Tuesday was so wonderful, we got together again on Saturday. I want to marry him and have his babies," she swooned. "He wants me to spend a whole weekend with him in Frisco in July to celebrate his birthday."

I snickered, shook my head, and blinked. "Damn, girl. Was he that good?"

"It was not just about sex. Calvin Ramsey is a very deep man."

I scratched my chin and gave Lola an inquisitive look. "Deep? Hmmm. That's an interesting way to describe him."

"Well, he is *deep*!"

"So is a bottomless pit. So is a black hole. So is an abandoned well. 'Deep' is such a creepy description to —"

Lola cut me off with a dismissive wave. "Stop tripping. You know what I mean."

I nodded. "Yeah, I think I do. He was the fantasy you hoped for, right?"

"And then some. Girl, Calvin is everything I want in a man. The fact that he has a lot of sympathy for Bertha, and admiration for me still taking care of her, tells me *she'd* even like him."

"Do you think she'd like him more than that dickless choir director you've been dragging along with lately who shares a house with his mama?"

"What's wrong with you, Joan? You know better. Elbert Porter is just a friend and . . . and . . . that's all he'll ever be to me." I noticed the hesitation and uncertainty in my homegirl's voice, and it puzzled me. I decided not to mention it for the time being.

"Well, Elbert is good-looking, and almost everybody I know buys most of their meat from the market he owns, so I know he's got a nice bank account. Besides, he suits Bertha — which is something nobody can say about any of your other men. Elbert is everything *she* wants in a man, or maybe I should say son-in-law."

"I don't love Elbert." Lola stopped talking, glanced around, and then looked me straight in the eye. Her lips barely moved as she told me, "Joan, don't laugh and please don't tease me, but I think I'm in love with Calvin. After our brief hookup on Tuesday, he actually drove behind me all the way to my street because I told him I didn't like to be on the road by myself in the dark. Yesterday, he was even sweeter. And the sex was better than it was the first time. I love him twice as much now."

As giddy as she had been acting over this man, I had been expecting her to tell me something like this anyway. "Oh? How do you know it's not just a crush?"

"I know the difference between a crush and real love. I've had a 'crush' on Denzel Washington since I was a teenager. Well, I'm a mature woman now, and I know what love feels like."

"Uh-huh. My next question is, do you 'think' Calvin is in love with you?"

"Joan, I wish you'd be more supportive of —"

I had to interrupt Lola in the middle of her sentence. "I asked you a reasonable question, and I am being supportive. You say Calvin is everything you want in a man. Do you think you're everything he wants in a woman?"

She hunched her shoulders and gave me a weary look. "I hope to find out real soon. He did say that he wanted to see me again, so that means there is some hope. He even called me up when he got home to tell me how much he'd enjoyed my company."

I shook my head and gave Lola a pitiful look. "Is that all you have to go on? He was a good fuck and he wants to see you again? Honey, the man picks women to sleep with through an online sex club! That's how he picked you!"

Lola gasped so hard, a hiccup followed. "Look who's talking! I can't believe what you just said! How is Calvin any different from your Mr. *LongJohn* Walden?"

I kept my lips pressed together because I was afraid my jaw would drop open low enough to hit the table. I rubbed the side of my face and blinked rapidly several times and then I locked eyes with her. "You leave John out of this! For one thing, he is a married man. He has made it clear that he will never leave his wife, so I will never be anything more to him than a piece of tail. How do you know that's not all you are to Calvin? If he is looking for a wife, do you honestly think he'd pick a woman like you?"

Lola gasped again. This time her eyes got big and her nostrils flared. The puppy-dog look that suddenly appeared on her face was so profound, I thought she was about to start barking. Instead, she spoke in such a low and gentle tone I could barely hear her. "A woman like me?" she wheezed. A split second later, her voice turned on a dime and she snarled, "What the F do you mean by that?"

Before I could respond, our server approached with our orders. She took her time arranging our plates and saucers on the table. We remained silent until we were alone again. Lola immediately gobbled up a few fries and bit off a huge chunk of her burger. "You know damn well what I mean. Answer my question, please," I ordered gruffly.

"Which one?" she snarled after she had swallowed her food.

I softened the look on my face and the tone of my voice. "Never mind, I guess." I started eating my fries, but I'd lost my appetite. "Hey, listen. I know it sounds like I'm giving you a hard time —"

"*Sounds* like? Joan, I know I make fun of you and some of your men, and I'm sorry. I'll watch what I say from now on. And I wish you would do the same for me." Lola gave me a pleading look. "Now, if you don't mind, let's change the subject." She sniffed and promptly resumed her end of the conversation. "What else is up with Long— uh, I mean, *John*?"

At the end of the day, no matter what she said or thought about being "in love" with a sex club member, I thought it was crazy. I didn't want to tell her that, because I figured she'd find out soon enough. My relationships with club members were just as outlandish as Lola's, and just as dead end. The only exception was John Walden. I had no choice but to refuse his repeated requests to be his mistress . . . for now.

"You want to talk about John some more?"

"Why not? If you ask me, he's as interesting to discuss as Calvin."

"Oh well. What the hell," I heaved. I was glad Lola laughed along with me. "You know something, if John's wife died or up and left him and he wanted to marry me, I just might do it."

"Uh-uh." Lola shook her head and wagged a finger in my face. "Not as long as Reed is still breathing down your neck. By the way, how has he been acting since you got back?" I was glad that Lola was now speaking in a more pleasant tone. And she seemed to be in a much more jovial mood. There was a mischievous gleam in her eyes and a smile threatening to form on her lips. "We haven't roasted him much lately."

"Same old same old," I said with a very heavy sigh. "I'd rather not talk about him right now," I added with my voice cracking. "It's too depressing."

"Can you at least tell me if he's still in the good mood he was in before you went to Phoenix?"

I gave Lola a thoughtful look and shrugged. "When I told him that I'd like to go off somewhere by myself more often, and for a longer period of time, you would have thought I'd just told him I had a terminal illness. He asked me point-blank if the reason was so I could sleep with other men. He's got this notion that all married women who go away without their husbands pick up strangers and sleep with them."

Lola gave me a guarded look. "He's probably right. You didn't pick up a stranger, but you did sleep with another man. It seems like the more things change for you, the more they stay the same."

"You got that right. The last time I was online, I noticed a couple of new club members I'd like to get to know." I paused and lifted another fry, waving it in the air like a magic wand. "You know, I think we both need to keep 'getting' while the getting is still good."

"What do you mean by that?"

"Well, if you and Calvin get serious about one another, I know you won't want to stay in the club."

Lola nodded. "You're right about that. Calvin is more than enough man for me. What about you? Do you think things will ever get better between you and Reed so you won't want to stay in the club either?"

"I hope so, Lola. I hope so."

CHAPTER 55
JOAN

I had not been home even twenty-four hours before I was ready to scream again. Reed's euphoria had ended and he was once again as moody and suspicious as ever.

"Joan, I hope your little vacation helped in bringing you back to your senses," he began. It was Monday morning and Junior had just left for school. Reed was still at the breakfast table nursing his third cup of coffee. I sat across from him, making out a grocery list.

"What do you mean?" I asked sharply.

"I allowed you to go away on your own so you could pull yourself together. Now that that's done, we need to move forward with our lives. But now you seem even more distant and distracted than before."

Bile rose in my throat, and I had to hold my breath to keep from puking. I dropped the pen I had been writing with onto the table and shot Reed a hot look. "Let's get one thing straight now. You didn't *allow* me to do anything. You're my husband, not my father," I hissed.

"I'm only trying to —"

"Trying to drive me crazy is what you're 'trying' to do!" I interrupted, shaking my finger in his face. "And after all that talk about how you want me to be happy."

"I do want you to be happy!"

"Then make me know it! I enjoyed going away by myself. I need to do more things like that so I can feel a little more independent." I paused and softened my voice. "I've even been thinking about getting a job —"

This time he cut me off. "A job? Woman, you don't need to work. I told you before we got married that you'd never have to work a day in your life."

"I get bored sitting around here looking at the walls all day, every day. I need to interact with people more. I need something to get me out of the house on a regular basis."

"What about that book club you belong to?"

"Huh?"

"Just last week you spent three hours with them discussing the latest book by Mary B. Morrison, whoever the hell she is."

I had almost forgotten about the bogus book club I told Reed I had joined. I wasted no time doing some damage control. "Oh! The book club! Well, this book club gets together only once or twice a month. I need to find something to do that'll get me out of the house more often than that."

"More often? *Pffft!* What about that disabled Liza Mae Ford woman you and Lola help out? That and your beauty shop visits, shopping, hanging out with Lola and your family, and now book club meetings — I think you already get out of the house on a regular basis."

"That's not enough. I want to get a job."

"Fine. Get a job if that's what it takes to make you feel more 'independent.'" Reed waved his hands in the air. I didn't like the exasperated look on his face and I didn't like what he said next. "My receptionist is getting married in a few weeks and she'll be moving to Sacramento. She gave her two weeks' notice last Monday, so I've been interviewing applicants from an employment agency. So far they've sent nothing but dingbats, sea hags, and grandmotherly frumps. You can fill in until we find a replacement. If you like it, you can stay on as long as you want."

The thought of working with Reed made my skin crawl. Having to spend time with him at home seven days a week was bad enough. The last thing I wanted to do was work with him in the same office five days a week too!

"Reed, I don't want to be anybody's receptionist. Every person I know who works in an office hates it. I was thinking of something that would be more fun, like waiting tables. Booker's Barbecue is looking for help."

Reed gulped and looked at me as if I was speaking Arabic. "Waiting tables?" The way he said the two words, with his lips twisted and a look of disbelief on his face, you would have thought I'd said I wanted to perform in a porn movie. He narrowed his eyes and glared at me. "You want to be a waitress?"

"Yes, I do! I think I'd like to be a waitress at Booker's. Their business is booming, and I heard that some days his waitresses make over a hundred dollars in tips."

"Bookers?" he growled. This time his eyes got as big as golf balls. "You want to work in that greasy rib joint in the heart of the ghetto? Have you lost your mind, woman? That place is thug city! For one thing, you don't need the money, so I don't care if his waitresses make a thousand dollars a day in tips. I'd rather see you working on a chain gang! When I was in that hellhole last week, two low-life creatures were flirting with their server and she didn't look half as good as you!"

"When men flirt with me, I let them know right away that I'm a happily married woman." I couldn't believe I could tell such an outrageous lie with a straight face.

"That doesn't matter! Thugs don't care if a woman is married or interested in them or not! They take what they want! A woman as pretty as you would get raped every day in that fucked-up jungle of a neighborhood!"

"I can take care of myself, Reed. I grew up around thugs but I never got raped until that night . . . you know what you did to me."

"Joan, you know how sorry I am about what I did to you that night. I've prayed about it, and I'm convinced God will keep me on the straight and narrow from now on. All I want is for you to be happy."

"I'm sure I'd be very happy working for Booker Watson. Too Sweet used to do his wife's hair, and I went to school with two of his daughters. His youngest daughter and I were born on the same day. We celebrated our sweet sixteenth birthday together, so the Watsons are like family to me."

"No — HELL NO!" Reed hit the table

with his fist so hard, the salt and pepper shakers fell over. "You being a waitress is absolutely out of the question. I won't allow it. Can you imagine how something like that would upset my family? And what would I say to my colleagues during social gatherings? Dr. Kline's wife is a newspaper reporter. Dr. Maitland's wife is a pediatrician. What would they think of me if I told them my wife worked as a *waitress* in a rib joint in the ghetto?" The mocking tone in his voice made me wince. "That's one notion you need to get out of your head right now!"

"You can't tell me what to do and what not to do. I am not going to put up with you controlling me, Reed. You know me better than that."

"I know Lola put this idea of working in your head. I never wanted to say this, but I'm saying it now. That woman is a bad influence! I wish somebody would marry that heifer and keep her pregnant so she can stop dragging you down with her!"

I chuckled.

"Tell me what's so funny," Reed demanded.

"You might not have to worry about her for long."

"Why not? Is she moving to another state or something?"

"There's a new man in her life and she thinks she wants to marry him. If she does, I'm sure you'd like to dance at her wedding."

"Humph. I'd rather dance at her funeral . . ."

My heart almost stopped beating and a lump formed in my throat. Reed's morbid comment stunned me and made me feel unbearably sad. I never expected him to say something so callous about someone who meant so much to me. "Reed, that's the meanest thing I've ever heard you say about another human being. Lola is my best friend. If something happened to her, I don't think I could go on."

"I know *that* feeling," he said with a mournful look on his face, and that didn't surprise me. He cleared his throat and stood up. "I'm sorry, Joan. I shouldn't have said that about Lola. You know I'm not a mean person. I like her and I want her to be happy too. Who is this man?"

"His name is Calvin Ramsey. He lives in San Jose, but I haven't met him yet."

"What does he do for a living?"

"He's a long-haul truck driver."

"That figures. And where did Lola meet this truck driver?"

"I'm not sure. I think she met him at a

party a few months ago."

"Well, a few months is not enough time to get to know a person. We both know that, now, don't we?"

I stared at Reed. I wanted to slap that smug look off his face. "You didn't have to marry me."

"But I wanted to marry you. And I'm going to stay married to you." What he said next made me sick to my stomach. " 'Til death do us part. . . ."

CHAPTER 56
LOLA

"You sure are in a cheerful mood this evening," Libby began when I walked in the front door humming Rihanna's "Umbrella," which was one of my favorite old tunes.

I had just returned from my dinner with Joan. Bertha was in the kitchen banging pots and pans together. Jeffrey and Kevin were outside in the driveway fixing a flat tire on Kevin's bike. Libby claimed her usual spot on the living-room couch. She had a bottle of beer in one hand and her smartphone in the other. I gently eased down on the love seat facing her. "Is there something wrong with a person being in a good mood?" I asked, not sounding as sarcastic as I normally would have.

"It is when the person is you," she sneered, and then snickered.

For the first time in my life, I smiled at her and was sincere about it. Since she'd told me the real reason she was so nasty to me, I didn't resent her presence so much now. And even though she still said mean and stupid things to me, it was not nearly as offensive as before. I was mildly convinced that there was a chance we could eventually become real friends and behave more like sisters. It was a pleasant thought. And it was all because I had caught her with another man. That and Calvin. He had already changed me in ways I never imagined.

But even if my relationship with Libby did improve, I still planned to feed her with a long-handled spoon. She was such an oddball, I would never be able to determine when she was being serious or only trying to get a rise out of me. Some of the stuff she said was meant to be funny, and sometimes I laughed along with her. I didn't feel like laughing this time. I should have ignored her, but I couldn't. "Well, if you really must know, I'm in love," I announced. I didn't realize Bertha was listening until she shuffled into the living room, wiping her hands on her apron.

"You're in love, Lola? *Already?* You don't even spend that much time with Elbert!" Bertha yelled. "My goodness," she added with a grin. "Hmmm. And the last couple of times he dropped by when you were out, he was happy to spend a few hours with me. He's such a sweet and innocent man."

"Bertha, Elbert and I are just friends. That's all we've ever been and that's all we'll ever be," I clarified. I decided that the sooner I made it clear that "sweet and innocent" Elbert was not a potential husband for me, the better. "He's getting real pushy about us spending more time together. I don't want him to get his hopes up, so I'm not sure I'm going to continue going out with him." And I decided that the sooner I revealed my "relationship" with Calvin, also the better. I couldn't wait to see Bertha's reaction when she met and got to know him and heard *from him* how he "encouraged" me to continue taking care of her even after I got married. "I'm in love with a man named Calvin Ramsey." For me to be a woman in my thirties, and one with common sense, I was surprised that I seriously thought I had a future with Calvin. Especially when I didn't even know if I'd ever hear from him again.

"Oh? When and where did you meet him? I hope you're not going to tell us you met this man in Reno yesterday and you're already in love with him," Libby said, looking disturbed and concerned at the same time. "And I advise you not to bring him to this house before you really get to know him. He could be an ax murderer."

"Bertha, he's the man I told you about last month who I had coffee with. Don't you remember?"

Libby and Bertha looked at one another at the same time and then back at me.

"I thought you told me you met him in the mall?" Bertha said, giving me a suspicious look.

"Actually, I did. We chatted for a few minutes in the mall and then we went across the street to the coffee shop."

"Poor Elbert. I hope he doesn't take your dumping him too hard," Bertha groaned. "He's been so good to you — and for you. And he has so much to offer."

"True. Well, now he can offer it to a woman who wants it," I said sharply.

"Does this Calvin have a job? So many women like you settle for a jackass with no job, sleeps on his mama's couch, and lives off other women," Bertha sneered.

"Calvin has a real good job. I told you he's a long-haul truck driver. He owns his house and he goes to church."

"Is he married?" Libby asked, looking at me out of the corner of her eye.

"Is he married?" I gasped. "*I* don't fool around with married men. Why would you think he was married?"

"From what you just said about him, he must have dozens of women chasing after him — unless he's butt ugly."

Had I been thinking about it, I would have asked Calvin to let me take a selfie of us together with my cell phone before he left the hotel. I made a mental note to do just that when, and if, I saw him again. "He's very handsome," I reported.

"Well, is he a geezer or handicapped?" Libby laughed.

"Libby, that's not a nice thing to say," Bertha said sternly. Then she turned to me and gave me a sympathetic look. "Is he an elderly man or missing a leg or something? I have to agree with Libby. If this man is all you say he is, he must be beating the women off with a stick."

"He's in his thirties, he's divorced, and he's not handicapped." I stood up and started walking toward the stairs. Libby and Bertha followed me, so I abruptly stopped and turned to face them.

There was a confused look on Libby's face. "I can't wait to meet your truck driver so I can check him out. If I get a bad vibe, that'll tell me he's a straight-up loser. And you'd better believe Marshall and I are not going to allow some strange truck driver to make himself comfortable and kick back in the house our daddy paid for," she declared as she shook her head. "Mama, don't you let that man start hanging around here too often until we all get to know him and his people."

"How does Calvin treat his mama, Lola?" Bertha asked. I felt like I was being cross-examined. And I guess I was. "What kind of woman is she?"

"His mother is deceased," I replied. "When I told him how I take care of you, he couldn't stop talking about how proud he was of me for being so caring. . . ."

"Oh? You told him all about *me*?" Bertha responded with an anxious look on her face. "That's nice. . . ."

"I thought I mentioned that to you already," I added.

"Um, you probably did, but you know my memory is not what it used to be," Bertha mumbled, and scratched the side of her head. She looked more confused than Libby.

"Mama, don't you do anything stupid. Don't you let your guard down and get too friendly with that strange man too soon. He could be bad news," Libby warned.

"*Pffft!*" Bertha blew out. "I am not going to worry about that. I'll pick this Calvin's brain as soon as I meet him." Turning back to me, Bertha added, "I'm glad you told this man you promised your daddy you'd take care of me. If he won't have a problem with you and me being so close and dependent on each other, I won't have a problem with him." She sniffled and wiped a few tears from her eyes with the tail of her apron. "Poor Elbert. If he stops coming around, I'm going to miss him. I hope he finds another woman who he likes as much as he likes you."

"Elbert will find himself another woman," I declared with a vigorous triple nod. Bertha smiled. I smiled back.

I was so glad I'd told her about Calvin and how I felt about him. How he really felt about me was something I didn't know. Despite what he had told me about wanting to see me again and how compatible we were in bed, he was still a man. Some of the best of them could turn on a dime and sever a relationship without a warning or an explanation, so I was not going to get my hopes up too high. I prayed that he was *the one* for me, but that was something he had to let me know in his own time. Until then, all I could do was hope, pray, and wait. . . .

AUTHOR'S NOTE

Please continue to e-mail me at Authorauthor5409@aol.com and visit my website at MaryMonroe.org. You can also communicate with me on Facebook at Face book.com/MaryMonroe and Twitter@Mary MonroeBooks.

All the best,
Mary Monroe
April 2017

■ ■ ■ ■

READING GROUP GUIDE: NEVER TRUST A STRANGER

MARY MONROE

■ ■ ■ ■

ABOUT THIS GUIDE
The suggested questions that follow are included to enhance your group's reading of this book.

DISCUSSION QUESTIONS

1. A lot of people find true love and excitement with someone they meet on the Internet. But do you think joining an online sex club like Discreet Encounters is a bit extreme?

2. Have you ever considered looking for love (or sex partners) on the Internet?

3. If your answer is yes, would you keep it a secret from your friends and family the way Lola and Joan did? Would you date as frequently as they did?

4. Lola took a lot of abuse from her stepsister. When Libby "explained" why she was so mean, did you feel sorry for her? If you know any plain Janes who have been picked on and bullied because of their looks, are they as bitter as Libby? Or are they nice people with lots of friends and

men who love them?

5. Libby's husband, Jeffrey, was handsome and successful. He had a great personality and he adored her. If you were in Libby's shoes, would you risk your marriage by having an affair?

6. Joan was drop-dead gorgeous, and her handsome husband, Reed, was a very successful dentist. But he was controlling, paranoid, and lousy in bed. Do you think he drove her to cheat?

7. Joan's mother-in-law, Mother Riley, looked down on her and all black people from the "hood." Do you know a woman like her? If so, do you ignore her comments or stand up to her?

8. Joan's favorite married Internet lover, John "LongJohn" Walden, repeatedly asked her to leave Reed and move to Phoenix to be his mistress. Would you consider a serious relationship with someone you met through an Internet sex club?

9. Joan and Lola were only interested in hooking up with doctors, lawyers, and men in other high-end professions in the

club. They refused to consider janitors, dishwashers, busboys, and other low-income members. Would you turn down dates with men only because of their line of work?

10. Even though Discreet Encounters did thorough background checks on prospective members before they allowed them to join the club, there was no way they could have known that Calvin Ramsey was a serial killer looking for more victims on the Internet. Is this reason enough for you to never consider online dating?

11. Before Calvin and Lola got together, he stalked her and she didn't even know it. She had revealed a lot of information about herself on social media, so it was easy for him to track her. Will you be more careful now when you post personal information about yourself on the Internet?

12. Calvin was the man of Lola's dreams, so her plan was to marry him and have his babies. She was the woman of his nightmares, so his plan was to kill her. Have you ever read a story with lovers

whose goals were as conflicting as these two?

13. Calvin's "girlfriend," Sylvia, was totally clueless. She believed everything he told her, so he was in complete control of their relationship. She had no idea that he had a dark side. Do you think that a lot of people have a dark side on some level?

ABOUT THE AUTHOR

Mary Monroe, the daughter of sharecroppers, is the author of the award-winning and New York Times bestselling God series that includes *God Don't Like Ugly* and *God Don't Make No Mistakes*, among other novels. Winner of the AAMBC Maya Angelou Lifetime Achievement Award and the PEN/ Oakland Josephine Miles Award, Mary Monroe currently lives in Oakland, California, and loves to hear from her readers via e-mail at AuthorAuthor5409@aol.com. Visit Mary's website at MaryMonroe.org.